Caught in a Storm

Perfect Storm
Book 3

Mari Carr

Copyright © 2025 by Mari Carr

MARI CARR® is registered in U.S. Patent and Trademark Office.

All rights reserved.

No part of this book may be reproduced in any form or by any electronic or mechanical means, including information storage and retrieval systems, without written permission from the author, except for the use of brief quotations in a book review.

Cover Photography: WANDER AGUIAR PHOTOGRAPHY LLC

Cover Design: Qamber Designs & Media

Editor: Kelli Collins

Final Line Editor: Nan Mabbitt

Caught in a Storm

In the storm of life, some passions can't be tamed.

Mila has spent her life working on Stormy Weather Farm, alongside her fiercely loyal, slightly eccentric family. The Storms believe in hard work, the importance of tradition, and—most of all—love at first touch. It's a family legend, passed down like a vintage bottle of truth: when you touch the one meant for you, you'll just know.

Mila always thought it was just a romantic notion... until Boone.

A rugged, brooding single father with a past that still smolders, Boone has one priority: giving his twelve-year-old daughter a stable, quiet life. Love? He's been there, done that, burned the T-shirt. Or so he thinks...until Mila.

She's all sunshine and cinnamon, and she makes Boone ache with cravings he thought were long dead. Every time she blushes, every time she touches him by accident, the tension coils tighter.

Soon, late-night harvests turn into stolen glances, and shared

Caught in a Storm

glasses of wine become heated whispers in the dark. But love is risky business, and Boone's heart isn't the only thing on the line—his daughter's trust, and Mila's future, hang in the balance.

Chapter One

Mila stepped out onto the front porch and pulled her coat around her more firmly. While it wasn't bitter cold, there was still enough nip in the air to keep most people inside. She would have been one of those people if not for the strong wind last night that had blown half the holiday lights down on the B&B Aunt Claire and Uncle Rex ran on Stormy Weather Farm.

Despite the chill, Mila took a moment, just as she always did, to enjoy the view. As far as she was concerned—winter, spring, summer, or fall—the view down into the valley from her lofty perch right here on the side of the mountain was never bad. While the valley was awash in every hue of green during the spring and summer months, and a colorful palette of oranges, purples, and reds in the fall, the winter provided its own beauty. Right now, the world below her was painted in a white so bright, she should have put on sunglasses.

Most of the year, the scene before her was all watercolors and pastels. In winter, it was more like a pen-and-ink drawing. Less vibrant, harsher, but just as beautiful.

She'd stopped by the B&B to see if Aunt Claire needed any help getting ready for the guests who were set to arrive this afternoon. Uncle Rex had taken a tumble a couple of days earlier and sprained his ankle. He'd been good-naturedly grumbling from the couch about not being an invalid, but that wasn't stopping Aunt Claire from fussy over him like a protective mother hen.

The fact her strong-as-a-bull, never-sit-still uncle was reclined under a blanket with his foot propped up on a pillow spoke to just how bad the injury was. Because Mila had watched him work with bad head colds, nasty coughs, and even a twisted back once.

Aunt Claire assured her she had everything in hand, with the exception of the holiday lights. Her aunt had intended to ask one of her sons—Mila's countless male cousins—to stop by to fix them, but Mila offered to take on the task. After all, she and Uncle Rex had been the ones to hang them, so it wasn't like she wasn't familiar with the process.

Part of her countless duties on the family farm—in addition to maintaining the rental cabins, pitching in at the B&B, maintaining the flower and herb garden with her aunt, and managing the kitchens at the brewery and winery, both located on the property—was that of chief decorator. She had her very own dedicated shed where she stored decorations for every holiday on the calendar and some fun ones that weren't, like May the Fourth's *Star Wars* Day and October Third's *Mean Girls* celebration.

Stepping around the house, she found the ladder Uncle Rex had stashed there. No doubt he promised Aunt Claire he would put it away multiple times, while never managing to actually do the task.

Pulling it to the front porch, she set it up, then sighed. While she always found special occasions to celebrate, she loved the Christmas holidays more than any other time of the year, which made January particularly depressing. Taking down all the

Caught in a Storm

Santas and Grinches and Snoopies and angels and snowmen and...well, if it dealt with Christmas, she had it...and packing them away for another whole year always made her melancholy.

It had been a particularly nice holiday season this year, as they'd added new "family" to her already overloaded list of relatives. In addition to her seven male cousins and her two sisters—her oldest sister, Lucy, had celebrated Christmas with her boyfriends in Philadelphia—they'd added a couple of girlfriends. Her cousin Levi had fallen madly in love with Kasi Mills, so she, her father, Tim, and brother, Keith, had joined them for the opening of gifts on Christmas Eve and the big meal on Christmas Day. And her cousin Theo had also been struck by Cupid's arrow, so he'd invited his girlfriend, Gretchen.

Adding new ladies to the mix was exciting to Mila, as she and her sisters, Nora and Remi, were painfully outnumbered on the farm. It had been nice with the extra females around. With the addition of Kasi and Gretchen, it felt like they were starting to even the numbers.

Ordinarily, she left the holiday lights up longer, as it was only a couple of days past New Year's, but thanks to that damn wind blowing a large section in the center down completely, she'd decided to follow Mother Nature's lead, taking the rest down now. Better that than rehanging them, only to have to ascend the ladder again in a couple weeks.

Beginning at the edge of the porch eave, she started the slow, arduous process of unhooking the lights, then descending and moving the ladder a few feet to the right before ascending again.

After the fifth trip down, she wound the first strand of lights carefully. There was nothing more annoying than getting all excited about decorating for the holidays, then being slowed down by tangled lights. She was a professional when it came to storing Christmas lights. The trick was notched cardboard. Her cardboard pieces were even labeled, so she knew where each strand of lights was hung. An important addition, considering she draped twinkle lights from the front of all three of the farm's houses, as well as in and around the brewery, winery, event barn, and any cabins that were rented in December.

Not to mention the lights for the countless Christmas trees they decorated in various places. Her lighting game was legit, and one she started in mid-November, as it usually took her a couple of weeks to hang them all.

Once the first strand was wrapped on the cardboard, she started to climb again, only to stop when Nora approached from the path that connected the farmhouse she shared with her sisters to the B&B.

"Why are you taking them down?" Nora asked. "Thought you usually left them up well into January."

Mila leaned on the ladder. "Mother Nature and that storm last night had different plans."

"Ah." Nora glanced at the cardboard pieces she'd arranged on the porch and grinned. It was Nora who, after too many years of listening to Mila bitch about using the wrong light strands in the wrong places, had suggested she label the cardboard.

Not that that was surprising. Nora took organization schematics to new levels because her OCD wouldn't let her rest if something wasn't exactly so. No one minded Nora's quirkiness because, in truth, she had a goddamn gift when it came to arranging and categorizing, and Mila always figured that if they hadn't been born on the farm, Nora would have been one of those professional organizers.

"What are you doing here?" Mila asked. Nora ran Lightning in a Bottle Winery and spent the majority of her days there—either in her office or in the tasting room, working with employees or chatting with patrons.

Nora held up a wine bag Mila hadn't noticed. "Aunt Claire asked if I'd drop off a few bottles of wine for Sunday dinner tonight. Apparently, we depleted the supply she had on hand on New Year's Eve."

Mila rubbed her temple, grinning. "Don't remind me. I swear I can still feel twinges of that hangover."

"Yeah. It was a hell of a party," Nora said. "One Uncle Rex is still suffering for."

Mila laughed. "Poor guy. He was the soberest of us all."

"Leading a conga line is no joke."

Uncle Rex's sprained ankle had been the result him catching his foot on the edge of the dining room table while leading them all through the house, conga-style, to Harry Belafonte's "Jump in the Line." He'd been shaking maracas with his pointed Happy New Year paper hat hanging off the side of his head, making him look like a lopsided rhinoceros. If there was one thing the Storm family loved, it was a conga line.

"Aunt Claire is taking good care of him. He's currently under one of Grandma's handmade quilts, drinking hot tea."

Nora snorted. "Twenty bucks says he added a shot of rum when Aunt Claire wasn't looking."

"Not taking bets I won't win," Mila joked.

"You were up and out early this morning," Nora said. "I didn't get to ask you how your date with Pastor Joshua went last night."

Mila gave her sister a casual shrug. "It was okay."

"Just okay?"

"It was nice," she amended. "He's a nice guy. You know he is."

"I know *nice* is really just code for boring," Nora pressed.

Mila sighed. "Not really. I mean, we're never hurting for conversation and he's super polite and friendly and…" She was aware that her tone wasn't exactly proving her sister wrong. Because despite everything she just said, there were absolutely zero sparks between her and Joshua, a local minister.

"Why do you keep going out with the guy if he bores you?"

"We've only been out a few times, and it's not as if we're a couple or anything. We haven't even done anything more than kiss."

Three times. And they were three of the most lukewarm kisses in the history of kissing.

For pity's sake, they'd all been close-mouthed. Not even a hint of tongue.

"He's a pastor. He probably can't do anything more than kiss you outside the confines of marriage or he'll go to hell."

Mila closed her eyes. "You're ridiculous."

Nora smirked. "Just think about it. You could be leading a man of the cloth down the path to sin. Which is hot in romance novels, but I'm pretty sure Pastor Joshua isn't sporting a six-pack under that clergy robe."

This time, Mila couldn't help but laugh. "Shut up, you idiot. I'm not leading him to sin."

Nora relented on teasing her. "You're obviously not into the guy, so why keep saying yes when he asks you out?"

Mila grimaced. "Because I can't think of a reason to say no. I mean, he really is a nice guy and it's not like he's done anything wrong on our dates."

Nora rolled her eyes, clearly unimpressed by that answer. "He hasn't done anything fun, either. The guy is too serious about being holy. It's honestly kind of annoying."

Mila agreed but didn't say so out loud. "He's the minister. It's not like he can go out every night and get wasted or sleep around. He has a reputation to uphold as a spiritual leader in the community."

Nora held her gaze, not responding to that with anything more than one quirked eyebrow.

"Besides, it's not like there are a ton of single guys running around town, and I can't help it if the only ones I seem to attract are the…" She realized how stupid her next two words were going to sound, but they were the only ones that worked. "Nice guys."

God. What the hell would she give to go out with a bad boy just once? No, not a bad *boy*. A man, a dominant, commanding, strong, virile man.

Her fantasies ran dark and dirty and kiiiiiinky, something she'd never been able to explore because, well, her dating pool consisted of nothing but a bunch of nice guys…like Pastor Joshua. The type who asked before they kissed her, who held her hand like she was made of glass…and who'd freak out if she begged them to pull her hair or spank her.

What she wanted more than anything was a man to lay claim to her—every part of her—and she didn't want him to say "pretty please."

She just wanted him to say "kneel" or "bend over" or—best of all—"good girl."

"Mila, I say this with all the love in the world, but you are too fucking sweet, and you need to knock it off."

Mila laughed, but deep down she hated the *sweet* descriptor. She'd always hated it, even though nine times out of ten, the first thing anyone ever pointed out about her was how sweet she was.

The problem was she'd lived in Gracemont, Virginia, the smallest town in the world, for her entire life. As such, the locals —as well as her family—had pigeonholed her into that category. They'd placed *all* her sisters into specific categories.

Lucy was the adventurous one, the one who'd always dreamed of leaving the farm and seeing the world. And she was currently doing that with her two boyfriends.

Nora was the quirky one because her OCD had OCD. Remi was the wild one, and Mila was the sweet one.

Gag.

Now that she thought about it, there was a good chance

Pastor Joshua probably found *her* just as boring as she found him.

That idea stung. Because she knew there was a much different Mila chomping at the bit to escape. But that Mila was one she'd never revealed, too afraid of…well, she didn't know what she was afraid of, exactly. All she knew was, holding that woman inside was starting to chafe.

Nora, still on a roll, added, "Next time Pastor Joshua calls, say no."

Mila didn't respond to that. Mainly because she hated letting someone down. She was worried he'd ask if he'd done something wrong—which he hadn't—and she couldn't come up with an excuse to break things off that wouldn't hurt his feelings. Confrontation was not her strong suit, and pair that with her deeply ingrained people-pleaser personality and it was a recipe for a quiet, mundane life, as well as few and far between, lackluster dates. A lifetime of them, to be exact.

"You need help?" Nora offered, gesturing to the strand of lights still hanging. The B&B had a large wraparound porch, but she'd only hung lights from the two sides visible from the driveway and road that ran beside it.

"Nope. I've got it. Only a few more up and downs on the ladder and I'll be done. I'm counting this as my daily cardio."

Nora snickered. "That's more than I'm going to get in. I better run this into Aunt Claire. I'm training Lark to work as a server part-time and she's due to show up soon." Nora waved and walked into the house.

While the Storm family was large, they ran so many different businesses on the farm that they needed to hire a lot of outside help. It was that hiring that had brought Theo's new girlfriend to them in September. Gretchen had been employed to serve as Stormy Weather Farm's event coordinator, setting up special celebrations at the winery and brewery, as well as overseeing their new event barn. She was just one of countless people employed to keep things running smoothly on the farm.

Mila blew on her hands to warm them, then decided the sooner she got the lights down, the sooner she could join Uncle Rex for a nip of his special hot tea. She hadn't exactly exaggerated about that New Year's hangover lingering, so hair of the dog and all that.

Reaching inside her coat pocket, she pulled out her phone and fired up Spotify. Music always made work feel less like work. Despite her de-Christmasifying the house, she remained loyal to the holiday playlist that had been her go-to since November.

She cranked up Mariah's "All I Want for Christmas" because, seriously, who could ever get sick of that song?

"One side down and one to go," she murmured to herself, as she began the arduous process again, singing along with the Queen of Christmas.

Mila had underestimated how many trips up and down the ladder would be required, her knees killing her after the seventh climb.

She was so close to finishing.

Maybe…

Mila stretched forward, attempting to reach the final hook without having to move the ladder yet again.

Unfortunately, her laziness wasn't working in her favor, because that last stupid hook was just an inch or so out of—

The ladder began to wobble, so she reared back too quickly, overcorrecting. The top of the ladder shifted away from the roof, hovering with no support, and her along with it.

She jerked from side to side like a new clown trying out stilts for the first time.

Mila was too off-balance to push the ladder forward again.

Despite her efforts, she was going to fall. There was no combating gravity, but she fought it for as long as she could.

One last-ditch attempt at recovery failed as her foot slipped. While the ladder fell forward, she went back. Closing her eyes, she cried out as she braced herself for the painful impact.

It didn't come.

Instead, she heard a grunt that didn't come from her.

Opening her eyes, she realized she *had* hit the ground. Or at least, the guy under her did, leaving her sprawled in his lap. He'd caught her and broken the fall. She blinked a few times, fighting to focus, and when she did...

Holy shit.

The rugged mountain man seriously looked like he'd stepped straight out of her fantasies.

He was large and muscular, with a thick beard and piercing brown eyes so dark they looked black. There was a slight crook in his nose that indicated it had been broken before, but rather than detract, it simply reinforced his attractiveness. His tanned skin was indicative of someone who spent a lot of time outside and reminded her of her farmer cousin Levi's complexion.

Those words *bad boy* flashed through her mind, but she dismissed them instantly because there wasn't one boyish thing about the stranger.

He was all man.

"Miss," he said, and she realized it wasn't the first time he'd said it.

Mila shook herself for staring so hard at the sexy man. "I..."

"Are you okay?" he asked, his voice deep and delicious.

Dear God. She'd knocked them both to the ground with her fall.

"I am." She tried to wriggle her way off his lap, but the man held her still. His large, calloused hands rested on her waist—

underneath her jacket—and the tight, protective grip sent her thoughts to some very naughty places.

"Stop," he practically barked.

She instantly froze in response, gasping slightly, her body reacting before her brain could catch up.

The man's eyes narrowed briefly, his head slightly tilted as if she was familiar to him. Which was unlikely because there was no way in hell she'd ever forget meeting this man.

"Take it slow, darlin'. Make sure you didn't break anything." His words were spoken softly, but with an edge that said he expected her to do exactly as ordered.

It took a few seconds for Mila's brain to start to function again, and when it did, she was tempted to point out that he'd taken the brunt of the impact, but there was something about him... About *her* that longed to obey, to please him. And not in her normal people-pleasing way, but in a visceral, instinctual way she couldn't fully understand.

"I'm fine," she murmured, aware she was still sitting on his lap. She shifted slightly, her eyes widening when she felt something hard press against her hip.

Holy. Crap. Was *he* hard?

Embarrassment kicked in and she tried to stand again.

He pinned her with a hard stare. "I told you to take a minute. I don't like repeating myself."

Oh yeah. This guy was dangerous...in all the right ways.

His hands tightened, gripping her waist harder, and she wished they weren't just under her jacket but under her sweater as well. The idea of his hands on her bare skin made her dizzy.

Mila mentally shook herself out of whatever spell this man was casting. She lifted her own hands and made a show of wiggling her fingers and then her feet for him. She even managed a grin as she did so, though given his stern look, it was clear he either wasn't convinced or amused. Not that it mattered how he felt because she was definitely floundering—drowning—in an ocean of lust, her thoughts hazy with a need she'd never experienced in her life.

"I'm, uh, fine," she repeated, intending to reassure him but failing because, woo-damn, her tone was way too breathless to sell it. She cleared her throat and tried again. "What about you? Did I hurt you?"

The man chuckled. "A little thing like you? Not likely. All I have is a bruised ass and wounded pride."

"Pride? Why?"

"Because I'm pissed I didn't manage to catch you midair without falling. Falling makes me look a lot less like a stud."

Mila giggled—until another voice entered the conversation.

"Gross, Dad."

Mila peered over the man's shoulder and saw a young preteen girl.

Great, Mila. Nothing like ogling a man while his daughter was watching.

She scrambled to her feet, the man rising as well.

When she swayed slightly, he reached out, gripping her hands to steady her.

And that was when she felt it.

It.

The thing her uncle Rex and Levi and Theo all talked about.

Lightning strike.

Earthquake.

Tsunami.

Love at first electrifying touch.

This man was the one. The one she'd spent a lifetime dreaming of while terrified she'd never find him.

She'd known since birth she would never leave this mountain. After so many single years, she'd recently started to fear her fantasy man didn't live in Gracemont. While she hadn't lied to

Nora about attracting a certain type, what she didn't add was, she didn't even attract many of those. Her dating history was so pathetic, she wasn't sure it classified as history. More like a handful of tiny little footnotes. Given the fact she knew exactly what Gracemont had to offer, as far as available bachelors, and the fact she rarely left town, she was most likely destined to live alone or—God forbid—become the pastor's wife.

Now, as Mila looked into this man's eyes, it felt as if her world had suddenly clicked into place.

Levi had said it was the same way for him. Kasi had passed out in his arms, and he'd realized she was his.

Theo claimed all it took for him was one handshake, and every fiber of his being recognized Gretchen as his soul mate.

The man was steadying her while at the same time, rocking her world down to its foundation. She'd never felt so lost, and yet so found.

And as amazing as that should have felt, there was something she couldn't ignore.

The man had a daughter.

Did that mean he also had a wife?

God.

How cruel could fate be? To put this man in her orbit when he couldn't be hers.

While it was utterly ridiculous, Mila mourned the loss of him, feeling as if her heart was breaking.

Over a man who wasn't even hers.

Chapter Two

Boone looked down at the beauty in front of him, trying to figure out what the fuck was wrong with him. He didn't flirt, didn't call women darlin', and he sure as shit didn't let his inner caveman out. That asshole had been locked away for years.

However, he was suddenly overwhelmed by something he hadn't felt in a very long time.

Something he hadn't *allowed* himself to feel…by design.

Attraction.

And not some run-of-the-mill, oh-she's-pretty attraction. Nope, this was a dick-twitching, chest-beating, feral kind of attraction. The kind that had his mind and body in perfect agreement, screaming at him to get the woman naked in his bed and under him immediately.

Fuck. Me.

The caveman was back in full force. He'd kicked the fucker out over a decade ago, not just locking the door behind him but barring and painting right the hell over it until he couldn't tell there'd ever been a door.

Now, dammit, as he stared down at this lovely woman, with her light brown eyes and cute upturned nose, the caveman had broken down the door, barging in like the bastard he was. Every single one of Boone's instincts were insisting he not just protect and care for her but claim every inch of this woman—body and soul.

He didn't have a clue how long the two of them stared at each other, but it stretched well beyond social normalcy.

Something his daughter noticed.

"Um...hello?" Sadie said, in that recently acquired smart-ass tone that drove him up the damn wall. Of course, it also had the desired effect, because it helped him pull his head out of his ass.

After all, she was one of the main reasons he'd exiled the caveman.

He dropped the woman's hands and took a step back, putting a proper distance between them. Clearing his throat, he forced himself to offer her a polite handshake, even though the idea of touching her again was...perilous. Shit. His long-dormant cock was awake after an eternal hibernation. His jeans were loose, but not enough to hide a full-blown hard-on. He needed to get his shit together, and fast.

"I'm Boone Hansen. This is my daughter, Sadie."

The woman's expressive eyes widened, making it clear she recognized his name. "Oh! Of course. I should have known. Levi said you were arriving this weekend. I'm afraid I've lost track of what day it is. Curse of the holidays, right?" She accepted his hand, and Boone felt the slight shiver that went through her.

She felt the attraction too. It was evident in the flush in her cheeks that grew more pronounced and the way she subtly, quickly darted her tongue over her lower lip. Then she offered him a sheepish grin as she pulled her phone out of her pocket and turned off Wham blasting out "Last Christmas."

Boone was amused that she was still listening to holiday

music, despite the fact he was usually sick of the crap before December even hit.

"I'm Mila Storm. My family owns Stormy Weather Farm."

Shit. She was one of the Storms. That made his attraction even more problematic. Boone had been hired by Levi Storm to work in the vineyard, and the man had explained that the farm, as well as the businesses on it, were run by his large family.

Boone was looking forward to this job because, at last, he would be the vineyard manager rather than just the assistant, something he never would have achieved in his last place of employment. The owner of that vineyard held the role of manager, and he'd been grooming his son to take over when he retired.

With no room for advancement, Boone jumped at the offer when Levi contacted him to see if he'd be interested in working on Stormy Weather Farm. He and Levi had met more than a few times over the years at trade shows and conventions, and they'd struck up an acquaintanceship, emailing from time to time with questions about crop concerns, etc.

As Mila released his hand, she turned her attention to his daughter, giving her an adorable wave. "Hi, Sadie."

Sadie smiled at Mila and said hello. He was sure the greeting seemed pleasant enough to Mila, even though Boone knew Sadie's smile was forced and there was an edge to her voice.

He blew out a long, slow, quiet breath, counting to ten in his head. He'd been doing that a hell of a lot lately in regards to his young daughter. Now, as always, he dug deep for patience, something that was in thin supply these days.

Boone shoved his hands in the pockets of his jacket, warding off the cold. Then he scowled as he considered Mila's ruddy cheeks. How long had she been out here in the elements? Where were the men on the farm? Why the hell were they letting her climb a ladder to take down holiday lights?

He considered asking all those questions, then realized he'd already come on too strong, demanding she take care before standing.

"Levi said he'd greet us and give us a tour of the farm, but we got here earlier than expected. Didn't hit any traffic and we managed to get out of Williamsburg without any issues." Boone didn't want to start off on the wrong foot, so he'd made sure to leave plenty of time for the three-and-a-half-hour drive.

"That's no problem at all," Mila said. "If you want, I can show you the cabin where the two of you will be living, then text Levi to meet you there. That way you can take some time to unwind before his tour of the farm."

"I don't want to put you out. If you give me directions—"

"Oh, it's no problem at all. I'd be happy to do it."

Boone couldn't think of a way to turn her down without appearing rude, even though it was probably wiser to put some distance between him and the beauty until he was able to shake off whatever the fuck this was. "Okay. We'd appreciate that."

"It's not far from here." Mila bent down to pick up the ladder.

"I'll do that." Boone beat her to it, hefting it off the ground before leaning it against the porch to unfasten the last of the strand of lights. He handed them to her as she deftly wrapped it around a piece of cardboard. He noticed the neat, feminine writing on it that said, *B&B Front Porch.*

Mila thanked him, blushing again as he lowered the ladder, then asked her where she wanted him to put it. She directed him to the far side of the house, where he rested it against the wall.

"One of my cousins will put it away later," she said. "The cabin's not too far from here. If you have room, I can just hop in your truck with you. If not, I'll run inside and tell my uncle Rex I'm borrowing his. I've gotta go in any way to get the keys to your cabin. I stashed them there a couple days ago for Levi to pick up when he met with you."

"We have room in the truck."

"Cool. I'll be back in two secs." Mila was true to her word, dashing inside the B&B, returning almost instantly.

Boone gestured toward his truck, walking around to the passenger side to open the door for Mila. Glancing toward the backseat, he caught the way Sadie rolled her eyes at his gesture, and it occurred to him his daughter had probably never seen him open a door for a woman…because there were no women in his life.

Mercifully, Mila didn't notice Sadie's rude reaction.

God save him from twelve-year-old girls. Up until the beginning of seventh grade, his daughter had been sweet as pie. Since then…not so much.

Climbing behind the wheel, he followed Mila's directions, traveling farther along the mountain as she explained they'd be living in one of the cabins her family had previously rented out to fall foliage seekers, bird-watchers, nature lovers, and anyone else looking for a serene, scenic getaway.

"Don't you guys worry," Mila said over her shoulder, glancing toward the backseat, though neither he nor Sadie had expressed any concern. "I picked you out a good one. The best one, actually."

"You picked it out?" Boone asked.

"One of my duties on the farm is to maintain the rental cabins. I guess you could call me the landlord-slash-maid," Mila said with a laugh. She continued chatting, pointing out where each of the dirt roads attached to the main one led. Not that he was listening. He was too distracted by her.

Boone tried to figure out how old Mila was. If he had to guess, he'd put her in her twenties, though he didn't think she was newly out of her teens. Not that it mattered. Whatever her age, she was too young for his forty years.

The second he had that thought, he kicked it out because attraction or not, he wasn't starting anything with pretty Mila Storm.

He didn't do relationships. Been there, done that, burned the fucking T-shirt.

He'd made that vow ten years ago and nothing had shaken his resolve since.

Which was why he was equal parts surprised and annoyed by the way Mila fired needs in him that he was usually much better at controlling.

"And that lane leads to the farmhouse where my cousins live. Seven men—well, six, now that Levi has moved in with Kasi—all under the same roof. My sister Remi calls it the frat house."

God, she had a pretty voice. Soft and lilting with just a touch of a southern accent.

Boone snuck a glance at the passenger seat, trying to figure out what it was about Mila that had captured his attention. She was certainly a lovely woman, but he'd met countless beauties in his life. She had a cheerful, friendly demeanor, a gorgeous smile, and one of those personalities that reminded him of something his grandmother used to say. Mila was the type of person who'd never met a stranger.

Given the easy way she'd climbed into his truck and started a conversation without a second's hesitation, he suspected she probably charmed the hell out of all the guests who came to visit the farm. More than that, she probably had a dozen young men all swarming around, fighting to claim her. He wasn't about to toss his hat in that ring, although the thought of her with another man actually had him growling.

The sound captured Mila's attention, and he cleared his throat in an attempt to play it off as a cough.

She only paused for a moment, then started talking about the stables on the farm and how many horses they had. "Remi leads trail rides, and I'm sure she'd love to show you around the mountain if you're fond of riding."

Boone nodded noncommittally, letting her continue to carry the conversation. He recalled watching Mila teetering on that ladder as he was climbing out of the truck. He'd taken off running, certain he wouldn't reach her before she tumbled. He didn't want to think about how hurt she might have been if he hadn't been there to break the fall.

The thought of her injured had him seeing red.

Jesus Christ. He'd just met the woman, and he was overwhelmed by the desire to keep her safe. He wasn't surprised by that impulse. Boone was a born protector. His mother used to say he'd missed his century, claiming he was most likely a knight in a previous life, the kind of man who fought to the death to protect his woman.

He'd been that way with his ex, Lena, and she'd accused him of smothering her because of it.

Ever since Lena walked out on him and Sadie, those protective instincts had transferred to his daughter. And *only* her.

No other woman had stirred this desire in over a decade, and Boone didn't like it, didn't want a complication like Mila interrupting his well-ordered life.

"That's the road to my farmhouse," Mila continued, oblivious to his inner turmoil. "I live there with my sisters, Remi and Nora."

Obviously, he was tired from the drive and stressed about the move and Sadie's bad fucking attitude. Those were the only excuses he could come up with for this instant desire to claim Mila Storm and make her his.

He was typically accomplished at keeping his libido under control. Not that he lived like a monk. In Williamsburg, he'd known a couple of women who were okay with occasional hookups, neither of them interested in relationships. They were nice women, but emotions hadn't been involved. He hated the term fuck buddies, but that's all his past liaisons could be classified as. And even those hookups were few and far between, because it wasn't like he was going to have sex at his place with Sadie sleeping down the hall.

There was something about Mila, however, that had his dick stirring with more than just a casual interest. She was the type of woman a man would keep in his bed for a good long time.

With so much blood residing south of the border, his dick was currently functioning as his brain, reminding him that while he wasn't looking for love, slaking his lust was a different matter.

Jesus. Get a grip, Hansen.

He might not answer to Mila directly, but she was practically one of his new bosses, so there would be no casual hookups with her. Once he got more settled in his new job, he'd start looking around to see what Gracemont offered in the way of women who were fine with no-strings-attached affairs.

Mila was off-limits.

Because she was too young.

Because she was a Storm.

Because she was dangerous. There was no room in his life for any other woman than Sadie. She had to be his top priority, had to come first. He'd made that vow to himself after Lena abandoned them when their daughter was just two years old.

Glancing in the rearview mirror, his jaw tightened when he saw Sadie slumped back in the seat, staring out the window, though he doubted she was listening to anything Mila was saying either, that too-familiar scowling sulk on her face.

The same guilt he'd felt since accepting this job swamped

him, but he was resolute in his decision to move to Gracemont, certain it wasn't just him who would benefit from a fresh start.

Sadie had made a new best friend, Stella, at the end of the last school year, and she had not been a positive influence on his daughter.

Stella had a smart mouth, didn't take her schoolwork seriously, and basically got away with bloody murder with her inattentive parents. If he'd had to hear Sadie complain one more time that Stella's parents always let *her*...fill in the fucking blank...he figured he'd go out of his goddamn mind.

Separating her from Stella had felt like the solution to something that was becoming a big problem. Of course, now she was pissed as shit at him for dragging her to this small town and away from all her friends in the middle of the school year. She'd raged for weeks when he'd told her they were moving, and when she finally ran out of angry words about how he was "ruining her life," she turned to silence.

Strangely, he preferred the shouting to the quiet.

It had been a long, wordless drive from Williamsburg to Gracemont today, but it didn't matter what he did to try to convince Sadie this change would be great for both of them. She wasn't having any of it.

Boone, on the other hand, was more hopeful. Because between spoiled Stella and the fact his ex, Lena, had moved to Florida last year with the latest in a long line of boyfriends, Boone realized there was absolutely nothing holding him in Williamsburg.

When Levi called to offer him the position of vineyard manager at Stormy Weather Farm, it felt like the answer to a prayer, a new beginning for him and Sadie.

"Here we are," Mila said, pulling him from his wayward thoughts.

Boone was pleasantly surprised by how quaint the cabin

looked. The word *cabin* itself had him thinking rustic and perhaps even a bit run-down, but this small home, fashioned from logs, was beautiful. It was tucked in the woods, providing privacy, but someone had taken the time to cut down just enough trees that visitors would have a stunning view of the valley from the front porch.

"Come on." Mila hopped out of the truck excitedly. Her enthusiasm wormed its way into him, and even Sadie, who for the first time since they'd hit the road this morning, seemed mildly intrigued.

Mila led them up the four steps, stopping and turning on the porch to point out the view. "Wait until fall. The colors are so beautiful, you'll never want to go inside. On that side of the house, just around the corner, there's a firepit that will be perfect for roasting marshmallows and making s'mores when the weather warms up."

Unlocking the door, she handed Boone the key, then dangled a second key chain, looking at him, then tilting his head toward his daughter, seeking permission. Boone nodded his head once, and Mila turned, offering Sadie her own front door key. Sadie smiled slightly when she looked at the tiny crocheted kitten attached to her key chain.

"Didn't know if you liked cats," Mila said to his daughter. "If not, just let me know and I'll crochet you a different animal."

Sadie lifted her gaze from the key chain. "You made this for me?"

"I might have a wee crocheting addiction. Or maybe it's more accurate to say yarn addiction. I own way too much," Mila joked.

"Thanks," Sadie said, and this time her smile was genuine, one that Boone hadn't seen in months. Some of the weight crushing his chest lifted.

Unfortunately, this unwanted attraction to Mila was now

laced with gratitude, because she'd managed—in less than twenty minutes—to bring back a bit of the daughter he'd been missing.

The three of them walked inside, and Boone decided the charm of the outside of the cabin was more than matched by the interior. The entrance brought them straight into the great room, which consisted of a large living room, separated from the kitchen by an island, as well as a dining nook tucked inside a bay window that offered a view of the surrounding woods at the rear of the house. There was a stone fireplace on one wall, a big-screen TV on another, a vase of flowers in the center of the table, and a plush rug on the floor in front of the couch.

The entire place was warm and cozy, and it was clear someone had taken care to make it special for them.

No. Not someone.

Mila.

If the word *home* had a picture beside it in the dictionary, it would be this room.

When Levi offered Boone the job, he said it came with furnished living accommodations, which had been a very nice perk. It hadn't been hard for Boone to say goodbye to his old furniture, a combination of cheap Goodwill buys and IKEA stuff that decorated the apartment he and Sadie shared. None of it had held any sentimental value, so he'd simply called up Habitat for Humanity and donated it all.

"I put a few essentials in the kitchen, like condiments, bread, coffee, eggs, milk…stuff like that. Just to hold you over until you can make it to the grocery store. And I've included a sample pack of Rain or Shine beer and a few bottles of our wine for you to try."

"You didn't need to do that," Boone said.

"Oh, it was no problem at all. Your room is over here," Mila said to Sadie, guiding her to a door on the right side of the cabin.

Boone followed, so he was close enough to hear Sadie's soft gasp as they entered.

"This is mine?"

He understood his daughter's surprise. The room was double the size of her previous one, and instead of a twin bed, Sadie would now be sleeping in a four-poster queen.

"Yep. I wasn't sure if you'd be bringing bedding or not. If so, I can take away the quilt." Mila walked over to the bed, running her hand over the handmade quilt. "My grandma Sheila made it. She was Queen of the Quilting Bee around here, so we're in possession of many, *many* quilts. If you don't like this one, I can show you some other options and you can pick your own. I wasn't sure if you were a pastel or primary color girl."

Sadie giggled, the sound nearly knocking Boone over. How long had it been since he'd heard her little-girl laugh?

"This one is perfect. I love it." Sadie crossed the room to climb onto the bed, bouncing a couple of times on her knees before flopping to her back dramatically, sighing as she sank into the soft mattress.

Boone took a moment to glance around. In addition to the bed, the room also had a dresser, two nightstands, and a full-length mirror. There was a large window, covered with gauzy white curtains, as well as a door that led to the front porch.

"And this is your bathroom," Mila said.

Sadie's eyes widened and she climbed off the bed to look. "My own bathroom?"

Boone was pretty impressed by that feature as well. The two of them had shared one bathroom in their old apartment, something that had led to countless arguments the past six months, as Sadie had discovered makeup and curling irons and straighteners and a whole bunch of other shit that covered the sink counter.

Boone marveled at Sadie's awestruck face as she spun around the room, dashing over to open the closet doors. It wasn't a walk-in, but the way his daughter reacted, it might as well have been.

"There's so much room for all my stuff!"

Mila smiled. "I'm glad you like it." Then she looked at him, pointing across the great room. "Your room is on the opposite side of the cabin. It's similar to this one, but a bit bigger."

Again, Boone followed Mila's lead, but Sadie didn't join them, too busy exploring her own space.

Mila opened the door, stepping in more timidly than she had when showing Sadie her room, hovering in the doorway. That shyness stirred something in Boone that he was hard-pressed to ignore.

Forcing one foot in front of the other, he entered the room. It was similarly decorated to Sadie's, but he had a king-sized bed and, instead of just a shower, his bathroom also had a whirlpool tub.

"We upgraded half of the cabins a few years back, making them less rustic and more luxurious. That way, guests can decide if they want the pampered experience or if they'd rather rough it," Mila explained.

"We didn't need anything this fancy. We would have been fine in a more rustic one."

Mila glanced over her shoulder toward Sadie's room. "I'm sure *you* would have, but I was twelve once, and I would have killed for my own bathroom. My sister Remi was the worst when it came to globs of toothpaste in the sink and wet towels on the floor."

Boone was touched by the way Mila continued to consider Sadie's feelings. Lena had left him—*them*—when Sadie was two, declaring she didn't want to be a wife *or* a mother anymore. She'd given him full custody as she flitted off, doing whatever the hell captured her fancy. Back when she'd lived in Williamsburg, she'd take Sadie for one weekend a month, and in the summer, she'd keep her for a week. Since moving to Florida, the visits had dwindled down significantly. In the past year, Sadie had only seen her mother twice, once when Boone had paid to fly her to Florida for a week, and then one day over the holidays.

During Sadie's time with Lena, bedtime was forgotten, meals consisted of junk food or McDonald's, and showers and toothbrushing was optional. It took a good couple of weeks for Boone to break the bad habits Lena instilled during her time in charge and get his daughter back to her normal, healthy routines.

Boone had taken to calling Lena Sadie's fun aunt—only in his head, not in front of Sadie—because she sure as shit wasn't a mother to her daughter.

Since their divorce, Boone had sworn off love and relationships, because he was dedicated to raising Sadie in a stable environment. Dating, in his mind, was too chaotic and not at all conducive to that goal. He'd been burned bad in the romance department, and he was not about to sign up for that shit again.

Boone caught sight of Sadie taking a picture of her new bed with her phone. He'd finally broken down and gotten her one for Christmas because, of course—according to Sadie—Stella and every other kid in her class had their own. He tried to convince himself it was because she was old enough, but he knew the gift was also a way to assuage his guilt over the move.

No doubt she was texting pics of her room to Stella and Lena, the latter of which—despite moving all the way to fucking Florida—had been pissed about him taking the job in Gracemont, claiming it would make her infrequent visits to Virginia more difficult.

He racked his brain to try to remember when Lena had ever taken Sadie's needs into account, and he came up with nothing.

Meanwhile, Mila, a stranger, was going out of her way to make sure Sadie felt comfortable in her new home.

"Speaking of Sadie…" Once again, Mila checked behind her

to make sure they were still alone, then lowered her voice. "My family always does a big Sunday dinner. What don't you and Sadie join us tonight? After all, you've had a long drive, and I know Levi will drag you all over the farm because he loves showing it off, so I doubt you'll have time to go the grocery store today."

Boone opened his mouth to refuse, because he really was tired and he didn't want to crash a family meal, but Mila cut him off at the pass.

"And before you say no, trust me when I say that Sunday dinner isn't limited to just family. We always have friends joining us. Plus..." Mila leaned toward him, speaking even more softly. "If you'd like...I was thinking of inviting Lark McCoy to come tonight. She performs weekends at the brewery and winery. She's an amazing singer and guitar player."

Boone didn't have a clue where Mila was going with *that*. Was she trying to set him up? He wasn't sure why the idea of her trying to hook him up with another woman pissed him off, but the idea of *Mila* not wanting him...

Boone clenched his jaw. *Mila is too young. She's a Storm. She's dangerous.*

Dangerous.

"Mila," he started again, but she clearly wasn't planning on taking no for an answer.

"Lark's little sister, Piper, is in seventh grade at Gracemont Middle School. She'll be in Sadie's classes. I was thinking maybe it would help make Sadie's first day easier if she had a friend going in. I'm sure Lark wouldn't mind coming to dinner and bringing Piper along."

Boone's refusal vanished into thin air, and he struggled to respond. Not because he didn't want to accept, but because Mila was truly going the extra mile to make not only him but his daughter feel welcome.

He wasn't sure he'd ever met anyone so damn thoughtful and sweet.

"That's a kind offer." Boone knew his daughter well enough to know that a lot of her quietness today was driven not so much by that damn silent treatment of hers, but because she was genuinely nervous about starting at a new school.

Between finishing at his previous job, the holidays, and packing their apartment, Boone hadn't been able to get them here before now. Which meant that, in addition to him beginning work tomorrow, Sadie was starting at her new school. It was a less-than-ideal situation, but there simply hadn't been enough time to do everything they needed to.

"Piper is super-outgoing. I swear the girl never stops talking, but she's also very nice and makes friends easily. I'm sure she'd show Sadie around school and introduce her to the other kids. And I promise you, Piper is a really good kid. One of the top students in the seventh grade."

With every word Mila spoke, Boone felt himself more and more drawn to her. She was honey and he was the bee. If he was smart, he'd put as much distance between them as he could.

However, she'd just made him an offer he couldn't refuse.

"We'd love to come to dinner." Giving his daughter the chance to make a friend prior to sending her into a new school where she knew no one was the least he could do, considering he was the one who'd uprooted her and dragged her across the state.

"Awesome." Mila pulled her phone out of her pocket. "Let me step outside to call Lark really quick and see if they can make it. I don't want Sadie to overhear me and get her hopes up if they're busy."

Boone followed Mila through to the great room, then out onto the front porch, where she could speak to her friend in private.

Sadie had already grabbed one of her suitcases from the truck and was dragging it to her room, looking a lot less sullen than she had an hour ago.

"You got it, Donut?" he asked his daughter. "Need help?"

"I'm good," Sadie called over her shoulder.

Boone listened as Mila explained the reason for the last-minute dinner invitation, then he walked to the truck to retrieve a couple boxes, not wanting to eavesdrop. Returning to the porch, he heard Mila say, "That's fantastic. See you both at six." She hung up the phone. "It's all set. Piper's excited to meet Sadie."

"Thank you for this, Mila. It's a very thoughtful offer."

Mila brushed away his gratitude with a wave of her hand. He couldn't help but notice she wasn't good at accepting compliments, always downplaying her actions. "It's nothing, really. One of the great things about small towns is everybody knows everybody else, so it's easy to know who to call on for help with pretty much any situation. Of course, the bad thing about small towns is, everybody knows everybody else."

She had a light, tinkling laugh that Boone found incredibly adorable.

"I texted Levi when I was grabbing the cabin keys to let him know to come straight here for your meeting. He's probably on his way."

"Is Levi your brother?" Boone asked, in the dark about who was who on the farm.

Mila shook her head. "He's my cousin. I have seven of them, all guys."

"Ah, that's right. The frat house." Boone dug deep to recall all the things Mila had said in the truck on the way here, while he'd been lost in thought about her pretty smile and sexy body and… "And you have two sisters," he said.

"Nope. Three. My third sister moved to Philadelphia just over a year ago, so that's why it's just me, Nora, and Remi in our farmhouse. You'll meet everyone tonight, and I promise to give you a rundown of who's who."

He smiled appreciatively. "Should I bring a notebook?"

Mila laughed. "Might not be a bad idea. Okay," she said. "I've overstayed my welcome. I'm sure you two are exhausted and anxious to unpack. Dinner is back at the B&B where we met, at six."

Boone nodded, then frowned when Mila stepped off the front porch. "Wait. Where are you going?"

"Home," she replied simply.

"I drove you here," he reminded her.

She lifted one shoulder casually. "I know, but I'm not walking back to the B&B. Just to my house. It's a lot closer."

"No," he snapped. "It's cold out, Mila. I'm driving you."

Mila froze for just a moment, her pupils dilating in response to his tone, which had been sharper than he'd intended. However, she recovered quickly, brushing his words away with a sunny smile as the sun hit her chestnut-colored hair, revealing auburn highlights. "Walking is the main form of transportation around the farm…in all seasons," she explained.

Boone was about to insist she let him drive her, unhappy with the idea of her traipsing through the woods on a winter's day, but as she turned away, another vehicle appeared.

Mila glanced over her shoulder at him. "There's Levi now," she announced, she and her cousin exchanging waves as he drove by her and Mila continued down the lane.

He watched her go, his hands itching to drag her back and spank that perky little ass of hers until she promised to do as he said. But that was a completely ridiculous thought. Because she wasn't his and she never would be.

He sighed as Levi parked his truck next to Boone's.

Yep. Mila Storm was dangerous.

And the worst part was…he wasn't as afraid as he should be.

Chapter Three

Mila pulled the pies from the oven as Aunt Claire returned to the kitchen from setting the huge dining room table. After returning to her house to tackle a few things on her to-do list, Mila walked back to the B&B to help her aunt cook dinner for tonight. She couldn't begin to count how much time she'd spent in this kitchen with her aunt, preparing meals. It was Grandma Sheila who'd taught her how to crochet and Aunt Claire who'd taught her to cook.

Following the death of Mila's parents when she was nine years old, her grandmother and aunt had wrapped her—and her sisters—in their arms, smothering them with the most wonderful motherly love in the world. So much so, Mila considered Aunt Claire more mother than aunt.

Mila drew in a deep breath, her mouth watering as all the scents in the kitchen hit her at once. The sweet smell of the apple pies mingled with the savory beef stew simmering on the stove, and underlying all that was the scent of fresh-baked bread. No place on earth ever smelled better than Aunt Claire's kitchen on Sunday night.

While this house functioned as a B&B six nights a week, Aunt Claire considered Sundays sacred. Meaning, no reservations were taken and the entire family was expected to gather for dinner at six p.m. sharp.

The boys teased their mother about her insistence that they share the meal together, reminding her that they saw each other all the time. With the exception of Lucy in Philadelphia, and Levi, who now lived down in the valley with Kasi, the rest of the Storms all lived and worked on the farm.

"Lark and Piper just got here. My goodness, that Piper is getting tall. She's going to be a beauty like her big sisters," Aunt Claire told her. Lark's bird-watching-obsessed mother had four kids. The twins, Lark and Wren, Robin, the only son, and then Piper, the baby. "Inviting them was a good idea, sweetheart."

"I hope Sadie and Piper hit it off. Sadie was pretty quiet most of the time I was with them this afternoon, and I couldn't help but think how hard it would be at that age, having to walk into the school cafeteria at lunchtime and not know anyone. Middle schoolers are brutal."

Aunt Claire grinned. "I suppose they are. It was such a sweet thing for you to suggest."

Mila shrugged. "Anyone else would have thought of it. I just happened to get there first."

Aunt Claire rolled her eyes but didn't say anything else. Mainly because she didn't need to. Mila had been subjected to countless speeches from her aunt about her inability to accept compliments.

"Tell me about Boone," Aunt Claire said. "You've said quite a bit about the girl, but you haven't said anything about him. Is he nice? Friendly? Do you think he'll be a good fit for the farm?"

Mila hadn't said much about Boone because she was struggling to think about the man without blushing, and she was worried her astute aunt would pick up on her insta-crush on their new vineyard manager.

No. Not crush.

Mila dismissed "crush" because it was too gentle a word for her instinctual reaction toward Boone. That tumble she took into his arms might have been earlier this afternoon, but she could swear she'd been in a free fall ever since. Not that she could tell anyone that.

Well, maybe she could pull Theo and Levi aside and ask them if what she'd felt when he touched her was truly the same as their experiences.

She shut that idea down. Mainly because she didn't want to look like an idiot if her feelings were one-sided and not returned. She didn't have enough experience with dating and attraction to read his expressions. A couple times, she felt as if he was looking at her with something like desire, but just as many times, she'd caught his scowl and wondered if she'd done something to anger him.

Wow. Reading too much into thirty minutes, Mila, or what?

She hadn't spent more than half an hour with the man, and she'd already analyzed every word and expression approximately four million times.

"He's a very nice man," Mila said, as she turned her back on Aunt Claire, stirring the stew, even though it didn't need to be stirred. "I think he'll fit in fine on the farm. We didn't really talk about the vineyards. I just helped them get situated in their new home."

God. She hoped it would be their home for a good long time. The thought of him leaving before she could figure out what *this* was made her stomach hurt.

Mila closed her eyes briefly, aware she was getting far too carried away over a man she'd just met. She knew precious little about him. And the stuff she did know was just tidbits Levi had dropped along the way after hiring him. He was divorced, a single father, and his previous job had been as an assistant vineyard manager in Williamsburg. Those three piddly facts were it.

Except that she knew Levi thought highly of Boone's skills with the grapes. She'd overheard him mention that Boone had been the one to help Levi identify an issue he'd been having with the Cabernet Franc grapes a couple of years ago, and how they'd researched together to solve it. She was certain Levi had probably said more about the man when they were discussing offering the job to him, but Mila hadn't been interested enough to pay attention, completely unaware of the effect Boone would have on her before today.

"What did he and Sadie think of the cabin?" Aunt Claire asked.

"Oh, they really liked it. While they didn't say as much, I got the feeling their last place was smaller. They both seemed impressed, and Sadie was delighted to have her own bathroom."

"It *is* one of the nicer cabins on the farm. I'm surprised you chose to let that one go. It's typically one of the first to get rented."

Mila wasn't sure why she'd selected that cabin, because her aunt was right. It was one of their most popular rentals. When the family decided to put Boone and his daughter up in one of the cabins, because Levi insisted it was in their best interest to keep the manager close to the vineyard in case of bad weather or other issues that might arise, she'd been charged with choosing which one. Because, as she'd told Boone, somewhere over the years, the cabins had become her domain. Not that she was particularly happy about that.

If she was smart, she would have chosen a different cabin. Boone had even said they would have been fine in a smaller, more rustic one, but as Mila considered the options, she decided the one she'd selected was best suited to be a permanent home. The cabin had always been her favorite, and she liked the idea of a family living there versus a different group of strangers every week.

"I want them to be comfortable," Mila said. "It could be their home for years."

Aunt Claire walked over and wrapped her arm around Mila's shoulders, giving her a squeeze. "Of course, you did, sweet girl. Always going the extra mile to make others happy."

Mila smiled, but before she could refute her aunt's words, Kasi stepped into the kitchen.

"Need any help?"

"Hello, Kasi, dear. When did you get here?" Aunt Claire asked, walking over to give Kasi a hug. Aunt Claire had begun to worry she'd never have grandchildren, given the way all seven of her sons had been stubbornly hanging on to their bachelor statuses. When Levi fell for Kasi last summer, Aunt Claire had been over the moon, and she'd been dropping the occasional hints about how beautiful spring weddings were ever since.

Kasi, Remi's best friend forever, had practically grown up on the farm, thanks to countless playdates, so she didn't take Aunt Claire's comments as pressure, but rather a compliment.

"Dad, Keith, and I got here just now. Walked in at the same time as Levi and the new vineyard manager."

Mila's heart instantly began to race, knowing that Boone was in the very next room.

Aunt Claire wiped her hands on her apron. "Oh good. I've been anxious to meet him. Do me a favor, Kasi, and keep an eye on the bread for us. Mila, are you coming to introduce Sadie and Piper?" Her aunt didn't wait for a response, leaving the room as if Mila following her was a given.

Mila tried to move, but her feet felt as if they were sunk in

Caught in a Storm

mud, her nerves kicking in. She'd fretted all afternoon about Boone's first impression of her. After all, her first act had been to fall on him, knocking both of them on their asses. Then she became a bundle of nervous energy, talking way more than usual. She worried he'd found her constant chatter annoying, because he'd been so quiet himself.

"Mila?" Kasi asked, her brows furrowing. "You okay?"

She nodded, fighting to calm down. She was losing her damn mind. "Yeah, I'm fine. I'll be back in a few minutes."

"Take your time. I know my way around this kitchen." Kasi was as good a cook as Aunt Claire, which was saying something.

Mila stepped out of the kitchen, following the sound of voices, all of which were in the living room.

Peering into the room, she saw Piper had already made her way over to Sadie, engaging her in what appeared to be a complete rundown of all the seventh-grade teachers. Sadie was listening intently, but more importantly, smiling. The young girl had been far too serious this afternoon, so Mila was pleased to see her looking a lot less scared.

She let her attention linger on the girls for a little longer because she feared once she turned her gaze to Boone, she wouldn't be able to look away.

"It's a beautiful farm," she heard Boone say to her aunt and uncle. Uncle Rex was standing somewhat gingerly on one leg as Aunt Claire hovered, clearly concerned he might fall again and hurt himself worse.

Mila wasn't sure what Uncle Rex said in response, because she'd managed to force herself to look at Boone. He'd showered before coming, and he was wearing a different shirt. He'd arrived at the farm in a warm flannel, but this shirt was a nice light blue button-down, and he'd exchanged his faded jeans for a crisp new dark denim pair.

His eyes drifted over to the girls in the corner, and Mila saw his shoulders relax.

Then he turned his attention to her.

His eyes slid down, taking in all of her, as she'd just done to him. His gaze felt like a touch, her body reacting to it as if he were stroking those large hands over her curves. She'd also put some thought into her outfit, exchanging her bulky winter sweater for a silky blouse and swapping out her comfy, loose-fitting jeans for the skinny pair that meant she couldn't eat much at dinner. It was worth it as Boone's gaze lingered.

"Mila." Boone nodded his head just once, and she felt herself flush because damn if she didn't like way he said her name. It was the same way everyone else did, but somehow he made it sound like both a compliment and a command, two things that shouldn't go together.

"Hi, Boone." She bit her lower lip, hoping no one else in the room caught the breathiness of her greeting.

Mercifully, Remi chose that moment to crash into the room. Or at least, that's what it always felt like. Remi did nothing quiet or subtle. "Hey, you must be Boone," she said, crossing the room, her hand outstretched.

Boone took it, smiling. "I am."

"I'm Remi Storm." Then she gestured over her shoulder to Nora, whose entrance had been overshadowed. "And this is my sister Nora. You already met Mila."

Remi had been home when Mila returned from showing Boone and Sadie the cabin, and she'd hit her with a million and twelve questions about them. Mila held her breath as Nora and Remi both spoke to Boone, part of her terrified that perhaps they'd also feel an attraction toward him. Because how could they not? The guy was sex-on-a-stick hot.

The three of them—or actually, just Remi—conversed for a few minutes, the conversation seeming nothing more than friendly as her youngest sister offered to take Boone and Sadie on a trail ride the following weekend to show them around the mountains, proclaiming they'd yet to see the prettiest views on the farm. Sadie and Piper overheard the offer, both girls coming over, clearly excited by the invitation.

"Can we go, Dad?" Sadie pleaded.

"I have a very gentle horse, perfect for new riders," Remi reassured him.

Boone considered it for a moment, then nodded. "Sure. I haven't ridden a horse in years."

"Can I go too?" Piper asked.

"If it's okay with your parents, then of course."

Mila grinned when the two girls bumped shoulders enthusiastically, acting like they'd been friends forever.

Boone saw the reaction as well, and Mila's heart began to thud when his gaze returned to her. Her analytical mind went wild, trying to figure out what she was seeing, because she couldn't tell if it was gratitude, desire, or indifference. Maybe all three, which made no sense.

Boone hadn't been on the farm more than six hours, and she was already completely lost in her head. At this rate, Mila would be completely insane by dawn.

One by one, more of the family appeared, each of her cousins introducing themselves to Boone and Sadie. Jace, her youngest cousin, joked that there'd be a test after dinner, regarding who was who.

"Dinner's ready," Kasi announced from the doorway.

"Oh my goodness," Aunt Claire exclaimed. "I completely lost track of time. Kasi, you are a dear for setting it all out."

Everyone filed into the dining room, taking seats around the huge farmhouse table. Because the family was so large, Uncle Rex had commissioned a local carpenter to build the table, which seated twenty. Tonight, they all fit, but on quite a few occasions, they had to set up a smaller "kids' table" to ensure everyone had a spot.

Sadie and Piper sat next to Mila, the two girls still chatting away. Mila had to stifle a laugh as Piper began filling Sadie in on who the hottest boys in their class were. Boone had selected the seat directly across the table from Mila, so she caught the way he briefly closed his eyes when he heard their conversation. When he opened them and looked at her, Mila offered a quick "girls will be girls" shrug that was met with an amused smirk.

The food was passed around, everyone helping themselves to the beef stew and bread. Boone devoured the dinner like it was the best thing he'd ever eaten in his life.

"This beef stew is delicious, Mrs. Storm," Boone said to Aunt Claire.

Aunt Claire lifted one finger, wiggling it. "No, no, Boone. I insist you call me Claire. And that compliment belongs to Mila. She made the stew. My assignments for tonight were the bread and pie."

Boone's gaze slid to her. "You're a woman of many talents."

Mila brushed off the compliment with a wave of her hand, lowering her head and praying no one saw the way she was blushing. She kept her eyes locked on her bowl for a few minutes as the conversation continued to flow around her, Sam talking about some of his goals for Gracemont, now that he'd won the mayoral election. Starting tomorrow, he was officially the mayor.

When she raised her eyes again, she realized Boone was still looking at her, and, once again, she was overwhelmed by the wealth of emotions he was shooting in her direction. She couldn't understand how this man, a virtual stranger, impacted her so strongly, making her want things—dark and dirty and oh-so-sexy things—she'd never experienced.

Mercifully, Grayson pulled Boone's attention away,

discussing the grapes they'd been growing and what wines they currently had on hand, aging in oak barrels. Mila listened, mesmerized by Boone's deep voice and the passion with which he discussed his work.

Unfortunately, she had to stop eavesdropping when Aunt Claire pulled her into a conversation she and Gretchen were having regarding this year's Valentine's Dance. Typically, most community events happened in Gracemont Community Center, but it was shut down prior to the holidays due to a leaky roof. Rather than cancel the town's annual Christmas party, they'd held it in her family's new event barn. The party was such a success, the town council proposed holding the Valentine's Dance there as well, so they could take their time repairing *all* the issues at the aging community center instead of just the roof.

Mila listened with half an ear as Gretchen and Aunt Claire discussed the decorations. Typically, she offered a ton of input, but tonight, she couldn't focus enough to do more than agree with their suggestions.

The second Mila reached adulthood, Aunt Claire had begun dragging her to all the ladies' auxiliary meetings, the local women in charge of organizing community events. As such, Mila had planned more Harvest and Valentine's dances, Christmas parties, and Fourth of July picnics than she could count. Not that she minded. It was the only time she could truly indulge her love of catering.

The whole time she spoke with Gretchen and Claire, Theo had his arm wrapped around the back of Gretchen's chair, occasionally resting his hand on her shoulder or stroking her hair, as if he couldn't stop himself from touching her. Every time he did so, Gretchen leaned closer to him, gazing at him with such love, Mila found it difficult to look away.

Gretchen had arrived at Stormy Weather Farm in September, after escaping an abusive relationship, so it had taken some time and effort for her cousin to earn the skittish woman's heart and trust.

Theo bent his head lower, whispering something into Gretchen's ear. She grinned, then he gave her a kiss on the cheek.

Mila longed for that kind of closeness, dreamed of finding a man who would be so enamored of her, he couldn't make it through dinner without giving her a kiss or running his fingers through her hair. Her gaze slid across the table to Boone…and she realized he was watching Theo and Gretchen as well.

When he turned his attention to Mila, his brows were furrowed, his eyes troubled.

Shit. She needed to stop staring at the man like some love-struck teenager.

For the rest of dinner, she worked overtime to avoid making eye contact.

Once the meal wrapped up, the guys rose, clearing the table, taking over the kitchen duties. Aunt Claire was a firm believer in the concept that the cooks didn't clean. Once the dishes were done, and leftovers were packed away and distributed for everyone's lunches tomorrow, people began to leave.

Boone probably would have followed suit, but Sadie had begged him to let her go to the stables with Remi, Piper, and Lark to see the horses. He'd agreed, clearly pleased that Sadie had found a new friend. Remi promised they'd be quick, but Mila knew that was a lie. Remi loved her horses and loved showing them off, so she suspected they'd be a while.

Eventually, it was just her, Boone, Aunt Claire, and Uncle Rex left.

"Okay, Superman," Aunt Claire said to her husband, pointing at his foot. "I *knew* you should have stayed in the living room with it reclined. Your ankle is swollen again. Time for bed and ibuprofen."

Uncle Rex didn't put up a fuss, which told Mila he was likely in quite a bit of pain.

"Mila, why don't you and Boone wait in the living room for the girls to come back? It'll be more comfortable."

Mila wasn't sure if Aunt Claire was attempting to play matchmaker or if she was simply charging her with entertaining their guest, since they were the last ones here. Now that Levi and Theo had succumbed to love, her aunt was bound and determined to see the rest of the Storm kids partnered up. While Mila didn't know for sure, she suspected it was Aunt Claire who had encouraged Pastor Joshua to ask her out that first time.

Mila sighed. She should probably stop thinking of him as *Pastor* Joshua, considering they'd gone out three times, and just call him Joshua.

While Aunt Claire helped Uncle Rex back to their master suite, she led Boone to the living room. She took a seat on the couch, hoping he would join her, so she was disappointed when he opted for one of the armchairs instead.

"Ready for the family test?" Mila joked, aware Boone had been pushed into the deep end on his first day, meeting the entire family in one fell swoop.

Boone chuckled. "Maybe not quite yet, though I think I'm getting a handle on it. I know that Rex and Claire have seven sons, but God help me if you ask me to name them all. Kasi was with Levi, and Gretchen was with Theo. And you have three sisters, though only two were here, Remi and Nora."

"Not too bad for first time."

"You said your other sister lives in Pennsylvania?" he clarified.

Mila nodded. "Lucy moved to Philly just over a year ago with her boyfriends."

Boone frowned, probably trying to figure out if he'd heard her correctly. "Boyfriends? Plural?"

Mila was aware Lucy's relationship with Miles and Joey wasn't exactly normal, but there was no denying what the three of them shared was magical. "Yep. Plural. She lives with two guys, Miles and Joey, as a throuple." Lucy was the one who'd started referring to her relationship status that way. Mila loved the word and thought it worked well.

"Wow. A real-life threesome."

Mila was relieved when she didn't hear any judgment in Boone's tone. There'd been more than a few locals who'd expressed their concerns over what they considered a sinful relationship.

While Pasto—err, Joshua—hadn't come right out and condemned it, he'd asked Mila what her family thought about it, and when she said they thought it was awesome, he'd promptly dropped the subject. She wasn't sure, because he hadn't said as much, but she got the sense the pastor thought the family should be showing Lucy the error of her ways rather than embracing the relationship.

"To be honest, I can't imagine trying to make a relationship work with two people. It's hard enough with one."

Boone opened that door, so Mila was going to walk through it, because she had a hundred questions she wanted to ask him.

"You and Sadie's mom are divorced?"

Boone nodded. "Over ten years now."

Mila's eyes widened in surprise. She expected to discover the divorce was more recent. "But that would mean that Sadie was only…"

"Two years old."

Mila opened her mouth, then closed it because what did she say to that? What mother left her daughter when she was still practically a baby?

Fortunately, Boone didn't need any prodding, giving her

answers to questions that would be too inappropriate to ask someone she'd just met.

"Lena decided after Sadie was born that the wife-and-mother routine wasn't for her."

Mila bit her lip, tempted to say that was a little late to make such a realization.

"Lena was younger than me. I'd just turned twenty-seven when we met. She was twenty. In hindsight, I can see we rushed the marriage thing, walking down the aisle just ten months later. Sadie was a honeymoon baby, appearing nine months after that."

"A whirlwind romance," she said, aware she was putting a positive spin on something she knew nothing about.

"Or just me being stupid. A couple of my buddies had taken the marriage plunge, and I decided I was ready to settle down and start a family too. Lena suffered from postpartum depression after Sadie was born, spending hours, sometimes days in bed, sleeping and crying. She barely even looked at Sadie the first few months. I thought once that passed, things would get better. She'd see Sadie and fall in love with our child the same way I had."

"She didn't?"

Boone didn't reply. Instead, he just lifted one shoulder noncommittally.

Mila's heart ached for the baby, even though she'd met Sadie and could see the young girl was healthy and happy. Sure, she was quiet today, but that was to be expected. Moving to a place where you didn't know anyone was scary.

Mila vowed right then and there that she would reach out to Sadie, offer her friendship, try to be a positive female influence. She knew all too well what it was like to grow up without her own mother. She'd been blessed with Aunt Claire and Grandma Sheila, and she wanted to pay that love and kindness forward.

"When Sadie was two, I picked her up from daycare and

came home to find Lena sitting on her suitcases, waiting for me. Said she was leaving." Boone ran his hand through his hair, the memory clearly still a painful one after all these years. "So, we got divorced, and she gave me full custody."

It felt like he'd skipped over a whole lot regarding his relationship with Lena and her reasons for leaving, but Mila didn't feel like it was her place to push for more. However, she was too curious about one part not to follow up. "Full custody? Does that mean she never sees Sadie?"

"Lena takes her one week each summer, and any other visits are typically at her convenience. When she lived in Williamsburg, she saw Sadie one weekend every month or two. Since moving to Florida a year ago, she's only seen Sadie twice, once when I flew her down for the summer visit, and then one day over the holidays. Lena's sister still lives in Williamsburg, so she flew up to see her family for a week and made some time for Sadie."

While Boone didn't say it aloud, Mila got the sense the Christmas visit wouldn't have happened if Lena hadn't already been traveling to Williamsburg. Again, Mila couldn't understand a mother who didn't want to see her child, didn't want to watch them grow up and spend every single day with them.

Mila wanted kids more than her next breath, and she knew when she had them, they would never spend a minute doubting her undying love.

"I'm sorry, Boone. None of that could have been easy for you or Sadie."

"I don't mean to sound bitter," he said. "Because I'm not angry or upset about the way things turned out. I'd go through all of it again because it brought Sadie to me. The rest is ancient history."

She wasn't sure she believed him, but she pretended she did. "You're right. It is."

"And I've learned from that history."

"What do you mean?" Mila asked, confused.

"It's not going to repeat itself. Not with me. I made a promise to myself the day Lena walked out the door that Sadie would always come first."

"That's how it should be."

Boone continued like she hadn't spoken, but there was no denying he was looking straight at her, his words meant for her. "I don't date because dating would bring chaos to Sadie's life."

"I don't think that's tr—" Mila started, but Boone cut her off, his tone sharper, harder.

"I'm forty years old and too set in my ways. Dating is a precursor to a relationship, and I'm not interested in that—at all. And I'm sure as hell not having any more kids. I'm happy with the life I've built with Sadie, and I'm not looking to change it."

Every word Boone spoke felt like a dagger.

Because she knew he wasn't just making conversation.

She'd given herself away. He'd caught her stealing too many glances, recognized the desire and hope in her expression…and now he was warning her away.

Mila's throat clogged and that stupid blush she'd worn all day was back. Only this time, it wasn't driven by attraction or arousal, but by embarrassment.

Boone was silent, as if waiting for her to reply.

Even if she wanted to speak, Mila couldn't, so she simply nodded.

Boone studied her closely. When he spoke again, his voice was gentler, softer. "Marriage was something I thought I wanted when I was younger, closer to your age, but I figured out it's not for me. I'm not good husband material. It's best that it plays no part in my future." He offered her a smile, but there wasn't a bit of happiness in it. In fact, it was downright miserable.

She supposed she should be grateful. He was attempting to

let her down easy before she let this—she sighed and used the hated word—*crush* go too far. It felt more accurate than it had before, especially since he'd made sure to point out the differences in their ages.

She told herself to speak, but she couldn't find any words.

Mercifully, she was saved by footsteps climbing the front porch, Remi and Sadie's voices shattering the silence that had descended between her and Boone.

Her sister and Sadie walked into the living room, Sadie's face ruddy from the chill in the air but her smile the biggest one Mila had seen yet. The sound of a car in the driveway told her that Piper and Lark were heading home.

"Hey there, Donut," he said, calling his daughter by her sweet nickname. "You have fun?"

"Dad," Sadie said, rushing over to Boone. "You should have come with us! Remi has ten horses, and she's getting a donkey soon, and I got to feed them carrots, and they were *so* sweet. One of them, Misty, put her head against mine. I love her so much! I can't wait to ride her. And Remi said I can visit them whenever I want. She's going to teach me all about the tack and everything too."

Despite the ache in her chest, Mila smiled, thrilled by Sadie's excitement. This was the most words she'd heard her speak all day.

And she obviously wasn't the only one blown away.

Boone listened to his daughter with something akin to awe on his face.

"She even said I can help her out around the stables after school if you say it's okay. Can I, Dad?"

Boone glanced up at Remi, who placed her hand on Sadie's shoulder, grinning widely.

"She'd be a big help," Remi reassured him. "She's a born horsewoman. The horses really took to her."

"That sounds great," Boone said, his voice suddenly thick. With emotion? "If you're sure she won't be in the way."

Remi ruffled Sadie's hair as the girl smiled up at her. "This kid? Hell...uh, heck no. She's awesome."

"Maybe we can revisit the idea in a week or two, once the two of us are unpacked and settled," Boone said. "This week is going to be too busy with Sadie starting school and me learning the ropes of the new job."

"Perfect." For the first time since entering the room, Remi's gaze swung in her direction...and the slight narrowing of her sister's eyes had Mila scrambling to paint a smile on her face.

"Well, we need to get back to our place, Donut," Boone said, standing. "Got to get up early in the morning. Say thank you to Remi and Mila."

"Thanks for taking me to see the horses, Remi. And for dinner, Mila. It was really good." Sadie waved as her dad guided her to the front door, she and Remi following in their wake.

Once they were gone, Remi turned to her. "You okay?"

"Yeah," Mila lied. "Just super tired. It was a long day."

"So much for Sunday being a day of rest," her sister added, thankfully buying Mila's excuse. The two of them left the B&B, aware Aunt Claire would come down around ten for her nightly cup of chamomile tea. She'd lock up then.

Remi carried the conversation as the two of them took the path from the B&B to their farmhouse. She hadn't lied to Boone about this being a "walking" farm. While they all owned vehicles, it was rare they used them to travel from one part of the farm to the other, even in the winter months.

She bid her sister good night as she climbed the stairs to her bedroom. Walking in, she sank down on the edge of the mattress wearily, hating how much Boone's words had hurt.

Mila was perfectly aware she was being stupid. She'd just met the man today, after all.

It was just, for the first time in her life, she'd felt real hope that the future she wanted might be within her grasp.

To have it instantly ripped away…

Well. It hurt. A lot.

So she was going to take tonight to throw herself a pity party and then tomorrow morning, she was snuffing out all the hope and putting Boone behind her.

Something told her that would be easier said than done.

Chapter Four

Boone had realized halfway through Sunday dinner on his first night on the farm that he needed to put the kibosh on whatever had been brewing between him and Mila.

Because he'd caught her shooting glances in his direction far too often.

Of course, the reason he'd caught all those glances was because he'd been looking right back at her, his gaze drawn to her time after time. The way she looked at him stirred needs that had lain dormant for ages. So he'd joined her in her aunt's living room after the meal and made it abundantly clear he wasn't about to revoke his membership to the bachelor's club.

Ordinarily, he never would have engaged in a conversation like that with a woman he'd just met, but it had felt like the quickest, simplest way to snuff out the attraction between them.

Hell, most of what he said hadn't even been for *her* benefit, but for his. A reminder of why he couldn't give in to his instantaneous desire for Miss Mila Storm.

Because he meant what he'd said. Lena introduced enough

instability into Sadie's life with her revolving door of boyfriends. He refused to do the same.

And if Boone had only been physically attracted to Mila, he would have been fine, because he could combat that. After ten years of practically living like a monk, it wasn't like he was a stranger to denying himself. When it came to self-care, he and his hand were intimately acquainted.

No, the problem with Mila was that, in one afternoon, she'd captured his attention in other, even more desirable ways.

First, because of Sadie. She'd found a way to make his angry daughter smile and given her the gift of a friend when she truly needed one. As Boone sat across the Storms' table and watched his daughter come to life, gratitude toward Mila bloomed, mingling with the attraction.

Then Boone had driven Sadie to school on her first day, because he had paperwork he needed to fill out. Piper had been right there waiting for Sadie, the two girls linking arms and walking into the building together.

The second reason he'd needed to put some distance between him and Mila was entirely superficial but, honestly, just as powerful in his mind. Because when it came to him, there was real truth to the statement that the way to a man's heart was through his stomach.

Once he was thrust into single fatherhood, it fell to him to feed him and Sadie. Sadly, time had always been in short supply in his world, so his cooking skills were limited to simple fare.

When he'd tasted Mila's beef stew… Jesus. It had taken everything he had not to circle the damn table, drop to one knee, and propose. That stew was a goddamn masterpiece, and he'd had to restrain himself from moaning in bliss after every single mouthful. He hadn't even realized until that moment that a woman's cooking could be a serious turn-on.

However, the main reason he forced himself to push Mila

away wasn't even because of something she'd done...but because of something she'd revealed without even meaning to.

Mila had a soft submissive side that called to him.

Between her adorable blushes, the way she looked up at him through lowered eyelashes, and her unintentional, instinctual reactions to his commands, he knew he was in deep trouble. Especially when he caught her watching Gretchen and Theo, a look of longing in her eyes.

Mila was young and looking for love, for a husband, for her own happily ever after. And it didn't matter how much desire or gratitude he felt toward her, he simply couldn't be that man. The most he could give her was sex without strings, and Mila was not that kind of woman. She deserved everything she wanted, which left it to him to erect some walls, put some distance between them.

So...he'd spelled that out for her, even though she hadn't said anything outright about her interest. He figured if he'd misread the situation, there was no harm, no foul. It was just a conversation.

However, it was apparent he hadn't mistaken her feelings at all. Because she'd listened well, giving him a wide berth ever since that night.

Since he was new to the farm, Boone didn't know if his and Mila's paths naturally didn't cross often or if she was making the effort to avoid him. If it was the latter, she was doing a damn good job.

It had been three weeks since that Sunday supper, since he and Sadie had arrived at Stormy Weather Farm, and overall, he thought the move had been one of the best decisions he'd ever made. He absolutely loved his new job, loved the trust the Storms had already instilled in him. His previous boss had been a decent guy, but he was a micromanager, something that chafed more with each passing year. Boone felt as if he was constantly cast in the role of student with no hope of ever graduating. It was one reason he enjoyed talking shop with Levi over the years. Levi treated him as an equal, so it was the only time he got to share his expertise without being questioned.

While it was winter, that didn't mean there wasn't a great deal of work to be done. The vines weren't dormant during the cold season and still required care. He'd spent the last fourteen days pruning the vines, trimming away excess growth, while focusing on the healthiest canes. He'd also taken measures to protect the vines from frost and safeguarding the roots by mulching with straw, which would act as a cozy blanket to protect against extreme temperatures.

Maverick and Grayson, the vintners, had welcomed him into the winery, the three of them discussing flavor profiles, tasting the progress of the maturing wines, and planning for the next harvest. His comments and suggestions were encouraged, and both men made him feel like a valued part of the team.

So as far as the job went, Boone couldn't be happier.

The same went for Sadie. The sullenness and silent treatment he'd endured all fall appeared to be a thing of the past as she and Piper became fast friends. His cheerful, fun-loving daughter was back. Hell, in some ways, Boone felt as if he'd never seen her this happy. Apparently, being the new girl in a school where all the kids had known each other since birth made her the shiny new toy. According to her, she was one of the popular girls, something made obvious by the ungodly amount of texts she got every night.

Boone had been forced to insist that dinnertime was a no-texting activity, and twice, he'd had to confiscate her phone for the night when he'd discovered her and Piper FaceTiming well after bedtime.

School wasn't the only place Sadie had assimilated to with ease. She was also loving life on the farm. Of course, he had

Remi to thank for part of that. There were two hours between the end of Sadie's school day and his quitting time, and he'd worried about leaving her on her own.

The anxiety had been wasted, because Sadie spent a lot of that time at the stables with Remi, which was a positive outlet for her. True to her word, Remi had put Sadie to work with the animals, teaching her how to care for them, giving his daughter some real responsibility, something that would serve her well as she got older.

In Williamsburg, Sadie had been on her own too much as well. Their neighbor across the hall, Mrs. Wilburn, an older widow, watched Sadie during the hours between her getting off the bus and him getting home, but the majority of that time had been spent doing God only knew what with Stella, who lived in the same apartment complex. Boone had even caught the two of them vaping once, Sadie saying the vape was Stella's older brother's and they'd only wanted to try it. Then she'd gotten a detention for skipping class, losing her mind when he'd grounded her for it, because *Stella's* parents hadn't.

Sadie's iPad had a filter as well as a time limit installed, but Stella's had been wide open. And while he didn't actually catch them—Stella was too quick on the draw—Boone suspected they'd been watching porn one afternoon when he came home early.

Sadie's grades had begun slipping, her first-semester marks less than stellar, something he hoped she'd be able to recover from in her new school. And if the grades coming home on tests and papers the past two weeks were any indication, she might be on her way to making the honor roll.

He also had to give credit to Mila for Sadie's current happiness, because while the woman was keeping her distance from *him*—which had been his intent, even though he hated it—she hadn't deserted his daughter. Like Remi, Mila had found ways to entertain Sadie without him even asking.

She was teaching Sadie how to crochet and bake.

Boone stepped into the cabin, inhaling deeply, enjoying the sweet scent of cookies. That alone was enough to make his mouth water—until he caught sight of Mila bent over, pulling a tray out of the oven. Goddamn, she had a perfect ass.

"What's this?" he asked, closing the front door behind him.

Sadie and Mila both whirled around.

"Dessert!" his daughter exclaimed. "Mila taught me how to make Snickerdoodles. We used her grandma's recipe."

"It smells incredible."

"Sadie's turning into quite the baker. Told her we have to keep that a secret or Aunt Claire will start recruiting her for kitchen duty."

Sadie's wide grin told Boone she wouldn't mind that at all. Aunt Claire, as she'd insisted Sadie call her, was quite the character. She'd invited the two of them to Sunday dinner every week since that first, but Boone had offered excuses, unwilling to tempt his control when it came to Mila.

If he thought distance would lessen the attraction, he'd been a fool. If anything, absence had made his cock grow fonder and harder.

This was the first time the two of them had been in the same room in three weeks, and just the sight of her pretty smile was enough to weaken his resolve.

Mila glanced at the clock. Clearly, she hadn't expected him to be home early. "Well," she started, gesturing toward the tray. "All that's left is to put those on the cooling rack. I'll leave you in charge of that, Sadie, and I'll get out of y'all's hair."

"Aw," Sadie whined. "Don't leave yet. Please! You were going to check my chain stitch and make sure I counted right."

"We can do that tomorrow. Promise," Mila said, clearly in a hurry to make her escape.

He hated that he'd made her so uncomfortable that she didn't even want to be around him. "Don't rush out on my account."

Mila glanced his direction, her gaze holding his for just a moment, before those gorgeous long lashes lowered shyly. This woman would be the death of him.

"Maybe you could stay for dinner," Sadie added. "Dad took out chicken and…well…" His daughter, the little minx, shot him a look that proved she didn't have much faith he'd produce anything edible.

Ever since tasting Mila's beef stew, Boone had decided to include fewer processed foods in their diets, buying more fresh vegetables and meat. So far, that experiment had been a great big bust.

Given the sly smile that passed between Sadie and Mila, it was obvious his daughter had shared just how bad his attempts at cooking had been.

"What were you planning to do with the chicken?" Mila asked.

"I looked up a recipe for chicken parmesan. I've got all the ingredients. There's more than enough if you'd like to join us." Boone silently cursed himself the moment he issued the invitation. Seeing Mila in passing was one thing, but spending an entire evening with her was another.

"I really don't want to impose," she said, and he could tell she was searching for some excuse to leave.

"You aren't," Sadie insisted. "Please stay. Please?"

Mila looked toward him, as if seeking permission. The simple glance was enough to send too much blood to his dick.

He smiled. "We'd love for you to stay."

What in the sweet motherfuck was wrong with him? She was ready to leave, so why was he stopping her?

"I'll stay on one condition."

"What condition?" Boone asked.

"You let me help with the cooking."

Sadie jumped up and down. "Deal!"

Boone chuckled. "Fine. Why don't you two do that crochet thing you planned while I go get showered and changed out of my work clothes?"

Mila nodded, following Sadie to her bedroom. The two of them climbed onto Sadie's bed, their heads bent together over the scarf Sadie was crocheting. He watched them for a moment, touched by the patient attention Mila gave his daughter. And while he hated that Lena was creeping into his thoughts, he couldn't help but feel sad that Sadie hadn't received the same attentiveness from her own mother.

Forcing himself to look away, Boone walked into his room, closing the door behind him. Pruning and mulching was dirty work, so he stripped off his clothes, dumping them into the hamper, then took a shower. Ordinarily, he took a nice long hot one, letting the steam ease his aching muscles. Today, he opted for a shorter, chillier one, using it to cool down his libido.

Once he was dressed in a comfortable pair of jeans and a T-shirt, he returned to the great room to find Mila pulling ingredients out of his refrigerator. Glancing into Sadie's room, he could see she was still on the bed, her hands working with the colorful yarn.

"I feel bad inviting you to dinner then making you cook. You really don't have to," he insisted, walking over to take the chicken, cheese, and mushrooms out of her hands to place on the counter.

"That's okay. I love cooking. The kitchen is my happy place."

"Even so," he started.

"Chicken parm is one of my favorite dinners. I can teach you how to make it if you want. It's pretty simple, really."

Boone grumbled, "I can see Sadie's been telling tales about my cooking."

Mila laughed softly, and the cold shower Boone had taken was suddenly a distant memory. "Not really. She just mentioned that you've been trying to make different stuff since moving here."

"And burning most of it," he admitted. "I've taken to keeping a large supply of soup and cereal on hand for nights when disaster strikes."

Mila grimaced. "Cereal isn't dinner."

Boone chuckled. "It is in the Hansen household."

"What things did you make before moving here?"

Boone reached into the fridge for a beer, lifting it to see if she wanted one. Mila nodded, so he uncapped a couple bottles of Rain or Shine IPA and handed one to her. Leaning against the counter, he took a long swig and felt his shoulders relax. This was his favorite time of day. Right after work and a shower, nothing but a quiet night ahead of him. Somehow having Mila here made it just a little bit better.

"I'm a regular Julia Child," he joked. "King of the microwave. Sadie and I tend to eat prepared foods like those tubs of pulled pork, mashed potatoes, mac and cheese, shit like that. Sadie's favorite meal is yellow dinner."

"I'm afraid to ask."

"Chicken tenders, Tator Tots, and a can of corn."

Mila didn't bother to hide her wince. "So much processed food."

"Yeah. I know. That's why I decided I should start making more of an effort. I will say that once a week, we do a little fine dining."

"What's that involve?"

Boone couldn't tell if Mila was grimacing or grinning. Probably both.

"Spaghetti—jarred sauce and boxed noodles—or frozen lasagna."

"Yikes."

Boone laughed. "It's not that bad, really. It's why I figured I could handle chicken parmesan. It's really just spaghetti with a piece of chicken on top."

"Well," Mila said, walking to the sink and washing her hands. "It sounds like we have our work cut out for us."

Boone sipped his beer, watching as Mila grabbed her cellphone from the pocket of her winter coat, hanging on a hook by the front door.

Waving it at him, she said, "Cooking music."

He tilted his head, amused. "I didn't realize there was such a thing."

Mila didn't reply. Instead, she pulled up Spotify and started playing a familiar old tune, "Amie," by Pure Prairie League.

"That's a good one."

"Aunt Claire always listens to seventies music when we're cooking together. Doobie Brothers, Steve Miller Band, Bob Seger—I love it all."

The sound of music pulled Sadie out of her room, and she joined them in the kitchen. Cooking had always been a solitary thing for him, as his style of cooking didn't require much effort.

Boone was pleased when his daughter asked Mila if she could help.

"Absolutely. You're on salad duty." Mila returned to the refrigerator, rummaging around and handing things out to Sadie, who stood next to her. "Here's lettuce, a tomato, and carrots." She stood up, looking at him. "No cucumber?"

He shook his head, making a mental note to add it to his grocery list. He wasn't sure what the hell he'd do with a cucumber, but it was obvious she was disappointed. Boone was strangely bothered that he couldn't provide something she wanted.

He had to shut that idea down. Hard.

"No problem. This is enough to make a decent salad. Do you have croutons?"

Again, Boone had to shake his head.

"Excellent. Gives us an excuse to make homemade ones," she replied with a cheery smile—and the croutons he'd mentally added to the list just got deleted. She'd already spotted the couple loaves of crusty bread he had on the counter. If Boone had one vice, it was bread. Toast with butter and jam was his favorite snack, so he always had a few loaves of sourdough bread from the grocery store on hand.

Mila held up one of the loaves. "We can use the rest of the loaf for garlic bread, if you'd like."

Homemade croutons *and* garlic bread?

Yeah. This was why Boone had been skipping Sunday dinners. Too many more of Mila's meals, and all the willpower in the world wouldn't be able to keep him away from her.

Sadie carried the salad fixings to the island and started peeling carrots.

"You and I can prepare the chicken," Mila said, stepping closer.

Boone drew in a quiet breath. She smelled like sunshine and cinnamon.

For the next twenty minutes, she talked him through the steps in preparing the chicken, pounding it flat, then dipping it in flour, eggs, and breadcrumbs. While he worked on that, she opened the jar of spaghetti sauce, crinkling her nose in distaste.

"Let me guess, you make your sauce from scratch," he mused.

She nodded. "I do. I keep a vegetable garden going most of

the year. This past year's tomato harvest was bountiful, so I canned it a few different ways. Sauce, salsa, whole and diced, even tried sun-drying some for the first time. The next time you get a craving for spaghetti, let me know and I'll bring you a jar of my sauce to try."

"We like salsa too," Sadie chimed in.

"Donut." Boone started to chastise his daughter, but Mila merely laughed.

"I'll bring you a couple jars of that too. I seriously have tons."

Bob Seger's "Old Time Rock & Roll" started playing and Boone was amused when both Sadie and Mila began dancing in place. When Sadie did a spin, he was reminded of when she was a little girl, no more than four or five. He'd gotten her a yellow princess dress for her birthday, and she insisted on him playing the Beast to her Belle, giggling at the way the skirt twirled around her.

Boone had spent the better part of the past summer and fall trying—and failing—with his daughter in every regard. Somewhere in the middle of last June, he'd become the villain of her life story, the one who made her miserable, who always said no, who didn't understand her. It killed him because for most of Sadie's life, she'd been a daddy's girl, the two of them wrapped around the other's little finger. He'd missed the closeness, the fun.

Before he could overthink it, he reached out to Sadie, taking her hand and spinning her around the kitchen floor. Her loud laughter felt like rain on parched earth. He'd half expected her to pull away, to reject him, and the fact she hadn't, felt amazing.

Mila stepped back, giving them a larger dance floor, but Boone didn't like her being so far away. Reaching out, he pulled her in, spinning both of them at the same time, and Sadie and Mila laughed as they bumped into each other. They continued dancing until the song ended, all of them slightly breathless.

"That was fun!" Sadie exclaimed, finishing her salad. Her task was taking longer than it should because she kept stopping every few minutes to reply to Piper's unending texts. Apparently, there was some serious middle school drama at play, as a boy in their class had just broken things off with one girl to go out with another.

Boone didn't have a clue what constituted "going out" in seventh grade, because he sure as shit had no intention of letting Sadie date until she was sixteen and could drive. And even then, he'd have to meet the boy first.

Fortunately, that was a problem for another day. However, considering Sadie wasn't even a teenager yet, and she'd already been putting him through his paces, he wasn't looking forward to it.

Once dinner was ready, Boone plated the chicken parmesan, his mouth watering over how good his kitchen smelled right now, thanks to the tomatoes, the garlic, and the bread. The three of them sat together at the small table by the bay window. Because it was winter, darkness had fallen over an hour ago, so the trees were barely visible in the moonlight.

It was a pleasant meal, the conversation easy as they talked about their days.

After they'd eaten their fill, Sadie went to her room to do her homework, while he and Mila quietly cleaned the kitchen.

"Well..." Mila started.

She was planning to go, but Boone wasn't ready to say goodbye yet.

"Stay for a glass of wine." He'd intended his words as a question, but they hadn't come out that way.

Mila hesitated, which made sense. *He'd* done this. Built this wall between them. He'd done it on purpose, thinking it the best way to get a handle on Mila's effect on him. After tonight, he understood all the distance in the world wasn't going to dim this attraction.

"I, um..." She was searching for an excuse to leave.

Boone didn't like the idea of her lying to him, so he gestured toward the couch.

"Go make yourself comfortable while I pour us each a glass."

She bit her lower lip. "I really do need to—"

"Mila. Sit."

Boone's cock twitched when she blushed and walked to the couch, sitting down without further complaint.

This was why being around Mila was a bad idea. Not that he could stop himself now.

He poured the wine, then joined her on the couch. A wise man would have taken the armchair.

Mila thanked him for the wine, taking a small sip, as Boone searched for a safe conversational topic. In the end, they discussed the wine they were drinking. Despite her roles involving aspects other than the making of the wine, she was quite knowledgeable about the grapes and the wine-making process.

"Obviously this is our slow season," she said, when they began talking about the winery. "In the spring, summer, and fall, the winery and the brewery are both very popular with locals and tourists, especially on the weekends."

"Probably has everything to do with the quality of the beer and wine made here." One of the first things Boone had done when Levi called to offer him a job was try the wine. While the job had fallen into the too-good-to-be true range, Boone wouldn't have accepted it if the quality of the wine was poor. He'd been impressed by just how good Lighting in a Bottle wine tasted.

"And the view," Mila added. "On a clear day, we can see all the way to D.C."

"It *is* an amazing view. I'm assuming you've lived here your whole life?"

Mila nodded. "Yep."

"Never considered moving away and living somewhere else? Like Lucy?"

"No. Never. This is home. I don't have to see the world to know there's no place better than this."

Boone smiled. He'd lived in various towns up and down the East Coast, his father never satisfied to settle in one place. Boone had hated the transient lifestyle, so when he landed the job at the winery in Williamsburg, he'd been determined to live out his years there. He was glad he'd made the decision to uproot and move to Gracemont, because it already felt more like home than Williamsburg ever did.

"I'm pretty sure you're right," Boone agreed. "This town and this mountain…they're damn fine places to grow old."

Mila's pleased expression told him just how much pride she took in her hometown. "Sadie seems to be settling in well," she said softly, not wanting his daughter to overhear.

"She is. Thanks to you. Introducing her to Piper was a stroke of genius."

Mila shook her head, downplaying his compliment. "I'm sure they would have found each other either way."

He didn't like the way she constantly belittled her acts of kindness, making them less than they were.

"Why Donut?" she asked. She'd obviously noticed his nickname for Sadie.

"When she was little, she loved donuts. Wanted them for breakfast, lunch, and dinner. I bought one of those bags of the little white powdered ones once, when she was four or five. I was doing chores…and *thought* I was keeping half an eye on her.

Obviously, I wasn't. Found her in the kitchen, the bag of donuts empty, her face, hair, and hands all covered in white. Told her she powdered herself so much, she'd turned into a donut. She giggled and the name stuck."

Mila giggled as well. "That's sweet."

"She had a good time Saturday night with your sisters." Nora and Remi had invited Sadie to join them for pizza and a movie a few days earlier. And while the invitation had been kind, that wasn't Boone's reason for bringing it up now.

"She's a fun girl, and she's got a wicked sense of humor. Gets that from…you?" Mila asked.

Boone shrugged noncommittally. "No comment."

Mila laughed.

When Boone went to pick up Sadie, not wanting her to walk home alone after dark, he'd arrived the same time Mila's date was dropping her off.

"How was your date?" He should mind his own business, because Mila's dating life was none of his concern, but he'd stepped out of the woods just in time to witness the good-night kiss. It had been a goddamn travesty. Zero heat. If Mila was his, there was no way he'd offer her a tiny peck on the lips.

No. If she was his, he'd devour her, consume and claim her lips until they were red and swollen so every man who saw her would know she was taken.

Boone had struggled to sleep that night, forced to admit it bothered him when he discovered she'd been out with someone, even though he wasn't about to toss his hat in the ring.

Relationships were for other men. The most he could offer her was sex, and Mila wasn't the type of woman a man made his fuck buddy.

She was wife material.

And he wasn't husband material. Lena had driven that point home.

Boone equated marriage with betrayal, abandonment, and failure, three things he wasn't signing up for again. His walls weren't just up—they were well fortified. Wedding vows were nothing more than lies told in pretty clothes.

And if that wasn't reason enough to stay away from Mila, there was the fact she was a Storm. He'd uprooted his entire life and Sadie's to bring them here. Doing anything to risk their fresh start would be the height of stupidity.

Mila's brows rose, indicating she was surprised he knew about her date.

"I saw the man dropping you off when I came to get Sadie."

"Oh. Yeah. It was…okay."

Boone noticed the pause before the word *okay*. It told him that the date *wasn't* okay, but that wasn't what he really cared about. Cursing himself for a fool, he dug deeper. "Is this guy a boyfriend?" He tried to make the question casual and light, but he didn't pull it off.

Mila quickly shook her head. "No. Not at all. Pastor Joshua is—"

"Pastor?"

Mila gave him a rueful grin. "I really need to stop calling him that. Saturday was my fourth date with Joshua, but he's not a boyfriend. He's, uh, just a nice guy."

Yeah. She made the word *nice* sound as shitty as *okay*. Of course, given the lackluster kiss he'd witnessed, he could understand her lack of enthusiasm.

He had a million things he wanted to say about Mila's nice pastor, but it wasn't his place.

Because the things he thought in regard to Mila Storm weren't *nice*. Hell, they probably weren't *okay*, either. There was something about her that called to him in a very primal way.

Boone wasn't an easy lover. In fact, he was downright rough. He had a penchant for bondage, demanding total control over his lovers. Lena had responded to his dominant side. It was one reason he'd been so quick to marry her. Her sexual desires had matched his. Unfortunately, good sex wasn't enough to make a successful marriage.

He really should change the subject.

But...

"Why do you make 'nice' sound like such a bad thing?" he asked, apparently a glutton for punishment.

Mila flushed. Jesus, he loved her blushes. "I didn't mean to. It's just, well...Pastor Joshua is very polite and..." She blew out a long, slow breath. "The dates are boring."

Boone chuckled. "Got it."

"But I need to just get over it, because nice, boring guys are the only ones I attract."

Mila wasn't wild and outgoing like her sister Remi. He wouldn't call her a wallflower, but she projected a quiet, sweet, almost timid personality. Apparently, it made it easy for most men in Gracemont to overlook her, though he couldn't understand how. Their paths hadn't crossed more than a few times in the past three weeks, and yet any time she was in the vicinity, every single one of his nerve endings flared to life, his attention drawn to and locked on her.

She was the only thing he could see.

"So what kind of man do you want to ask you out?" Even as Boone asked the question, a bright light and siren blasted in his mind, screaming "red alert!"

Mila took a moment to consider her answer, though Boone suspected she knew *exactly* how to respond. When she looked away, he realized she didn't intend to answer honestly.

"I don't know."

Yep. Liar.

Despite knowing better, Boone reached out and cupped her cheek, forcing her to face him again. "Yes, you do."

She swallowed heavily, and he lowered his hand, even though it felt wrong *not* to touch her.

"I want a man who'll challenge me," she whispered. "Someone strong and gentle at the same time. Confident, not shy or weak, but not arrogant. I want someone who sees me for who I am—who I *really* am—and likes me, flaws and all."

Her words struck deep, because Boone saw who she was. He had from the first moment she fell off that ladder and into his arms.

Mila was submissive and sweet. And if he let himself claim her, she would most likely be his perfect match.

But he thought he'd found that perfect match before, and she hadn't been. God, she *really* hadn't been. It made him question his instincts because it was clear he couldn't tell the different between love and lust, and that was a problem.

Boone backed away from her on the couch. Just slightly, but enough that she noticed. He saw the instant that damn wariness he'd provoked the first night they met returned. For most of the evening, she'd been at ease, comfortable with him, and it felt good.

Now, he ruined it again.

"Thank you for the cooking lesson, Mila. Dinner was delicious. You're an incredible cook."

Mila lifted one shoulder. "You did most of the wor—"

Boone reached out, her chin pinched between his thumb and forefinger before he could even think about it. "Don't diminish your actions. You prepared the lion's share of that meal, so I'm paying you a well-earned compliment."

Mila unconsciously licked her lips, though he wasn't sure if that was from nerves or arousal.

"I…" she whispered breathlessly, her eyelids fluttering.

"Say thank you," he murmured in a deep, commanding tone.

"Thank you."

"Good girl," he praised.

Boone heard Mila's quick intake of breath, felt the shiver that coursed through her. Or maybe that was *him* shaking.

He lowered his hand, resting it in his lap to hide his rapidly growing erection.

Those two words had jerked them both, impacted them more than they should have.

Mila's blush grew darker, and Boone had to look away before he did something insane—like drag her to his bedroom and tie her to his bed for the rest of their lives.

He closed his hands into fists to resist that urge.

He wasn't sure what Mila saw, but whatever it was, clearly it was enough to have her standing quickly.

"I should head home."

Boone stood as well, glancing outside and frowning. Mila walked everywhere, traipsing along the farm's paths no matter the time or temperature. He hated it, but she wasn't his. It wasn't his job to forbid it.

"I'll drive you."

She shook her head. "I'm fine." He watched as she attempted a carefree smile. Like him, she wasn't selling it. "I can walk around this farm with my eyes closed."

His scowl darkened enough that her grin faded. "It's pitch black outside and seventeen degrees. You're not walking home."

Before Mila could disobey—fuck, *disagree*—with him, he crossed over to Sadie's room, knocking on the door before opening it. "I'm going to run Mila home really quick, Donut."

Sadie bounced off her bed, approaching him. "Okay." Peering through the door, she added, "Good night, Mila. Thanks for dinner!"

"You're welcome."

"Can you come give Dad another cooking lesson tomorrow? I'm in the mood for meatloaf and mashed potatoes."

Boone shook his head as Mila laughed. Then, he grabbed his keys as Mila pulled on her coat.

He kept his hands by his sides as they walked to the truck, careful not to touch her again when he opened the passenger door for her.

Climbing behind the wheel, he drove the less than a mile between his cabin and her farmhouse. She gave him an exasperated "I told you so" grin when they made it to her place in under two minutes.

Because he wanted to make sure his lesson stuck, he said, "Thank you for dinner."

"It was your—" She pulled up short, quickly changing directions. "You're welcome."

It was on the tip of his tongue to say good girl, but if he did that, he'd follow it up by pulling her over the console and onto his lap and fucking her until she understood exactly what it meant to be his *good girl*.

Shit. First thing he was going to do when he got home was take another cold shower, because his thoughts had turned on him and were suddenly enemy number one.

"Thank *you* for dinner." Mila had just the right amount of brattiness in her tone, and he chuckled.

"You're welcome."

She reached for the door handle. "Well, I guess I'll see you around."

After spending the evening with her, Boone wasn't looking forward to her going back to avoiding him again. Self-preservation flew out the window when he said, "I wouldn't mind another cooking lesson. Maybe early next week?"

She was clearly surprised by his request. If he was lucky, maybe *she'd* find the strength to keep the distance between them.

If not…

"I'd like that. We could make it a weekly thing if you'd like. Every Tuesday?"

Boone signed his own death warrant when he nodded. "Every Tuesday would be just fine."

Mila smiled widely. "We'll start with meatloaf for Sadie. I have a great recipe I think you'll both like."

"Text me the ingredients and I'll make sure we have everything we need."

"Okay." Mila opened the door.

He got out as well.

"You don't have to walk me to the door."

"Yes, I do," he said, the two of them climbing the front steps side by side. "Your sisters home?"

"Yeah."

"Good. Lock the door behind you."

She nodded. "I will. Good night, Boone."

"Night, Mila."

He waited until he heard her throw the lock, then he walked back to his truck.

Sighing as he put it in drive, he was painfully aware that he was in big, big trouble when it came to Mila Storm.

Chapter Five

Mila laughed at Remi's outrageous, yet impressive dance moves before fanning herself dramatically and pointing toward their table to indicate she needed a break. Not that anyone really noticed; they were all too entertained by Remi.

She returned to the table she'd been sharing all night with Remi and a couple of her cousins, dropping down into the chair and chugging the lukewarm water she'd been ignoring all night in favor of the spiked punch.

Mila was going to pay for drinking so much vodka tomorrow, but her tipsy brain reasoned it away by pointing out it was Valentine's Day, and she was still painfully single. If she wasn't going to get kissed at the end of the dance, the least she deserved was a decent buzz.

A large part of Mila was secretly delighted this party was almost over. Not because it hadn't been fun, but because Aunt Claire, Gretchen, Edith Millholland, and the other half dozen women in the ladies' auxiliary who helped organize the event had talked about nothing else since New Year's. They'd rethought the decorations and food so many times, Mila nearly lost her mind. Especially since the majority of the cooking had fallen to her, Aunt Claire, and Kasi.

In years past, the Valentine's Dance had been just that. A dance. This year, the ladies had decided to up the ante and make it more family friendly by adding a dinner beforehand. The original plan—and the reason Mila had agreed to incorporating a meal—was because the food would be easy fare…spaghetti, garlic bread, and salad.

Somewhere in the middle of January, the simple pasta was deemed "not enough," and suddenly Mila was making four large lasagnas—two veggie, two meat—and a mountain of chicken parmesan, as well as the spaghetti sauce. She'd spent countless hours in the kitchen the past few days, preparing enough food to feed an army.

Given the lack of leftovers, she supposed it had been a hit.

Once her glass of water was empty, Mila set it down and reached for her half-full glass of Cupid's Punch, something Edith Millholland had whipped up, calling it their "signature cocktail." Edith had heard the term at some fancy wedding she'd attended in D.C. and decided their small-town dance needed a bit of classing up, hence the themed cocktail with the cute name.

Mila didn't care what Edith called it, just that it was doing the trick. Helping her forget that she was attending another one of these damn Valentine's Dances alone. That hadn't been much of a hardship prior to this year, because all her cousins, Nora, and Remi had always attended single, too.

This year, she'd been sharing a table with Theo and Gretchen, as well as Levi and Kasi, both couples so sweetly in love, Mila was risking a cavity just being close to them.

She chastised herself for the ungracious thought.

Mila was thrilled to her toes for Theo and Levi. They'd met their true loves, and seeing them so happy warmed her all the way to her soul. Even if it *did* cast too bright a light on her own...loneliness was probably the word, even though it felt wrong.

Probably because the only time Mila was alone was in bed at night. The rest of her day was spent in constant company, beginning with her aunt each morning, as Mila helped her prep desserts for the B&B guests. From there, Remi typically served as her assistant, the two of them cleaning any vacated cabins, while preparing them for the next visitors.

After that, she moved to the winery to get their food options set up before moving on to do the same at the brewery. Both businesses had employees who worked in the kitchens, filling the orders as they came in, while Mila served as manager as well as prep chef.

Once her regular chores were completed, she found herself helping various family members or friends with a variety of other tasks, more often than not. Gretchen, still fairly new in her position, often asked for help setting up the event barn for upcoming celebrations. The ladies' auxiliary was in the middle of a huge charitable project, knitting and crocheting scarves and hats for the underprivileged, so whenever she had a free moment, her hands were flying fast and furiously as she attempted to finish the ten pieces she'd promised to donate. And up until tonight, the rest of her spare time had been spent planning, decorating, and cooking for this dance.

The only time she took for herself lately was the Tuesday night "cooking lessons" with Boone and Sadie. Since the initial one, she'd been back twice, teaching them how to make meatloaf —which Sadie loved—and the beef stew that Boone had enjoyed so much at Sunday dinner.

After Boone had warned her away his first night on the farm, Mila had taken special pains to steer clear of the man. Not because that was what she thought *he* wanted, but because she'd hoped not being around him would help her shake off the effects of that stupid love-at-first-touch curse.

It hadn't worked.

The less she saw him, the more she thought about and obsessed over him. Something his daughter had inadvertently fueled, because while she'd been maintaining a distance from Boone, she refused to do the same with Sadie. In many ways, Mila felt like she and Sadie were kindred spirits. Mila knew how hard it was to grow up without her mom. Sure, the circumstances were different—Mila's mom had died, while Sadie still got to see and talk to hers occasionally. But it was clear they both missed their mothers, and Mila hoped to fill a tiny bit of that void for the young girl.

Mila suspected if Boone hadn't come home early a few weeks ago, when she'd been teaching Sadie how to bake cookies, she would have continued to give the man a wide berth. That determination or self-preservation or whatever it had been was squashed somewhere in the middle of watching him pound chicken for the Italian dinner.

Ever since telling her that he wasn't interested in dating or relationships, Boone had done nothing to make her think that was a lie, or that he'd changed his mind. Tuesday nights might be the highlight of her week, but apart from friendly conversation, Boone hadn't offered even the slightest bit of hope that he was interested in her romantically.

Nope. She'd been friend-zoned.

Story of her life.

She'd spent most of high school and even the years since playing the matchmaker, her guy friends asking for her help in setting them up with whichever one of her girlfriends had struck their fancy. Mila wasn't sure, but she suspected she might hold the Gracemont record for most times serving as a bridesmaid.

She had eight godawful dresses she would never wear again hanging in her closet as proof.

She was perfectly aware that she was giving off all the wrong vibes to prospective suitors. Apparently, quiet, soft-spoken, goodie-goodie types weren't in high demand when there were lots more outgoing, fun girls around. Mila suspected most people in Gracemont still believed she was a virgin, which was another strike against her, since men her age also weren't looking for someone so inexperienced in the bedroom.

Of course, while she wasn't a virgin, that fact was true by such a small margin, she wasn't sure she could defend it. In actuality, she'd slept with only two men, one time each, and neither of them lived in Gracemont to tell the tale to other prospective suitors. Which, in hindsight, might be a blessing.

So…yeah. She was the living model of the phrase, "Always a bridesmaid, never a bride."

Mila looked at the time on her phone and noted it had been eleven minutes since the last time she'd snuck a peek at Boone. She'd made a game of only rewarding herself with glimpses of him after restraining for at least ten minutes. Clearly, her life was very small if granting herself the chance to look at the sexy man felt like a huge prize.

Glancing in his direction, she was pleased to see he was engaged in a conversation with Uncle Rex. It meant she could steal a good long look of his gorgeous profile.

Mila had never considered herself one of those shallow women who placed too much stock in a man's appearance and physique, believing it was the inside that mattered. Boone was testing her on that because, holy shit, the man was *built*. He was no stranger to hard physical labor, and it showed…in his thick muscular arms and legs, his wide, strong shoulders and back. The man was a mountain she was dying to climb.

And if his great body wasn't enough to send her thoughts down wicked, wicked paths, there was his handsome face. Actually, handsome didn't begin to describe how freaking hot the man was, with his piercing dark eyes, his sharp jawline, and full lips that, when he smiled, had her longing to taste them. He kept his light brown hair short, though there was enough length that she could run her fingers through it if she ever got the opportunity.

He also had a beard.

God, Mila was a sucker for bearded men.

Pastor Joshua was clean-shaven. Actually, his face was so smooth, she wasn't even sure the man *had* to shave. Not that whether a man had a beard or not should matter.

It was what was on the inside, she thought, even though she followed that with an internal eye-roll. Maybe she was shallower than she thought.

Mila spent most of her days now in constant denial.

Because in addition to the lie she was telling herself about looks not mattering, Mila was also operating under another doozy, pretending that if all she could have was Boone's friendship, she would take it and be happy.

Yeah, right.

Liar, liar, pants on fire.

"I'm exhausted," Kasi said, dropping down into the chair next to hers and distracting Mila from her wayward thoughts. "I'm not sure why I ever think for *one* second that I can keep up with Remi on the dance floor."

"You've been her friend long enough to know better," Mila pointed out.

"I think I view it as a challenge, one I'm determined to win just once in my damn life."

Mila smirked. "While you're at it, why not try to outdrink her, too? Dare ya."

Kasi laughed at her sarcasm and threw her hands up in

surrender. "You're right. You're right. I should just admit defeat."

"But you won't."

Kasi and Remi had been best friends since birth, so in a lot of ways, Mila had always viewed the woman as another sister, one of the heart. Now that Kasi was marrying Levi and becoming an official member of the Storm family, Mila couldn't be happier.

"But I won't," Kasi echoed. "Where'd Nora go?"

"The original party animal?" Mila joked. "She headed out with Sadie right after dinner. The two of them had plans to binge-watch some reality show."

Because the dance was a community event, there'd been a lot of kids here for the dinner part of the evening, including Piper. However, as the evening wore on, most of the parents here with children had called it a night and headed home, leaving behind the younger generation, which was showing no sign of packing it in until the final song was played.

"I really like Sadie. She's a neat kid. Remi said she's a natural with the horses, which is high praise coming from the original horse whisperer. And Levi was worried about giving up the role of vineyard manager, but having Boone here has really set his mind at ease."

"Maverick said Boone really knows his stuff. Said we were lucky to get him," Mila added.

"I'm glad they've started coming to Sunday dinners. They're a nice addition to the table."

Mila nodded, though she wasn't in total agreement.

Apart from their cooking lessons, Mila only saw Boone in passing at the farm and at Sunday dinners. She wasn't exactly sure why he'd started joining them on Sundays again, though she suspected it was because Aunt Claire wouldn't continue taking no for an answer. He'd offered excuses that had gotten him out of a couple Sundays, but Aunt Claire was made of sterner stuff, and she was determined to pull the Hansens into the fold.

Like Mila and her sisters, Aunt Claire had taken Sadie under her wing as well, so now, most Sundays, it was Mila, Sadie, Kasi, and Aunt Claire preparing the meal together.

Boone always claimed a spot at the opposite end of the table, well away from Mila, talking shop with Grayson, Maverick, and Levi. She suspected the distance was an intentional act on his part, which hurt more than it should.

Sunday dinners had always been her favorite time of the week, but with Boone sitting right there in the same room, yet too far away to talk to, they'd become downright torturous.

Kasi leaned toward her, her voice lowered. "Sooooo…I couldn't help but notice Pastor Joshua made his way over here earlier to claim the first slow dance with you."

Mila fought to school her features, trying not to wince. With the exception of Nora, she hadn't told anyone in her family that she wasn't really interested in the man. So it was her fault Kasi mistakenly believed Mila and the pastor were getting serious. Although Mila wasn't sure four dates in two months equaled "serious." But what did she know?

Her dating experience was as limited as her sexual knowledge.

"It was just one dance," Mila said. "He's danced with other women tonight, as well."

"Yes, all of them grandmothers. According to Remi, you've gone out with the pastor four times, and it's obvious he's into you."

Oh shit. Was it?

How was it obvious? Apart from asking her to dance one time, Past—er—*Joshua* had spent the remainder of the dance moving from table to table, socializing with the parishioners who attended his church.

"I'm sure that's not true," she said softly.

Kasi clearly wasn't convinced. "He's a nice guy," she said, stating the same thing Mila said when describing the man to both Boone and Nora, but Kasi obviously viewed that as a perk, not a boring fact. "Though I'll admit, he seems a bit socially awkward on the dating scene. Not that that's necessarily a bad thing."

It was, but Mila held her tongue.

"And it's no mystery why he's so smitten with you," Kasi continued.

Mila felt her nose begin to crinkle but managed to stop herself. "Smitten. What?"

"Mila, you're one of the sweetest women I know. People are comfortable with you. They turn to you when they need help because you're generous—and not just with money but with your time. You're compassionate and empathetic. I can imagine those are all attributes Pastor Joshua would find attractive."

Mila shrugged off Kasi's compliments, uncomfortable with the praise and annoyed that other men didn't seem to be attracted to those traits in her...but mainly upset because she'd gotten hung up on that stupid word.

Sweet.

It sucked as much as *nice.*

Before Mila could figure out how to respond to Kasi without letting her depression seep out, the deejay announced it was the last dance, and Levi was by their table within seconds, reaching out for Kasi's hand and pulling her back to the floor.

Mila smiled because she loved Alex Warren's song "Ordinary," but the grin faded when she spotted Past—dammit!—Joshua walking in her direction.

She glanced toward the food table, wondering if he'd change course if she started cleaning up. Unfortunately, the older women who weren't dancing had taken care of clearing everything away. Hell, they'd already put a dent in taking down the decorations, so there wasn't going to be much to do once the party ended.

She sighed, resigning herself to dancing with Joshua again, when she felt a firm hand on her shoulder.

"Dance with me."

The deep voice belonged to the one man she'd spent the entire night longing to dance with.

She looked up at Boone and smiled.

He'd spent the evening at the table next to hers. There were enough Storms in attendance that they'd filled not one, not two, but three tables. When Boone first walked in tonight, it looked like he'd been heading to the seat next to her at this table. But he'd gotten waylaid by Maverick, who waved him over to sit at his table, while Sadie sought out and found Piper.

Damn cock-blocking cousin.

As Mila stood, Boone briefly glanced in the pastor's direction, frowning slightly.

Wait.

Was that why he'd asked her to dance? Was he just trying to save her from having to dance with the other man again?

Of *course* he was, she thought with disappointment.

She'd already mentioned that she found her dates with Pasto —*motherfucker*—Joshua boring, so Boone was clearly stepping in to save her from enduring another dance.

Just what she wanted.

A pity dance.

Regardless, Mila accepted with a nod, even though his request hadn't been a question. Nor did it feel like her response was necessary, considering he'd already claimed her hand and was pulling her toward the dance floor.

She caught a glimpse of the pastor hesitating for a moment, before turning and asking eighty-something Edith Millholland for a dance.

Mila shivered as Boone pulled her into his arms, his large palm at her lower back, just a shade above her ass. She expected him to keep a proper distance between them, so she was shocked when he drew her closer, her chest pressed firmly against his.

Unlike—fuck it—Pastor Joshua, Boone was not leaving room for Jesus.

Throughout the night, every time a slow song played, and Boone didn't ask her to dance, Mila comforted herself with the fact that he hadn't danced with anyone else, either. Up until a minute ago, she was convinced he was just one of those guys who didn't dance. Or at least not in public, she amended, recalling that one silly dance in his kitchen with Sadie.

So much for that assumption.

He was an incredible dancer.

Boone guided her through the slow dance with a strong, confident grip that had her melting under his control. Mila had read enough spicy romance novels in her life to have a good grasp on what floated her boat, though it wasn't something she could ever admit to anyone.

How the hell would Kasi have responded if Mila had said she'd never marry Pastor Joshua because she longed for a man who would demand her submission in the bedroom?

How could she confess that every single night since Boone's arrival at the farm, she'd played out some pretty hardcore fantasies of the man ordering her to her knees, commanding her to crawl to him, demanding that she—

Mila shut down that line of thought *hard*, because she was already getting too turned on. Her nipples were budded and ultra-sensitive, so every time they rubbed against Boone's chest, she felt a tremor of need that had her very wet pussy clenching.

She released a shaky breath, keeping her face averted, lest Boone see her blush and know what kind of an impact he was having on her.

She'd never been this affected from just a dance. God, if the song went on any longer, there was a very good chance she could come.

Especially when his thumb stroked circles into her lower back, his thighs brushed against hers, and she felt his hot breath against her cheek.

"Thank you for saving me from…" Mila paused, wishing she hadn't spoken. Mainly because it prompted him to shift away an inch or two, making it obvious she was speaking to his chest, unable to look at his face. Not when he was this close.

"From?" he prompted.

She shook her head, hoping he'd let it go. "Nothing. Never mind."

Boone didn't let her off the hook. "From the pastor?" he asked softly, mindful of the fact Joshua was somewhere nearby on the dance floor as well.

She nodded, her gaze still locked resolutely on the second button of his dark blue shirt.

"Look at me, Mila."

That commanding tone was quickly becoming her kryptonite, and her eyes raised without a moment's consideration.

"I asked you to dance because I wanted to, not because I was trying to cock-block the pastor. I knew I needed to move fast, because I was tired of every other guy in the place getting to you before I could."

He'd wanted to dance with her all night?

Pastor Joshua had been quick on the draw for the first slow dance, then Uncle Rex had been standing next to her when the second began, so he'd grabbed her hand. The third dance was claimed by one of the brewery employees, Billy, who'd dated her sister Lucy back in high school—which meant he viewed her as a little sister and nothing more. She'd hidden in the bathroom during the fourth slow dance, because Gracemont's former mayor, Scottie Grover, had been heading in her direction. And she'd rather boogie barefoot on a bed of red-hot coals than dance with *that* asshole.

"I'm glad you asked," she said, her breathlessness a dead giveaway of her current state.

His eyes narrowed slightly, drifting to her lips when her tongue darted out to wet them. She wasn't intentionally flirting —or at least, she didn't think so—but she couldn't help the overwhelming effect he had on her.

This was the closest they'd been physically since the day he'd saved her from her fall off the ladder.

"You look pretty tonight."

She'd bought the flowy red skirt just for this dance, pairing it with a white blouse. "You look nice too."

Boone was wearing khaki pants with a dark blue button-down shirt. He'd left the top two buttons undone, giving her a tiny peek of a hairy chest.

"I like your hair like this." Boone brushed her hair over one shoulder, his fingers sliding through it.

Mila was typically queen of the ponytail, simply because she spent the majority of her days in kitchens and around food. Tonight, she'd taken special pains, curling her hair to achieve the waves that hung loose down her back.

Tucking her close again, Boone pressed his cheek against the side of her head, the two of them swaying in time to the music. When the chorus played, he gripped her hand, spinning her away from him the way he'd done the night they'd danced in the kitchen with Sadie.

Mila couldn't help but giggle when he reeled her back against him, her breasts flat to his chest again. With one hand held tightly in his, she rested the other on the side of his waist awkwardly.

"Wrap your arm around me, darlin'. There's no need to be shy with me."

She didn't have to be told twice. Sliding her hand around him, she rested it on his back, tempted to stroke him there, mimicking his caresses. The vodka was making her bold. Mila wished there weren't so many clothes between them.

The song ended way before she was ready, and the lights that had been dimmed after dinner were raised again, signaling the party was over.

Mila reluctantly stepped away from Boone, instantly missing his arms around her. God only knew when she'd get the chance to be that close to him again.

"Do you need help cleaning?" Boone offered.

Mila shook her head. "The ladies have already taken care of most of it. Gretchen and I plan to tackle whatever's left tomorrow."

They walked back to the table where Remi, Kasi, her cousins, and several other friends had gathered. Mila wasn't surprised to discover they were planning to move the party, none of them ready to call it a night.

"We're heading over to the brewery, making our own private after-party," Remi said to her and Boone as they approached. "You guys want to join us?"

Mila didn't reply, waiting for Boone's response. Truthfully, she was exhausted after rising early to cook and put the finishing touches on the decorations, but if Boone said he was in, she would find a second wind…somewhere.

Boone shook his head. "No. Sadie's with Nora, and it's way past time for her to be in bed. Weekend or not."

"I'm going to say good night here too," Mila replied. "It's been a long day."

"Ooookay," Remi drawled, before playfully singing her party

pooper song. *"Every party has a pooper, that's why we invited you."*

Boone chuckled, shaking his head, as Mila rolled her eyes, unoffended. Because she was usually the first one to cry uncle, she'd been subjected to Remi's ridiculous song countless times before.

"I'll walk you home," Boone said to Mila, after they grabbed their coats and stepped out into the chilly winter air. "Since I'm heading your direction anyway."

Mila nodded, thrilled by the opportunity to spend even just ten more minutes with Boone as they took the path toward her farmhouse. The rest of their gang headed in the opposite direction, making their way down to the brewery.

She shivered, pretending it was the cold affecting her and not Boone's hand resting on the small of her back, steadying her as they walked.

Stormy Weather Farm had countless paths connecting the businesses to the homes and cabins. A few years earlier, they'd lined every single one of them with solar-powered lights that made nighttime walking easier. Prior to that, they were always stumbling around in the dark, using the flashlight app on their phones.

"Do I have you to thank for that delicious dinner tonight?" Boone asked.

Mila shook her head. "Not really. It was a group effort."

He turned his head, looking at her too seriously. "And how much of that effort was yours?"

She lifted one shoulder. "The lasagna and the chicken parmesan. And the sauce for the spaghetti."

"Jesus, Mila. That was practically the whole meal. There must have been over a hundred people there. You made all that food?"

"I'm used to cooking for large groups. Look at the size of my family," she joked. "Although, I have to say, I'm in no hurry to go back to the grocery store anytime soon. Took me three trips over three days to get it all. But to be fair, I didn't cook the whole meal. Kasi baked the garlic bread, while Aunt Claire cooked the spaghetti noodles and made that humongous bowl of salad. She was chopping vegetables for hours. The rest of the ladies prepared the desserts."

"You made most of it," he stressed.

"I didn't mind."

Boone stopped, his hand gripping her elbow so he could turn her toward him. She blinked a few times as he used a finger to gently touch the spot just under her eye. She'd pulled some late nights and early mornings the past few days, so she knew what he was looking at. Dark circles were hard to hide.

"I've watched you around the farm, Mila. Jumping from one task to another, taking on duties no one else wants to do. You work too hard," he said.

She tried not to let him see how thrilled she was that he'd noticed her at all. Of course, she gave herself away, revealing she'd been watching him, too. "That's the pot calling the kettle black. You're up with the sun like me every morning, and I've seen you walking home way past quitting hours more times than not since starting work here."

"I'm trying to prove myself worthy. There's a lot to learn. Plus, winterizing a large vineyard takes time. However, we're not talking about me. We're talking about you."

"I'm fine, Boone. Now that the Valentine's Dance is over, things should slow down a bit."

He shook his head. "Why do I get the feeling you'll get swept up in some other big project?"

She laughed but didn't bother to deny it. Gretchen was already talking about organizing a St. Patrick's Day celebration she wanted to host at Rain or Shine Brewery. She'd scheduled a meeting for the two of them Monday afternoon to discuss food ideas and decorations.

They started walking again.

"What TV show were Nora and Sadie so fired up about watching?" Boone asked.

"Oh God. I'm not sure you want to know."

Boone paused once more, not that Mila was complaining. She'd stand out in the cold all night if it meant more time with him. "She said it was some reality show?"

Mila grinned. "They're getting caught up on the latest season of *Love is Blind*. It's this show where single people try to fall in love without seeing the other person's face."

Boone grunted. "Sounds ridiculous."

"Honestly, I wouldn't know. I've never seen it. I don't watch a lot of TV. Spend most of my nights reading or crocheting."

"Sounds like a better use of your time."

She wondered if he'd feel that way if he saw the stack of steamy romance novels on her nightstand. She and her sisters—and now Gretchen—were constantly passing books back and forth, so much so, they'd discussed starting what Remi was calling their own "dirty book club."

She and Boone glanced at the full moon shining through the trees. If it was just a little bit warmer, it would be a beautiful night.

"I appreciate you and your sisters taking Sadie under your wings. She wasn't looking forward to moving here, leaving her friends. The transition has been a lot easier than I anticipated, thanks to you, Remi, and Nora."

"Yeah, well, you might regret letting her spend too much time with us," Mila said jokingly. "Lest we're a bad influence."

He grinned. "How so?"

"Well, Nora loves her reality TV. God help you when she exposes Sadie to *Jersey Shore* or teaches her the wonder of

89

online shopping. It's a rare day when there's not a package delivered to our door. You might want to hide your credit cards. Of course, by comparison, Nora will be the better influence, because while Remi is teaching her to ride and care for the horses, she cusses like a sailor. I've warned her to curb the four-letter words around Sadie, but half the time, I swear Remi doesn't even realize she's letting the F word fly. And that's the *least* offensive in her vocabulary, because she tends to get creative."

"Creative?"

Mila bit her lower lip as she lowered her head.

"You blushing, darlin'? Now you're going to have to give me an example."

She huffed out a breath, feigning annoyance. "Cuntcake and twatwaffle are some of her most used."

Boone laughed, unconcerned. "Sadie's not a stranger to bad words. For one thing, she's in middle school."

Mila grinned. "True."

"And for another, Lena makes zero attempts at cleaning up her vocabulary in front of our daughter. Never has. I had to sit down with Sadie and give her the 'do as I say, not as your mother does' speech when she was in first grade, and the teacher called to let me know Sadie had told a little boy in her class to go fuck himself."

Mila's eyes widened. "No way."

"She'd spent the previous weekend with her mother, and when I asked her where she'd heard that word, she admitted it was Lena who'd said it to the boyfriend she'd been having a fight with. I called Lena and read her the riot act, but she accused me of overreacting, then insisted Sadie had most likely picked it up from the guys I was working with at the time. My ex-wife is very good at deflecting blame." Boone sighed. "Shit. I don't want to talk about Lena tonight. So what about you? How do you plan to corrupt my daughter?" he joked.

Mila paused, trying to come up with something, though nothing popped to mind. "I actually wish I could think of something, but unlike my sisters, I'm the boring one."

Boone frowned. "You don't really believe that, do you?"

"Not really," she lied, wishing she hadn't said that aloud. "I'm just not adventurous like Lucy, or quirky like Nora, or wild like Remi. I'm just sort of the..." She sought a word that might make her seem even a little bit interesting, because she'd be damned if she said *sweet*.

"The good girl," Boone said, filling in the blank with words that should have supported her assertion that she was boring. But he said the words in such a way that Mila didn't just feel interesting, but sexy. Surely that couldn't have been his intent.

She drew in a slow breath, liking it more than she should when he called her that. When Boone ran his finger along her cheek, she knew her damn blush had given her away. It was virtually impossible for her to hide the way Boone made her feel. She'd never felt an attraction like this, so she had no shields.

He dropped his hand, and they started walking again. When they reached the edge of her yard, Boone grasped her hand, pulling her to a halt.

"Happy Valentine's Day, Mila," he said.

"Thanks. You too."

Something in her tone must have given away her true feelings about the holiday, because he tightened his grip on her hand. "Not a fan?"

"It's just another day, isn't it?" This time, she didn't bother to temper her words.

"I thought women loved the romance of the holiday. What the hell was that dance just about otherwise?"

Mila grimaced. "It's only romantic for those in love."

"I see," he said, and she could see he did.

"Want to know a secret?" Mila asked, the vodka she'd drunk loosening her lips more than was wise.

He nodded.

"I've never had a date or even gotten a kiss on Valentine's Day."

"Never?"

"Never." She was touched by his look of disbelief. It soothed the parts of her that felt undesirable as one Valentine's Day after another passed without her finding love.

"What's wrong with the men in Gracemont?"

She laughed, secretly pleased by how aghast he seemed. "Thanks for pretending it's them, not me."

"You really *don't* see it, do you? Guess it's up to me to correct that wrong."

Mila didn't have time to respond or even analyze what he meant before Boone's hands grasped her shoulders, and he pulled her toward him.

She gasped the moment his lips touched hers, Boone capitalizing on that by brushing his tongue against hers.

She tasted the cinnamon and apples from the pie Edith Millholland had baked.

That was the last sane thought she had as Boone deepened the kiss, claiming her lips like they were the spoils of war.

She wrapped her arms around his neck, her fingers digging into his hair, grabbing it tight enough that Boone groaned. She immediately opened her fists, sorry for hurting him, until he murmured, "Keep holding on, darlin'," without lifting his lips from hers.

Mila had been kissed before, but never like this. Boone's lips were hard and soft at the same time. His hands strong, yet gentle. She was struggling to breathe, to stand, to do anything other than drown in this kiss.

Time stopped moving as the two of them got lost in the

silence of the night, the soft light of the moon, and the shelter of the trees.

Mila sucked in a harsh, much-needed intake of air when she felt the rough bark of a tree at her back. When did they leave the path?

None of her brain cells were functioning, every single one short-circuiting when his large thigh somehow found its way between her legs.

She moaned, rocking her hips, her body shifting into overdrive as Boone's hands drifted beneath her coat, cupping her breasts and squeezing, the lace of her bra stimulating her nipples until she was panting for breath.

Her panties had been damp from the dance they shared, but now they were downright soaked. Her entire body tingled when he pressed his thigh against her core harder, higher, making sure her clit was now part of the action. Everywhere Boone moved her with those strong, powerful hands, she followed, desperate for more.

His hands lowered to her hips, gripping hard as he increased the pace of her movements.

"God, yes! Please, Boone," she cried, her head falling back against the tree, hard enough it should hurt. However, all she could feel was the relentless pulsing between her legs.

Sadly, her words broke whatever spell had fallen over them.

Boone froze, stiffened, then pulled away.

She started to demand he finish what he'd started, but speaking was beyond her abilities now. He'd robbed her of air for too long with those drugging kisses. By the time her vision cleared, and she could focus again, she'd swallowed down the demands—hating the regret suffusing his features.

"Mila," he started, huskily.

All she had to hear was her name to know where this was going. He was going to warn her away again, probably even start offering a million excuses why this couldn't happen. She didn't want to hear them. She'd been on the receiving end of his "I'm not looking for a relationship" speech before, and she couldn't stand to hear it again. So she cut him off.

"Wow. You really know how to correct a wrong," she said, smiling the lightest, most carefree, nothing-to-see-here grin she could muster.

Given his frown, she suspected she'd managed nothing better than a pained grimace.

"Mila," he started again, his voice softer. If he apologized for that kiss, she would die. "Listen—"

"It was just a kiss," she hurried to lie. While she wasn't overly experienced, she was smart enough to know that was way more than a kiss.

Boone's shoulders were stiff, his gaze studying her too intently. Somehow, she found the strength to push away from the tree, though she was wobbly enough that Boone quickly reached out, placing a steadying hand on her elbow.

"Too much vodka," she whispered, hoping perhaps she could convince him she was tipsy enough that this would be forgotten.

Ha fucking ha.

She'd remember that kiss on her deathbed.

Pulling her winter coat around her, Mila was grateful the wool was thick enough to hide her nipples, which were now hard enough to cut glass.

Boone looked like he wanted to say more, but if he did…

His features softened, something like worry creeping into his eyes. Great. She probably looked emotionally fragile or some horrifying shit like that.

Turning away, she started walking across the yard to her house. It took a couple of seconds, but then Boone moved as well, taking his place at her side. They made the rest of the short journey in silence.

Because what the hell could they say after that?

Sadie must have heard them climbing the stairs, and she met them at the door. Their goodbyes were short and quick, and less than two minutes later, Mila was climbing the steps to her bedroom. Her body hadn't quite gotten the message that Boone and their heated interlude in the woods was over, because every part of her was still vibrating, shimmering...anticipating.

Mila stripped off her skirt and blouse, her bra and damp panties, then crawled into bed without bothering to put on her pajamas.

They would just be in the way, since there was no way she was falling to sleep tonight without taking care of unfinished business.

It took less than five minutes for the memory of Boone's kiss and her tried-and-true vibrator to produce the much-needed orgasm. And it wasn't one of the lukewarm ones she usually managed, the ones that got the job done but just barely.

Nope. This one was legit, mind-blowing, and proof that what she'd been doing in the past would never satisfy her again.

So...great. Boone wasn't just the kind of guy who would ruin her for other men. But also for masturbation.

She was screwed—figuratively, but never literally.

Chapter Six

Boone roamed around the kitchen, opening the refrigerator, looking inside, then closing it without pulling anything out. He'd done the same thing four times already, not because he was hungry but because he was bored.

It was midafternoon on Tuesday, and he should still be in the vineyard or at the winery, working with Maverick and Grayson. However, he'd cut the hell out of his hand right after lunch. Maverick tried to convince him to go to the ER, thinking he might need a few stitches, but

Boone refused.

He was no stranger to injuries, and while this one throbbed like a motherfucker, it would heal just fine. At Maverick's insistence—the man wouldn't take no for an answer—he'd taken the rest of the day off to come home, treat the wound, then take it easy so he wouldn't keep reopening it. Antiseptic and a butterfly bandage had done the trick as far as stopping the bleeding, but now he was left with too much time to think about what had distracted him and caused him to cut his damn hand in the first place.

Mila.

He hadn't been able to think of anything except her since that ill-advised kiss after the dance.

What in the sweet mother fuck had he been thinking?

Actually, he knew the answer to that.

He *hadn't* been thinking. He couldn't.

His cock had drawn every drop of blood from his brain the second he'd walked into that Valentine's Dance and seen Mila in that flouncy, flirty, sexy red skirt. Between that and the silky white blouse that kept giving him sneak peeks of her perfect cleavage, he'd been reduced to a silent, smoldering mass of testosterone. He didn't need anyone to tell him he'd been the least-stimulating conversationalist at the table he shared with Maverick, Grayson, and several other Storm brothers. His contributions throughout the night had been little more than one-word replies and a few grunts of agreement in between stealing a whole lot of glances at Mila.

Boone supposed he should be grateful to Maverick for inviting him to join his table, Sadie claiming a spot with Piper and her family. Upon arriving, his dick had homed in on Mila, seeing nothing but her and the empty seat beside her. God only knew what kind of damage he could have done if he'd been sitting next to her the entire evening. The simple whiff of her floral perfume during their dance had sent his thoughts down dirty, dirty paths.

Boone figured Maverick had done him a solid, saving him from himself by drawing him away from her and presenting him with a much safer place to sit.

If his cock hadn't been running the show, he never would have asked Mila to dance. He'd been proud of himself for remaining in his seat as each slow song started, his "don't do it" pep talk running on repeat. Unfortunately, his resolve only persisted—barely—until the deejay called out "last dance."

He'd seen the pastor making his way over to Mila, and all common sense flew out the window. Boone had already white-knuckled it through Pastor Joshua holding Mila through one dance. He didn't have it in him to do it twice.

The slow dance with her had wreaked havoc on his libido, and he'd had to take special care to make sure Mila didn't feel the half-chub he sported throughout.

The dance had been just the first of several missteps that night. Because he should have accepted Remi's invitation to the after-party, simply to keep him in a crowd of people who could distract him from Mila.

The problem with that option was, he suspected Mila would have said yes to attending in that case, and he hadn't liked the dark circles under her eyes. She'd worked herself into a state of exhaustion, preparing the food and decorating the barn. He hated that no one in her family seemed to notice how tired she looked, that no one was making sure she took care of herself.

So he'd offered that lame excuse about Sadie needing to get to bed, even though he didn't enforce bedtimes on the weekend, something his night owl daughter took full advantage of.

From that point on, his list of fuckups grew exponentially when he offered to walk Mila home, then stopped several times along the way, simply so that he could draw out his time with her.

Most of his other interactions with her since he'd moved to Gracemont had involved other people. Even the glasses of wine they shared after their Tuesday night cooking lessons were tempered by the fact Sadie was in the next room.

As Boone recalled that walk home—and the kiss—he was overwhelmed by guilt and regret.

Sadly, neither of those emotions were driven by the fact he shouldn't have kissed her.

Nope. They were the result of him pulling away from her. Because, as incredible as it seemed, he was damn sure Mila had been on the verge of coming...from nothing more than his hands on her breasts and his thigh between her thrusting hips.

And he'd left her hanging.

She'd said his name, along with that breathless "please," and it felt as if someone had dumped a bucket of cold water on his head. But it wasn't until he broke the kiss and stepped away that he'd realized just how close she was—her pupils blown wide, her breathing labored, her hard nipples straining through her bra and blouse as her chest rose and fell heavily.

Boone prided himself on his control, on his ability to handle difficult situations calmly and rationally, but none of that had been present as he watched her fight to lock down her body's needs before walking away.

Hell, he couldn't remember managing to say more than her name as Mila had done her best to put them back on firmer footing with humor. She'd let him off way easier than he deserved, and he'd spent the three days since kicking his own ass for...well...all of it.

But mainly for leaving her wanting.

Boone dropped down on the couch and rubbed his brow wearily. Sadie would be home from school soon. He had no idea if Mila was coming for their weekly cooking lesson. There was a good chance she didn't want a damn thing to do with him, and he wouldn't blame her. He and Sadie hadn't gone to Sunday dinner because she'd had a bad headache and asked if it was okay if she just stayed in bed. While he hated that his daughter had been hurting, she'd offered him a much-needed excuse to avoid Mila until he got his shit together.

His shit was *still* not together.

Leaning his head back against the couch, Boone closed his eyes, revisiting that moment in the woods again. No matter how he tried, he couldn't put the memory of it away, couldn't stop dreaming about Mila's hands in his hair, how sweet her breath tasted, the way her breasts filled his hands perfectly.

Groaning, he shut those thoughts down.

Mila was too young.

She was a Storm.

She wanted more than he could give.

While they hadn't discussed her desires for the future, Boone suspected she wanted what most women her age did. Marriage, kids, a home. And she deserved all of that with a man closer to her age, and with a hell of a lot less baggage.

When his cell rang, Boone shifted, leaning toward the coffee table where he'd set his phone after getting home.

He scowled when he saw Lena's name on the screen. For a moment, he considered letting it go to voicemail. After all, she knew he worked until well after five every day. Even though he was home right now, *she* didn't know that. Not that it mattered. Lena called when the spirit moved her, not when it was convenient for him.

Mercifully, she didn't call that often, which was why he reached for the phone and answered.

"Lena."

"Hello, Boone," she said sunnily. Lena was very good at ignoring things she didn't want to see, so she'd never given any indication that she felt the annoyance and impatience that rolled off him in waves whenever they spoke privately. "I'm so glad I caught you. It's been a crazy day already."

Lena launched into a five-minute recitation of how her boyfriend's car had broken down and left her stranded at the manicurist, how her new boss had gotten pissed off and fired her for being late, and how she didn't care about the loss because she'd planned to quit the job anyway because it sucked.

Lena went through minimum-wage jobs the way most people went through underwear. In addition to her commitment issues, she also struggled to deal with rules—like showing up to work on time, not texting while there, and not getting into it with customers when they complained. As such, she spent at least half the year looking for work, the other half bitching about her job. She managed to get away with her part-time unemployment because she excelled at finding guys who would foot the bills.

Lena's overactive dating life after their divorce was the main reason Boone had eschewed relationships. He figured it fell to him to provide stability for Sadie, since nothing in Lena's life was constant. He'd lost count of how many men Lena had told Sadie to call "Uncle Whatever." Like her jobs, the men never lasted long, something that had bothered Sadie a great deal when she was younger. Nowadays, his daughter took Lena's breakups in stride, and to be honest, he didn't know which was worse. Boone worried what long-term effects Lena's revolving door of lovers might have on Sadie when she was older.

"Was there a point to this call?" Boone interjected, when Lena came up for air.

She sighed. "You don't have to be rude," she snapped. "We haven't spoken since the holidays. I thought you might be interested in what's been going on in my life."

"I'm not sure what I've ever done that's given you the impression I care about what you do."

Lena laughed as if he was joking. "Same old grumpy Boone. It's no wonder you're still single after all these years. I'm the only woman in the world who could put up with all that growling for more than ten minutes."

Boone closed his eyes, praying for patience. "What do you want, Lena?"

"Since I'm between jobs, I thought I'd come home for a visit. I'll be staying with my sister in Williamsburg, and I thought it might be nice to see Sadie. She's getting older now, and she needs more time with her mother. I can teach her how to straighten her hair and put on makeup and stuff like that."

It was sad that Lena believed all Sadie needed from a mother was surface-y bullshit like hair and makeup tutorials. Not that he should be surprised. Lena had always treated Sadie like a doll she could play dress-up with.

"When are you coming? Because she's in school and she can't miss."

"Oh, for God's sake, Boone. She's in seventh grade. I'm sure it won't be the end of the world if she misses a week."

"A week? Not happening. I told you, her grades slipped first semester. She's been turning it around since we moved to Gracemont. I don't want her to backslide."

"She can get the missed work from her teachers, and I'll help her do it."

Riiiiiight. And Boone was going to ride a unicorn bareback and start shitting rainbows.

"No."

"Don't be difficult, Boone. If you hadn't dragged Sadie away from Williamsburg, this visit would be much simpler because I could just pick her up after school every day. You're the one who added this wrinkle."

Of course. Boone should have known. Lena's call wasn't so much about seeing Sadie as it was designed to punish him for moving. The irony of that was, she'd moved first, and farther away, but that would be totally lost on his ex, so he didn't bother mentioning it.

"Which week are you coming home?" He wasn't conceding, but he knew Sadie would want to see her mom, so he'd have to find some compromise.

"The week of March seven through fourteen. I'm flying in Sunday morning, and then out again late the following Sunday evening. You can just drop her off on the seventh at Carol's house and—"

"She's not coming the whole week, and I'm not driving all the way to Williamsburg." Boone had hit his limit on jumping through Lena's hoops when it came to her visits with Sadie. All the responsibility for getting Sadie to Lena had fallen on him in the past. He always dropped her off, picked her up, and when the flight to Florida was involved, he'd paid the airfare. He was done with that. If Lena was serious about seeing Sadie, some of the effort had to be hers.

"I don't have a car."

"You can borrow Carol's." Lena's sister worked from home and rarely went anywhere. She'd never been diagnosed as agoraphobic, but Carol certainly ticked all the boxes, getting her groceries delivered and never eating out. He knew for a fact she went out once a week just to start her car in the driveway to keep the battery charged.

"I don't see why you can't just drive here."

"Because I'm not driving a combined fourteen hours round trip to drop her off and pick her up. Spending hours on the road isn't my idea of a good time. Besides, I have work." He put Lena on speaker while he loaded Google maps, searching for a midpoint between Gracemont and Williamsburg. "We can meet in Fredericksburg."

Lena huffed her displeasure. "Maybe you didn't hear me, but I just lost my job. I can't afford gas money to—"

"You found the money for a plane ticket," Boone interjected. "So I'm sure you can figure out how to pay for a couple tanks of gas."

"Need I remind you that I was vehemently against you moving my daughter away from Williamsburg."

"Need I remind *you* that you don't get a say in my life. This move was the best thing for *both* Sadie and me. If you saw her more than a couple times a year, you'd know that."

"Oh, you just love throwing that in my face, don't you? Don't you think I'd see her more if I could?"

The answer to that was a resounding no, but he wasn't interested in engaging in a fight with Lena. Especially when the front door opened and Sadie walked in.

"Who's that?" his daughter mouthed, probably surprised to find him home early and on the phone. Neither were common occurrences.

"Your mom," he replied.

"Is that Sadie?" Lena asked, her voice loud through the speaker. "Put her on. Let me talk to her."

Boone knew exactly where this was going to lead, but it wasn't like he could refuse. Especially given the way Sadie's face lit up when she found out he was talking to Lena.

He handed the phone to Sadie, who excitedly said, "Hi, Mom."

Boone listened with half an ear as Lena shared her tale of work woes with Sadie, who was much more sympathetic than he'd been.

He tried to hide his displeasure when Sadie started to tell her mother about her day at school, only to be cut off.

"Listen, Sadie. I don't have a lot of time to talk."

Boone growled low in his throat. Lena never had time to talk unless it was about *her*.

"I'm coming to Virginia in March," Lena said.

Sadie cheered excitedly. "That's awesome! You can see our new house and my bedroom and the farm. I can introduce you to all the horses and—"

"Oh no, Sadie. I'm not coming to Gracemont. You're coming to Williamsburg to see me. We'll stay with your aunt Carol."

Sadie's enthusiasm dimmed considerably, mainly because Carol was a genuinely miserable person. Her two twenty-something-year-old kids, who should have been out of the house years ago, also lived there, and they were about as much fun as oral surgery. "Oh. Okay. But I have school."

"I was just telling your dad it won't matter if you miss a week—"

"She's not missing a week," Boone said, entering the conversation, aware Lena was setting him up as the bad guy with Sadie…just like she always did. "I said you could go for a long weekend. I don't want you missing more than two days of school."

"But, Dad," Sadie whined, "we're not even doing anything. I won't miss much."

He shook his head. He was sure her teachers would love to hear that apparently their lessons didn't count for anything. "I'll drive you down Wednesday after work and pick you up on Sunday. That's a long enough visit."

"Boone," Lena started, ready to pick up the argument.

He wasn't having it. "Take it or leave it, Lena. And don't forget we're meeting in Fredericksburg."

Lena huffed. "I don't know why you're being so stubborn about this. I hardly ever get to see Sadie."

"Yeah, Dad," Sadie chimed in. "I can get the missed work from my teachers before I go."

"And I'll help you do it, sweetheart," Lena chimed in.

It took all the strength in Boone's body not to scoff. He knew all the way to his bones that upon Sadie's return, his daughter would be stressed out because none of the schoolwork would be done. On top of that, it would take him a couple of weeks to get Sadie back to the responsible daughter he'd raised as she continued hitting him with the old, "But Mom always lets me…"

"Wednesday to Sunday and we meet in Fredericksburg, Lena."

"Fine, Boone." Lena's tone let him—*and* Sadie—know that she thought he was being unreasonable. "I need to skedaddle. I'm meeting a girlfriend for drinks later."

"I'll text you a location where we can meet," Boone added, aware Lena wouldn't do it.

She didn't acknowledge his comment, which meant she wasn't finished fighting that fight.

Something to look forward to, he thought sarcastically.

"Bye, Mom." Sadie hung up and handed Boone his phone. "I don't see why I can't—"

"I'm not changing my mind, Donut. You've got good grades right now, and I think you've got a shot at making the honor roll. There's no way you're missing a week of school."

Sadie scowled. "Fine. Whatever."

It just occurred to him that he hadn't heard that tone in weeks, and he hadn't missed it.

At. All.

Rather than call Sadie to task, he remained silent as she went to her room and closed the door just a smidge too hard.

Wonderful.

As if his day hadn't sucked enough. Now he got to look forward to a night of Sadie stomping around the cabin.

He glanced at the time on his watch and sighed. Boone wasn't one for napping, but he considered going to lie down. Dealing with Lena was exhausting. Every time he spoke to her, it drove home just how stupid he'd been to marry her in the first place. It was clear they'd had nothing but good sex going for them, so a large part of him was surprised they'd made it as long as they did as a married couple.

Boone had long ago accepted that he'd had his head turned by Lena's pretty face and her adventurousness in the bedroom.

Lena was the first woman he'd slept with who wasn't turned off or overwhelmed by his dominance. While she wasn't naturally submissive, she played the role because she got off on bondage and dirty talk. He'd been young enough and stupid enough to think she was his forever match.

It was another reason he'd avoided the dating scene. Boone didn't trust his instincts when it came to matters of the heart. He'd dated a few women prior to Lena, ones he might have thought were the one as well, if he'd been older and looking to settle down, which he hadn't. Lena was the first woman he'd seriously considered spending the rest of his life with.

What if he fell for another woman only to discover—once again—that he'd mistaken lust for love? Sadie had already been hurt once by his poor decisions, forced to grow up with an absent mother. He wouldn't subject her to that again.

While Boone was still annoyed by Lena's call, it had come at a good time, because it reminded him why he'd been an idiot to kiss Mila. There was no denying he was attracted to her, but he couldn't let himself get carried away thinking it was more than physical desire.

Boone rose from the couch, bypassed his bedroom, and walked over to the kitchen drawer where he kept the medicine. His hand was fucking throbbing. Grabbing the bottle of ibuprofen, he popped a couple in his mouth and washed them down with a glass of water from the tap.

He turned when he heard a brief knock on the front door, followed by the sound of it opening.

"Sadie?" Mila called out, stopping when she spotted him in the kitchen. "Oh, Boone. I didn't realize you were home." She glanced at the door she'd just walked through, as if he'd be mad at her for coming in without waiting for an invitation.

Despite the fact he'd just told himself he needed to keep his distance from Mila, there was no denying the way his crappy attitude gave way to happiness the second he saw her. Part of his distraction today had been him wondering if she would come tonight, and getting pissed at himself for potentially ruining the cooking lessons with that kiss.

Boone held up his injured hand. "Cut myself at work. Maverick told me to take the rest of the day off. Otherwise, I was just going to keep splitting it open and bleeding all over the place."

Mila crossed the room to the kitchen, taking his hand in hers, instantly concerned. "Does it need stitches?"

He shook his head. "I've squeezed the skin together pretty good under that butterfly bandage. It'll be fine. I…" He hesitated. "I wasn't sure you were coming tonight."

"It's Tuesday." She was smiling, but Boone got the sense it was a bit forced. "Sadie asked if we could make homemade pizza." Mila lifted a canvas bag he hadn't noticed her carrying. "I grabbed some of my sauce and I've brought some veggies, pepperoni, sausage, and shredded mozzarella. Oh, and yeast. The rest of what we'll need, you already have."

"Which means flour and water, right?"

Mila snickered. "Yeah. Pretty much."

"Let me give you some money toward the ingredients," he insisted.

Mila shook her head. "Nope. Tonight's dinner is on me. You've provided all the ingredients for our last few lessons, so it was time for me to take a turn."

Before Boone could argue, Sadie came out of her room. "Hey, Mila."

Mila must have noticed the less-than-enthusiastic tone. "You feeling alright, sweetie?"

Sadie shrugged casually. "I'm fine." She disproved that assertion by shooting an angry look his direction. Boone narrowed his eyes in warning. The last thing he wanted was for Sadie to start up their argument in front of Mila.

Mila glanced from Sadie to him and back, forcing that cheerful smile again as she started unpacking her tote bag. "Good. Because we have a lot of work to do. I thought you and I would make the pizza dough first, since it has to rise."

Mercifully, Sadie perked up as she took in the vegetables and meats now covering the island. "That sounds cool."

Mila reached into the refrigerator and pulled out a beer, offering it to him. She'd been in their kitchen enough to feel at home, and he liked it way too much. "Why don't you relax on the couch? I'm worried about your hand."

Her comment captured Sadie's attention. "What did you do to your hand?" For the first time since arriving home, his daughter noticed his bandage.

"Just a little cut. It's fine."

"I wondered why you were home early," Sadie mused aloud.

If Mila was curious why the two of them hadn't already discussed that, she didn't let on.

Boone took the beer from her, popping the cap on the bottle. Then he scooted behind her, trying to hide the impact her close proximity had on him when his chest brushed her back. "What about you, ladies? I'm not going to be much help on the food prep tonight, but I'm willing to serve as bartender and deejay."

Mila laughed. "I'd love a glass of wine."

Sadie climbed on one of the stools by the island. "Sprite, please."

Boone poured their drinks before claiming his own stool next to Sadie, fiddling with Spotify until he found Mila's favorite seventies playlist.

Despite the music and Mila's lesson, Boone still felt the strain between him and Sadie. Things had been so good since moving to Gracemont that it was hard to return to the hell that was their previous fall. He'd lived through months of his daughter's anger and silence, and he'd genuinely believed they'd turned a corner.

Wishful thinking on his part.

He should have realized it was a honeymoon period.

Leave it to Lena to fuck things up.

While the pizza dough was rising, Mila and Sadie chopped the green peppers, onions, and mushrooms, discussing their favorite toppings.

Boone chimed in whenever they asked him a question, otherwise, he simply sat and listened to them chat. Between his hand, Sadie being pissed at him, and this unending internal battle he continued to wage over his feelings for Mila, he was too out of sorts to be good company.

Once the pizza prep was over, Mila and Sadie went to her bedroom to work on the scarves they were crocheting for the underprivileged. Boone was usually at work during this time, so it was interesting to see the routine Mila and Sadie seemed to have established. They talked too quietly for Boone to hear them from the living room, though he picked up bits and pieces, mainly Sadie talking about her school day.

He didn't know if his daughter was filling Mila in on his perceived unfairness over not letting her miss school. Part of him suspected if Sadie did, Mila would be on his side because— unlike Lena, who said she'd help with homework but never followed through—Mila was never too busy to tutor his daughter in history and science, or proofread a paper she'd written.

Boone had turned on the TV, though he kept the volume low, uninterested in the repeat of a sitcom he'd seen a million times.

Eventually, Mila and Sadie returned to the kitchen, and he followed in their wake, watching as the two of them rolled out a crust for each of them. Mila covered the crusts with her delicious-smelling sauce and cheese, then he and Sadie each decorated their own before popping them into the oven.

Boone refilled all the drinks as Sadie set the table. Dinner had been quite lively and fun the past few weeks, but tonight, it seemed neither he nor Sadie could kick their foul moods, so it fell to Mila to keep the conversation rolling.

As soon as the table was cleared, Sadie excused herself to go do her homework. Mila wiped the counter, then turned.

"I'm going to head out."

The two of them usually had a drink on the couch after dinner, and despite the fact he was probably coming across like a bear with a thorn stuck in his paw, Boone didn't like the idea of her skipping out early.

"Stay for a drink." As always, he intended his words to be an invitation, not a demand.

Yeah. So much for that.

Of course, it hadn't escaped his notice that Mila responded better to the demands. "Are you sure? If your hand is hurting—"

She was blaming his bad mood on pain. "It's not. My hand is fine. I took a couple ibuprofen earlier, and they've kicked in." Rather than wait for her to respond, he walked to the fridge to pull out the wine she'd been drinking. Filling her glass, then pouring one for himself, he gestured toward the couch.

Mila took the glass, thanking him as she walked to what had become their usual spots. Each of the three weeks prior, he'd made sure to keep a proper distance between them, but tonight, he was feeling contrary and ornery enough to shrink it.

So much for learning from his fucking mistakes.

"Is everything okay?" Mila asked. "Did you and Sadie have a fight?"

"Lena called this afternoon. She's going to be in Virginia in March and wants to see Sadie."

"Oh. That's cool. Sadie has been chomping at the bit to show her mom the farm and—"

Boone cut her off. "She's staying in Williamsburg with her sister, so we're meeting halfway, and Sadie will visit her there."

"Does Sadie not want to go?" Mila asked, clearly confused. "I got the impression she and her mom were close."

Boone didn't even know how to reply to that. He was sure Sadie *did* think she and Lena were close, but that was only because the relationship they shared had always been like this, with Lena making time for Sadie when it was convenient for her. Since moving to Florida, that had been reduced to Lena calling or FaceTiming once every couple of weeks and the way-too-occasional visits.

"They are," he lied, not wanting Sadie to overhear what he really thought about her relationship with Lena. He'd decided a long time ago he needed to love his daughter more than he despised his ex. While it was sometimes difficult to temper his tone, especially today, when Lena had gone out of her way to push all his buttons, he thought he'd done a decent job of following through when it came to hiding his true feelings for Lena. "The problem is, Lena wanted to take her out of school for a week."

Mila's wince proved Boone right. "That's a long time. Wouldn't Sadie miss a lot?"

"That's what I said, which is why I agreed to only let her miss two days. I'll drive her down on Wednesday after work and pick her up on Sunday."

"That sounds fair enough," Mila said.

Boone chucked mirthlessly. "Tell that to my daughter."

Mila grinned. "Given a choice, kids will always choose to miss more school."

"True. But as you can see, I'm currently the villain, a role I'm getting damn tired of playing."

"I don't see a villain. Just a good father. Give yourself a break, Boone. You're doing terrific with Sadie."

He was grateful for her words, unaware until she spoke them just how much he needed to hear that.

Mila twisted on the couch to face him more fully. "Take it from me, divorce isn't easy on kids."

Boone frowned, confused, because it sounded like she was talking from experience. He'd learned from Maverick that Mila's parents had been killed in a car accident. Since Mila had never mentioned her folks, that was all he knew about them. Regardless, he wasn't sure how to broach the subject, in case it was hard for her to talk about.

Mila saved him from having to try. "My parents were in the midst of getting a divorce when they were killed in a car accident."

Jesus.

As he looked into Mila's pretty brown eyes, he saw the compassion she felt for him and Sadie, despite how much she'd suffered herself.

His heart swelled and broke at the same time.

He'd known Mila Storm was dangerous, but he didn't realize just how much.

Chapter Seven

"How old were you when they died?" Boone asked her.

"Nine, but I was eight when Mom left us."

"She left you?"

Maybe now, Boone would understand why she'd been going the extra mile with Sadie. She knew from experience how it felt to live without a mother.

"She and my dad had a whirlwind romance. Married three months after they met, and Lucy came along nine months after that."

Boone grimaced. "I can't help but recognize some similarities between your parents' relationship and mine with Lena. Impetuous choices made in the heat of the moment."

"That's not always a bad thing," Mila said, though she could tell her words were falling on deaf ears.

"So your mom wasn't from Gracemont?" he asked.

She shook her head. "She was a photographer. She'd just graduated from college and was in the midst of a cross-country road trip. She was adventurous. Lucy takes after her that way."

Mila had told him quite a bit about her sisters with Sadie and Boone during their shared meals. She was extremely close to them, so they were one of her favorite subjects. She supposed it made sense that they were close, considering they'd been orphaned so young. That kind of devastating loss forged strong bonds.

"Mom and Dad were happy for quite a few years, but after a time, Mom's wanderlust started to kick in. They fought a lot because Mom wanted us to move."

"Where?"

Mila shrugged. "I'm not even sure that she cared where. She just wanted off the farm."

"I guess your dad didn't want to leave."

"He and my uncle Rex were very much alike, both wholly devoted to this land. They hit an impasse, so Mom left. Packed her bags and hit the road the second we left on the bus for school one day. Dad was waiting for me and my sisters when we got home. He said Mom went on a vacation, but I knew she wasn't coming back. Lucy, however, hung on to that lie for months. She and my mom were very close."

"You weren't?"

Mila smiled sadly. "I was a daddy's girl. At least, I was until…" Mila leaned back against the arm of the chair and stopped talking. She hadn't meant to go into any more detail than she already had.

Of course, Boone prodded. "Until?"

She bit her lower lip, hesitating. "I've never talked about the year Mom was gone with anyone. Not even my sisters. Nora and Remi were too young to really grasp what was going on. Lucy and I… Well, without saying so, I think it was obvious we'd both picked sides. Lucy wanted Mom back, and I was mad at her for hurting Dad. Because he…changed."

"Changed how?" Boone clearly regretted the question the

moment it slipped out, because she had to quickly look away, unwilling to let him see the tears she was fighting the very devil not to shed. "You don't have to talk about this, Mila."

She blinked a few times, beating back the sadness before turning to face him again. She'd come this far, and besides, strangely, it felt good to be able say these things aloud. She'd been carrying them around inside for far too long.

"It's okay. It happened a long time ago. I guess seeing you with Sadie…it's made me remember things I haven't thought about in years. My dad was a hard worker. He loved getting his hands dirty, digging in the soil, caring for the vines. Just like you. I would wait for him every day on the porch and the second he walked through the clearing, I'd run to him, and he'd pick me up and spin me around over his head. Then I'd tell him about my day while he washed up for dinner. He always called me his little chatterbox."

"Chatterbox, huh?" he asked with a grin.

"Back then, there was no shutting me up. I swear I was worse than Remi."

Boone feigned a shudder, and Mila laughed.

"He told the greatest bedtime stories ever, making up the most outlandish tales about princes and knights fighting off fearsome dragons, or trolls, or even vampires to rescue their princesses. The stories were never the same, always fraught with drama and big battles, and we loved them."

Mila's smile faded. "After Mom left, he worked longer hours. My grandma and Aunt Claire started taking care of us, feeding us dinner, even putting us to bed some nights when he was really late. No more of his bedtime stories. He stopped spinning me around, and while I still told him about my day, it never felt like he heard what I was saying."

"I'm sorry. That couldn't have been easy on you."

"Sometimes it felt like I hadn't just lost my mother, but my father as well. So I spent the better part of that year furious at my mom, and overwhelmed with guilt because I didn't miss her the way Lucy did. I thought I should, and that there was something wrong with me because I didn't."

"You were eight years old, Mila. That's a lot for someone so young to deal with."

"It was—" She stopped, because the only word she could think of was *hard*. She couldn't minimize how difficult that time of her life was, but she felt guilty, sitting here unloading nearly two decades' worth of emotional baggage.

"It was difficult," he answered for her. "You don't have to pretend for my sake. I'd prefer it if you didn't. But I'm confused," Boone continued. "You said your parents died in a car accident. Did your mom come back?"

Mila squeezed her hands together, wringing them, because this was where the story got tougher. So tough, she debated not telling it because once she did, the pain she'd buried all those years ago would be revealed, the vein cut open.

Boone reached out and placed his over hers, grasping and holding them tightly. "Take a breath."

She did as he suggested, then she took another.

He smiled. "Good girl."

The nervous flutters in her stomach instantly stilled as a wave of calm washed through her.

She swallowed deeply. "One night, I was talking to my dad while he washed for dinner. He'd come home on time that night, and I was thrilled because I hadn't seen him for three days straight. No matter how early I got up, he was always out of the house before then. That night, I was trying to make up for lost time, talking a mile a minute when he sort of…exploded."

Boone frowned. "What's that mean?"

"He told me I needed to stop talking so much, that I needed to stop constantly being under foot because I annoyed people.

Then he said he was tired and just wanted me to leave him alone."

"Mila," Boone started.

"I skipped dinner that night. Dad didn't bother to call for me or try to drag me to the table. I don't know if that's because he was still mad or because he felt bad for what he'd said. I cried myself to sleep and by the next morning, I set my mind to being quieter, less annoying."

"Mila, I don't think that's what your dad wanted at all. He was clearly struggling with your mom leaving and he took it out on you. What did he say about it the next morning?"

"Nothing. I didn't know at the time that he was stressed out because Mom was coming home the next day. She'd filed for a divorce, and the two of them were going to sign the papers."

"He *did* talk to you about it, though, right?"

Mila blinked several more times, but a few tears escaped anyway. She tried to wipe them away but Boone beat her to it, brushing them with his thumb, his hand caressing her cheek so sweetly, she leaned into the touch.

They stared at each other without speaking for a few moments, and Mila resisted the desire to shift toward him, to kiss him.

Boone shook himself free of whatever spell had fallen over them first, moving back a few inches. "Tell me the rest." From his tone, it almost felt like he was mentally preparing himself for what came next. She was touched that he cared so much.

"When I got home from school that afternoon, Grandma was there to watch us. Mom and Dad had gone to the lawyer's office —not that I knew that until later. I guess they were planning to sit us down over dinner to tell us about the divorce, but…"

"But?"

"Nora had ridden the bus to a friend's house. Mom and Dad picked her up after their meeting with the lawyer. On the way back up the mountain, they hit a patch of black ice and the car ran off the road, hit a tree head-on."

"Nora was in the car?"

"Yes. She wasn't hurt badly—just some scrapes and bruises and a nasty bump on the head—but she was trapped for several hours. Mom and Dad were... The police officer said they were killed instantly."

Boone flinched. "She was in the car with them for hours?"

Mila nodded, unable to continue, the lump in her throat too thick.

Boone took her hand again, to hold it, she assumed. Instead, he tugged on it, pulling her toward him and wrapping his arms around her.

Mila accepted his hug. Actually, she sank into it, because she needed it so damn bad. Closing her eyes, she breathed in Boone's masculine scent.

Cedar and bergamot with the faintest overtone of tomato and garlic from the pizza sauce.

She hadn't intended to share so much with him regarding her parents. Not because it was a secret or because it was difficult to talk about, since everyone—family and friends—already knew what had happened.

What she'd never told another living soul was the last conversation she'd had with her father.

Realistically, she knew Boone was right. That her dad had been on edge and if he'd had the opportunity, he would have apologized and made things right.

But he died before he could do that, and for too many years afterward, his words stuck, and the wound refused to heal.

She suspected her grandparents had blamed her newfound quiet disposition on grief, but that emotion was only one small part of why she'd changed so drastically after her parents' deaths. Mingled with the pain was also a lot of anger toward her mother, whom Mila blamed for basically everything, as well as shame. Mila had swum in an ocean of it, hating that she'd disappointed her dad by being too loud, too chatty, too annoying.

Looking back now, she could see that wasn't true, but nine-year-olds weren't exactly known for handling their emotions well, and hers had gone completely haywire the evening Granddaddy had walked into their farmhouse, sat Mila, Lucy, and Remi down, and broke the news that their parents were dead. Uncle Rex and Aunt Claire had gone to the hospital with Nora, so she didn't get home until much later that night.

By the time Mila reached adulthood, she was able to reflect on Dad's words without all those intense emotions coloring them, but by then it was too late. Her personality had been reshaped and reformed, and there wasn't any going back to the carefree, wild, young chatterbox she'd been.

She loosened her grip and pushed away from Boone, feeling guilty for holding on so tightly for so long.

"Thanks," she said softly. "I shouldn't have unloaded all of that on you."

Boone cupped her cheek in his large, calloused hand. "You didn't unload anything that I didn't ask to hear. Who raised you after your parents' passing? Rex and Claire?"

Mila shook her head. "We moved in with our grandparents. Not that Uncle Rex and Aunt Claire didn't help a lot. It was just that they had seven boys of their own to raise, all between the ages of nineteen and nine."

Boone, bless him, made a horrified face, clearly meant to lighten the mood. It did the trick and she laughed, agreeing when he said, "I can't imagine having seven kids in ten years. I've got one twelve-year-old and she's putting me through my paces."

"Aunt Claire says she would have had more, but Uncle Rex put the kibosh on that, claiming seven was more than enough."

"Was she going for a girl?" he asked.

"She's always said no. She just wanted a big family. I think she got whatever girl fix she might have needed from me and my sisters. She helped Grandma make our prom dresses, she taught us how to French braid our hair, and she put us in the kitchen alongside the boys and made sure we all knew how to cook."

"Now I see who inspired your cooking lessons."

"I was blessed with amazing role models because Aunt Claire is seriously the greatest cook ever, and Grandma taught me everything I know about crocheting."

Boone rested his arm along the back of the couch, his hand very close to her shoulder. She wished he'd touch her again, cup her cheek or hold her hand. Sadly, he didn't. "Did you like living with your grandparents?"

"I did. They took us in and worked overtime to make sure we knew we were loved and safe. I can't imagine acquiring four young girls at their age—Grandma was sixty-seven and Granddaddy was seventy."

Boone's eyes widened. "Wow. Yeah. That would have been an adjustment. For all of you."

"It was fine...for a while."

"For a while?"

Mila held up her hands. "Oh my God, I swear I'm going to stop now. I don't mean to keep dumping my tragic past on you."

She was delighted when Boone reached over and squeezed her shoulder. "Don't stop. I want to hear the rest."

She could tell he was sincere. She was also strangely grateful to him for listening. She'd kept all of this bottled inside for so long that it felt cleansing to get it out.

"Grandma was diagnosed with dementia when she was seventy-five. I was eighteen and had just graduated. Lucy had been out of school a year. Granddaddy continued to work in the vineyard, and Lucy was ensconced in the brewery with Theo and Sam, so I stayed with Grandma during the day. Then at night, we were all there with her, making sure she was comfortable and safe. A couple years after that, Granddaddy got lung cancer. For a year, my sisters and I took care of the two of them, along with Aunt Claire and Uncle Rex, of course. They died within an hour of each other. Grandma died first, while Granddaddy held her hand, then he passed once she was gone. It was sad, but also kind of beautiful, because I've never known two people so much in love."

"Jesus, Mila. You give so much."

"Not at all. They took us in and raised us. And I know it wasn't easy. Nora was…" Mila hesitated, unsure how best to describe her sister's mental state. "She was messed up after Mom and Dad died. She started stuttering, and that was when a lot of her compulsions began, the extreme organizing, her disdain for even numbers. Grandma took her to see a therapist."

"Good. I'm sure she needed that."

"And then there was Remi, running wild. I can't even count how many hours poor Granddaddy spent searching for her on the mountain because she always took off, forgetting to come home, even after dark."

Boone smiled sadly. "Not sure that's changed much."

"It hasn't, but I hated it when she didn't come home on time because I could see how much it worried Grandma and Granddaddy. Lucy tried to pitch in too. I guess as oldest, she thought it fell to her to help 'raise the little ones,' so she played surrogate mom to Nora and Remi as much as they'd let her. Which was basically not at all."

"What about you?"

"What *about* me?" she asked, confused.

"Were you still a chatterbox?"

Mila licked her lips uncomfortably. "No. I just tried to be quiet. I didn't want to add to anyone's stress. Didn't want to anno—" She stopped short.

"Annoy anyone?" Boone shook his head, and Mila was swamped with misery, feeling as if she'd disappointed him somehow. "Mila. You were a little kid. No one expected you to be perfect."

"I'm not saying I was. I just…"

"You purposely made yourself small, put yourself in the background." Boone reached out and placed his hand on her knee to stop it from bouncing nervously.

"I didn't want to be a burden."

"They're your family. They wouldn't have seen you that way. They love you, Mila. But I wonder sometimes if you're not still hiding the real you."

How could he know that? How could he see it when no one else could?

Regardless, this conversation had gotten way too deep, and she needed out before she fell apart completely.

"I told you I should stop." She gave him what she hoped would pass as a playful smirk. "Everyone has sad stories in their past. Those were mine. And you're right. I'm blessed. My family loves me, and I live on this gorgeous farm, doing work that fulfills me. Nothing that happened when I was younger broke me. It just molded me into the person I am today."

Boone looked like he might continue the argument that she wasn't truly being herself, but she didn't want to talk about that, so she tried to throw him on the hot seat. "I'm sure there're things that have impacted the man you are today, as well."

Boone nodded in agreement. "There are."

"Maybe one day, you'll share them with me."

He grinned, taking her hand in his again. "Maybe I will." He looked at her in a way that not only made her feel seen but, God, cherished. "You're an amazing woman, Mila Storm."

Her cheeks grew warm—damn blushing—and she ducked

her head at his compliment. "Amazing is probably a bit strong," she joked, though it fell way short.

Boone scowled, and his grip on her hand tightened. "Amazing isn't strong enough."

Her heart raced, thudding loudly in her ears. In what world did she think she could settle for mere friendship with this man? Every word sent her tumbling deeper and deeper. She was falling so fast and hard for him, there was no way she wouldn't wind up with bruises on her heart and soul.

The silence between them hovered, as Mila tried to figure out where to go from here.

Sadly, Boone made the decision for them. "It's a nice night. We should take advantage of the break from the cold. How about I walk you home?"

"You don't have to." She'd said the same thing after every cooking lesson, though she knew it wasn't an argument she was going to win.

Boone rose despite her assertion, helping her into her coat before pulling on his own.

They walked over to Sadie's room, Mila knocking softly before opening the door. "I'm heading home. Night, Sadie."

"Night, Mila. Thanks for the pizza."

"You finished your homework, Donut?" Boone asked.

Sadie lifted her notebook and grimaced. "Everything but math," she grumbled.

"I'll help you with it when I get back from walking Mila home."

Sadie nodded, and Mila got the sense that her anger toward Boone was passing. She was glad, because she knew it weighed on him when his daughter wasn't happy.

They headed out of the cabin and down the dirt road toward her farmhouse. The moon was bright in the sky, just like it was the night of the Valentine's Dance.

They walked in companionable silence for a few minutes. Since they were out of earshot of Sadie, Mila decided to ask about today's argument.

"How long do you think Sadie will stay mad at you?"

He shrugged. "Probably until the trip has come and gone. Shades of the Sadie I thought we'd left behind in Williamsburg reappeared today. The attitude and door slamming."

Mila laughed quietly. "That was always coming back. She's a twelve-year-old girl. Believe me when I say, she has not yet begun to fight."

Boone grumbled a few choice words under his breath, and she laughed harder.

"Thanks for the pep talk, coach," he joked, sarcastically. "Sadie's been so good here. So happy. I forgot how tough the fall was."

"She really didn't want to move?"

"Not at all. Maybe if she'd been doing well in school and hadn't been getting into trouble, I might have thought harder about making Williamsburg work for us, but I was desperate to get her away from that Stella girl."

Boone had mentioned the troublesome Stella a few times, so Mila could understand. "It's scary how much influence friends can have during middle school and high school."

"It is. I couldn't keep watching her go down bad paths."

The farmhouse was dark as they approached.

"Your sisters already in bed?"

Mila shook her head. "Not here. Levi proposed to Kasi after the Valentine's Dance."

"Maverick told me," Boone said.

"So Nora and Remi are at Kasi's tonight, diving into wedding planning."

Boone stopped and turned to face her. "You didn't want to go? You could have skipped the cooking lesson."

Mila waved her hand. "The girls will be planning that wedding every damn day until it happens. I'll have at least a million opportunities to weigh in. Plus, I'm pretty sure the wedding planning was going to take a backseat to the three bottles of wine Remi took with her. Twenty bucks says they either wind up spending the night at Kasi's or getting Koda to Uber them home."

Boone glanced at the dark house, scowling. "You gonna be alright here alone if they don't come back tonight?"

"Of course. I'm a big girl."

Boone's expression darkened, and he didn't seem to share her humor. She was secretly thrilled by his concern for her.

They crossed the yard to the front porch.

Mila had spent most of the night on the hot seat, divulging things she'd never meant to say. Which meant Boone now knew a hell of a lot about her, while she still knew practically nothing about him.

That was the only reason she could think for opening her mouth and sticking her foot in it…big-time. "So you haven't dated anyone since you divorced Lena?"

Jesus. She'd spent the entire day practicing her "happy face," determined to walk into Boone's this afternoon like that kiss had never happened. So much for that.

That kiss had rocked her world. It had also given her a hope she probably shouldn't be harboring but couldn't snuff out.

Boone was quiet as they climbed the steps, and she wondered if he was going to ignore her.

"I'm not sure dating is the right word. I've gone out with women since the divorce, but it's been less about dating and more about…" He was clearly hesitant to finish.

"Hookups?"

He smirked. "Yeah. There were a couple of women in Williamsburg who I knew through work. They were both divorced as well, and neither were looking to take a second trip down the aisle. Whenever Sadie was with her mom, I'd call one of them, we'd grab some dinner, and then..."

"The hookup," she added, grinning.

Boone nodded his head. "Yeah."

"Sounds kind of depressing," she said.

"It was sex, Mila. Scratching an itch. Emotions didn't play a part."

Mila was starting to think she was a glutton for punishment. Everything she learned about Boone backed his assertion that he wasn't looking for love or a relationship. Maybe if he hadn't kissed her like the world was about to come to an end on Valentine's Day, she'd be better at moving on. Unfortunately, that had merely stoked her desire for the man even more.

"Do you want to come in for a drink?" she asked.

He shook his head. "I need to get back to help Sadie with her math homework."

"Oh, right." Mila bent down and retrieved the key she and her sisters stashed under the mat.

"What the hell is that?"

She jerked upright, not expecting Boone's sharp tone.

She dangled the key between her fingers. "Key to the front door. Of course, knowing my baby sister..." she thought aloud, realizing Remi was the last one to leave this afternoon. Mila reached out and, sure enough, the front door was already unlocked. "I don't need it," she said with a sigh. "Remi never remembers to lock it." She bent down to put the key back where they'd kept it for years.

Remi always moved like a force of nature, which meant she was forever forgetting her house key. All of them walked to and from work, only driving when they were going into town, so it was easier to just stash a key under the mat rather than fool around with carrying one. They'd made that decision after the twentieth time she, Nora, or Lucy had had to leave work to let Remi inside.

Before she could replace it, Boone stopping her, his large hand gripping her upper arm.

Mila shivered, just as she always did whenever he touched her. Theo and Levi hadn't mentioned that the lightning strike they experienced when they'd realized Gretchen and Kasi were theirs didn't stop with that first hit. Every time Boone touched her, Mila's entire body awoke, shimmering with electricity and heat.

"What's wrong?" she asked.

"You leave a key to your house in the most obvious place in the world?"

While she was fighting off powerful arousal, Boone didn't seem to be suffering the same. If anything, he looked pissed.

"We live on the side of a mountain, Boone. There's very little traffic. No, scratch that. There's none."

"There are two businesses and an event barn on the property," he pointed out.

"And the turn-off for all three of those is before anyone gets here. It's only a few of the cabins and the stables that stretch beyond us, and we always know who's there."

Boone crossed his arms. If he was hoping to look intimidating, he was missing the mark, because all his stance did was draw her attention to his thick arms and broad chest.

"You're three women living alone," he said.

"Anyone driving this road at night would pass the frat house and the B&B. You must know by now, the guys are protective of us. Whenever headlights flash by, there's almost always a text from one of my cousins asking if we're expecting company."

Remi always got annoyed by those texts, insisting they were grown women, but Mila found them sweet, and they set her mind at ease.

"What about during the day? Everyone is at work during the day. Who's guarding your unlocked house then?"

"Nora's usually the last out each morning, and she never forgets to lock the door. That's just Remi."

"Mila. I don't like that you're leaving your key where anyone could find it." Boone finished opening the door as he spoke.

She wasn't sure how to reassure him they were fine leaving it there. They'd done so for years. Instead, she followed him into her house, her insides warming as Boone systematically turned on lights, doing a quick scan of all the downstairs rooms. It was obvious there wasn't anyone in the house, but she was still touched by his actions.

"Boone," she said, when he returned to her. His gaze traveled to the stairs, and she suspected he was only just barely restraining himself from doing a full-house search for some make-believe boogeyman hiding under the beds. "No one's here but us."

He sighed, his frown still prevalent. "Don't leave that key under the mat again."

His words were spoken like a command he expected to be followed, and the devil inside her was too tempted to ask what would happen if she did.

Boone must have realized that, because his eyes narrowed and he took a tiny step closer. "You won't like what happens if you do, so don't test me."

"What would happen?" she whispered, cutting a few more of the inches between them.

Boone stopped tiptoeing around, leaning down until his face was in hers, his breath hot against her cheek. "I'd take you over my knee and spank your ass until you couldn't sit for a week."

Yep. That key was going right back under the mat.

Her smirk must have given her away.

Boone scowled. "Goddammit, Mila. *Wrong* reaction."

His hands flew to her upper arms as he pulled her roughly against his chest, his lips devouring hers the same way they had Valentine's night. Because of his tight grip, holding her arms pinned to her sides, all Mila could do was crook her elbows, grasping his jacket.

For several minutes, it was a battle of wills, tongues, teeth, and lips.

Mila had to turn her head to draw in much-needed air, something Boone didn't seem willing to allow. One large hand wrapped around the back of her neck, his thumb pushing her face toward him once more, his lips stealing hers for another—God, yes—hotter kiss.

His other hand started to roam, stripping off her coat and dropping it to the floor before slipping under her sweater to squeeze one of her breasts roughly. He pinched her nipple, the lace of her bra adding to the sensations as she saw stars.

Mila had no idea her breasts were erogenous zones. Most—okay, *all* of her masturbation focused on the regions south of her stomach.

"God, Boone," she breathed into his mouth. "That feels so good. I didn't know." She wrapped her hands around his neck, throwing her head back as his lips descended the side of her throat, nibbling and licking. "I've never…"

Her words fell away when Boone abruptly broke off the embrace, stepping away from her like she was a bonfire and he'd gotten too close.

"Shit," he muttered, running a hand through his hair.

"Boone."

"That was a mistake, Mila."

"No, it wasn't."

He sighed, but mercifully, one side of his mouth quirked in an amused grin. "Ten years and I've never once struggled to do the right thing."

She hated that he thought their kisses were a mistake because as far as she was concerned, they were the greatest things she'd ever experienced.

"I've only been on this farm a month and a half and I'm doing all the wrong things with you."

"They don't feel wrong," she whispered.

"Trust me...they are." He crossed his arms once more, his brows furrowed. "Especially since..." He studied her intently. "Finish what you were about to say before. You've never what?"

Mila was instantly besieged with regret for her wayward tongue. "Nothing. I—"

"Finish it, Mila."

That tone of his was deadly, making her want to give him what he asked for, making her desperate to please him.

"I didn't realize my..." She bit her lower lip, her face suddenly a thousand degrees, and no doubt bloodred. "I've never gotten so turned on from just a kiss." She skipped over the breast discovery, because that would reveal way more than she wanted.

Boone's arms lowered, and he slid his hands into the pockets of his coat. "Who were you dating before the pastor?"

Mila hesitated, because she already suspected his reasons for holding her at arm's length had as much to do with her age as her name. While Boone hadn't spelled things out for her, she wasn't an idiot.

There was thirteen years' difference in their ages, something that didn't bother her, but she didn't think the same held true for Boone. Add to that, her last name was Storm, and he'd just uprooted his life and Sadie's to move here for a new job. She could get why he wouldn't want to risk his livelihood by taking a chance with her.

"I've done a bit of dating, but it's sort of challenging in Gracemont. It's a small town and it's not like the pool of available men is big." She stopped there, hoping he'd accept that answer and move on.

She should have known better.

"Keep going," he demanded.

"It actually gets smaller with each passing year. A lot of the guys I went to school with have settled down with someone, or they're the men who are still single for very good reasons." She added the last with a grin, hoping once again to escape the conversation...this time with humor.

"I'm hearing a lot of words, yet none of them have answered my question."

Mila scowled, then crossed her own arms, loving the way his eyes drifted lower—for just a second—before landing on her face again. It was those brief stolen glances that told her she wasn't alone in this attraction and made her want to continue fueling the flames. Because his eyes were saying very different things than his words.

"I had a boyfriend in high school. Senior year. Todd and I dated for all of four months. Which I don't have to tell you is a long time by high school standards," she joked.

Boone didn't grin. In fact, his expression grew darker. "Your last boyfriend was high school?"

"No," she added quickly, even though it was a pretty stupid thing to say, because in truth, Todd *was* her first and last boyfriend. "I'm just saying he was the first."

"Mila, are you a virgin?"

Mila didn't think her face could grow any hotter. At this rate, she was bound to give herself a sunburn from the inside out. "No. I lost my virginity to Todd in the backseat of his piece of shit Dodge. We broke up a few days later because I found out he'd started texting another girl in our class right after that. She was a good friend, so she told me he was coming on to her. I dumped him."

Boone scowled. "Sounds like a dick."

"He kinda was. Moved to Houston after graduation, so at least I don't have to see him anymore."

"Who else?"

"I've gone out on quite a few first dates, but none of those translated to a second."

"Define 'quite a few.'"

She licked her lips nervously. "I don't know. Six or seven?"

"And that's it?" Boone asked in disbelief.

"A couple years back, I met a guy from Henley Falls. Dylan. We started meeting at Whiskey Abbey every Wednesday to dance. One night, he invited me home with him. I went. It was… just okay. For both of us, I guess. He didn't show the next two Wednesdays, and when he came the third week, we were back to polite acquaintances. No dancing, no talk of a repeat. Not that I was interested in doing it with him again. That was the last guy, I guess."

"And the pastor?" he asked.

"He hasn't done anything more than kiss me good night."

Boone nodded, clearly waiting for more, but there wasn't anything else to divulge.

"My grandparents got sick right after I graduated, Boone. I spent the next three years taking care of them. There wasn't time for dating or relationships. By the time I hopped back into the pool, a lot of the guys around my age were in serious relationships or even married."

Boone was silent for a few moments—and it wasn't a good silence. When he spoke, it was clear just how much she'd hurt her chances with him.

"You've had sex with two guys," he repeated, though it almost sounded like he was reiterating that for his own sake, not hers. "One time each?"

She didn't want to answer that, but before she could figure out some way to mitigate the damage, he sighed.

"You've had sex twice."

"Boone," she started.

He shook his head, stepping even farther away, her chest growing tight as she watched him shut down.

"I'm sorry," he said, his apology confusing her. Until he added, "For those kisses. They were a mistake."

"No. They weren't."

"They were. Mila, I know what you want from me, but I'm trying to do the right thing here."

"Boone," she tried to hop in again, but he was finished listening.

"Let's forget the fact you're much younger, and a Storm, you have to trust me when I say, I'm not the man for you. My…" He paused, swallowing deeply, and she could almost see the debate he was waging with himself over whether he should keep explaining.

"Say it," she demanded. He wasn't the only one who could give commands.

"My needs—sexually—run too dark for someone like you."

"No, that's not—" she began, shaking her head.

Once again, he talked over her. "Mila, this thing between us, it ends here. All of it."

She blinked a few times, wishing her eyes weren't clouding with tears. "I don't understand."

"No more cooking lessons."

"But Sadie—"

"You and Sadie can continue hanging out just like you have been, but you and I…I think it's for the best if we keep a polite distance. Just until these feelings…" He waved his hand between them. "Die down."

Her feelings for him were never going to die down. But Mila

could see Boone had made up his mind, and he wouldn't be swayed.

If she was a stronger woman, she'd fight him on it, insist she wanted exactly what he offered in the bedroom. But she was too close to falling apart, and she refused to cry in front of him. Tears would only serve to convince him even more that he was right.

"I need to leave."

She nodded but didn't speak.

"Good night, Mila." He walked to the front door, opening it.

For a split second, she hoped he might have changed his mind when he turned back around to look at her. That hope was dashed when he said, "Lock this door behind me. And don't put that key back under the mat."

He didn't even wait for her to agree. Instead, he walked out, closed the door, and then she listened as his footsteps thudded down the porch stairs.

Unable to hold back, Mila dashed upstairs, not bothering with the lock. Nora and Remi wouldn't have a key, and she wanted to be safely ensconced in her bedroom before they returned. Because there would be no hiding...

She stumbled up the last few steps, her vision blurred with tears. Entering her room, she locked the door, fell into bed, and sobbed her heart out until she fell into a restless sleep.

By the time morning arrived, Mila did what she always did.

She became the person who made everyone else's life easier. She'd spent years perfecting her talents, managing to blend in with the wallpaper. Never annoying. Never talking too much.

If Boone didn't want to see her, he wouldn't.

And hopefully, somewhere down the road, years from now, maybe being invisible wouldn't hurt as much as it did at the moment.

Chapter Eight

Boone leaned back in the chair, watching several of the Storm guys out on the dance floor of Whiskey Abbey, swinging around pretty girls. He sipped his beer, regretting for the millionth time tonight that he'd accepted Maverick's invitation to join him, Jace, and Everett for a guys' night out. Problem was this was at least the fifth time Maverick had extended the invitation since he'd started working on the farm, and he'd finally run out of excuses.

"Hey, Boone. Sorry I'm late. Where is everybody?"

Boone smiled as Theo joined him, pointing toward the dance floor. "Taking advantage of ladies' night. Good to see you. You know, the guys were just taking bets on whether you'd show up at all. Appreciate you coming. While they all said you'd choose Gretchen over them, I had faith you wouldn't leave us hanging. I'm about to be fifteen bucks richer."

Theo chuckled. "That was a brave bet on your part because, believe me, if it'd been up to me, I'd still be with Gretchen. But she and Edith have this little romance book club of two, and tonight, they were getting together for dessert, tea, and book talk.

Though I think they're also making plans to expand the group. Apparently, Mila, Remi, Kasi, and Nora all want in. Remi's demanding they make it a dirty book club."

Boone had met Gracemont's unofficial first lady, Edith Millholland, on many occasions, as she was a familiar face at Stormy Weather Farm. The woman was quite a character, and he'd grown fond of her, despite her continual attempts at setting him up with local women. Each of the last few times they'd run into each other, she'd slipped him a different woman's phone number, singing the woman's praises, giving him her backstory, and telling him he should call her.

Boone had politely taken the numbers, even though he had no intention of calling anyone.

He taken the fact Edith hadn't suggested Mila as a potential date as proof that he'd been right to put the brakes on that train before it became a runaway. Obviously Edith, who had a reputation around town as a matchmaker, could see they weren't suited to each other, or else he had no doubt the woman would have started shoving him in Mila's direction.

It had been two weeks since that ill-advised kiss in Mila's foyer.

And two weeks since the woman had essentially dropped off the face of the earth, as far as he could tell.

While she'd taken his wishes to heart, avoiding him with the skill of a stealth bomber, she hadn't cut Sadie out, something he was very grateful for. Even if it did mean he was subjected to all of the little "Mila tidbits" his daughter dropped without realizing he was hanging on her every word.

Apparently, Mila had encouraged Sadie to start coming to her farmhouse once she got off the bus, the two of them continuing the cooking lessons, though so far, they seemed to be focused on the baking end. According to Sadie, Mila was in charge of making all the desserts served at the B&B—yet another duty

Boone didn't realize she'd taken on. So every day, Mila put Sadie to work, the two of them baking up a storm. Not that he was complaining, because Sadie's payment for helping was usually a miniature version of whatever cake or pie they'd made, or a pile of cookies, always enough for two. Boone was going to have to start running if the desserts kept rolling in.

"Hey, hey, hey," Maverick said, slapping Theo on the back as he and the other guys returned to the table. "Look who finally decided to show."

Then Maverick looked at Boone, sighing heavily as he reached for his wallet, recalling he'd lost the bet.

Boone chuckled as Everett, Maverick, and Jace each slapped a five-dollar bill into his hand. "Next round is on me," he said, to soften the blow of losing.

Jace waved the waitress down to ask for an extra glass, filling it from the pitcher of Rain or Shine IPA for Theo. It was their second pitcher, though Boone was still nursing his first cup.

"I'm surprised the girls aren't here," Theo mused.

"They're all obsessed with that cat that wandered into the stable the other day," Jace said. "Remi and Nora are apparently setting her up with a comfortable spot to rest until the kittens arrive."

Boone was up to speed on all the news on that front, because Sadie was just as crazy about the cat. Remi had adopted it on the spot when she realized the tabby was pregnant and the vet confirmed there was no microchip.

However, the cat news wasn't enough to distract him from wondering why Mila wasn't helping them create the cat's new home. Sadie mentioned Mila and Kasi both wanted a kitten, and Remi was worried there wouldn't be enough to go around.

That concern was proven valid when Theo said, "Gretchen's hoping to take one of the kittens after they're born and old enough to be weaned."

Boone was pretty sure he was going to end up with one of the damn kittens as well, given Sadie's off-the-charts excitement about the coming birth. "Sadie's the same. Begging me nonstop."

"Where is Sadie tonight?" Theo asked, probably because his daughter was his typical go-to excuse for not being able to join them.

"She's having a sleepover with Piper McCoy," Boone replied. Tonight was Sadie's first-ever sleepover, which was another reason why he'd said yes to coming. He figured if Sadie decided she didn't want to stay all night for whatever reason, he'd already be in town and close enough to call an Uber and pick her up.

He tried very hard not to be one of those helicopter parents, but that didn't mean he wasn't protective of his little girl. He'd met Piper's parents a couple of times at school events. Mrs. McCoy was more than a little eccentric, with her flowy hippie dresses and flowered headbands, while Mr. McCoy was so ordinary and nondescript, it was easy to forget he was in the room. However, they were both very nice and he trusted Sadie with them.

Jace muttered under his breath when a woman walked too close to their table, bumping into his chair and brushing her hand against his shoulder.

"Sorry, Jace," she said, with a come-hither smile.

"No problem, Janice," he replied, turning away from her, as Janice walked away dejected.

"Another one," Everett said in hushed tones, once she'd moved on.

"Another what?" Boone asked.

Everett grinned. "Edith has been spreading tales about the Storm family."

Boone frowned. "What tales?"

"Not sure you can call them tales if they're true," Theo said, correcting Everett.

Maverick rolled his eyes. "Dear Jesus. They're *tales*," he insisted, though Boone didn't get the sense Everett or Jace agreed.

"Somebody wanna fill me in?" he asked, completely in the dark.

"Can't believe you've been on the farm all of two months and haven't heard the myth about the Storms," Theo said.

"In his defense," Jace piped up, "he spends most of his time with Maverick, a disbeliever, and Grayson, who'd have to actually open his mouth and speak words instead of grunts, snorts, and scoffs."

Boone chuckled at Jace's apt description of Grayson. Not that the man never spoke, but he was certainly a quiet one. Boone figured that was because it was hard for him to get a word in edgewise around Maverick at work, but it sounded like his quietness was also part of his nature.

"According to my dad," Theo began, "he fell in love with Mom the first day he met her. They were introduced, he reached out to shake her hand, and *boom*."

Boone took a sip of his beer, waiting for Theo to continue. When he didn't, he prodded, "Boom?"

"Love at first touch," Theo said, as if he didn't sound completely insane.

"Ooookay," Boone drawled.

Maverick laughed, but Theo ignored his younger brother.

"We all grew up hearing that story countless times, but we never really thought anything of it—until the same thing happened to Levi," Theo said.

Boone had spent a good amount of time with Levi, especially at the beginning of his tenure as vineyard manager, the other man showing him the ropes. Levi talked about his girlfriend a lot, something Boone accredited to the fact it was a pretty new relationship, not even a year old. He'd been tempted to warn the other man about the dangers of getting too wrapped up in new love, because that had been Boone's downfall with Lena. He'd let himself be blinded to all her faults, thinking with his dick and heart rather than his head. However, he'd held his tongue, aware he didn't know Levi well enough to offer advice.

Of course, when he'd learned Levi and Kasi had known each other forever, he decided their relationship wasn't like his at all.

"I thought Kasi basically grew up on the farm, best friends with Remi," Boone pointed out. He'd learned a great deal about the Storm family during his weeks in Gracemont because they were all so open and friendly. They constantly pulled him and Sadie into the fold, treating them as honorary Storms.

"She did, but because there's a big age difference between them," Jace explained, "it wasn't like they spent a lot of time together."

"How big an age difference?" Boone knew Kasi was younger, but he obviously hadn't bothered to do the math in his head because Levi and Kasi fit together perfectly.

"Thirteen years," Everett replied.

That was exactly how many years separated him and Mila—and Boone's thoughts detoured down a bad path, the part of him that still wanted Mila pointing out how age wasn't a problem for Levi and Kasi.

Theo topped off everyone's glasses. "Every single day for years, Levi drove down to Lucky Penny Farm and bought a pie from Kasi's fruit stand. Day after day, he paid for that pie and left. Then one day last summer, it was hot as blue blazes. Kasi passed out, and Levi caught her. He said he knew in that moment she was his."

Boone nodded, trying to stop himself from comparing him and Mila to Levi and Kasi. Doing so wasn't helping his resolve.

Not that he'd caught Mila when she fell off that ladder and knew she was his. Shit like that didn't happen. But there was a contrary voice in his head insisting he'd definitely felt *something* when Mila landed in his lap.

He shut that voice down. All he'd felt was lust, because it had been a long time since he'd had a beautiful young woman in his arms.

"That's a nice…story," Boone said, not sure how else to reply.

Theo must have heard his skepticism, because he continued trying to make his case. "I was once exactly like you," he said, mimicking the voice of an old man. "But then I saw the light."

They all chuckled.

"The first day I met Gretchen, the same thing that happened to Dad, happened to me. I shook her hand and *boom*. It was like I'd been struck by lightning. I knew in that second that I'd met my soul mate, that she was meant to be mine."

Boone leaned back in his seat and crossed his arms. "And Kasi and Gretchen just went along with these revelations?"

Maverick shook his head. "Of course not. Kasi thought Levi was off his rocker at first, especially when he started beating on his chest like goddamn Tarzan, pointing at her and declaring her 'his woman.'"

Theo smirked. "But he wore her down eventually. I've had to take a slower approach with Gretchen, because she's just gotten out of a very bad relationship. I'm not going to lie though. It's been hard not to release my inner caveman and carry her off to my lair. I've had to learn how to practice patience."

Theo's three brothers cracked up when he declared himself patient.

"Bro, I'm not sure you can brag about being patient when you hit her with that 'you're mine' line five weeks after meeting her," Jace joked.

"Hey," Theo protested. "That was five weeks longer than Levi made it."

"He makes a valid point," Maverick said, before turning to Boone. "Theo and Levi made the mistake of telling Edith about the love-at-first-touch curse and—"

"It's not a curse," Theo corrected.

"Curse, legend, whatever," Maverick continued. "Edith has been spreading the story far and wide around Gracemont, and now, whenever one of us single Storm guys goes out, we've got these women we've known our whole lives going out of their way to bump into us. Literally. Like we're going to fall head over ass in love with them or something."

Boone chuckled. "Glad I'm not one of the Storm brothers, then."

Theo shrugged. "Not sure it's only the male Storms affected. Lucy fell pretty hard and fast for Miles and Joey. There's just as good a chance Nora, Remi, and Mila are going to find their true loves the same way."

With one touch.

Boone wanted to kick his own ass for wondering if perhaps Mila had felt something like that for him that first day. There was no denying the spark between them had flashed hot and in an instant.

"Not sure the curse extends to the girls," Maverick said, refusing to give up his terminology. "Because Mila hasn't mentioned the lightning, and she's out on yet another date with the pastor tonight."

Boone was instantly overcome with a jealousy he didn't want to feel, because she wasn't his. After what he'd learned about her inexperience, she couldn't be. Christ almighty, he'd break a woman as sweet and innocent as Mila.

Jace waved the waitress down, ordering a platter of wings for the table. "I can see Mila as a pastor's wife. God knows she's sweet enough."

The other brothers seemed to agree—but Boone didn't.

Sure, Mila was sweet as pie, but there was something more. He recalled her description of her ideal man. How that man would look at her and see her for who she really was. Mila was inherently sweet and kind, but underneath, there was a woman kicking and screaming to be seen, to go wild.

Then, he recalled her last conversation with her father, how it had impacted her, shaped and molded her into the woman she was today. How different might Mila be if her parents hadn't been killed in that car accident? Would she still be a chatterbox? Still be as wild and unrestrained as Remi?

He wasn't sure why it felt as if he was the only person who could see all the things Mila tried to hide about herself. After all, he'd only known her a couple of months, while her family had been present for every part of her life.

Regardless, he had to hold himself back from contradicting them outright, though Mila deserved more than the pastor, and that wasn't jealousy speaking. It was the fact he'd seen them dance, witnessed one of the man's lackluster good-night kisses. There was no spark between her and Joshua, and Mila deserved a goddamn spark.

"I'm surprised Mila went out tonight," Theo said, pulling Boone from his thoughts.

"Why?" Jace asked, before Boone could.

"Gretchen said she looked pretty wiped today. She was actually worried maybe she'd gotten the flu from Mom and Dad," Theo replied.

Maverick mentioned that Rex and Claire had caught some nasty bug a few days earlier, but so far, no one else on the farm had gotten sick.

"Wouldn't be surprised if she did," Everett said. "She was the one who took care of them and kept things going at the B&B. I stopped by to check on them and found Mila in the kitchen making chicken noodle soup and baking her sourdough bread. Apparently, the only thing Dad could keep down for a couple of days was tea and toast, so Mila made sure he had a steady supply."

"Damn," Maverick said with a grin. "Might be worth getting sick for some of Mila's homemade bread. Heaven on earth."

All four brothers seemed to be in agreement on the bread, but Boone couldn't get past the fact that Mila had once again taken too much on her shoulders, playing nurse while running the inn and, no doubt, keeping up with her countless other chores.

"Do you think she looks worn out because of all that extra work?" Boone said, pissed that the other guys weren't seeing it on their own.

"Yeah. She probably is." Theo rubbed the back of his neck. "Damn. I guess we should have stepped in and each of us taken a shift. But Mila always just takes over, and she makes it look so easy. Never complains, never asks for help."

Boone was slightly mollified when each brother agreed they shouldn't have placed all the care of their parents on Mila's shoulders. He couldn't deny she had a way of simply assuming tasks without ever complaining or letting on that it was too much.

Despite Boone's determination to stay away from Mila, he was helpless to keep from watching her. As such, he saw all the hours she put in at the brewery and winery, how she was using the "slow winter months" to do a deep cleaning of the cabins, how she spent hours with Claire, preparing Sunday dinner. He'd watched as she slowly redecorated every business, replacing the Valentine's décor with St. Patrick's Day shamrocks, and God only knew how many scarves and blankets she'd crocheted for the less fortunate so far.

She worked tirelessly, never saying no to anyone who asked for help. And on top of all that, she still found time for Sadie each day.

"Hey, guys."

Boone glanced up as a woman approached their table.

"Hiya, Tina," Maverick said cheerfully. "Have you met Boone Hansen, our new vineyard manager?"

There was something about the way Maverick introduced him that made Boone wonder if the man was taking a page out of Edith's matchmaking book.

"I haven't," Tina said, her smile wide. She looked to be about his age. She was pretty enough, though she'd used a heavy hand when putting on her makeup, and he was sure her blonde hair wasn't natural. She had a curvy figure, but she wasn't trying to show it off with overly provocative clothing. "I'm Tina Reynolds. Edith Millholland mentioned there was a new vineyard manager at Stormy Weather Farm."

Boone recognized her name as one of the women Edith had told him about. And now he was wishing he'd paid better attention, because he couldn't recall if Tina was one of the two divorcees or the widow.

"Nice to meet you," he said. Tina reminded him a little bit of Hope, one of his occasional hookups from Williamsburg.

"You too. How are you liking our little town?"

"Gracemont is great," he replied. "It's a terrific place to live."

"It really is." Tina glanced over her shoulder as a slow song began to play. "Could I interest you in a dance?"

He didn't want to, but he saw Maverick watching them with great interest, so he accepted. Maverick was the primary source for information on the farm, as gossipy as a gaggle of old women. Boone didn't doubt for a moment that his dance with Tina would make its way through the grapevine to Mila. And

Caught in a Storm

while his goal wasn't to hurt her, he thought perhaps it would help her move on if she believed *he* had, as well.

He followed Tina to the floor. A wise man would have concentrated on the woman in his arms, but Boone spent too much of the dance comparing it to the one he'd shared with Mila.

What he decided was there was no comparison.

"Edith tells me you have a daughter," Tina said, breaking the awkward silence between them.

"I do. How about you? Any kids?"

She nodded. "Two boys. Eight and ten. I moved home about a year ago after my divorce. I've got full custody, and I needed my parents' help since I work full time."

"I have full custody too," Boone said, trying to maintain his side of the conversation.

"It's hard, isn't it? I mean, we spend so much of our time raising our kids, there's never time left for us. This is the first night I've been out in months," she confessed.

"Same," he agreed.

"My ex was a real piece of work, so I'm glad to have him out of my hair. But even so, a woman has needs, and with kids…it makes it so hard to date or spend any real time with someone."

Tina toyed with the hair at the nape of his neck, pressing herself more firmly against his chest. She was making it perfectly clear she'd like to get to know him in a more carnal way. If Boone had a lick of sense, he would take her up on the offer. She was exactly the kind of woman he should be pursuing.

"I'm sure it does." That was the wrong answer, but Boone had no interest in going home with Tina.

"You know, my parents have my boys all night. Maybe we could move this party to my place, get to know each other."

The song was coming to an end—mercifully—so Boone

147

slowly lowered his arms, taking a step away from Tina. "I'm afraid I need to get home to my daughter," he lied.

Tina took his rejection with good grace. "I understand. Maybe some other time."

He nodded noncommittally. "Maybe."

"Edith said she gave you my number."

"She did," Boone said, not bothering to add that he'd thrown it away.

"Great. Well, call me sometime," she said, giving him a finger wave before rejoining her friends at a table in the corner.

Boone returned to his own table, sinking down heavily, wishing he'd brought his own vehicle. Glancing around, he realized they were down one man. "Where's Theo?"

"Gretchen texted to say she and Edith were wrapping things up. He hightailed it out of here so fast, I swear he kicked up a cloud of dust behind him," Jace joked, sliding over the platter of wings that had arrived while he was dancing.

Boone grabbed one, dipping it into the ranch, trying to hide his frown when the waitress brought over another pitcher.

Thankfully, they consumed that one more quickly than the first two, Maverick and Jace feeling no pain by the time he and Everett convinced them to call it a night. Boone offered to drive Maverick's car, since he hadn't had more than one beer.

Pulling up in front of the frat house, he shut off the engine, all of them climbing out.

Maverick gestured toward his car. "Go ahead and drive it to your place. I can come get it in the morning."

Boone had walked from his cabin to the house, and he didn't mind doing that again. "I'm fine walking. It's not cold tonight and I wouldn't mind the fresh air." He didn't dare mention he had an ulterior motive for making the trek on foot.

Maverick nodded, stumbling up the stairs with Jace, as Everett said good night.

Caught in a Storm

Boone headed along the path that led to all three farmhouses. Ordinarily, he would leave it just after the B&B, taking the right fork that led to his cabin. Tonight, he continued on the left fork, walking toward Mila's.

He wasn't sure what his intentions were. He sure as shit didn't plan to knock on her door. But he knew he wouldn't be able to sleep without knowing if she'd made it home from her date safely.

There were no extra cars in the driveway, so it didn't look like Pastor Joshua had come in for a nightcap. Part of him was tempted to sneak onto the front porch to make sure she hadn't put the key back under the mat.

He shook his head. Yeah, he wouldn't be doing that.

Instead, he skirted around the rear of the house, hanging close to the tree line, feeling like the world's biggest creeper. There was a light on in the kitchen…and he could see Mila's face through the window.

She was doing dishes.

Boone shook his head. Eleven o'clock at night and she was doing the damn dishes.

He growled to himself when she rubbed her eyes wearily, stretching her head from side to side to get the kinks out of her neck.

Boone remained where he was, watching as she made herself a cup of tea before leaving the kitchen, turning the light off behind her.

She needed a man to take care of her, to force her to slow down, to set boundaries so she didn't work herself to the brink of exhaustion night after night.

Boone sighed.

He couldn't be that man.

Moving on, he walked back to his cabin alone.

Chapter Nine

Mila pulled a tray of scones from the oven and placed them on the cooling rack. Ordinarily, she would have been in bed a couple hours ago, but today was the gift that just kept giving. She'd started her day at five a.m., so ending it at midnight was pretty painful. Unfortunately, she'd gotten slammed from all directions today.

Gretchen, who was doing an amazing job as event coordinator, had managed to schedule a large wedding at the barn last weekend. Weddings in early March weren't exactly unheard of, but they also carried a bit of risk, given the possibility of winter weather. Damn if it hadn't been a huge hit. Mercifully, the weather more than cooperated, offering three mild, sunny, fifty-degree days in a row. Thanks to the large wedding party and family members in attendance, the B&B as well as every cabin had been rented out as well.

While they'd been thrilled by the business during what was typically their slow season, it had added a lot to Mila's plate, as she spent the past three days systematically cleaning her way through all the rental cabins. It wasn't a quick or easy process, since the wedding party and guests hadn't limited their celebrating to the event barn, so nearly every cabin looked like it had been hit by college kids on spring break. Because she still needed to do her other daily chores, she hadn't managed to clean more than three cabins each day—and that was with Remi's help. Today, they'd tackled the final—and dirtiest—two, but it had taken them the better part of the morning and early afternoon.

Originally, the farm had ten rental cabins, but that number had been shaved by two in the past few months. Boone and Sadie occupied one, and Theo was in the process of renovating the cabin he wanted to share with Gretchen. Or maybe it was more accurate to say they were already sharing it…part time, at least.

When Gretchen first arrived on the farm last September, she'd escaped an extremely abusive relationship, and it had taken Theo some time and effort to earn her trust. While her cousin was no doubt chomping at the bit to get to the next part—forever —with Gretchen, Theo wasn't pushing her into anything she wasn't ready for. So nowadays, they were splitting their time between living together at the cabin and Edith Millholland's boarding house, depending on which part of the cabin was torn up during any given week. Mila suspected once Theo completed all the renovations, they'd make the cohabitation plan permanent.

In addition to cleaning the cabins this week, Mila had continued to keep the brewery and winery kitchens stocked, the food prepped, as well as decorating the brewery for a big St. Patrick's Day event and helping Aunt Claire at the B&B.

When one of the winery cooks called in sick today, she'd volunteered to work the shift, even though it set her behind on her baking for the B&B. She could have asked Aunt Claire to take care of the baking for tomorrow, but her aunt's sciatica was acting up again, so she knew it was hard for her to be on her feet too long.

Mila was exhausted, but at least she was starting to see a light at the end of the tunnel as far as today was concerned. Wrapping the scones, she placed them and the two apple pies she'd baked aside. She would deliver them to Aunt Claire first thing tomorrow morning.

Putting the kettle on to boil, she dropped down into one of the kitchen chairs. Despite her exhaustion, she struggled to fall asleep each night, so she'd picked up her aunt's habit of drinking a glass of chamomile tea before bed.

She knew why she wasn't sleeping, but she didn't see that problem resolving itself anytime soon. She revealed too many cards during her last encounter with Boone, and she saw the very moment he'd shut down. So, for the past three weeks, she'd tried to do a system reboot, returning to the Mila she'd been pre-New Year's. Sure, that Mila had been slightly overwhelmed and not entirely happy with her life, but at least she'd held on to a minimal amount of hope that she would still meet "the one," fall in love, and find some sort of happily ever after.

That Mila was blissfully unaware of Boone Hansen.

She wanted to be her again.

Because this—living so close to the man who made her heart race, who made her body sing, who made her feel protected and seen and even sexy—was torture.

Mila rubbed her eyes wearily, recalling Maverick stopping by this afternoon while she was working in the kitchen at the winery. Three p.m. seemed to be his witching hour, as far as snacking was concerned, so it wasn't unusual for him to arrive in search of food. While she made him a pepperoni flatbread pizza, he leaned against the counter, regaling her with gossip. She'd been so busy with the wedding—prep and then cleanup—that she'd been out of the loop, too tired and depressed to pay attention to the chatter. Boone had begun sending Sadie on her own to eat with them on Sundays, offering his regrets with some fill-in-the-blank excuse.

While Maverick waited for his pizza to bake, he told her about Boone joining him and a few of the guys for ladies' night at Whiskey Abbey. Mila had tried to look uninterested, even though she'd wanted to ask him a million questions. Fortunately —or unfortunately—questions weren't necessary when Maverick was involved, because he never skimped on details.

So, she got to hear all about Boone dancing with Tina Reynolds, who'd moved back to Gracemont after her divorce. Tina had gotten married right after graduation to her high school sweetheart, Donnie, her first and only boyfriend, so nowadays, she was ready to sow some wild oats. Maverick, who always had an opinion on *everything*, remarked that Tina and Boone were probably a good match, since they were about the same age, neither of them looking to get married again, and were both single parents.

Mila wasn't sure which part of Maverick's story had bothered her more. That Boone was better suited to Tina than her, or that Maverick knew about Boone's desire to remain a bachelor for the rest of his days.

As much as it hurt her to admit, she agreed with Maverick… because Tina was perfect for Boone in ways she wasn't.

Mila rose as the kettle boiled, pouring the steaming water over the tea bag, intent on drinking it in bed. She paused for a moment when she heard a tapping on the front door.

Who the hell was knocking on the door at midnight?

Leaving her tea on the counter, she left the kitchen, walking toward the door, her stomach clenching nervously. Late-night visits and calls were never good news.

She was shocked when she spotted Sadie standing on the front porch, shivering.

"Sadie! Are you okay? Did something happen to Boone?" Mila couldn't think of a single reason why Sadie would be here in the middle of the night on her own.

"Dad's fine. Can I come in?"

Mila swung the door open, shivering as a blast of cold air hit her. She looked at the empty driveway and the young girl's ruddy cheeks. "Did you walk here?"

Sadie nodded. "I'm sorry I'm here so late. I just—"

"Mila?" Nora's voice sounded at the top of the stairs. "Is someone here?"

Mila watched as Nora and Remi bounded down the steps together, Remi clenching a baseball bat, her idea of home security.

They pulled up short at the bottom.

"Sadie," Remi said, lowering the bat. "What are you doing here?"

The young girl's cheeks turned a darker shade of red, and Mila began to wonder if it was the cold or embarrassment driving the color. "I, um…" Sadie shuffled her feet uncomfortably.

Mila reached out, taking Sadie's freezing-cold hand in hers. "Sadie, it's just us. You're safe here. What's going on?" she asked, infusing as much comfort into her tone as possible, even though she was starting to worry.

"Igotmyperiod and Idon'tknowwhattodo." Sadie spoke so rapidly, her words all blended together into one.

"Oh, Sadie," Mila said, relieved. "First time?"

Sadie nodded.

"It's okay." Mila pulled the girl into her arms and gave her a hug.

Remi grinned, and she and Nora joined them.

"Well, you've come to right place," Remi said, gesturing

around her grandly. "Because this is a house of women only. We've got this."

Nora rolled her eyes at Remi, taking Sadie's hand. "We've all been where you are, Sadie. There's nothing to worry about. We can fix you right up."

"Does your dad know where you are?" Mila asked.

Sadie shook her head. "No. I waited to come here until he went to sleep. He'd kill me if he knew I snuck out, but I was just… It started after dinner. I tried to use some toilet paper, thinking I could wait until I saw my mom tomorrow, but…" She shrugged, still talking a mile a minute. "That didn't work very well. And now my sheets are ruined and I can't go to school like this tomorrow and I didn't want to tell my dad because…" Sadie huffed. "That would be mortifying!"

"Take a breath," Mila said, placing her hand on the young girl's shoulder. "Remi's right. We've got this. Come upstairs and we'll get you what you need. Okay?"

The four of them walked upstairs, stopping by a hall closet—organized by Nora—that held all the feminine hygiene products…possibly in the world. While Mila was used to the closet, it wasn't until she heard Sadie's gasp of surprise that she realized just how over the top it was.

"Jesus," Remi muttered. "You would think we were running a hospital."

Nora, who'd bought the wide array, ignored Remi. "These two shelves are my 'I am woman. Hear me roar' shelves."

Remi leaned closer to Sadie, lifted her hands in the paw position. "Rahrrr."

"Call it what you will," Mila added. "It's still a lot." In addition to the "roaring" shelves, there was also an overabundance of pain and cold medication, hot and cold compresses, heating pads, vitamins, bandages, and God only knew what else.

Nora put her hands on her hips. "I think you're both forgetting that I only have this closet because Mila's decorations collection was so big it didn't fit anymore, and Uncle Rex had to build a shed to hold it all."

Mila attempted to correct the story. "He built the shed for me and Aunt Claire. She has four artificial trees she puts up in the B&B every year. Uncle Rex said they were slowly being buried alive by Christmas crap."

"He didn't say crap," Remi chipped in, winking at Sadie.

"I know the word shit, Mila," Sadie said with a giggle.

She sighed. "Boone's gonna lose it if he finds out you two are cussing up a storm in that stable."

"Hey," Remi said, putting her hands on Sadie's shoulders. "She's riding the beast now. She's gonna need a safe space and an outlet for all that…roaring."

Sadie mimicked Remi's paws. "Rahrr!"

Nora laughed, then launched into an explanation of how each pad was different, claiming a woman needed options to fit different outfits and daily plans.

Remi rolled her eyes as Nora rambled on and on, but Sadie listened intently, then pointed to one of the pads. "That one sounds okay."

Mila leaned toward Sadie. "I need to call your dad and tell him you're here. If he wakes up and finds your bed empty, he'll be worried."

"He's gonna be mad at me."

Mila shook her head. "No. I'll explain, and he'll understand. It'll be okay. Promise." Mila wasn't looking forward to placing the call. She'd avoided the man for three weeks, only catching peeks of him from a distance. Since that last kiss, she'd convinced Sadie to start coming here after school for crocheting and baking lessons. Regardless, Sadie had asked every single Tuesday if Mila would have dinner with them again. Mila hated constantly coming up with excuses for why she couldn't.

Nora led Sadie to the bathroom, telling the young girl to come to her bedroom when she was done. Mila walked down the hallway to her own room, quietly closing the door behind her as she dialed Boone's number.

"Mila?" His voice was gruff, and it was obvious she'd woken him.

"Boone, I'm sorry to call so late."

"Is everything okay?"

"It's fine. It's just...Sadie's here."

"What?"

She heard movement, and she could picture Boone getting out of bed and crossing the great room to look into Sadie's bedroom.

"How the hell? What's she doing there?" he asked, once he'd confirmed Sadie was gone.

"She got her period," Mila whispered.

"Fucking hell," Boone muttered. "Why didn't she tell me?"

Mila grinned. "She's twelve, Boone, and she was embarrassed."

"Yeah, but I would have..." He paused.

"You would have handled it just fine," Mila reassured him, hating that he sounded upset Sadie hadn't confided in him. "But there are just some things it's easier to tell another woman."

"I should have realized this was coming. Should have... prepared somehow. Did she walk there?" he asked. "In the freezing cold?"

"Yeah, but she's fine. Nora, Remi, and I have set her up with what she needs. She's taking care of it right now. I'll bring her home in a few minutes."

"No, I can come get her."

"Boone, I know I got you out of bed. I'm still awake and dressed. We'll make sure she's okay, answer all her questions, and then I'll drive her."

Boone sighed. "Okay. I appreciate you taking care of her, Mila."

"Of course. See you in a few."

She disconnected the call, then followed the sound of voices to Nora's room.

Sadie looked at her apprehensively when Mila walked in, joining the three of them on the bed. "Was he mad?"

"Nope. Just worried about you. Feel better?" Mila asked, stroking Sadie's hair.

She nodded.

"I got my first period on the last day of school, sixth grade, and of course, I'd been wearing white shorts that day," Mila said. "I felt something as I stood up to get off the bus. Mercifully, we were the last stop, so all the other kids had already been dropped off. Lucy knew what it was because she'd already gotten hers, so she took me to Grandma, who showed me what to do and answered all my questions."

"And then she called Aunt Claire," Nora piped in.

"Yep," Mila confirmed. "Who showed up armed with chocolate and a celebratory soda, loudly proclaiming I was a woman now and hugging me half to death. Talk about mortifying."

Mila and her sisters laughed, because Aunt Claire had done and said the same thing for all of them.

Sadie giggled when Remi leaned across the bed, wrapping her in her arms and dramatically saying, "You're a woman now!"

"Next week, when you get back from your trip to Williamsburg, the four of us can get together for chocolate and sodas," Nora said.

They talked for a few more minutes about the joys—all listed sarcastically—of periods.

"Come on," Mila said, rising from the bed. "It's a school night, and I promised your dad we wouldn't be long."

Nora grabbed a tote bag, loading it with enough pads to carry Sadie through a year's worth of periods.

Sadie took it gratefully, hugging Nora and Remi, and thanking them for their help.

Once she and Sadie had put their coats back on, they made the short drive to the cabin, Sadie gripping the handle of the tote bag nervously.

"He's not mad," Mila tried to reassure her.

Boone was waiting at the open front door when they parked and got out of the car. Mila issued her girlie bits the old "down, girl" when she saw him in his lounge pants and long-sleeved tee, his feet bare. She'd never seen him in such casual clothing, certain there was nothing hotter than Boone in his faded jeans, flannel shirts, and work boots. She stood corrected.

Even on their cooking nights, he always put jeans, long-sleeved tees, and sneakers on after his shower.

God help her when summer arrived, and she saw him shirtless. She'd probably spontaneously combust on the spot.

"You okay?" he asked Sadie, as she climbed the front steps.

"Yeah."

The three of them walked inside, and Boone gave Sadie a big hug. "Good. I changed your sheets."

Sadie flushed, lowering her eyes.

Boone tapped under his daughter's chin, forcing her to look at him. "Donut. You can talk to me about anything."

Sadie gave him a guilty smile. "I know, but…"

"I get it," Boone said. "I'm glad you reached out to Mila." He looked her direction, gratitude giving way to a frown when he saw the overstuffed tote bag she handed to Sadie.

"Did you all run to Walmart? How long were you gone?" he asked Sadie.

"Nora has a bit of a shopping addiction, remember?" Mila

said, responding for Sadie. "She claims women need options during that time of the month."

Mila and Sadie laughed, the sound growing louder when Sadie said, "Because I'm a woman now."

Boone shook his head, clearly amused. "Okay, woman. It's a school night and it's late. And while I know you think you had a good reason, the two of us are going to have a long talk about how you will *never* sneak out of the house in the middle of the night again."

Sadie grimaced until Boone bopped her nose playfully.

"Night, Donut."

"Night, Dad. Thanks, Mila."

Sadie walked to her room and closed the door.

Mila hovered by the front door as Boone crossed over to the couch, dropping down heavily. "I'm not ready for this part."

"You'll do just fine."

"She used to tell me everything when she was little. I thought we had a relationship where she could confide in me. I mean, I took her to get her first bra last year. I thought I handled that okay, even if there were a few awkward moments."

Mila hated seeing Boone so down on himself. "She trusts you and loves you, Boone. It's just…as she gets older…you have to be prepared for some bumps in the road." She remained where she was by the door, until Boone noticed she hadn't moved and patted the couch next to him.

She considered refusing. Because it really was late, and being close to him again was only proving what a shitty job she'd done the last few weeks trying to get him out of her system.

"Please, Mila," he pressed, when he noticed her hesitance. "Just for a minute. I know it's late."

She walked over, joining him on the couch but keeping her distance.

"What bumps in the road?" he asked.

"The hormones coursing through her right now are going to introduce you to a new Sadie you've never met before. There are times you're going to think she was possessed by the devil, but trust me when I say possession would be the lesser of two evils."

Boone's lips kicked up at the corners. "You trying to give me nightmares?"

She shook her head. "Just trying to prepare you for what's to come. Because between this and her teen years when she discovers boys..."

"I'm nailing her windows shut and sealing that door in her room."

Mila laughed. "Yeah. That never worked for Granddaddy where Remi was concerned."

"What about you? He never nailed your windows closed?"

Mila shook her head. "Nope. Eternal good girl, remember? Remi was challenging enough for Grandma and Granddaddy. I didn't want to add to their plates, especially with Nora—" Mila abruptly stopped talking.

"Nora?"

Mila sighed. "I told you. After the accident, Nora developed a stutter. She hated it so much, she went silent. Grandma and Granddaddy were worried sick. That therapist they took her to see helped a lot, but it took time. Between that, and Remi running wild all over the mountain, I tried to behave, not wanting to add to their stress. So...I did my chores, got good grades, tried to give them one less thing to worry about."

Boone reached over and placed his hand atop hers. "You have empathy in spades, darlin', and while that's a good trait to have, you might want to try sparing some for yourself."

Her heart thudded rapidly, a combination of him calling her darlin' and then gently running his finger under her eye, the same way he did after the Valentine's Dance.

"Why were you awake at midnight?"

"Long day. Or week, I guess."

He chuckled. "It's only Tuesday."

"The wedding this past weekend was a lot. Took me a few days to work my way through the cabin cleaning. Things should slow down now."

Boone huffed disbelievingly. "Pretty sure they never slow down for you."

"It's my family's farm, Boone, and there are always a million chores to be done. I'm just pulling my weight, doing my share."

"Feels like more than that."

"What do you mean?" she asked.

"Everybody around here has a role, and while I'm not saying the Storms aren't some of the hardest working people I've ever met, it feels like you're spread thinner than the rest. You don't even get Sundays off because you're always cleaning cabins and cooking Sunday dinner with Claire for the whole family, and that's after working at the brewery and winery."

"I don't mind," Mila said, though lately…she did. She was exhausted, but over the years, she'd volunteered to take on more duties, and now she didn't want to burden her family by *unvolunteering*.

"When's the last time you went out and did something fun?" he asked.

It was on the tip of her tongue to say their cooking lessons, but he probably wouldn't like that answer. "The Valentine's Dance was fun."

"You worked yourself into exhaustion that day too, so try again."

"Boone," she said, when she couldn't come up with a suitable reply. "I'm fine, really."

"You're too young to work from sunup to sundown. You should go out more," Boone said.

"I go out," she said, though in truth, she'd only been out once since Valentine's. But her date with Pastor Joshua hadn't even made a blip on her radar when paired with the word *fun*. The night had been downright uncomfortable, because at the end of another eternally long, boring dinner, she'd finally worked up the courage to tell him she didn't think they should see each other anymore. He'd taken it with good grace, though she could tell she'd surprised and upset him, which made her feel even worse, since it seemed Kasi had been right. He *had* been into her.

However, she didn't say any of that to Boone because she was still fighting a little demon called jealousy.

"Mm-hmm." Boone clearly didn't believe her.

She decided that was enough focus on her. "I heard you went out with the guys last week."

"I did," Boone nodded.

"Heard you danced with Tina Reynolds."

Boone chuckled. "Maverick has a big mouth."

He was obviously hoping to break the tension with humor, but Mila wasn't as good at masking her emotions. "Are you going to call her?" *Way to fucking overstep.* She tried to backtrack. "I mean, Tina's really nice, and the two of you have a lot in common and—"

"I'm not going to call her," Boone interjected, saving her from herself.

Then she ruined it by sticking her foot in her mouth. "Oh. Right. Not interested in dating. I forgot."

Boone didn't reply to that, which made the fact she'd said it at all feel a million times worse. Time to cut and run.

She bounded from the couch quickly. "It's late. I need to get home." She waved her hand, trying to stop Boone when he slid on his boots and jacket. "You don't have to—"

"I'm walking you to the car, Mila."

She knew that tone well enough to know arguing would be pointless. "Thanks."

They walked the short distance to her car in silence. Thick clouds had rolled in, so the woods were pitch black and foggy, the front porch light barely cutting through.

"Thanks for being there for Sadie tonight."

Mila nodded. "Of course. I'd do anything for her."

Boone ran a hand through his hair, then rubbed his hands together to ward off the chill in the air. "I'm taking Sadie to see her mother tomorrow. Planning on taking half a day from work and getting her out of school early to try to beat that weather that's coming tomorrow evening."

Yet another reason why the wedding party had been lucky. March was a veritable wild card, and while last weekend had been beautiful, tomorrow was calling for one hell of a snowstorm. Apparently, this year, March was going out like a lion rather than a lamb.

"Not canceling?" Mila was somewhat surprised, because the forecasters were calling for a foot of snow. Most of tomorrow's workday would comprise of battening down the hatches, preparing to be stuck in for a couple of days.

Boone shook his head. "Only calling for two to four inches in Williamsburg, and I suspect the roads will be cleared by the weekend, so I'll be able to pick her up on Sunday with no problem."

"Drive safe."

She started to turn, but Boone stopped her, pushing her back against the car door.

"Boone," she whispered, when his hands cupped her cheeks.

He didn't reply. Instead, he lowered his head and kissed her.

Unlike his previous kisses, this one was softer, gentler…God, downright romantic. He wasn't claiming her this time; rather, he was worshipping her.

Mila wrapped her arms around his waist, under his coat, loving the way he shifted closer, sharing his body heat with her.

His tongue brushed against hers, the taste of his toothpaste adding to the intimacy of this moment. That, paired with his casual attire, was the strangest yet most potent of aphrodisiacs. Her lack of boyfriends—and the fact she lived with only her sisters—meant she'd never really been around a man who wasn't fully dressed and ready for his day.

Mila tightened her grip when she sensed he might pull away, so she was delighted to discover he wasn't finished. Instead, his lips slid along the side of her neck, his hot breath a welcome contrast to the cool winter breeze.

Their last two kisses had been passion personified, as they came at each other like ravenous beasts. This kiss held nothing but an almost calm desire. Boone's hand gripped her ponytail, using it to twist her head this way and that, clearing the path for his soft lips, his seeking tongue.

A small peep escaped when he nipped her earlobe, a low chuckle rumbling from him in response before he returned to her lips, kissing her senseless once more.

When he finally stepped away, minutes later, it wasn't with the same abrupt halt that had ended their first two embraces. Instead, he simply gentled the kiss before breaking it.

"Another mistake?" she asked quietly, too well-versed in what came after Boone's kisses.

"No," he admitted, surprising her. "Mila, I don't know what this is, darlin'…but it's not a mistake."

She waited for him to expound on that, but he didn't.

He grimaced. "If you're looking to me for an answer to this," he waved his finger between them, "I don't have one."

She did, but it wasn't one he wanted to hear. She'd been walking around with her heart on her sleeve since Boone saved her from that fall off the ladder. Standing here now, telling him about the romantic "love at first touch" legend her family believed in, sharing that she'd been struck by lightning the day they met, that she thought fate had brought them together, would definitely send Boone running for the hills, once and for all.

"It's late," she said. "And we're both running on fumes. Granddaddy always used to say things look clearer in the morning light."

"He sounds like a wise man."

Mila stepped away from the car and Boone opened the door for her. Climbing in, she gave him a quick grin and a wave, loving the way he returned both.

He'd looked like a man on the way to the gallows after their first two kisses, his expression drowning in guilt and regret. None of that was present tonight.

Which meant that as Mila climbed into bed way after bedtime, pre-New Year's Mila was back.

For better or worse, hope had returned. Now, she just had to pray that Boone saw the same thing she did when that morning light appeared.

Chapter Ten

Boone squinted through the windshield and cursed the weather.

"Fucking weather forecasters," he muttered, not for the first time since pulling off the highway and making his way down a snow-covered Main Street, fighting to see the turnoff to Stormy Weather Farm.

He'd stupidly trusted the timing of when the predicted storm was going to start, not anticipating that the last thirty minutes of his return trip to Gracemont would be made white-knuckling the wheel in a veritable whiteout.

The storm wasn't supposed to start until later this evening, but apparently it was moving faster than anticipated. The eight to twelve inches they'd been calling for had now been upgraded to twelve to sixteen, and he was starting to think he'd made a mistake not canceling Sadie's visit.

He breathed a sigh of relief as he made the turn to the farm—then immediately sucked it right back in and held it, because these last couple of miles were going to be the most hazardous. Levi insisted they'd improved the road leading to the farm over the past decade or so, but there were still too many twists and turns for his peace of mind. The prospect of teaching Sadie to drive one day was daunting enough, but the idea that she'd eventually be behind the wheel on this road was enough to give him night terrors. He wondered if the family would be open to more suggested road improvements. There was one hairpin turn in particular that was a real bitch.

Speaking of, Boone slowed his speed as he made the tight turn, hoping his truck would make it the rest of the way up the mountain. He had four-wheel drive, but he probably would have been smart to invest in snow tires or chains, too. His truck was fine for driving in snow on flat roads, but the farm road had one hell of a sharp incline.

He made the turn just fine, trying to maintain enough speed that he wouldn't get stuck. In addition to the thick snow, the wind was beating a gale, blowing the white stuff in every direction. His windshield wipers and the defroster were only just about doing the job.

He drove past the winery and was coming up on the brewery when he slammed on the brakes, spotting a figure plodding along on the road.

The back end of his truck fishtailed and the tires slipped off the side of the road as he fought to correct course.

Squinting through the windshield, his temper exploded when he saw a shivering Mila huddled in the ditch. No doubt he'd surprised her, and the sound of his brakes and the truck skidding had sent her hightailing it off the road.

He rolled down his window. "What in the fuck are you doing out here?" He hadn't meant to shout, but the thought that he could have hit her scared him spitless.

Mila trudged over to the driver's side, but he shook his head when he saw her bright red cheeks. "Get in."

As she crossed around the hood, he cranked the heat.

"Thanks," she said as she climbed in. "It's like a blizzard out here."

"What the hell are you doing walking in it?"

"The storm wasn't supposed to start until later tonight. We opened the winery and brewery, but obviously no one was coming to drink with the forecast, so we closed early to let the employees get home safe. I made a bad call and decided to clean the walk-in pantry and fridges at the winery, since no one was around. I've been meaning to do it for months—Nora's actually been threatening to do it herself, which would have driven me crazy—so I thought I'd tackle it before the snow started. There are no windows in the pantry, and I didn't even think to look outside—"

"I almost *hit you*, Mila. I didn't see you until you were right there." He tried to loosen his grip on the steering wheel, aware he was still white-knuckling it.

She bit her lip. "I'm sorry. I didn't realize you hadn't already gotten back, and I sure as hell didn't expect anyone to be driving on this road."

He took a deep breath, trying to calm his rapidly racing heart, but it wasn't easy. While she'd obviously miscalculated the storm the same way he had, Boone couldn't get over the fact she'd put herself in serious danger.

Too many times during the past couple of months, he'd considered how Mila's life would be different if she was his. Because there was no way he'd let her continue to work herself to the point of exhaustion, and hell would have frozen over before he'd let her walk a mile in a fucking blizzard.

When the first few deep breaths didn't work, he gave up hope and put the truck in drive. The tires spun, traction a thing of the past, thanks to the blowing snowdrifts. Getting the vehicle moving on a flat surface would have been challenging, but no amount of shifting from reverse to drive was going to budge the thing out of the ditch.

"I'm sorry," Mila said, shivering quietly as he put the truck in park, cursing under his breath.

"Not your fault."

She shot him a look. "Of course it was. If you hadn't had to slam on the brakes, the truck wouldn't have slid off the road."

Boone debated whether it was smarter to give her a few minutes to get warm in the truck or to get the damn hike through the snow over with, so she could put on some dry clothes. Glancing outside at the thick, fat snowflakes and the ever-growing drifts, he decided their best bet was to get to his place. "Looks like we're going to have to walk." He nodded to the wine bag in her hands. "What's that for?"

Mila gave him an adorable grin as she gestured toward the six bottles of wine. "I'm facing being snowed in for two days with Remi and Nora. Felt like provisions were necessary."

He chuckled. "Well, my cabin is closer. What do you say you get snowed in with me?" Boone was perfectly aware he was sealing his fate with that invitation, but after nearly hitting her with his damn truck, he couldn't shake the need to keep Mila close, where he could protect her and ensure she was safe and sound.

Sure, he thought sarcastically. *That's all you want to do.*

Mila hesitated just long enough that he regretted phrasing his invitation as a request. Because it wasn't.

"Stay there," he said, turning off the truck and climbing out. Circling, he opened her door and took the bag of wine. "Come on. This trudge is only going to get harder the longer we wait."

Mila took his hand, the two of them hunched forward, pushing against the strong wind as they slowly made their way to his cabin. Neither of them bothered with conversation, as it was too damn cold to make the effort.

She hadn't verbally agreed to stay with him, but when he made the turn down his lane, she didn't say anything, just let him continue to guide her.

He sighed in relief when they made it to his place, the warmth of the cabin welcome after the freezing-cold walk. Facing her, he helped her out of her hat, scarf, gloves, and coat, depositing them all on the hooks hanging by the door.

She gave him an amused grin. "I can do that myself."

Boone ignored her as he knelt down, untying her boots and pulling them off. Once that was done, he repeated the process for himself before reclaiming her hand and taking her to his bedroom.

"Let me find you something to wear that's dry, then I'll go start a fire for us. Loaded the woodbox yesterday, so we're set there." Boone rummaged through his dresser drawer as Mila stood quietly by his bed. He forced himself to ignore how easy it would be to push her down on that mattress and get her nice and warm without clothing.

He discreetly adjusted his growing erection, pulling out a couple pairs of lounge pants and some warm socks. Walking to Mila, he started to hand her the clothes, aware he'd be smart to leave her to change on her own while he closed himself inside the bathroom to do the same.

He wasn't feeling particularly smart right now. That kiss last night by her car had shaken something loose, and all those well-rehearsed reasons he had for staying away from her had already started to fade. Now, the storm raging outside had blown them away once and for all.

So instead of leaving her alone, he tossed the pants and socks on the bed...then reached for the button of her jeans.

Mila gasped, her trembling hands flying to his.

"You're shivering too much. Put your hands down."

Now, as always, Mila responded to his commands instinctually, acting before the part of her brain that needed to consider stuff could kick in.

She closed her hands into fists at her sides, as if forcing herself to keep them there, while he drew down the zipper. Her jeans were soaked clear through from the knees down, but when he reached behind her to tug them down, he realized the ass of them was wet too.

He gave her a curious look.

"I slipped in the winery parking lot."

Boone frowned, as she reminded him again how much danger she'd put herself in. Slipping the jeans over her ass, he worked the clinging denim down until she was able to step out of it.

Mila's cheeks were red, but they'd been like that since they walked into the cabin, so he couldn't tell if the color was from the cold or if arousal driving it. When she licked her chapped lips, tugging on the bottom one with her teeth, he got his answer.

She started to reach for the lounge pants, intent on covering up, but he rose and grasped her wrist, stopping her.

"Boone?" she asked.

"Turn around."

She frowned.

"You fell. I want to make sure you're okay."

Her soft intake of breath reminded him that she was relatively inexperienced. Hell, inexperienced didn't even cover it. Mila was practically a virgin, which should have been the biggest fucking red flag in the world. He had no business taking her to bed, and yet, that inner caveman was beating his chest, determined to claim her.

Slowly, Mila turned around until she faced away from him. Her sweater was long, covering most of her ass, so he lifted it as he peered down.

Her panties were as innocent as hers. Not granny panties, but she wasn't wearing a thong. The practical cotton covered a fair amount of her ass, though not enough that he couldn't see the small red marks that would probably be bruises come morning.

He growled, then stroked the sore spots, causing Mila to tremble harder. He didn't pretend she was shivering from the cold anymore.

"You're gonna bruise. Must have been a hard fall."

Mila lifted one shoulder as she glanced back at him, a mischievous grin appearing. "I was trying to save the wine."

Her humor faded in the face of his stern expression. "You getting hurt isn't funny, darlin'. Why were you walking on the road instead of the path?"

"I thought the road might be clearer. Jace put salt down this morning."

That made sense. And in a normal storm, the salt probably would have helped. Unable to resist holding himself away from her, Boone wrapped his arms around her waist, pulling her back against his chest, kissing the shell of her ear. He needed to hold her, needed to know she was safe and relatively unharmed.

"Never again, Mila. You ever find yourself in a position where getting home alone isn't safe, you hunker down and call me. I'll come get you."

"Boone."

Her tone told him she wasn't going to agree. It was the wrong tone to take with him right now. He was still on edge.

He tightened his grip. "You will call me," he stressed again. "This isn't something that's up for negotiation."

"I don't understand what's happening here," she whispered.

Boone wasn't surprised. He'd been the king of mixed signals, flashing hot before turning cold. Even now, he questioned the wisdom of what he was doing.

The problem was, he couldn't stop this. Mila was the moon and he was the tide, helpless to resist her pull.

He forced himself to let go, to take a step away. He was coming on too strong. Best to slow things down for a bit. "I'm going to get changed in the bathroom. Those lounge pants have a drawstring," he said, pointing to the pants he'd found her for. "Hopefully, that'll be enough to help you keep them up. Once we're changed, we can get that fire going and see about making some dinner."

"Okay." Mila grabbed the pants. "I need to text my sisters. Tell them where I am. I called Nora before I left the winery and told her I was walking home. She's probably starting to worry."

He nodded, slightly relieved to know she'd at least told someone she was heading home in the storm, so they'd know to come looking if she didn't make it.

Boone walked to the bathroom, closing the door behind him. Gripping the edge of the sink, he bent forward and took several steadying breaths. For a second, he considered jerking off because that was the only thing that was going to get rid of the raging hard-on being strangled in his jeans. It had probably been a mistake grabbing lounge pants for himself because at least denim managed to partially conceal an erection. The damn cotton pants were going to look like a pitched tent.

In the end, he decided against it, changed quickly and walked back out to his bedroom, which was empty. Heading to the great room, he spied Mila looking in the refrigerator. She glanced his direction when he joined her.

"Thought I'd see what I could make us for dinner," she said. They hadn't had a cooking lesson in three weeks, and he'd skipped Sunday dinners since that last impulsive kiss at her house.

"There should be plenty of options. I stocked up a couple of days ago, in case the storm hit as hard as they predicted."

Mila gestured toward the window, where it was still a virtual whiteout, the woods completely obscured and hidden behind the snow. "I think it hit harder."

"You're not wrong about that."

Mila pulled out a package of hamburger. "Burgers and fries?"

He grinned. "Sounds great. You want to start that while I build a fire?"

She nodded.

"Did you text your sisters?"

"I did," Mila responded, grinning. "They joked and said they'd see me sometime next week. If the snow keeps falling at this rate, they might be right. I'm assuming Sadie's with her mom now?"

"She is. Lena met us in Fredericksburg. The storm's not supposed to be as bad there."

"On the plus side, there's a good chance school will be closed tomorrow and Friday, so she won't miss anything."

"Hadn't considered that. That *is* good." Boone placed several logs in the fireplace, along with some kindling, then lit it. Took a couple tries to get it going, but before long, there was a roaring fire. The cabin was usually warm enough with just the heat running, but on exceptionally cold nights, it could get chilly.

Tossing one more log on, he rose and walked back to the kitchen. "Put me to work."

She tilted her head toward the bag of wine she'd placed on the coffee table. "Want to pick a wine for us?"

He grabbed a bottle of red, uncorking it and pouring each of them a glass as she flipped the burgers. Since the fries were already in the oven, he leaned against the counter, watching her fry the hamburgers. Despite the distance between them the past few weeks, they both fell back into the easy camaraderie they'd formed during the cooking lessons.

They sipped the wine, conversing about the weather and how it might impact the grapevines.

Once the timer beeped for the fries, Boone started pulling condiments out of the fridge. Mila plated their burgers and fries, and they each carried their own food and wine to the small kitchen table.

"I suppose Sadie was excited to see her mom."

Boone nodded. "She was. Lena usually plans fun activities for them."

"That's nice."

Boone smiled, pretending to agree. He worked hard to keep all his unkind thoughts about Lena locked away inside, never speaking them aloud, on the off chance Sadie overheard. Obviously, there was no danger of Sadie hearing his real thoughts about her mother if he chose to talk to Mila about Lena, but he held his tongue.

For one thing, he didn't want to think about his ex-wife tonight. Not when he was here with Mila. And for another, if he off-loaded his true feelings about Lena, there was no way he wouldn't come off sounding bitter and angry.

They'd just finished the meal when the lights in the cabin flickered a few times before going out completely.

"Oh no," Mila said, the room suddenly very dim. "Power must have gone out." She reached for her phone and quickly fired off a text to the family thread. The sound of several pings followed. "Looks like we've all lost it. Thankfully, the guys prepared for this and filled the generators with fuel. Theo's still at the brewery, so he's starting the one there, and Jace is going to plow his way down to the winery. Due to the forecast, there aren't any guests at the B&B. Snow scared everyone away."

"They need any help?" Boone asked. He hated the idea of trudging back through that snow again, but he would if they needed him.

Mila shook her head. "Nope. Sounds like they've got it covered."

"Hopefully, the electric company will manage to get here to sort it out." Boone rose, rifling through the kitchen junk drawer, pulling out several candles.

Mila was already walking around the room, lighting the decorative ones she'd put in the cabin prior to them moving in. Boone had never lit them, but seeing the cabin now, in the flickering light provided by the candles and the fireplace, he decided to utilize them more in the future. The cabin looked downright cozy.

Boone carried their dishes to the sink, then topped their wineglasses. "Sit by the fire with me."

Mila grinned as he did some quick rearranging of the furniture. The couch usually faced the television, but that wouldn't be necessary tonight, so he pushed the coffee table to the side and moved the couch until it faced the fire.

"Tonight's show," he said, as he and Mila sat down.

"My favorite," she replied.

He frowned when she claimed the opposite side, putting too much distance between them. He crooked his finger. "Come closer."

Mila moved a couple of feet but it still wasn't enough for him, so he reached over and dragged her over the cushions until she was pressed against him.

Twisting so that the arm of the couch was at his back, Boone parted his legs, placing Mila between them and reclining her against his chest.

She sighed, sinking into his arms, the two of them watching the fire spark and flash.

Silence fell, but it wasn't awkward. In fact, this was the most peaceful Boone had felt in ages. He grabbed the blanket that was draped over the back of the couch and spread it across their laps.

She glanced at him. "Thanks. After that walk in the snow, I

was a little afraid I'd never be warm again. This is so nice and toasty."

He grinned and placed a soft kiss to the top of her head. "I hope you don't get sick."

"I texted Jace and warned him your truck was stuck on the side of road. He said he'll plow it out as soon as the snow stops. Winter is that guy's season. Loves getting out on that tractor and pushing snow around. I swear it's when he's happiest."

"What's that expression? Boys and their toys? And how they get bigger and more expensive with age."

Mila laughed. "That definitely applies to Jace." She paused, then reconsidered. "Actually, it applies to all my cousins. Everett got that drone for Christmas."

"The aerial shots he's taken with it and put on the website are cool."

"They are, but I swear he's out every day flying the thing. Between that and Theo's new digital grill slash smoker thingie, I don't know who had the better Christmas. They're both still raving about their gifts."

Boone chuckled. "I've always considered myself a fair hand at grilling, but Theo puts me to shame with all his gadgets and recipes. It's nice that they take turns cooking for each other."

"I guess considering there are seven of them, and they're all pretty different, it's amazing how well they get along. Levi's always said they aren't just his brothers, but his best friends."

"Must be nice to have siblings and be close to them."

"Only child?" she asked.

He nodded. "Yep. My parents didn't meet and marry until they were well into their thirties, so I was a late-in-life kid."

"I don't know what I'd do without my sisters and cousins. We grew up on the farm together, so the guys feel more like brothers to me."

"You're a lucky woman, darlin', because your family is awesome."

She gave him a huge smile. "They really are," Mila gushed, "though I have to admit, I'm curious to see how things will change now that they're falling in love and planning weddings. Not that the guys won't still be close. It's just...it took some time to get used to Lucy leaving the farm and moving to Philly. We talk on the phone or FaceTime a few times a week, but I still really miss her."

"You think any of the other Storm kids will uproot and move away from Gracemont?"

Mila shook her head. "No. I think Levi moving down into the valley was probably as far as any of the others would ever consider venturing. I sort of expect the rest to follow Theo's lead, claiming one of the cabins as their own."

"You okay with that?"

"Absolutely. Taking care of the cabins isn't my favorite thing. I took it over from Aunt Claire about five years ago, when her sciatica started acting up and she couldn't clean them anymore. I expected her to take them back once she felt better, but," Mila shrugged, "she never did."

"Levi said everyone claimed their role on the farm after they graduated from high school."

"They did," Mila confirmed. "Though I was a little slower to chisel out my place because of Grandma's dementia, and then Granddaddy's cancer."

"Was running the kitchens at the winery and brewery your choice?" he asked.

"It was. I love to cook. I'd actually love to expand the menus at both places, offering something more substantial than the appetizers. I have this idea for signature hot dogs we could sell at the brewery, where we give them all stormy weather names with fun toppings. And for the winery, I'd love to add gourmet grilled cheeses to the menu, and we could even pair each to a Lightning in a Bottle wine."

"Damn. Both those ideas sound delicious."

"I have a million ideas because, as it stands now, most patrons come for a happy hour drink, share some of the light fare, then they leave to go somewhere else for dinner. If we offered a more substantial menu, they wouldn't have to leave at all, which would only mean better beer and wine sales."

"Solid business plan." Boone wondered why she wasn't suggesting it to her family.

"My *real* dream is to someday be able to start my own catering service. Gretchen could offer it as one of the add-ons at the event barn. We anticipate hosting lots of weddings and parties there, and I think it could be a real selling feature if we also made catering available."

"Why someday?"

Mila shrugged. "There aren't enough hours in the day right now."

"Well, then here's hoping your cousins start snapping up those cabins, so you'll have more time to do what you really love." He tapped his wineglass against hers, and they finished their wine.

Boone took her glass, placing them on the side table, so he could wrap his arms around her.

Mila looked over her shoulder curiously. She indicated earlier she didn't understand his sudden affection, and he wished he could offer her some answer as to what had changed for him.

He'd had plenty of time on the return trip to Gracemont to consider last night's kiss.

All he knew was that when she'd gotten out of her car with Sadie safely in tow, some cold, dead part of his heart came back to life. Sadie had been terribly upset…and she'd sought out Mila.

And Mila had taken care of her. Hell, she'd been taking care of Sadie since the first day they met.

And that was when he admitted the way to his heart wasn't through his stomach at all. It was through his daughter.

Mila was sweet and giving, and when he watched her and Sadie walk toward the cabin last night, Mila placing a comforting, almost protective hand on his daughter's shoulder, every so-called "good excuse" for keeping his distance from her no longer felt good enough.

Boone placed a soft kiss on her cheek, then turned her face so he could kiss her lips.

Mila followed his lead, twisting to face him, returning his kiss with a hunger that matched his own. Her hands slid through his hair as he grasped her waist, tugging her until she was straddling his lap.

Her eyes widened briefly when he pulled her more firmly against him, letting her feel the impact she was having on him. His cock was rock hard.

"Boone."

He stopped her from saying more because he wasn't interested in talking right now. He'd turned a corner, though whether for now or for good, he couldn't say. His physical needs were drowning out every voice of reason, and he let them. Let them take over.

Kissing her again, he cupped her ass, taking advantage of her gasp to push his tongue in to find hers.

Mila mewled as he caressed her ass, then slipped his hands under her sweater, unhooking her bra.

"I'm going to lay you down on this couch and take you, darlin'," he said. "If you don't want that, you need to say so now."

"I want that so much," she said, her lips tickling his throat as she spoke.

"Good girl," he said, praising her, loving the way her pupils dilated whenever he called her that. Reaching for the hem of her sweater, he pulled it over her head, her bra going next, both articles of clothing tossed to the floor.

Boone growled low in his throat as he looked at her gorgeous tits. "So beautiful," he murmured.

Mila's head flew back when he took one of her tight nipples into his mouth, sucking on it until she moaned with pleasure... and maybe a little bit of pain.

Her hands clung to his shoulders, her fingers fisting the material of his shirt.

"More," she gasped.

Boone pinched her nipples, loving the way her back arched and her eyes closed. She was responsive and more uninhibited than he'd expected. While he wouldn't call Mila shy, she was definitely one of the quieter Storms, more reserved and softspoken. Of course, it was probably hard to be seen when constantly in the company of Theo, Maverick, and Remi, who seemed to draw every eye with their larger-than-life personalities.

This Mila wasn't holding back *anything*, and he was here for it.

Pinching her nipples again, he tugged on them until her eyes —and her mouth—flew open. Her breathing was already ragged.

"It...feels..." she panted.

She didn't—or couldn't—say more, but Boone didn't need her words because everything Mila felt was written all over her gorgeous face, her expressive eyes screaming her needs.

He continued to play with her tits, sucking, pinching, nipping, squeezing. He could spend hours with her breasts and never get enough.

Mila's fingers were fisted tight in his hair, pulling it. Not that he cared.

Cupping both breasts, he placed a soft kiss on the tip of each nipple, then leaned back, studying her face, waiting until that moment…

It took a minute or so for her vision to clear and her brain to catch up, letting her know he'd stopped touching her.

"That…was…" Once again, she paused, then shook her head. "I swear to God I know more words than I'm managing to say."

Boone chuckled, lifting her off his lap despite her clinging, desperate to remain right where she was.

"Stop fighting me, darlin'. Go where I put you."

"But—"

"Don't question me, either."

Ordinarily, Boone tempered his tone, held back his gruffer, more demanding nature. He'd only ever truly let that side show with Lena, who'd enjoyed his rough bedroom play. With his last two lovers, he'd locked the dominant away, keeping things painfully vanilla. Not because those women couldn't handle a stronger touch. Hell, they might have even preferred it.

But Boone hadn't wanted to go there with them. He hadn't lied to Mila. Those lovers were there to scratch an itch, and stretching things beyond missionary and doggie felt too… personal. And since personal wasn't something he'd been looking for, he held back.

That wouldn't be possible with Mila. Because her submissiveness was so innate, so true, so real. Lena may have liked their bedroom games, but to her, that was *all* they were. Games. She assumed her role because it turned her on, but she could have just as easily flipped and played the dominant, as well.

However, this wasn't a game or a role to him. His dominance was a deeply ingrained part of who he was, and he'd hidden it away for far too long.

Mila wouldn't let him do that. Not because she'd make

demands verbally but because her nature called to his, and like opposing magnets, whenever they got too close, they were going to snap together. *Hard.*

She stopped struggling, letting him help her to her feet. She reached for him, but he gripped her wrists and placed them at her sides. "Keep them there."

He kept a strong hand on her elbow until she was steady, then he tugged on the drawstring of the pants he'd loaned her. Mila had rolled them several times to keep them up, but they'd come loose when she was straddling his lap, so it was a simple matter of untying the knot and shoving them down. They fell to her feet in a heap, and she stepped out of them.

That pretty flush on her cheeks didn't stop with her face, slowly creeping down her slender neck to her chest. She wasn't seeking to cover herself, and he was amazed by and proud of her courage.

Boone ran his fingers down her arms, then along her midriff and hips before teasing them around the elastic of her practical panties. "I like these," he said, lightly snapping the elastic.

Mila's hands rested flat on the outside of her thighs, even though he could tell she was itching to touch him. She was resisting that desire, obeying him.

"They're not very sexy," she said.

"They're the sexiest panties I've ever seen." Because they were on her. "But they're in the way." Boone slipped them over her hips, letting them drop like the pants. Once again, Mila stepped free. He was tempted to circle her, to take his time studying every scintillating curve of her body, but he could see from her slight trembling, from her shallow breathing, that her needs were becoming desperate.

Not surprising, considering it had been years since she'd been with a man.

Boone guided her back to the couch. "Lie down."

She did as he said, stretching out on the plush cushions. If Boone had to pick a favorite thing about his new house—after the stone fireplace—it would be this wide, comfortable couch.

He lifted one of her legs, positioning himself between her outstretched thighs. Kneeling there, he saw the confusion in her eyes, her brows furrowed.

"Your clothes," she whispered.

Boone winked at her. "Not there yet." He grinned as she huffed out an unsteady and impatient breath.

She gasped when he spread her legs farther apart, bent forward, and ran his tongue along her slit. Mila was already wet, but he was determined to ensure she was drenched when he sank into her tight pussy.

"Boone!" she cried, jerking, her hands returning to grasp his hair. He'd be bald by morning.

"That's right, sweetheart. Yell my name. Yell any damn thing you want. Let me hear you." He blew against her clit. Parting her folds with his thumbs, he set to work, feeling a bit desperate himself. Desperate to hear his girl come.

Boone sucked her clit into his mouth, the same way he had her nipples, and Mila began to rock, her hips rising to meet every stroke of his tongue, every nip of his teeth.

"God!" she cried out, when he added more fuel to the fire by pressing one, then two fingers inside her.

Fuck. He knew she'd be tight, but this…

Boone wasn't sure he could do this without hurting her. He wasn't a small man, and he wanted her with a passion he'd never felt in his life.

Regardless, he was determined to make up for her past shitty lovers.

Forcing himself to gentle his strokes, he slid his fingers in and out, slowly stretching her. As he did so, he toyed with her clit, using it to drive her arousal higher, hotter. For most women, penetration wasn't enough. However, paired with that magic button…

Firmly pressing the flat of his tongue against her clit, Boone somehow managed to add a third finger.

Mila exploded, erupted. Her back arched as her orgasm raced through her, and his sweet woman let loose with language that would make a sailor blush.

"Motherfucker. Holy Jesus! Goddammit, Boone. *Boone!*"

He lifted his head, wanting to watch as she fell apart. He held his fingers still inside her, savoring every pulse of her pussy muscles, waiting until they finally calmed before pulling out.

Mila's eyelids fluttered, and it took her another minute or two before she recovered enough to look at him. "No one's ever —" She stopped midsentence, but he wasn't going to let her stop there. He wanted the rest, needed to know.

No one had ever what? Gone down on her?

"Ever what?" he prodded.

"Made me come." She blushed with her admission, hastily adding, "Except me, I mean."

Boone shook his head in disgust, hoping he never ran into the two assholes who didn't realize or appreciate just how special Mila was when they took her to their beds…or backseat of their damn car.

Unable to resist, Boone crawled over her, caging her beneath him as he kissed her senseless, letting her taste herself from his lips. The kiss lingered for minutes. Hell, maybe hours.

Boone wanted her, but more than that, he wanted to make tonight a good memory for her. And him.

He pulled back and placed a playful kiss on the tip of her nose.

"You said you were a rough lover, but that—" she started.

Boone placed his finger against her lips. "You don't have to worry about that. Not tonight. Tonight is going to be your first time."

She frowned, confused. "But it's not."

"Darlin', those first two men didn't deserve you, and they obviously didn't give you what you needed."

"Boone?" she asked softly.

"Yeah?"

"Will you take off your clothes? I want to see you, touch you."

He grinned, because there was nothing he wanted more than Mila's hands on him. "Don't move."

Standing beside the couch, he tugged off his shirt, teasingly flexing when her eyes widened.

"I knew you were strong, but…"

Boone didn't consider himself a vain man or one who was overly concerned with his looks, but Mila's appreciative stare sure did make him feel good.

Reaching for the waistband of his lounge pants, he tugged them and his boxer briefs down, his gaze glued to her face.

Mila's eyes slid down his chest, her lower lip disappearing under her teeth as she took in his erection. It bounced against his stomach as he kicked off his pants.

Climbing back over her, Boone resumed their kisses, enjoying the way Mila took advantage of his newly bared skin, her hands roaming all over his chest and upper arms. He let his lips do a little exploring too, kissing her cheek, beneath her ear, around her throat.

"Please," Mila gasped, the first to cry uncle.

Boone reached between them, gripping his cock.

"Birth control?" he asked, suddenly aware he hadn't grabbed a condom. Jesus, he never forgot to wrap his dick. But the idea of stopping and walking to the bedroom right now for a condom felt as daunting as the prospect of scaling Mt. Everest.

"I get the shot," she replied.

"Your call, Mila. I'm clean, but—"

"I don't want you to use one. I just want to feel…you."

Boone had to fight to get air into his lungs. Sweet Jesus. He'd never been this turned on in his life.

Placing the head of his cock at her opening, he slowly pushed inside. It took every ounce of self-control to keep his pace easy, pausing along the way to give her time to adjust.

"So good," she whispered, once he was seated to the hilt. "So full, and so good."

Boone cupped her face in his hands and placed several soft kisses on her lips. "Tell me when you're ready."

She smiled. "I've been ready since the day I met you."

He chuckled. "Little minx."

Taking her at her word, he withdrew, then returned, repeating over and over, his pace steady at first but slowly building.

Mila lifted her legs, wrapping them around his waist, the shift in position allowing him to go deeper, something that had both of them groaning.

Boone had proclaimed tonight her first time, but it occurred to him that this was *his* first time as well. Because he'd never taken a woman like this, never let the sex, the physical act, be driven by pure emotion.

Because he'd never felt this way. Not even for his ex-wife.

That realization shook him to his core.

They continued to kiss as he thrust, every pulse of her pussy pushing him closer to the brink. What the fuck was wrong with him? He always had plenty of staying power, but he didn't have a prayer of maintaining control with her.

Reaching down, he drew his finger over her clit, felt the hard throb of her cunt around him. As he stroked her harder, Mila's hips began to rise and fall more rapidly, dragging him closer to the abyss.

Boone sucked in a deep breath and held it, determined she would get there first.

"God, Boone!"

Mercifully, she did, but damn if it wasn't a close call. The first spark of her orgasm triggered his, the two of them diving into the ocean together. Boone came hard, filling her with his come.

The fact that he had a flash of regret about her being on birth control, that he couldn't get her pregnant, told him how far gone he was.

Even after their orgasms subsided, Boone remained above her, his weight on his elbows, his soft cock still inside her as he worshipped her with kiss after gentle kiss.

And as he kissed her, Boone realized just how much trouble he was in.

Because while he wasn't looking for forever, there wasn't a doubt in his mind that forever would never be enough time for him and Mila Storm.

Chapter Eleven

Mila leaned back against Boone's chest, spooned between his legs, the two of them still naked. They were sitting on the plush rug in front of the fire, Boone propped with the couch at his back. He'd wrapped a fleece blanket around them, but they were generating enough body heat that it wasn't needed.

After the hottest, most incredible sex in the history of the act, Boone had cleaned them with a warm washcloth—sigh—then grabbed a second bottle of wine, refilling both their glasses. They'd polished off the first bottle right after dinner, and since they were housebound and definitely not working tomorrow, Boone suggested they open another as they cuddled by the fire.

Mila had agreed, though she was buzzed enough from the sex that the wine wasn't necessary. She took a small sip, snuggling closer, resisting the urge to pinch herself.

There was no way this was really happening. After two plus months of longing for Boone without hope of anything more than friendship at best, she couldn't believe how quickly it had changed.

Tonight was the single most romantic moment of her life, and she'd agreed to the wine because she didn't want it to end.

She wasn't sure what corner he had turned, but something had clearly happened that made Boone willing to give in to their shared attraction.

He hadn't indicated that this was more than sex, and she sure as shit wasn't bursting the bubble of bliss she was floating in to ask what he thought this was.

That was a conversation for tomorrow. Or…if it looked like they were going to be snowed in another night, the next day. She didn't want to say anything that might make him stop.

Because she did *not* want to stop.

Not after…

God.

She'd had two mind-blowing orgasms that had been miles better than the ones she gave herself. Those typically got the job done, but barely. Her cheeks grew warm as she recalled the way he'd knelt between her legs, going down on her like it was his job.

She took another drink of wine, glancing over at the bottle. It was nearly empty.

"Are you trying to get me drunk so you can have your wicked way with me?" she joked.

"Just had my wicked way with you, and I didn't even have to get you drunk, darlin'."

She giggled, thrilled by the way he called her darlin'. Surprisingly, she didn't feel drunk, and she was at least two glasses over her usual wine intake. Of course, she wasn't sure the first bottle they consumed counted anymore, given they had more than worked that off.

Along with opening the second bottle of wine, Boone had put on some music, playing a list he'd put together of favorite songs on Spotify. It was an eclectic playlist, and she was surprised to discover how similar their music tastes were.

When an old John Prine and Iris Dement duet started to play, she grinned. "In Spite of Ourselves" was a favorite, the funny lyrics never failing to make her laugh. When she started to sing the female part, Boone looked surprised.

"You know this song?"

She nodded. "I love it."

"Don't know many people who've heard it. How on earth did you?"

"My granddaddy was the world's biggest John Prine fan. Listened to him all the time. He loved a lot of folk singers. I swear one of the highlights of his life was seeing Peter, Paul and Mary perform at Wolf Trap. Once, when we were younger, Grandma and Granddaddy took us all—and I do mean *all*—to the National Zoo in D.C. Grandma played 'Goin' to the Zoo' the entire way there."

"I'm assuming 'all' means not just you and your sisters, but your cousins too?"

She nodded.

"How the hell did they get all of you there?" Boone asked, aghast.

Mila laughed, because she understood his shock. For one thing, it was rare—as in never—that they all left the farm at the same time, and while the zoo was only an hour away, loading them in vehicles was no small feat.

"Uncle Rex drove a nine-passenger van at the time, and Granddaddy bought a used minivan after inheriting four girls. The zoo had been Remi's only request for her birthday, and since it was the first birthday after Mom and Dad's deaths, Grandma went all out. She insisted we were all going, and she wouldn't take no for an answer from anyone. Granddaddy and Uncle Rex relented because Aunt Claire was on Grandma's side, so they knew they'd never win the argument."

Boone chuckled. "Powerful women in your family. I see where you get it from."

Mila stumbled for a moment, almost forgetting to finish her story because no one had ever called her powerful. Just sweet—blech.

She preferred powerful. Made her feel like a badass.

Boone chuckled. "I'm trying to picture fifteen of you rolling up to the zoo in those two vans."

"Oh, it was a show. Levi, Sam, and Theo grumbled about being forced to go, claiming they were too old."

"Well, to be fair, they probably were. Levi would have been what? Twenty? Twenty-one?"

"He was twenty at the time, Sam nineteen, and Theo seventeen. The three of them kicked up a fuss, claiming they were grown men, not kids. For two weeks before the excursion, they did nothing but bitch about it, but guess who had the most fun at the zoo?"

Boone laughed. "Loved it, did they?"

"Oh my God. They were hilarious, creating ridiculous backstories for the animals. Theo created an entire soap opera for us in Gibbon Ridge. So many scandalous affairs, and you wouldn't believe how many thieves, blackmailers, and backstabbing gibbons they had at that zoo," she joked. "Mom and Dad had been gone six months, and laughter was pretty scarce. That trip brought it back. It was probably one of the best days of my life."

She didn't mention it had fallen down a slot on the list after tonight skyrocketed to the top.

Boone placed a soft kiss on her bare shoulder. "Sounds like a great day. Your grandma was smart to insist you go, and I'm glad the guys embraced it in the end. I swear that Theo is a born storyteller."

"Yeah, he is," she agreed.

"Speaking of storytellers," Boone started. "I heard you went out with the minister again."

Mila smirked. "Maverick has a big mouth."

They both laughed.

"How do you know it wasn't Grayson who told me?" he asked, even though she knew it was meant as a joke.

"Because Grayson keeps to himself. He's a grumpy 'you do you and I'll do me' kind of guy. It's what I love best about him."

Boone nodded. "That's a good description. So…how was your date?"

Mila didn't even have to pretend it was jealousy she heard in his voice. It totally was. "It was okay. Pastor Joshua's a nice guy."

"You still calling him Pastor Joshua?" Boone asked.

Mila snorted. "I can't seem to stop."

"Are you a religious person, Mila?"

She shrugged. "I consider myself more spiritual than religious. Aunt Claire and Uncle Rex go to church on Sundays when they don't have guests checking out of the B&B, but I'm one of those C and E people."

"C and E?"

"Christmas and Easter."

Boone chuckled. "Not sure a pastor's wife could get away with that."

Her eyes widened. "Good God. I'm not marrying Pastor Joshua. In fact, I broke things off with him. Told him it wasn't working out."

"I'm glad. He wasn't good enough for you."

Mila drank in his dark tone laced with jealousy. She'd never made anyone jealous. Ever. It felt amazing.

"He's a good man," she said, because Pastor Joshua was perfectly kind. He just wasn't her type.

"That's not what I meant." Boone stared at her—and the light went on.

"Oh. Yeah. Well, you're right about that. He was still asking if he could kiss me good night after four dates." She rolled her eyes. "It was kind of exhausting."

Boone chuckled. "You don't like to be asked?"

"Every single time?"

"Fair point," he said, agreeing. Then he gave her a shit-eating grin as he cupped her cheek, planting one hell of an unrequested kiss on her lips.

She hummed as they parted. "I love your kisses," she said, the wine loosening her lips. "So much better than…"

"The pastor?" Boone asked, amused. "Not good kisses?"

Mila grimaced. "They were just like him. Nice and pleasant enough, but they sure didn't set the world on fire."

Boone brushed her hair over her shoulder, tickling the side of her neck with his nose. "You realize you have a tone when you say *nice*. Makes it sound like the word's made of manure."

Mila tilted her head, giving him better access because there was a spot behind her ear that she'd just discovered was a huge erogenous zone for her, and Boone had homed in on it. "I don't mean to do that," she said, struggling to follow the conversation when he playfully nipped her earlobe. "I've tried to come to terms with the fact that I only seem to attract that specific type of guy."

She cursed herself for still talking when Boone lifted his head. "The nice, boring guys?"

She nodded, then quickly said, "Present company excluded, of course."

Boone grinned. "I'm not nice?"

Mila twisted until she sat facing him. "You're very nice," she said, dragging one finger down the center of his chest. Maybe she *had* drunk too much wine, because she couldn't believe how comfortable she was, sitting here completely naked with him. "But not a bit boring."

"Good to know." Boone was teasing her.

"Jesus, can you imagine if I'd gone to bed with Pastor Joshua? No doubt he would have asked for permission before removing every piece of clothing."

Boone smirked. "You sure that's not your cup of tea?"

She narrowed her eyes. "You know it's not."

He reached out and pinched her nipple. "So why do you think you only attract a certain type of man?"

"Because I've been pigeon-holed in a box for most of my adult life, one I can't seem to break free from."

"What box is that?"

"The sweet one," she said, with the same disdain she used for the word *nice*.

"There's nothing wrong with being sweet, Mila. I think that's one of your best attributes."

Boone chuckled when she screwed up her face in disgust.

"You're going to have to explain to me why you think it's such a bad thing," he said.

"Because all anyone ever seems to see is this sweet, boring, unadventurous woman who blends into the background. I'm about as interesting to people as that couch," she said, pointing to the piece of furniture. "It's useful, but no one really looks at or thinks about the couch. It's just there, doing what it does, offering people a place to sit."

Boone's expression sobered. "Mila—" he started, but she'd held all of this in for weeks.

"*You* pushed me away when I told you about my sexual experiences."

Boone scowled. "Not sure you could call any of that experience."

"I'm twenty-seven years old, Boone, and while I may not

have a lot of practical experience, I don't live like a nun. I read dirty books. I watch porn. I know what I want from a lover."

"There's a difference between fantasies and reality, darlin'."

"Don't do that. Don't diminish what I'm saying by trying to tell me I don't understand my own desires."

"I wasn't doing that. I'm just saying—"

"I know what you're saying. You're warning me. You think you're protecting me," she spat out angrily. "Because apparently I'm too *sweet* and *virginal* and *stupid* to really know what I want."

Boone narrowed his eyes. "Don't put words in my mouth, Mila. Especially wrong ones."

"So you weren't playing the martyr? Saving my sweet, innocent self when you pushed me away?"

Boone ran a hand through his hair, clearly frustrated—because they both knew that was exactly what he'd done. "You've never been with a man like me. You might find yourself in over your head, might not like pain with your pleasure, might not like losing control."

She crossed her arms. "So I don't even get the chance to try? I'm too far gone for anything more than boring-as-shit missionary with beta men who ask permission every step of the way and treat me like I'm some fragile doll? Awesome. I wish I'd known there was a shelf life on kinkiness. I would have gotten out more in my early twenties."

Boone huffed out a harsh breath, half laugh, half annoyance. "Alright. Fine. You've made your point. So spell it out for me. Tell me what you want in a lover?"

No one had ever asked Mila that question, but that didn't mean she didn't have her answer ready.

"I want to be with a guy who knows what he's doing. I want someone who'll pull my hair and spank my ass, bend me over the nearest flat surface and fuck me until I can't walk straight. I want him to call me his good girl, and I want him to take charge, give me commands he expects me to obey. I want someone who wants *me* so much, he rips off my clothes the second he sees me."

Boone had said he was a rough lover, but he hadn't alluded to much more than that. What if her desires were too much for him?

Panic set in when he didn't reply, so she sought for a way to minimize the damage, turning her gaze toward the fire. "I think I'm drunk."

"Tipsy at most." Boone grasped her chin between his thumb and forefinger, drawing her face toward him. "Look at me, darlin'."

She did, but damn if Boone's poker face wasn't in full force.

"You don't want me to diminish your words, so you don't get to do it either. Did you mean what you said?"

She nodded.

"Would those words be different if you hadn't had wine?"

"Not a single one," she confessed.

"Are they going to change tomorrow?"

"No."

"So that's what you want," he said simply.

Mila leaned closer, reaching out to run her hand over his shoulder, down his muscular arm. Bending closer, she didn't stop until her lips brushed his cheek, his beard scratching the side of her face. "I want it all the way to the depths of my soul."

Boone's jaw grew tight as his gaze slid over her naked form. "You're beautiful."

Then he moved before she could react. She'd intended to kiss him, but Boone was too fast. One second, she was kneeling before him; the next, she was on her back, sinking into the plush rug.

Boone stared down at her, looking at her so intently, she

could barely breathe. She couldn't tell if he was getting ready to kiss her or walk away.

She gripped his upper arms, frightened by the idea he was going to push her away again.

When he chuckled, shaking off her hold, she frowned.

"I'm not going anywhere, darlin'."

"I didn't freak you out?" she asked.

Boone didn't reply. Instead, he lowered himself over her, kissing her so deeply, her entire body tingled. He was a large man, physically, and while that should feel intimidating, all Mila felt was safe and warm.

"Do I look freaked out?" he murmured against her lips.

She huffed out a soft laugh, but it quickly turned to a gasp when he bit her shoulder. Mila savored the burn, wanted him to leave his mark, wanted a reminder of tonight. Something she could look back on in a few days and remember this moment, how perfect it was.

She moaned when his lips trailed down her neck and chest, stopping at her breasts. Cupping them, he shifted back and forth, sucking on her nipples, plumping the flesh, teasing her with his licks and kisses.

Boone ran his tongue along the valley between them. "I'm going to fuck you here. Have you press these gorgeous tits together while I bury my cock in the middle."

"Do it now," she whispered, loving the sound of it.

"Miss Impatient."

"Please, Boone. I want everything. Every experience you'll give me."

"Maybe you should make me a list."

She knew he was joking, but she'd do it.

"Not tonight, though," he said. She started to panic again until he added, "Tonight, I've got my own list."

"Oh yeah?" she whispered.

"Tonight is all about taking our time and learning each other's bodies. You've only come twice. That's nowhere near enough."

Halle-fucking-lujah.

Boone bent his head and continued playing with her breasts until Mila was gasping for air and desperate for more. While his ministrations were definite turn-ons, they weren't nearly enough. Mila slipped one hand lower and started to stroke her clit.

Boone grasped her wrist and pressed it against the rug. "Bad girl."

"I need more."

"And you'll get it. When I give it to you."

"Please, Boone."

He gave her a hard kiss, followed by an equally hard look. "I do like the pretty way you beg. Hope you're prepared to keep doing it."

She shot him a dirty look, but all it did was amuse him. And dare him.

Boone returned to her breasts, taking his time. He'd said his intention was for them to learn each other, and she figured at this point, he knew the layout of her tits better than she did.

She shivered when—finally—he shifted lower.

"God," she whispered when he licked along her slit. Boone wasn't shy about his exploration. More than that, he made her feel like some sort of delicacy as he hummed in pleasure.

Placing a too-soft kiss on her clit, he followed with gentle strokes of his tongue that didn't offer enough stimulation.

Mila lifted her hips, hoping he'd get the point, that he'd up the ante, but if anything, he moved even slower, his touches so light they were almost imperceptible.

She huffed out a short breath of frustration, confused when Boone lifted his head and gave her a wicked grin. The bastard knew exactly what he was doing to her. Or, perhaps it was more accurate to say what he *wasn't* doing to her.

"I don't hear any begging, darlin'. Start with my name, then toss in a few pleases. And grab hold of my hair again like you did earlier. I don't want a quiet, *sweet* lover." He emphasized the word *sweet*, knowing it would set her on fire.

"Boone," she said, too wired to protest. She needed more of his heated, rough touches and she needed them now. "Please!"

Boone winked then lowered his head, turning the temperature from lukewarm to raging inferno. He left no part of her untouched, unkissed, unbitten. Her back arched as she loudly cried out his name when he shoved three fingers in to the hilt. The gentleness from their first encounter was gone, replaced by this powerful man who took without asking, who listened to her and was now making all her dreams come true. One rough thrust at a time.

Mila came within minutes, her thoughts going to pure static, and her body jerked as if electrocuted. Her orgasm hit so hard, she swore her bones rattled. Boone didn't give way like he did the first time. Now, he continued to stroke, driving the impulses out longer, pushing them so high, she feared she'd pass out.

"God. Please, Boone! *Please*." Mila wasn't sure if she was asking for mercy or more. Not that it mattered. Boone had his own agenda, and he was making it damn clear her input wasn't necessary.

Her climax only began to slow when his fingers did.

"Perfect," he mused, lifting his head. "Goddamn, you're pretty when you come, Mila."

Her cheeks heated. She was only able to offer him the weakest of smiles, her body still in recovery mode.

"I came so hard, it almost hurt."

If she'd expected him to apologize for that, she was destined to be disappointed, because her admission pleased him way too much.

Boone shifted over her, giving her a long, passionate kiss, the taste of herself lingering on his lips.

He reached between them, intent on taking her again, but there was something on *her* list that she was dying to try.

Mila placed her hand flat on his chest, pressing against him.

Boone paused, confused. "Are you too sore?"

She quickly shook her head. "God no. It's just..." She grasped his cock in her hand, sliding her palm along the length. This was the first time she'd held his dick. No wonder she'd felt so full when he took her before. Boone's cock was the perfect amount of length and girth. Maybe a little too perfect.

"You want to take me in your mouth, darlin'?"

She nodded.

"You ever done that before?"

She shook her head, her eyes narrowing in warning, lest he be tempted to tell her no. "You said tonight was about us learning each other's bodies, not just you learning mine."

Boone cupped her cheek. "Put your claws away, kitten. I'm not about to turn down what you're offering."

He gave her one more hard, fast kiss, then pushed off the floor, sitting on the edge of the couch, his thick thighs spread wide. "Get on your hands and knees and crawl over here."

Mila was in position before he finished the request, making her way toward him slowly, then kneeling between his legs.

Boone ran his fingers through her hair with one hand, the other gripping his cock.

Mila reached out, stroking one finger over the tip of his dick, collecting the precome beading there.

Boone groaned when she placed that finger in her mouth, tasting him.

Brushing Boone's hand away, she replaced it with her own, running her fist along him from base to head.

"Tighten your grip, darlin'. Pretend like it's my hair. Don't be afraid to tug hard."

She smiled, then did as he said, desperate to make him feel as good as he'd made her feel tonight. She stroked several times, closing her fist around him with as much force as she could.

Boone's eyes closed briefly when she used her other hand to cup his balls, juggling them, fascinated by them. More precome gathered on the head of his dick.

She licked her lips.

Boone's eyelids lifted, his gaze locked on her. "Give me that mouth, Mila. I need to feel your lips wrapped around me."

She didn't need to be asked twice. Shifting forward, she ran her tongue over the head of his cock, her own hum of approval rumbling out.

Boone gripped the side of her neck. "I'm not sure I can let you take control here," he warned her. "I want this too badly."

"Show me how much," she whispered.

Boone moved forward until his ass was just barely perched on the edge of the couch. Using his hold on her neck, he drew her face down until his cock brushed her lips. His large hand covered hers on his shaft, increasing the speed and grip so much, she worried it might hurt.

"Open," he growled.

Mila's lips parted and he pushed his cock inside. Thrusting shallowly at first, he went deeper on each return until he brushed the back of her throat. Mila fought with her gag reflex, wishing she could be like those women in her spicy romance novels. The ones who could deep throat the hero like a champ.

Her eyes began to water as his cock hit her gag reflex again. She tried to take in more, but Boone held her steady, his grip on her neck firm, unrelenting.

"Stop," he grunted, pulling out of her mouth completely when she kept trying to fight him.

Mila blinked, trying to clear her vision.

"Stop trying to take more than you can."

"But—"

"But nothing. I want to be with you, Mila. Just as you are."

"But in my books—" she started again.

"Books are fiction. This is real. And your mouth," he added, running his thumb over her lower lip, "is fucking perfection."

Mila had to blink away more tears, but this time, it wasn't her gag reflex to blame. It was her heart. Boone was stealing more and more of it with every word he spoke. She would take as much of this man as he was willing to give because if the past few months had taught her anything, it was that he was it for her. If that meant she was facing a broken heart somewhere down the road, then she'd deal with it.

Boone pushed his cock back into her mouth, and this time, she didn't fight him as he thrust in and out, taking what he needed without pushing her too far.

Mila held on tightly, moving her hand in tandem with her mouth, then she cupped his balls again.

After a dozen more thrusts, Boone withdrew, his breathing labored.

Mila tried to pull him back into her mouth, aware he was close, but he placed his hand around the front of her throat, holding her back.

"I want you to—"

"Not tonight," Boone interjected. "We're still learning. If I come down your throat, that ends things too soon." He gave her a crooked grin. "I'm forty, remember? Quick recovery is a young man's game, and I've still got a few items on my list for tonight."

Mila laughed breathlessly, any complaint she might have had fading away.

Boone reached down, tweaking one of her nipples. "Move back to the middle of the rug. Hands and knees."

As she shifted into position, Boone ran his fingers over her ass. "No bruises from your fall."

"Told you. Lots of padding."

"Is that right?" He swatted her ass playfully and she squealed with surprise. "Goddamn, you've got a gorgeous ass."

Mila giggled, the sound cut short when Boone knelt behind her, running his fingers down her spine.

She expected him to tease her more, so she was relieved when his cock brushed her opening. Mila hadn't anticipated the blowjob would impact her so strongly or make her so horny again. After all, he'd given her one hell of an orgasm. If she'd managed one of those on her own, she would have been set for months, maybe even a damn year.

That didn't hold true with Boone. It was as if the more orgasms he gave her, the more she needed. And it wasn't due to a lack of satisfaction. Nope. It was because she was becoming greedy as hell, addicted to the high only he could provide.

Gripping her hips, Boone slammed in to the hilt in one hard thrust.

Mila hadn't been prepared, her arms buckling until her weight rested on her elbows. If not for Boone hanging on to her lower body, she would have slipped facedown onto the rug.

"God!" she cried out, when he started fucking her in earnest. She'd told him she didn't want kid gloves, and Boone had taken her at her word.

Thank God.

Tonight wasn't just about proving to him that she could take what he gave her. It was about proving to herself that she'd been right about all those untapped desires.

Boone was giving her the greatest gift by letting her explore them, by giving her exactly what she asked for without constantly questioning if she was sure, or if she was okay. He was trusting her to tell him if she wasn't.

She wasn't used to being so…seen. So understood.

"Fuck, darlin'," Boone grunted. "This pussy…it was made for my cock. Squeezing me like a vise."

Mila's inner muscles clenched at his dirty talk. It was as heady as his powerful fucking.

"Boone! Yes," she screamed, when he tilted his hips slightly, his cock slamming against her G-spot until she saw stars. "There," she gasped. "Right there."

She repeated those same two words, her fingers clenching in the plush rug, seeking purchase, something—*anything*—to hang on to.

Lightning flashed behind her eyes, blinding her as her climax struck.

Mila froze, stunned into stillness, her mouth hanging open with no sound emerging. A silent scream.

It took several minutes before she realized Boone had followed her into the abyss.

By the time she pulled herself back to shore, she was lying chest down on the rug, her head twisted to the right, where Boone had collapsed next to her.

She watched his chest rise and fall, gradually growing slower. It wasn't until he spoke that she realized he was watching her too.

"There you are," he said softly.

"I think I blacked out."

Boone chuckled. "I like the sound of that. Been trying to make up for falling on my ass that day you fell off the ladder. Sounds like my stud status is back."

Mila giggled. "Definitely back."

Boone reached over, clasping her hand in his, the two of them lying there for nearly ten minutes in silence. Words weren't necessary.

Finally, Boone forced himself upright, sitting next to her. "I'm too old to sleep on the floor, darlin'. Let's go to bed."

Mila had never spent the entire night in bed with a man before, which was why—simple though it may seem—it was ranked fairly high on her list of things she wanted to experience.

She flopped over onto her back, still feeling boneless after that orgasm.

Boone rose, then reached down, helping her. She started to pick up the borrowed clothing she'd shed, but Boone tugged her toward the bedroom. "You're not sleeping in clothes in my bed."

She didn't bother to argue because...why would she?

Boone carried a couple candles with them, placing one by the bed before leading her to his bathroom, where he put the other on the counter. Reaching beneath the sink, he grabbed a new toothbrush. Opening it, he put paste on it and handed it to her before doing the same to his. They stared at each other through their flickering reflections in the mirror, grinning like fools as they brushed their teeth, the simple act incredibly intimate.

"Hopefully, the power will be back on by morning and we can take a hot shower. As for tonight, I don't want you washing me off you."

Mila felt the same way about him.

They returned to the bedroom, Boone pulling back the duvet so that she could lie down. Climbing in on the opposite side, he tucked her against his chest, kissing the top of her head.

"Night, darlin'."

"Night, Boone." Mila sank into his embrace, expecting sleep to take some time.

She was wrong. It came quickly.

Because, for the first time in her life, she was exactly where she was meant to be.

Chapter Twelve

Boone flipped the bacon, grinning when a sleepy Mila came stumbling from the bedroom into the kitchen. She must have rifled through his dresser because she was wearing one of his T-shirts. It covered her to mid-thigh and was sexier than any lingerie he'd ever seen.

She gave him an adorable grin. "Hope you don't mind," she said, gesturing to his shirt.

"Looks a hell of a lot better on you."

She stepped next to him. "I smelled bacon, but the power isn't back on."

"Grabbed my camp stove from the storage closet. Got enough propane that we can probably cook breakfast, lunch, and dinner on it if we need to. Problem is it's only a one-burner deal, so we might have to get creative."

"I can do creative." Mila glanced out the kitchen window. "It stopped snowing."

"Yeah, but the wind is still kicking up pretty good, so the drifts are going to be a bitch. Not to mention there's another pocket of weather heading this way, and forecasters are saying it could dump another two to four inches on us. Looks like we're stuck inside another day."

Mila perched on one of the stools by the kitchen island, watching as he loaded the cooked bacon on a paper-towel-covered plate, then cracked a few eggs in the pan. "I'm okay with being stuck here with you."

Boone chuckled, because he was *more than* okay with it. He was a bit of a workaholic and not the type of man who liked to sit still for long periods of time. If he'd gotten snowed in by himself, he would currently be climbing the walls, bored out of his mind.

"Afraid I can't make toast or coffee, but there's some orange juice in the fridge."

Mila rose and grabbed the juice, filling two glasses and taking them to the island as he followed her with plates loaded with bacon and scrambled eggs.

"Smells good," she said, picking up her fork.

"Cooking breakfast is where I shine in the kitchen," he joked, as he claimed his own stool. His gaze drifted to her legs, bare from mid-thigh down, except for the socks she'd also stolen from his dresser to add to her outfit. "You look cute as hell."

Mila grinned at his compliment, shifting slightly on the stool. The action caused the shirt to ride higher.

Boone narrowed his eyes. "What do you have on under that shirt?"

Mila's instant blush answered his question before she could. "Nothing."

"Show me," he demanded.

"Boone," she said, giggling.

"Lift that shirt, darlin'."

Mila grasped the hem, flashing him a way-too-fast peek at her lack of panties.

Unable to resist, Boone leaned forward, reaching around her hip to run his hand over her bare ass beneath the shirt. He gave it a playful squeeze, as she grasped his upper arm.

Mila was a very tactile woman, constantly exploring his body. Last night, he'd fallen asleep to her fingers slowly circling his nipples, toying with the smattering of hair on his chest.

He loved her hands on him, loved the way her eyes darkened with desire and appreciation. Boone figured he was in decent enough shape for a forty-year-old man, but Mila made him feel like he was a hell of a lot more than just decent. It felt good to know he could still turn the head of a beautiful young woman.

Once they finished eating, Boone rinsed their plates, leaving them in the sink. He'd do a proper cleaning when the power was back on.

Her phone pinged with an incoming message as he reclaimed his stool.

"Jace just texted the family group." She read the message, then summarized for him. "He's about halfway through plowing the main road. Trying to make it passable enough that the electric company can get here to fix the power lines. Said he probably won't tackle the side roads or driveways until after the next storm passes."

Boone nodded. "Smart. If we get another four inches, he'll only have to plow them all again. He's definitely going to have to give the main road another pass or two, thanks to the drifting. Got one of those auto-texts from the school. You called it. They've closed for today and tomorrow, so Sadie lucked out. She won't be behind at all."

"Have you spoken to her?"

Boone pointed to where his cell sat on the island. "She texted me when she and Lena made it to Williamsburg, and I got a good-night message late last night." Boone didn't mention the text had come through at two a.m., so clearly Lena enforcing any sort of reasonable bedtime was out the window. "I'll call her later." Given her late night, he suspected Sadie wouldn't be up before one.

She might not technically be a teenager yet, but she sure as hell slept like one. She'd remain in bed until the afternoon every weekend if he'd let her. Which he didn't. The weekends were when they did their chores—laundry, cleaning house, yard work, and so on.

If Sadie wanted her allowance—and she did—she was expected to chip in. Boone was determined to raise an independent, responsible young woman.

"I'm glad you didn't have to cancel her trip. She was excited about seeing her mom."

Boone nodded but didn't add to the conversation because the last thing he wanted to think about now, when he had Mila dressed in nothing but his shirt, was his ex-wife.

"So, what should we do?" Mila asked, though the twinkle in her eye let him know she had some definite ideas.

Boone placed his hands on her waist, tugging her off the stool until she stood between his thighs. He pressed his lips to her cheek. "Once we take care of the matter of your punishment, the day is ours to do as we please."

Mila shifted her face back, slightly confused but, more importantly, intrigued. "Punishment?"

If there'd been an ounce of fear in her tone, he would have backed off immediately, but the breathless, excited quality of her question had his cock rock hard in seconds.

"You put yourself in danger yesterday, Mila. You didn't think I was going to forget that, did you?"

She tilted her head. "And you think it's your place to punish me?"

He gave her a wicked grin. "You made it my place last night."

Boone could tell Mila had a million questions to follow that pronouncement, but she held back. And he understood why.

Neither of them had brought up what would happen once they got out of this cabin. He wasn't sure what was holding Mila back, but for him, he'd held his tongue on the subject because what he wanted wasn't...

Fuck. It wasn't smart.

Most of his reasons for not starting a relationship with Mila continued to exist. She was still, to some extent, one of his bosses, and he could be jeopardizing his livelihood if things ended poorly between them.

Not to mention there was thirteen years between him and Mila. Would that start to feel like too big a gap at some point? Kasi and Levi seemed to do just fine with the age difference, but their relationship was new too, so he wasn't sure he should be looking to them as a case study.

And then there was Sadie. He'd never brought a woman into their lives. But maybe it was time to take her off his list of excuses.

For the first few years after Lena took off, Boone clinging to his bachelor status wasn't as intentional as he liked to pretend. The truth was, he worked a full-time job, then came home to a very young child. Most days, it was all he could do to get Sadie ready for daycare, work a long shift, then come home to tackle the dinner, bath, and bedtime routine. Those early days of single fatherhood all blended together into one never-ending period of exhaustion and fighting to keep his head above water.

It had gotten somewhat easier when Sadie started school, but by that point, Lena had introduced their daughter to no less than three new "uncles," and Boone refused to add to his little girl's confusion.

With Sadie in middle school, wiser to the ways of the world, it was stupid of him to keep using her as an excuse to stop looking for romance or a second chance at love. The problem was, he'd let enough years go by that he really had become set in his ways. Before Mila, the idea of trying to meet women and going out on dates sounded fucking exhausting and like more trouble than it was worth.

She had him rethinking a lot of things, and it was terrifying.

At what point was he just too damn old to start over?

Jesus. Boone needed to get out of his head.

Especially when he realized Mila had gone quiet too.

"You're not answering," he said, "so let me do it for you. It *is* my place. To protect you, and to show you the error of your ways when you do something dangerous."

Mila bit her lower lip, but not from nervousness. He got the sense she was trying to stop herself from saying too much.

Boone hated that she felt like she had to hold back with him, even though he knew he had no one to blame for that but himself.

Placing a light kiss on her cheek, he tilted his head toward the couch. "Go stand by the couch. I'm going to put you over my knee. I appreciate you saving me the time of having to tug your panties off before your spanking."

Mila took two steps toward the couch before self-preservation overruled that sweet submissiveness of hers. She started to speak, but he cut her off.

"You remember what you said last night?" he prompted. "About what you want?"

"I remember," she whispered.

"You said none of that would change. Has it?"

She hastily shook her head.

"Good girl," he praised. "Then we're going to spend the day exploring those things, giving you a chance to test them out, maybe figure out where some of your limits are."

Mila's eyes brightened. "I'd like that. Does this mean we need a safe word or something?"

Boone chuckled. She'd already admitted figuring out her turn-ons through fiction. "I'm not that kind of guy. I don't wear leather or wield whips and chains, and I'm not going to make you call me sir or master or any of that shit. Nothing we do is going to be a game. It's just you and me here, Boone and Mila. If you don't like what I'm doing, you say stop and I will. Understand?"

"Yes."

"And I mean it, Mila. Don't let me continue doing things that hurt or make you uncomfortable just because you think I want it. All I *ever* want is to bring you pleasure. Got it?"

"Yes," she said again. Before adding, "God, you are so hot."

He chuckled. "I appreciate the compliment, but that's not going to make me go easy on the punishment. You scared the shit out of me yesterday when I turned that corner and found you walking alone in the middle of the road in that hellish weather. I could have run you over."

Just saying those words made his blood run cold. He could have seriously hurt her…or worse.

"I'm not going to repeat myself," Boone said, glancing toward the couch when she remained where she was.

Mila started moving again, walking over to the couch, waiting patiently for him.

Boone followed at a slower pace, wanting to give her a second to consider what he was about to do. He'd never put a woman over his knee in his life, never realized how much he wanted to until her.

Sure, he'd swatted his lovers' asses in the heat of the moment, but those were more playful taps than a true spanking.

She'd accused him last night of not taking her desires seriously due to her inexperience. He hated to admit that was exactly what he'd done. The irony was...here was Mila, exposing him to a new and previously unexplored kink.

She watched as he walked toward her, her cheeks flushed with obvious excitement.

Sitting on the couch, he spread his thighs, patting one. "Put yourself over my leg."

Mila dropped down so quickly, he had to stop himself from laughing. Several times during the night, he'd felt her tighten her hold on him, obviously worried he'd pull away. Wild horses couldn't pull him away from her at this point.

She rested one of her elbows on the couch, holding herself in a plank, but that wasn't how this was going to go. He'd spent the better part of the morning lying in bed, watching her sleep, playing out this scenario, and praying she'd agree to it.

He wanted her to feel just how much she was in his control, so he pushed on the nape of her neck.

"All the way down," he demanded. "You can hold on to my leg or place your hands flat on the floor, but the only thing that should be in the air right now is this gorgeous ass of yours."

Mila followed his instructions, gripping the leg of his lounge pants. He hadn't bothered with a shirt this morning, merely tugging on the comfortable pants. He was amused when he considered that the two of them were basically sharing one outfit at the moment, her in the shirt and socks, him in the pants.

Boone pushed the T-shirt up, baring her ass. He took a moment to admire it because *damn* if his girl wasn't built for sin. Curvy in all the right places.

She jerked slightly, then shivered when he ran his fingers lightly over the soft skin, circling the small bruises from where she'd fallen in the parking lot. He'd take care not to hit those areas, and he sure as shit didn't plan to spank her hard enough to add any other color to her ass but a bit of pink.

"Tell me why I'm punishing you."

She peered over her shoulder, but he shook his head.

"Eyes down, Mila."

She complied. "I put myself in a dangerous situation."

"That's right. You did." He punctuated his words with a stinging slap to her right ass cheek.

"Ow!" Mila cried out. One hand flew back as if to cover her ass.

"Hands down," he demanded loudly.

The hand hovered midair for a second or two before dropping back to his leg.

Perfect.

Boone spanked her left cheek, alternating back and forth, even adding a few smacks to her upper thighs. He didn't stop in between. He'd told Mila how to stop this if she didn't like it, and he trusted her to do so.

Not that trust was necessary. Given the way she gasped and squirmed, anticipating his smacks and shifting her hips to meet them, he'd say Mila had hit the nail right on the head as far as this particular desire.

Her panting breaths and soft mewls were going to be his undoing. Once her ass was pink and hot to the touch, he stopped, cupping one of her cheeks and squeezing it, loving the way she groaned.

Dragging his fingers along her slit, Boone grinned when they came away slippery as an eel. "This was supposed to be a punishment," he said, even though that wasn't true. Boone could have simply told her to get over his lap and called this spanking foreplay, but he needed it to accomplish more than just giving them a chance to explore a kink.

Mila was a people pleaser, that trait so deeply ingrained in her that it would seriously bother her to disappoint someone. He hadn't underplayed his terror of nearly hitting her with his truck yesterday. So he needed her to know, to understand just how serious he was about her taking risks with her own safety.

"What are you going to do the next time something feels dangerous?"

"Boone," she started, his name more breath than sound.

He gave her another smack, this one harder than the ones before. "What are you going to do?"

"Call you," she gasped. "Call you for help."

He caressed her ass softly. "Good girl."

Mila trembled, unable to mask the impact those words had on her. Hell, it was hard for him to hide how much they shook him to the core too.

Bending forward, he wrapped his arm around her, tugging her until she was sitting in his lap. She narrowed her eyes when he grinned at her wince. He didn't spank her as hard as he could have, and he doubted the sting and color would last more than an hour.

"Punishment, remember?" he reminded her.

Mila nodded.

"You okay?"

Mila took a moment and considered his question. Boone's gut clenched at the thought that perhaps he'd gone further than she wanted, and she hadn't spoken up.

"It hurt," she confessed. "But I liked it. I always sort of thought *that* part of the romance books was fiction. But it stung and my ass feels like it's on fire, but I'm also so horny I can't see straight."

Boone couldn't help it. He laughed because she was too fucking adorable. Then he gave her a kiss on the cheek. "I could probably take care of that. Want to crawl back into bed with me?"

Mila was off his lap so quickly, she almost clipped his chin with her shoulder. "Thought you'd never ask."

Caught in a Storm

Boone rose as well, amused by the way she raced into his room and dove into bed.

He followed, stripping off his pants when he reached her. Mila was sitting, tugging off the socks, then ripping the shirt over her head. She climbed beneath the duvet before flinging the covers on his side back and patting the mattress.

As good as she looked in his shirt, she looked even better naked and in his bed. Mila's gaze was locked on his erection. She licked her lips. For a second, he considered letting her finish that blowjob she'd started last night, but this thing between them was too new and too uncertain.

Boone didn't want to come anywhere except inside her.

Once again, he was shaken by the thought of getting Mila pregnant. Jesus. Breeding kinks weren't his thing, but again… Mila was provoking all kinds of unfamiliar needs in him.

He drew in a sharp breath when she crawled across the bed on her knees, reaching out and taking his dick in her hand. She was a quick study, because damn if she didn't find the perfect grip and pace right out of the gate.

He let her jerk him for nearly a minute before grasping her wrist and tugging it away. "Lie down. Middle of the bed. Spread those sexy legs for me."

Mila's eyelids were heavy as she assumed the position he demanded.

"Put your hands up, lay them flat on the pillow, by your head. One of these times, I'm going to tie you up, but I don't have the patience to look for something to bind you with right now."

Mila lifted her hands in surrender, her nipples erect, her breathing shallow.

"Would you like that?" he asked, holding his breath. Boone was a little too fond of bondage. He'd owned all sorts of stuff when he was with Lena—handcuffs, straps, even a spreader bar —but all of that had gone to the dump after she left.

"So much," Mila whispered.

"Soon," Boone promised, as he climbed between her outstretched legs. Running his fingers through her slit, he pressed on her clit, circling it until she was writhing beneath him, her skin flushed with need. She was still turned on from the spanking, so it didn't take long before she was begging him to take her.

Boone made a silent vow to himself that he'd slow things down after this, that he would draw out the foreplay, build the anticipation.

Maybe.

Placing the head of his dick at her opening, he thrust in, driving straight to the hilt. There was a sleeve of condoms in his nightstand drawer, only a few feet away, but now that he'd been inside her without one, he couldn't go back to using them.

Mila's back arched, her inner muscles pulsing around him. God, she was already close. Too close.

Her eyes drifted shut and her hands rose, looping around his neck. Boone grasped them, pressing them to the pillow, a silent reminder that she wasn't obeying.

Her gaze rose to his. Her pupils were blown, her pussy soaking wet. She liked being held down, liked that he was physically restraining her.

Keeping hold of her wrists, he started to fuck her in earnest, pounding in and out of her with more force than he should use with someone so inexperienced. But slowing down wasn't an option when she wrapped her ankles around his waist, tilted her hips, and cried out his name loudly.

Her pussy clamped down around his cock like a vise, and Boone stopped trying to fight it. Bending, he kissed her as she screamed into his mouth, his fingers still locked around her wrists, as he came inside her. Hard.

She'd said the spanking had hurt, yet she liked it.

He got it, because this was by far the most blissfully painful climax of his life. It felt as if his balls were going to explode.

"Mila," he groaned, as the last spurt of come erupted. "Darlin'. *Fuck*."

It took a full minute before Boone managed to let go of her, dropping to her side.

Mila flopped toward him, her hand finding its way to his chest again. He lifted it, placing a kiss on her palm, frowning when he saw the red marks circling her wrists.

"I hurt you," he grumbled.

She shook her head without lifting it from the bed. "Don't feel any pain," she murmured, her words garbled enough that she sounded drunk. "Only feel good."

Boone chuckled, placing a kiss on the top of her head, the two of them falling asleep within seconds.

THIS WAS the second time Boone had woken up in his bed today, and he discovered Mila watching him, much as he'd watched *her* sleep first thing this morning. She'd looked so beautiful and peaceful, he hadn't had it in him to wake her. So, he'd studied her sleeping face, committing it to memory, because even as happy as he'd been, there was still that small voice in the back of his head telling Boone he couldn't keep her.

It looked like Mila was hearing the same voice, her expression too pensive, too serious, given what they'd shared.

"What time is it?" he asked, clearing his throat.

"Just after one."

They'd napped for three hours. Boone couldn't recall the last time he'd slept in the middle of the day without being sick.

"You okay?"

Mila nodded, but the affirmative response didn't match her expression. "The power is back on."

Boone glanced over to his nightstand where, sure enough, his alarm clock was blinking, waiting for him to put the right time back in.

"Came back on about an hour ago," she added.

"You've been awake all that time?"

She shook her head. "I kept dozing, waking up, then falling asleep again." She gave him a sheepish grin. "Someone wore me out."

"Not as much as you wore *me* out. Because I just slept like the dead for three hours straight."

Mila giggled, delighted, but the soft tinkling laugh didn't last nearly long enough.

It looked like the rubber had hit the road, and it was time for that talk they'd both been avoiding since the night before last, when Sadie snuck out of the house.

Before he could start, his phone rang from the kitchen. He considered ignoring it.

"It's probably Sadie," Mila said. "You should go get it."

Boone agreed, so he climbed out of bed, not bothering to pull on his pants. Instead, he walked to the living room, grabbed his phone, and started back to the bedroom as he answered it.

"Hey, Dad."

"Hiya, Donut. You having fun with your mom?" he asked as he returned to the bed, leaning against the headboard. Mila pushed herself up, sitting next to him quietly.

"Yeah. We did a movie marathon last night."

"Oh yeah. What did you watch?"

"Promise you won't be mad?"

Boone closed his eyes, counting to ten. "Sadie."

"*Magic Mike* and *Bridesmaids*."

Awesome. Leave it to Lena to show their daughter an Rrated movie about strippers. If he wasn't sitting next to Mila, he'd probably ask to speak to Lena, but he was already facing one difficult conversation today and had no desire to double down.

Ignoring the movie selections, he asked, "How much snow did you get there?"

"Not much. Aunt Carol said there's not more than three or four inches. Piper said you all got a ton, and school is already closed for tomorrow too."

"We got a lot. But the weather is supposed to clear by the weekend, so I should be able to pick you up on Sunday like we planned."

"Okay," Sadie said. "Mom wanted me to ask if you'd just come here so she doesn't have to drive to Fredericksburg again."

Of course, Lena thought it was smart to put Sadie in the middle of that argument. "I'll text her later about that," Boone said noncommittally, because that text was going to be a big HELL NO.

"Do you have big plans for today?" he asked.

"Yeah!" Sadie replied, excitedly. "Mom said I could hang out with Stella, so I'm going over to her house today. If the roads aren't too bad, her mom is going to take us to the mall, and then we're going bowling, and afterward, we're getting pizza and chilling in Stella's room."

Fucking great. Boone had specifically asked Lena to limit Sadie's time with Stella, and now it sounded like she was leaving their daughter with the world's more irresponsible parents for the entire day.

"Thought you and your mom were spending time together."

Sadie's brief silence warned Boone he wasn't going to like what was coming next. "Mom's boyfriend, Uncle Adam, came with her. They're going to the movies and out to dinner because they want some alone time."

Yeah. Like they didn't get enough alone time in Florida, where it was always just the two of them.

But what the hell could he do or say to any of that? He was trapped in a foot and a half of snow in Gracemont, and even if he forbade Sadie from seeing Stella, Lena would still drop her off anyway, while making him look like the unreasonable hardass.

"Okay, well, behave yourself." Boone didn't have to see his daughter's eye-roll; he could feel it. "Have fun but make smart decisions."

"I will, Dad. I gotta go."

"Love you, Donut."

"Love you too."

The call disconnected, and Boone put his phone on the nightstand.

Mila leaned closer, shoulder-bumping him. "Everything okay?"

He nodded, even though nothing ever felt okay when Sadie was with Lena.

"You sure?" she pressed.

Boone must not have been very convincing, so he dug deeper. "Yeah. It's fine."

Mila didn't look assured, and it occurred to him he could talk to her about Lena's parenting, but this wasn't the time. For one thing, they were sitting together naked in his bed, and for another, they had their own issues to sort out.

He wasn't sure when Mila had become so attuned with his thoughts, but he could swear she'd just read his mind. Her shoulders slumped slightly, and she sighed.

"Boone," she started. "I've been thinking."

"So have I," he admitted, even though his thoughts were one giant swirling mass of conflicted feelings.

Mila put her hand on his forearm. "Can I go first?"

"Sure." Maybe hearing what she was thinking would help him figure out his own shit.

"I know that you're not interested in a relationship, and that your affairs since Lena have just been casual hookups, but—"

"This isn't a casual hookup, Mila," he all but barked.

Her nervous smile gave way to a genuine one. "It's not?"

"Good God, no."

She released a relieved breath. "Good. Because I was kind of hoping we could keep going."

He nodded, but wanting that and proceeding with it were the two conflicting parts. "I want that too, darlin', but—"

"You said I could go first," she interjected.

He lifted his hand, waving it in a proceed fashion.

"I know your primary concern is Sadie, and she should be. The two of you are making a life here, so we need to be careful. Boone, you haven't been in a relationship since Lena, and I've *never* been in one. We had sex, and it was amazing, incredible, mind-blowing," she said, her tone becoming louder with each descriptor.

Boone chuckled. "It was all that and more."

"But sex is only one part of this," she hesitated, before adding, "thing between us."

She was right about that. Sex was what led to his downfall with Lena. Because he'd gotten so carried away with the lust, as well as his desire to get to the next part—marriage—that he'd failed to see too many red flags regarding their relationship. While Lena had only been seven years younger than him, she was a hell of a lot less mature than Mila. He could argue that was because she'd been twenty when they met, but that maturity still hadn't grown as she aged.

"Sex is only one part," he agreed.

"And as amazing, incredible, and mind-blowing as it was," she repeated, "it's not the most important part."

"You're right."

"I think it's the other parts we should try to figure out, and it would be easier to do that if we weren't subjected to other people's opinions and thoughts on the matter."

Boone frowned. "What do you mean?"

"Until we see if this," again with the pause, "thing—"

"Relationship," he corrected her. "We're trying to build a relationship, Mila. You don't have to change the word because you think I'll go running for the hills."

"Okay. Relationship. Until we see if the two of us are as compatible as I think—I hope—we are, I don't think we should tell anyone about us."

Boone rubbed his jaw, stroking his beard as he considered what she was suggesting. "How would that work?"

"We both work on the same farm. I think we should reinstate the Tuesday night cooking lessons. Because it gives me a chance to spend time with you and Sadie, gives me a chance to continue to build a relationship with her as well. I think that would help when…if…we decide to make this Facebook official."

He chuckled at her description, but she was also right. Because his reason for not dating was because any woman he brought home wouldn't just be in a relationship with him, but with Sadie as well. He was touched that Mila saw that and was willing to put in the work.

"I agree."

"And I was hoping the two of you would start coming back to Sunday dinners. My family is a huge part of my life. I want them to know you, and you them."

For someone with no relationship experience, Mila had a firm grasp on the building blocks, on what would create a firm foundation for a successful one. Family was top of that list for both of them, and she recognized that.

"We'll come to Sunday dinner."

"Other than that, I think we need to chisel out some time where the two of us could be alone to get to know each other better. How would you feel about lunch dates? Sadie would be at school, and there are a million private places where we could meet."

In one short conversation, Mila found a way to take all the jumbled mess swimming in his head and tuck it away into neat piles. She'd broken things down bit by bit and made something that seemed virtually impossible to him not only possible but simple.

"I think lunch just became my favorite meal of the day," he joked.

Mila laughed. "Mine too."

"You know, Sadie doesn't get back until Sunday. Think we can come up with a reason for you to keep being snowed in here with me?" he asked.

Mila gave his question some thought. "I'll tell my sisters we're doing a puzzle."

Boone chuckled, thinking she was kidding.

When she didn't laugh, he asked, "A puzzle?"

"I don't do puzzles very often because I become sort of obsessed. Like, I don't look up or stop until it's done."

"And your sisters will buy that?"

"Nora will, because she's usually the one sitting beside me, just as obsessed. We might actually have to set a puzzle out on the table, just in case she tromps through the snow to help. As for Remi, twenty bucks says she's all but camped out in the stables, making sure her precious babies are warm and cared for. All her attention will be on them."

"Good. Because I'm going to be greedy and hoard you all to myself this weekend."

"Hoard away," she said with a happy smile.

Boone wrapped his arm around her shoulders, tugging her

against him. Now that they'd had the hard talk, he felt even closer to her than he had a few minutes ago. This woman got him, understood him better than he did himself.

Then, he considered Maverick's assertion that the Storms lived under that "love at first touch" curse, that they knew their soul mate the moment their hands touched.

Boone hadn't believed the story at the time, but now…

If it was true, Maverick was wrong. Because it was no curse.

Chapter Thirteen

Boone grinned as Mila hummed, flitting around the kitchen, flipping some chicken wings in a bowl, coating them in butter and garlic. The house smelled fucking awesome right now. He and Mila had basically remained sequestered in the cabin all weekend, only leaving on Saturday to help the rest of the family dig out all the businesses, clearing sidewalks and paths, before returning to "finish their puzzle," which, oddly enough, Mila's sisters totally believed.

Nora actually got mad that they hadn't invited her to join them. He and Mila had been hard-pressed to keep straight faces when Nora said, "Next time, call me. I don't mind walking through snow for something fun."

Boone couldn't help but wonder if Remi and Nora bought the lie because they'd hidden their interest in each other too well, or because her sisters considered the two of them an unlikely pairing. The second thought bothered him.

Life had returned to somewhat normal yesterday, as he headed back to work and Sadie to school. The only change had been at lunchtime, when Mila texted, inviting him to join her at the kitchen in the winery. The winery didn't open to the public until four, so it had been just the two of them, sitting on stools by one of the large counters. Yesterday, she'd made them grilled cheese sandwiches with tomato soup, and today, they'd had flatbread margherita pizzas. He really needed to revisit the running idea, because too many more lunches with Mila would be bad for his waistline.

Yesterday—somehow—they'd restrained from having sex, but after two days without being inside her, he caved after lunch today. Mila hadn't resisted at all when he'd tugged her into the pantry, told her to bend over and hold on to one of the shelves. They'd come together in a flurry of passion, fucking fast and furious. The more he was with her, the more he wanted her, and it seemed insane that there was ever a time when he thought he could get her out of his system.

He'd picked up Sadie on Sunday, and she'd been in a foul mood ever since. Reconnecting with Stella meant she was now pissed at him again for making her move. So he'd been subjected to the silent treatment for the past three days.

Mila arrived later than usual for their cooking lesson because she'd run to the store for tonight's ingredients. And while she tried, not even Mila could cajole Sadie out of her bad mood. Sadie bailed on helping them cook, then locked herself in her bedroom.

"Dinner's almost ready," she said, as he leaned on the counter next to her.

Boone glanced toward Sadie's still-closed door, then bent toward her to steal a quick kiss. "Smells delicious."

She smiled. "It's just wings and a big salad. Nothing fancy."

Boone would like to know what the hell Mila considered fancy. Because his mouth watered as he looked at the platter she was loading. She'd cooked a mess of wings, which she'd broken into three piles and coated in different flavors. They had a selection of teriyaki, garlic butter, and buffalo. And her salad was restaurant-worthy, with homemade croutons, shaved parmesan, and all kinds of vegetables, including corn and black beans. She'd topped it with a homemade buttermilk ranch dressing, which they were also using to dip their wings.

"Trust me when I say this is damn fancy." Boone reached out and snatched one of the wings, taking a big bite and closing his eyes in bliss.

Mila looked over her shoulder toward Sadie's room. "Do you think she'll come eat with us? She seemed kind of upset."

Boone probably should have warned Mila that Sadie's behavior right now was typical following a visit with Lena. In addition to the absence of rules, it was also hard for Sadie not knowing when she'd see her mom again.

That was what made this transition back to life as normal so difficult. Sadie was always sad/mad, and he tried to tiptoe around her for a few days because he didn't want to add to her pain.

"She's eating. You went to all this trouble," Boone started, pushing away from the counter.

Mila grasped his forearm. "Yeah. But if she's not hungry, it's no problem for me to pack a plate for later."

Boone was a huge believer in eating supper at the table as a family. Given the fact he worked long hours, even on the weekends, he needed this quality time with Sadie as much as she did. "It's dinnertime, and we eat together."

Mila nodded and let him go, carrying food to the table, as Boone crossed the great room and knocked on Sadie's door. "Donut, dinner's ready."

Sadie didn't open the door. "I'm not hungry."

"Didn't ask if you were hungry. Come and sit at the table with us. Mila's been cooking for nearly an hour."

"I'm. Not. Hungry."

Yeah. He was putting an end to this. He'd let her get away

with heating a bowl of soup and eating on her own last night because he'd worked late, and after his sex-filled weekend with Mila, he'd been exhausted. But tonight was a different story. Mila had gone to a lot of trouble for them.

Boone drew in a long, slow, steadying breath. Not that he felt much steadier after. "You going to come out, or am I going to have to ground you for two weeks? No phone, no iPad, no stables with Remi. How's that sound?"

Sadie's response was silence, followed by her door flying open. She stomped by him, pulled her chair out roughly, and plopped down at the table with her arms crossed. "It's stupid eating this early. What are we? Eighty? Mom and I didn't have dinner until nine."

Boone didn't bother to point out that six-thirty was hardly the early bird special and nine was bedtime, not dinnertime, because it wouldn't make a damn bit of difference right now. Sadie was pissed and determined to be a pain in the ass.

Mila gave him a sympathetic smile, then shrugged her shoulders slightly. She wanted to start their Tuesday dinners again so that she could get to know his daughter better. Figures Sadie would lead off with a doozy of an attitude.

He joined her and Sadie at the table, lifting the platter of wings and offering it to Mila first. He was glad when she piled a couple of each flavor wing onto her plate. He liked a woman with a healthy appetite. Given how hard Mila worked around the farm, and the fact she walked everywhere, she needed the calories.

Once Mila was finished, he held the platter out to Sadie. He knew his daughter well enough to know that she was waging an internal battle right now. She wanted to hold her ground and not eat, but the way she eyeballed the wings proved she wanted some.

Mila noticed her hesitance, so she helped him out, pointing to each variety. "That's garlic butter, which is my favorite, then teriyaki and buffalo. Your dad said you were a fan of spicy foods, so I included that last one for you." Mila widened her eyes dramatically. "Though I don't know how the heck you can eat something so hot."

Mila's easygoing nature worked as Sadie reached out, sliding four of the buffalo wings onto her plate. Then they passed the salad around.

Mila managed to get the conversation rolling when silence descended, filling Sadie in on how the pregnant cat fared during the snowstorm, letting her know how much Remi had missed having her help this weekend with the horses. She added that the donkey was slated to arrive next week, then she described the outrageous, super-comfy, warm cat house Remi had constructed in the corner of the stable, and how Mila had considered moving into the thing herself.

Sadie listened without much response, though she managed a few half-hearted grins.

Mila, bless her, was not deterred. Moving on from the stable gossip, she told a story about Jace almost plowing into Everett's car because it was completely buried in a snowdrift. The way Boone had heard the story from Maverick, Jace missed the thing by no more than two inches, Everett running from the house shirtless and barefoot through the snow to wave Jace down and warn him the car was there.

"How was your visit with your mom?" Mila asked, probably tired of being the only one talking.

Sadie shrugged. "It was good, I guess."

"Did you manage to do some fun things, or was the weather too bad? We got snowed in with no power. Had to find our own entertainment."

Boone hid his grin at the way Mila pointedly avoided making eye contact with him as she said the word *entertainment*. Fortunately, Sadie's eyes were locked on her plate and the carrot she was currently pushing around, so she didn't see Mila's blush.

"I went bowling and to the mall with my best friend, Stella," Sadie said when Mila paused, waiting for her reply. "Watched some movies at home with Mom and her boyfriend."

"Oh. I didn't know her boyfriend came to visit as well. What's he like? Nice guy?" Mila asked.

Sadie put her fork down and leaned back in her chair. "Adam's okay, I guess." His daughter had stopped putting any real effort into getting to know Lena's boyfriends when she was eight or nine. The clever girl figured out from a young age that it was a wasted endeavor. Boone was on the fence about whether that was a good or bad thing.

"Have they been dating long?" Mila was working overtime to keep any conversation going, but Sadie wasn't giving an inch.

"I dunno."

Mila took a sip of her wine, her gaze darting to Boone.

He grimaced, then decided to jump in himself. "How was school today, Donut?"

While it seemed like an innocuous question, Boone had apparently struck a match to the kindling.

"It sucked," Sadie spat at him. "It's a stupid backwoods school filled with rednecks and idiots, and I hate it!"

Boone scowled. "Sadie," he started.

"And I hate Gracemont! It's *boring*. I should go live with Mom in Florida. At least there's stuff to do there. Instead, you dragged me to the middle of nowhere!"

Boone wasn't sure exactly where shit had gone south, but he had a limit on how much rudeness he could take—and Sadie just hit it. "You were perfectly happy in Gracemont a week ago. Now stop slouching, clean up the attitude, and tell me what happened at school today that upset you."

Shit. His tone was as crappy as hers, but it'd been a long time since she'd pushed his buttons like this. He was out of practice with being patient.

Sadie crossed her arms, her lips pressed together tightly as she shot him a dirty look fit to kill.

"Maybe we can help," Mila offered gently.

Sadie exploded out of her chair, her face red with rage, her hands shaking. "We? What do you mean *we*? I don't need your help," she said. "You're not my mom, so stop pretending you are!"

"Sadie!" Boone yelled, but his daughter had already spun around, dashing to her room and slamming the door behind her.

Boone started to rise, but Mila placed her hand on his. "Give her a few minutes to calm down. If you go in there now, it's just going to get more heated."

"I'm not going to let her talk to you like that." Obviously, Sadie wasn't the only one who needed to calm down.

"It's fine, Boone. I'm a big girl and I know she didn't mean it." She lowered her voice. "Is she always like this after her visits with Lena?"

Boone nodded. "There's an adjustment period as we try to get back into our routines."

"She misses her mom. It's understandable. You said they don't get to see each other very often. Lucy was the same when our mom left."

Boone settled back in his chair, sighing tiredly. "She was?"

"I mean, it was a little different, because my mom left and stayed gone for a year. No visits. Just phone calls, and she sent us gifts on our birthdays. I told you that Lucy and Mom were really close, so when her birthday came along, we found out she'd been harboring this idea that Mom wouldn't miss it. Lucy was so sure Mom would come home to celebrate with her."

"But she didn't."

Mila shook her head. "Lucy hung out on the front porch from

the time she got home from school until dinnertime, even though it was windy as hell that day. My dad had come home on time, since it was Lucy's birthday, and Grandma had come over to make her favorite dinner—spaghetti with meatballs. It took Dad some talking to get Lucy to come in to eat. Then Grandma said something innocuous—I don't even remember what. Something about helping Lucy do something she'd wanted to do. Lucy erupted just like Sadie did. Yelled at Grandma. Said she didn't need any of them because Mom would be home soon. She stormed off to her room. Dad wanted to follow her, but Grandma said Lucy needed to get some of that pain out, and she was strong enough to bear it for her."

"You take after your grandma, don't you?"

Mila smiled. "I hope so. She was…everything. Sweet but stern. Thoughtful, generous, patient. I missed her when…"

"When her mind started to go?"

Mila nodded. "Dementia is like watching someone you love die in slow motion. Every day there was a little less of her there."

Boone reached over and held her hand, squeezing it.

Mila shifted her hand so that their fingers were interlocked.

"What happened with Lucy?" he asked.

"Ten minutes hadn't passed before we heard her crying. Grandma went to her, and I overheard Lucy apologizing, saying she didn't mean it. I didn't hear the rest of their conversation, but Lucy came back to the table for cake and presents, and she looked happier, more at peace. I wish I knew what Grandma said to her because maybe I could use her words to help Sadie."

Boone had been fighting a losing battle since the beginning with Mila. With those words, he gave up the battle *and* the war… because he was in love with her.

He cleared the lump blocking his throat as he tried to come to grips with that fact, and where the hell he was supposed to go from here. He couldn't drop those three little words on her already. She'd decided they should take things slow, and while he'd fallen hard for her, he wasn't sure Mila was there yet. Because as he'd learned the hard way at her age, there was a difference between love and lust.

Mila admitted after their lunchtime quickie that she understood how people could become addicted to sex. The time Mila had offered for them to get to know each other and to see how they fit together wasn't just for him. It was for her, too, and he hadn't given her enough of it. Hell, when he considered it, most of the personal sharing had come from her. He'd yet to tell her much of his own history.

They were both distracted by a sound coming from Sadie's room, and he bowed his head.

"She's crying." The sound broke his heart and he rose, ready to go comfort his daughter.

Sadie had been too young to feel the pain of Lena's desertion, but Boone had felt it for her...and for himself. In the past few years, Sadie had caught up to him, so at the end of every vacation, she suffered from the separation and from being left behind.

Mila stood too. "Do you mind if I..." She gestured toward Sadie's door.

Boone nodded without hesitation, considering the story she'd just told him about Lucy. He'd had countless conversations with Sadie about her mother, and he still wasn't sure he'd ever found the right words.

Mila walked to Sadie's room and knocked on the door. "Sade? Do you mind if I come in?"

While Boone heard Sadie's voice, he couldn't make out the words. It must have been some sort of invitation because Mila opened the door and slipped inside.

She pushed the door behind her but didn't close it all the

way, leaving a six-inch gap that he was certain was intentional. She wasn't closing him out or trying to overstep. She'd asked for a chance to speak to his daughter, ensuring he could hear it all and intervene if he needed or wanted to.

Boone hadn't asked her to carry his baggage, but damn if Mila wasn't proving she was strong enough to do so.

He silently crossed the room until he stood just outside Sadie's door. Peering around slowly, he saw Mila perched on the edge of the mattress, Sadie sitting. They were both in profile to him, so neither of them saw him standing there.

"I'm sorry I upset you," Mila said.

Sadie wiped her eyes, shaking her head. "I didn't mean to yell at you."

Mila grabbed a tissue from the nightstand and handed it to Sadie. "I know that. I'm sure it's hard having to say goodbye to your mom."

Sadie shrugged, trying to act like it didn't hurt her as much as it did. "I don't know when I'm going to see her again. It could be a long time."

Boone's chest tightened at her confession. While he tried to comfort her after each visit, Sadie didn't talk much about her feelings toward her mom, and suddenly Boone wondered if that was because she was protecting *him*.

"Boone said you spend a week with her every summer, right? I know that seems like a long time from now, but it's only a handful of months and I bet it goes fast."

Sadie sniffled, fresh tears falling. "Mom's not sure I can come this summer. She lost her job and said she won't have any money to do stuff. I said that was okay, but..." Another shrug that went through Boone like nails.

"Maybe she'll find another job before then. My grandma always used to say, don't borrow trouble."

"What's that mean?" Sadie asked, confused.

Mila reached out and ran her hand over Sadie's hair. "It means, it's too soon to worry about summer, but…I understand how you're feeling. It's hard being away from your mom. My mom left when I was eight."

"Remi told me your parents died in a car accident. I'm sorry."

Boone smiled sadly, so proud of his daughter for her compassionate words.

"Thank you. But they died when I was nine. My mom left us when I was eight."

Sadie frowned. "Remi didn't tell me that."

Mila sighed. "She was only five at the time, so I'm not sure how much she remembers of the year Mom was gone."

"Did your mom want a divorce?"

Mila nodded. "Yes. She wasn't happy living on this farm. She longed for bigger cities, more exciting places."

Sadie grimaced, recalling her comments at the table. "I don't really hate Gracemont. The people are nice, and I love this farm and the stables and the horses."

That confession from his daughter nearly brought Boone to his knees because he hadn't fully shaken his worry about that since the day he'd loaded the truck and drove them away from Williamsburg.

"I'm glad. Because you and your dad fit in here like you were born on this farm. Aunt Claire is already declaring you honorary Storms," Mila said, grasping Sadie's hand.

Sadie's smile proved those words meant as much to her as they did to Boone. "Were you close to your mom?"

Mila hesitated for a moment, and Boone recalled the anger she'd felt toward her mother. "We were," she said. "She used to call me her little Whippoorwill because when I was younger, I was as wild and crazy as Remi is now."

Sadie laughed.

"She used to brush my hair every night after my bath." Mila reached up, touching her own hair. "It always felt so good. And my mom gave the greatest hugs ever, whenever I was hurt or scared or sad."

There was something almost wistful in Mila's tone that told him she hadn't let herself remember the good things about her mom in a long time, too angry about the end.

"My mom gives good hugs," Sadie added. "Did yours come back for visits, after she left, I mean?" Sadie asked, proving she was still upset about leaving Lena.

Mila shook her head. "No. She was gone for a full year. And the only reason she came back was to sign the divorce papers. She and Dad drove to see the lawyer and…"

This time, it was Sadie who reached out to grab a tissue, handing it to Mila, who wiped her eyes.

"Was that when they died?" Sadie asked.

"Yes," Mila whispered, swiping her nose, then laughing self-deprecatingly. "I came in here to try to make you feel better, not start crying on your shoulder."

Sadie touched Mila's arm with genuine caring. "I don't mind. You really do get it, don't you?"

"I do," Mila admitted. "It sucks not having your mom around. But, Sadie, you're lucky the same way I was. You have your dad, and I had my grandparents, and Aunt Claire and Uncle Rex. And if you'd let me, I'd like to be there for you too. Not because I'm trying to take your mom's place but because I want to be your friend."

Sadie rose on her knees, hugging Mila tightly. "I'm sorry," she said, repeating her apology. "For yelling at you like that."

Mila pulled away, booping Sadie on the nose. "Forgiven."

Boone was touched by the way Mila treated Sadie so gently and respectfully—not like someone trying to "play mom," but as someone who saw his daughter and truly cared.

"Would you brush my hair?" Sadie asked. "My mom's never done that, and I want to know what it feels like."

Mila grinned. "Go grab a brush."

Sadie scurried to her bathroom, returning with the brush. Mila positioned herself on her knees behind Sadie, who sat on the edge of the bed. Mila ran the brush slowly through her hair several times, and Boone felt hypnotized by the smooth, gentle strokes.

"Now," Mila said. "What the heck is going on at school?"

Sadie launched into some serious middle school drama about the boy she liked suddenly sitting next to Piper in the cafeteria instead of her.

"Does Piper like him too?" Mila asked.

"She says no, because she knows I like him."

"Sadie, if you ever hear anything I say, please hear this—boys are dumb, and they are *never* worth losing a good friend over."

Boone had to fight to restrain his chuckle, then decided to walk away. Mila clearly had things well in hand.

He returned to the table, clearing away the dishes and packing the leftovers. He'd just started the dishwasher when Mila emerged from Sadie's room, closing the door behind her.

He raised a questioning eyebrow.

Mila grinned. "Piper called, upset that Sadie was mad at her. I didn't hear much, but I think they're going to mend things just fine."

Boone wrapped his arm around her waist, engulfing her in a hug. "Thank you for talking to her."

"Of course," Mila said, downplaying her role in making his daughter feel better.

Boone made a vow to compliment her every damn day until his woman learned her worth and realized just how special she was.

His woman.

Thinking those words felt right. Felt good.

"Come on. I'll drive you home." He knocked on Sadie's door, peeking his head in. "I'm taking Mila home."

She nodded and gave him a genuine, happy Sadie smile, then continued her phone call with Piper.

He felt twenty pounds lighter as he walked Mila to his truck, opening her door for her. Crossing to the driver's side, he climbed behind the wheel and they started down the lane.

Boone glanced over at her knee-length skirt, aware that she'd changed before coming to dinner because he knew *exactly* what he'd stripped off her at lunch. "Did you wear that skirt for me?"

She laughed. "Absolutely. Today was a bit challenging in that pantry, fighting with my jeans."

Boone chuckled. "So you were aiming for easy access?"

She shrugged, her face pure minx. "Maybe. If the spirit moved us and we had the opportunity."

Boone pulled the truck off the road, the two of them tucked in the privacy of the surrounding woods, far enough from both his cabin and her farmhouse that no one would see them. Pushing his seat all the way back, he reached out. "Consider the spirit moved. Get over here."

Mila giggled, climbing over the console until she was straddling his lap, facing him.

Boone had stolen a handful of quick kisses at the cabin, none of them enough for him. Kissing Mila was too good to be rushed. He gripped the back of her neck with one hand, guiding her this way and that as he deepened the kiss, his other hand slipping beneath her skirt.

Mila gasped, breaking the kiss when he slid his fingers beneath her panties. Her smile was sweet seduction when she started unfastening his jeans.

Sadly, they were both cognizant of the fact they couldn't take their time and draw this out. Not that they'd managed to do that this weekend, either, when they were alone with all the time in the world.

Boone might be a forty-year-old man, but with her, he felt like a teenaged boy. Every time he sank his cock inside her, it took everything he had to hold off. And the moment he left her body, he was aching to get right back inside.

Mila opened his jeans, drawing his boxers over his dick until it sprang free. Then she wrapped her hand around it, stroking until he moaned.

As she worked her fingers up and down his shaft, he did his own exploring, rubbing her clit several times before pushing two fingers deep. "You're soaking wet," he murmured.

"It's sort of becoming a problem for me," she admitted. "Happens whenever you're around."

Boone drew his lips down her throat, licking a path, before flicking the top two buttons open on her blouse. She still had her winter coat on, but it didn't hinder his progress when he shoved it and the blouse off, baring one shoulder so he could bite.

Mila gasped.

"Want you wearing my mark. Every day." Boone had never said anything like that to a woman. Hell, he'd never even thought it, but there was some deep, primal part of him that needed to leave proof that she belonged to him. Even if it was somewhere only he and she could see.

"Lift up, darlin'."

Mila complied, her hands digging into his shoulders as he guided his dick to her pussy. They groaned in unison when she sank down, not stopping until he was balls deep.

They froze there for a moment, just long enough for him to steal another kiss. Then he gripped her waist, helping as she pushed on her knees, and they were off to the fucking races.

Mila might have been inexperienced at first, but one week in proved she was a quick study. While he'd threatened/promised to tie her up, they'd never gotten there this past weekend. The sex too new and too exciting without bringing kink to the mix.

Mila rode him hard and fast, her chosen speed, and Boone used his grip to add his own force, loving the way she gasped and moaned and squeaked whenever his cock brushed different places inside.

Boone was getting close, but he hadn't come before her yet, and damn if he was about to break that record. He stroked her clit, aware it was her self-destruct button.

"God, Boone," she cried out, her body folding forward under the impact of his touch. "Too much. Too good."

"Ain't no such thing. Now be a good girl and come on my dick, darlin'. Squeeze all this come out of me." He'd also discovered that dirty talk worked just as well as her self-destruct button, when it came to making his woman orgasm.

Mila threw her head back, almost hitting it on the roof of his truck as her climax struck, pulsing through her and around him until she was milking him dry.

"Mila!" he groaned. "Darlin'…love."

They held on to each other, her hands wrapping around his neck, her forehead falling to rest on his shoulder as they struggled to catch their breath.

For a moment, she was so still and quiet, he wondered if she'd fallen asleep. If she had, Boone was fully prepared to spend the rest of the night right here, like this, holding her on his lap, his softening dick still deep within her.

Eventually, she lifted her head. "It keeps getting better."

He nodded. "It does."

"I'm never going to get enough of this," she admitted, before biting her lip, clearly concerned she'd said too much.

He tugged on her chin, dislodging her lip from her teeth so he could give her a quick kiss. "Me neither."

She smiled at him like he'd given her a dozen roses, and Boone huffed out a laugh. This woman was good for the soul.

They laughed together as they struggled to disentangle with their clothing messed up. Once she managed to get back to her seat, they took a minute to put themselves to rights. Mila buttoning her blouse and shoving down her skirt, Boone refastening his jeans.

He hoped her sisters were already in their rooms, because Mila had a dreamy, happy, just-fucked glow about her. Then he realized he didn't really care if Nora and Remi were awake or if they noticed. While he was prepared to give Mila time to be sure about them before they announced their relationship, he wouldn't be upset if the beans got spilled accidentally and sped up the process.

Then he considered Sadie...and he mentally slowed his roll. He wanted to tell her about him and Mila himself, not have her overhear it through the Stormy Weather Farm grapevine—aka Maverick.

Pulling back on the road, he drove Mila home. There was a light on in the living room, which made sense, considering it wasn't that late.

"Good night, Boone," Mila said, glancing toward the window, then bending close to give him a quick kiss.

"Night, darlin'."

"Meet me in the winery kitchen tomorrow for lunch?"

He nodded. "I'll bring the leftover wings and salad."

"Should I wear a skirt?" she joked, though there was no denying what answer she was hoping for.

"Mila, you could wear a damn chastity belt and it wouldn't stop me."

She laughed, blushing.

"Thanks again for helping Sadie. You handled it so well," he said, wanting her to know just how much he appreciated what she'd done for them.

"You're welcome," she said, wiggling her eyebrows playfully, showing off how well she'd managed to take his praise.

"Good girl. You're learning."

She got out of the truck, waving when she got to the front porch, then walked inside.

Boone backed out of the driveway and headed down the road, not aware until he'd walked into his own cabin that he'd been smiling the whole way home.

He was in love.

Hot damn.

Chapter Fourteen

Mila bent her neck to the left, then the right, trying to work out the kinks before continuing to mop the kitchen floor of one of the rental cabins. She was starting to think that maybe it hadn't been a great idea for her family to open an event barn and hire Gretchen. Not because both weren't doing fantastically but because they *were*.

It turned out, Gretchen and Everett made one hell of a team when it came to marketing the barn. Everett, the family's tech genius, had a gift when it came to online marketing, so he kept bringing in potential clients, and Gretchen, with her girl-next-door sweetness, managed to seal nearly every deal.

This past weekend, they'd hosted a massive family reunion, and once again, the B&B and every cabin had been rented. Ordinarily, she had a few days to clean the cabins and set them back to rights, but here she was on Tuesday and—she glanced at her phone—in three hours, a large group of guys was descending on the mountain, renting six of the cabins for a huge bachelor party. They planned to hit several of the breweries in the area, including Rain or Shine, while staying in the cabins for a couple of days. Once they left, she'd have to work overtime to turn them around again for another wedding next weekend.

Ordinarily she had Remi to help her clean the cabins, but her sister was out of town today, picking up their "beer" donkey. Gretchen had suggested getting a donkey as a fun add-on for the event barn, where the donkey would serve as a walking cooler, circling the barn with Rain or Shine beer in its packs.

The uptick in business was amazing, but between cleaning and running the kitchens, and trying to find time to sneak away to see Boone, Mila was running on fumes.

They were three weeks in on their secret romance, and every single day was better than the one before. Mila was certain her sisters—and a few of her cousins—suspected something was going on between them, because Boone, while never overtly crossing a line, wasn't great at subterfuge. Not that she minded.

For three weeks straight, he'd sat next to her during Sunday dinner, their chairs pushed together just a shade too close. Everyone was aware of their Tuesday night "cooking lessons," and her sisters had taken note of how Mila came home later and later after each one...typically with her hair askew and her clothes wrinkled.

While losing her virginity in the backseat of Todd's Dodge had sucked, she was a big fan of getting busy in the front seat of Boone's truck. And in the pantry. And in the winery storage shed. And once in the stable, where Remi had come *this close* to catching them.

Of course, even better than the sex—which was off-the-charts—was the lunch hour. More often than not, they simply sat side by side in the winery kitchen, talking about anything and everything under the sun. Mila had told Boone things about her and her past she'd never shared with anyone, and he always listened intently, like she was the most fascinating person on the planet. No one had ever made her feel so seen, so special.

With each passing day, he claimed a tiny bit more of her heart. It wouldn't take much longer before the whole thing belonged to him.

She was so distracted thinking about Boone, she didn't pay attention to her footing and tripped over the bucket of dirty water behind her. The bucket tipped, so she not only landed on her ass but also in a deep puddle.

"Shit!" she cried out, banging her fists on the floor, splashing more water on herself.

She didn't have time for this! Taking care of these cabins was the bane of her existence. At too many family meetings, she'd wanted to talk about relinquishing this part of her farm duties. She'd considered asking if someone else wanted to take them over, or if they could perhaps hire someone to do the cleaning part time, but she always held her tongue, hating the thought of letting everyone down. Her biggest fear was Aunt Claire would offer to take charge of them again. Her back wasn't strong enough for that, but knowing her aunt, she'd step in anyway.

"Mila?"

She turned her head as the door to the cabin opened and Boone walked in. She'd bailed on lunch today because she was on a time crunch in terms of getting the cabins cleaned.

"What the hell happened?" Boone rushed over, helping her to her feet when she tried to rise herself and slipped in the water.

"I tripped over the bucket." She stood and grimaced. Her jeans were dripping wet.

"Did you hurt yourself?"

She shook her head. "No."

"Are you sure?" he asked, as he ran his hands over her arms, hips, and legs, like he was searching for broken bones.

"I fell on my ass, which has plenty of padding," she said, attempting to wipe the concerned scowl off his face with humor.

It sort of worked when he shook his head, amused. "You have got to be the clumsiest woman I've ever met."

She wanted to protest that, but the truth was, she'd taken three tumbles since meeting him. "I swear I wasn't until I met *you*."

He snickered. "Blaming me?"

She winked. "Maybe. You distract me."

Boone pointed to the light red scar on his hand, a remnant from the bad cut he'd suffered a few weeks ago. "Ditto."

"What are you doing here?"

"You've been feeding me for weeks, so I thought I'd return the favor." He gestured toward the door, where she spied a couple brown paper lunch bags. "I know you're busy, but I didn't want you working through lunch. It's not good for you."

Mila sighed as she took in the dirty water covering the kitchen floor, then considered her soaking jeans. Cleaning the floor and herself would set her even further back on her list of daily duties.

"Come on," Boone said, taking her hand and pulling her out of the kitchen. "First thing we need to do is get you out of the wet jeans."

Mila giggled. "Always trying to get me out of my pants."

"Hell yeah, I am. Does this cabin have a dryer?"

Mila nodded.

"Great. Then let's toss these in there while we eat so that you're not walking home in wet pants. It's chilly today."

Mila held on to Boone's shoulders as he peeled her jeans over her ass and down her legs. She toed off her shoes, then lifted her feet so he could get them and her damp socks off. Then he reached around her, grasping her ass, tsking. "What a shame. Your panties are wet too."

Mila offered no complaint as he stripped those off as well, adding her sweater to the mix. The only thing that hadn't gotten wet was the long-sleeve tee she'd been wearing under the sweater and her bra.

Boone carried her clothes to the dryer, tossing them in and turning it on before returning to her. Taking her hand, he led her to the table, grabbing the lunch bags. He pulled out a turkey sandwich, bag of chips, and two of the chocolate chip cookies left over from Sunday dinner from one of the bags, and placed it in front of her.

"You tuck into that, and I'm going to mop the floor."

She reached out, gripping his arm. "Oh, you don't have to do that."

"Mila. Eat."

She wasn't sure what it said about her, but whenever Boone used that tone, she jumped to obey without thinking twice. Before she knew it, the sandwich was in her hands and she'd taken a big bite.

She didn't consider herself a weak woman, but she knew that wasn't what this was about. When she sought to follow his commands, it was because she wanted to please him, wanted to make him happy, wanted to hear him say…

"Good girl," Boone praised her, placing a kiss on the top of her head before walking to the kitchen. Within minutes, he had the water mopped, the floor looking better than it had when she'd cleaned it.

Dumping the water, he put the mop and bucket away, then joined her at the table, diving into his own sandwich and chips.

They'd nearly finished their lunch when Mila giggled.

"What's funny?" Boone asked.

"God help us if someone comes in and sees me and my bare ass eating lunch with you."

He chuckled. "That would probably require some fancy talk to explain."

"Not sure there's enough fancy talk in the world," she joked.

Boone rubbed his jaw, stroking his beard. "Of course, if we're going to all the trouble of explaining your half-naked state, maybe we should make it worth our while."

Before Mila could ask what he meant, Boone rose and reached for her hand, pulling her from the chair and planting the mother of all kisses on her lips. Mila responded in turn, wrapping her arms around his shoulders, lifting one leg around his thigh and humping it like a dog in heat.

Boone had opened a door inside her, revealing a legit sex maniac. Who knew that woman had been there all along?

The kiss went on and on, growing harder and hotter, until she was light-headed.

Mila pulled away when her back hit the wall of the kitchen, and she looked around, confused, wondering how they'd gotten all the way across the room. She didn't even realize they were moving.

Boone ran his fingers through her slit, smiling as he always did when he discovered her wet and ready for him. She would have thought he'd be used to it by now because she was *always* freaking wet and ready.

He slid his hands under her shirt, cupping her breasts over her bra, using the lace to stimulate her nipples when he pinched them. "Unfasten my jeans, darlin'. I know you don't have a lot of time, but it's been four days since I've been inside you, and I can't wait another second."

Mila's level of need matched his, and she was opening his pants before he even finished his request. She tugged his thick cock out of his boxer briefs, the two of them groaning in unison when she gave it a long, firm stroke.

She might not have a wide field for comparison, but there was no way Boone's dick wasn't on the upper end of average in terms of length and girth. Sometimes, she was amazed it fit inside her.

"Lift your legs around my waist and hang on."

Between the wall at her back and Boone's firm grip on her ass, Mila was able to do exactly as he asked, wrapping her legs around him, lifting until the head of his cock was in position.

Boone hadn't exaggerated his need as he thrust in deep, not stopping to give her time to adjust. Instead, he took her like a man possessed, pounding inside her like a jackhammer.

She loved when he took her this way, claiming her like it was their last day on earth. The way he needed her, wanted her... For a woman who'd been on her own for most of her adult life, it was a wonderful, magical thing.

Mila hit her head against the wall when she threw it back, the orgasm she hadn't seen coming striking hard and fast.

"God," she cried. "Boone!"

He didn't give way, fucking her through that orgasm and straight into a second, her vision going so cloudy at the edges, she couldn't see anything except him. His gorgeous face with those piercing dark brown eyes were locked on hers, a wealth of emotions swimming behind them.

They hadn't ventured into the "feelings" talk yet. Mila had offered Boone time because he'd had strong opinions about remaining single when they met, and she didn't want him to feel pressured into anything.

While Mila knew she hadn't needed time when she'd suggested it, she was glad now that they'd taken it. Because it was solidifying her belief that he truly was *the one*...based on a hell of a lot more than a "love at first touch" legend and great sex.

Boone cupped her ass, kissing her roughly, even as he continued to thrust. Mila was grateful for his strength because her body was limp after those two orgasms.

"Boone," she gasped.

"I'm there, darlin'. I'm there. Just hold on. One. More. Sec

—" Boone came with a harsh grunt, driving his cock deep once, twice, three times before erupting, filling her.

Panting for air, Mila let her legs fall, though they were as much good to her as wet noodles. Boone kept a steady grip on her hips, holding her upright until she was able to support her own weight.

As was his habit, he placed soft kisses on her cheeks, her forehead, the side of her throat, even the tip of her nose as the pleasure slowly started to fade and reality returned.

"We're getting pretty damn good at that," he mused.

"Sex while standing up?"

"I meant quickies, but yeah, we do tend to do it standing a lot. God, what would I give to get you in my bed for a night or fifty?"

She laughed, so happy he wanted more. She cupped his face affectionately. "Sometimes it's hard to remember we met just four months ago. I feel like I've known you forever."

"I feel the same way." His smile was brief, fading to a frown as he ran his finger under her eyes. "Getting tired of seeing you with dark circles under your eyes. You're spread too thin, darlin'."

"It's just been a busy week."

He scoffed. "You say that every single week. You're not taking care of yourself."

"That's not true."

"What did you have for breakfast?"

Mila closed her mouth because he wouldn't like her answer. She'd skipped it today, so she could get an early start on cleaning the cabins.

"Mm-hmm," he hummed, her response not necessary. "And you were planning to skip lunch."

"I would have grabbed something at the winery later."

Boone ignored her. "What time did you go to bed last night?"

"Boone," she started.

"Give me a time."

She lifted one shoulder. "It was sometime after eleven. Got caught up in wedding planning with the girls. Levi isn't going for a long engagement. I swear he'd marry her tomorrow if Kasi wasn't insisting on a big wedding. As it is, they've scheduled the event barn for the first weekend in May, which means we've only got a few more weeks to pull it all together. Kasi asked me to cater it."

Boone sighed. "You do too much."

"I love cooking, you know that."

He nodded, then glanced around the cabin. He also knew she wasn't fond of this part of her job, and he'd encouraged her to say so to her family. She kept intentionally avoiding bringing up the subject.

Before he could bring it up again, she rose on tiptoe, kissing him on the cheek. "I promise I'll go to bed early tonight."

"I'm going to hold you to that, Mila. I worry about you."

She smiled. "You do?"

Boone looked at her incredulously. "Of course I do."

Mila swore her heart grew seven sizes. She had zero experience with romance—apart from the fiction she read—so she wasn't used to a man saying such sweet things to her. Boone was turning out to be more swoon-worthy than any of the romantic heroes in her stories.

"Thanks," she whispered. It was all she dared to say, because if she kept going, she'd say way too much and drop three little words on him. While she grew more hopeful every day that this would bloom into a true relationship, she didn't want to ruin it by saying anything he might not be ready to hear.

Of course, not saying them didn't mean she didn't feel them. Deeply.

Boone must have misread her response, because his brows

furrowed. "You're important to me, Mila, so when you don't take care of yourself, it tweaks this part of me that…" He raked his fingers through his hair. "I can't always control."

"What do you mean?"

For a second, she wasn't sure Boone was going to reply. It didn't look like he was comfortable with whatever was bothering him. Then, he took her hand and led her back to the table, where they reclaimed their seats. Mila was still naked from the waist down, but self-consciousness wasn't a thing with her and Boone.

He took a swig of water, then finally answered her question. "When I care about someone, I become a bit overprotective."

Mila snorted. "I've seen you with Sadie. You're not exactly dropping state secrets here."

Boone shook his head, amused. "I'm not going to apologize for keeping a close eye on my daughter."

"And I wasn't suggesting you should. Especially not now. Preteen and teenage years are when you need to double down."

Boone chuckled. "Always trying to give me nightmares. What I'm trying to say—badly—is my controlling nature gets worse with…people I care about."

She was certain he was referring to his relationship with Lena, but she didn't say that for fear he'd shut down. Just like he always did whenever the subject of his ex-wife came up.

"In what way?" she asked, curious and maybe even a little bit concerned. So far, Boone's demanding nature hadn't scared, angered, or bothered her at all. In fact, all it ever did was make her so horny, she couldn't see straight.

"With people in the past, my inner caveman came out."

Mila grinned. "Inner caveman?"

Boone didn't share her humor. "Yeah. Started with my high school girlfriend, though it was slightly tamer with her. With each relationship, my controlling nature sort of got a bit stronger."

"How many girlfriends have you had?" Mila broke off a tiny bit of her cookie and ate it.

"Just the high school one, two women in my early twenties, then Lena."

Mila never quite knew what to make of the fact that Boone basically quit dating for all of his thirties. Sure, he was raising a child alone, but still...

"Give me an example of what you mean."

"When I was in a relationship in the past, I needed to know where my girlfriend was and who she was with."

She frowned. "Because you were jealous?"

He quickly shook his head. "No. I didn't give a damn if my girlfriends had friends who were guys, and it wasn't like I ever told them they couldn't go out. For me, it was about knowing they were safe."

"So you're not a jealous guy?"

Boone sighed, hesitated. "I haven't been in the past, but..."

She waited for him to finish his thought.

"I didn't like you dancing with the pastor at the Valentine's dance. I didn't like that one little bit."

Mila never thought she'd want to be with a jealous man...but clearly she was wrong, because Boone's admission made her insanely happy.

"What else?" Mila thought what he was describing so far sounded just fine.

"If we weren't together, I wanted them to call or text me as soon as they were home and in bed for the night. I liked being the last person they talked to each day."

"What happened if they didn't call or text?" she asked.

"What?" he countered, confused. "Nothing. I just liked hearing about their day. Liked saying good night and encouraging them to have sweet dreams...preferably about me," he added with a wink.

"Those wouldn't be sweet dreams, they would be dirty fantasies."

"Damn. If that's the case for you, darlin', I want you to start calling me every night."

"Okay, I will," she replied, not even sure if he was being serious or just making a joke.

Boone must have wondered the same about her, because he decided to clear it up. "Good girl."

"Nothing you've said seems over the top, Boone. It's all pretty sweet and romantic."

Her comment took Boone aback again, but she wasn't sure why.

"Did you tell your girlfriends how to dress? What they could and couldn't eat?"

Boone shook his head. "Of course not. I wear flannels, T-shirts and jeans ninety-nine times out of a hundred. What the hell do I know about fashion? And I wouldn't say anything about someone's eating habits unless they weren't eating *enough*, and I worried about their health."

"Is there anything else?"

"Little stuff." Boone cupped her jaw. "If one of them was working too hard, I'd make them slow down, make sure they got enough sleep." It didn't feel like Boone was talking about past girlfriends anymore. This time, she got the sense he was telling her how he'd be with *her*. If she was his.

"And if she had too much on her plate, I'd make her clear some stuff off. I wouldn't just watch her work herself to exhaustion, wouldn't let her say yes to everyone else at the expense of herself and her own happiness."

Mila bit her lower lip, because damn, if those three words weren't hovering right there again, poised and ready to be spoken.

If Boone thought he was scaring her off, he'd missed the

mark. She'd lost her parents when she was young, and while her grandparents loved her and took very good care of her, they were older, and they had already raised two sons and moved into the indulgent grandparent lifestyle. Which meant she and her sisters were given a lot of leniency.

Jace used to joke that as the baby of his family, he got away with bloody murder because his six older siblings had broken their parents' spirits. Obviously, he didn't mean it literally, but Mila always thought there was some truth to that.

So she liked the idea of someone watching out for her the way Boone spoke of.

"I think everything you've said sounds nice."

Boone's frown remained in place. "Not all of the others thought so."

Was his protective nature the thing that drove Lena away? Was that why he'd started this conversation like he was issuing a warning?

Mila rose when the dryer buzzed. While she redressed in mostly dry jeans, Boone cleared away the lunch garbage, then put a new bag in the trash can for her.

"I'll dump the trash on my way back to work."

She nodded her thanks. "I still need to tackle the bedrooms here, then I'll be finished with the cabins."

"I'd say good, but I know all that means is you'll be heading to the brewery and winery to start your next full-time job."

"True," she replied. "But...it's Tuesday, my favorite day of the week."

"I'm looking forward to you teaching us how to make quesadillas."

She laughed. "I appreciate you saying that like they're hard to make."

Boone wrapped his arm around her shoulders, tugging her toward him. "I thought wings and salad were simple fare until I saw the way you did it. You're an incredible cook. And the more I think about it, the more I think you should consider starting that catering business sooner rather than later. Kasi's wedding would be a great place to come out officially with the folks around town."

"I'd love that, but…" She glanced around the cabin. "I think it's still too soon."

Boone sighed but mercifully didn't push. "I gotta head back to work. See you at my place around five?"

She nodded. "I'll be there with bells on."

Boone gave her a soft kiss, one that lingered, though nowhere near long enough for her.

"Don't work too hard, darlin'."

She watched him walk back to his truck because *damn*, that man had a fine ass. Then she sighed and trudged to the bedroom.

Back to work.

Chapter Fifteen

A few hours later, Mila stifled a yawn, fighting like the devil to find a second—maybe third—wind. She hadn't napped since she was a kid, but God if she didn't long for one now.

She glanced from the cheese she was cutting to the kitchen doorway when Nora stuck her head in.

"Oh good. You're here. You got a minute? I was hoping we could chat in my office."

Mila nodded, putting the knife down and washing her hands before following Nora upstairs, to her office at the winery. She was surprised when she spotted Remi there, kicked back in Nora's chair, her feet on the desk.

Mila shot a look at Nora, who twitched a little when she saw Remi's dirty boots on her pristine desk. "Out of my seat," she demanded, circling the desk.

Remi dropped her feet and rose, grinning at Nora.

"You're a heathen," Nora murmured.

Remi snickered. "Someone's gotta keep you on our toes. All this perfection and cleanliness isn't good for you."

Nora rolled her eyes, claiming her own chair, as Mila took one of the two chairs across the desk from her, Remi the other.

"I thought you were getting the donkey today," Mila said to her sister.

"Just got back about an hour ago," Remi replied. "Hoping we can make this interrogation quick so I can make sure he's settling in okay."

Mila frowned. "Interrogation?"

"Intervention," Nora corrected, then tilted her head. "Although I don't think that works either. Investigation?"

"Come to Jesus?" Remi offered.

"What's going on?" Mila asked.

"We want to talk to you," Nora replied. Before adding, "About Boone."

"What about him?" Mila was hedging, but she wasn't sure how else to respond. She'd promised Boone they would keep their budding relationship on the down-low, but she also didn't want to lie to her sisters. Or continue to keep the secret. She'd always been close to them.

"Told you she'd play coy," Remi said, crossing her arms. "Why don't we just save you the trouble of trying to brush us off with a bunch of bullshit. Last week, you came home from your 'cooking lesson'," Remi air-quoted those two words, "with your shirt on inside out."

Dammit. Mila was really hoping her sisters hadn't noticed that.

"Oh. Yeah."

"Did this start when you two were snowed in or before that?" Nora asked.

"We'd kissed a couple of times before the blizzard, but yeah…things changed during the storm."

"Doing a puzzle," Remi said, shaking her head. "I nearly

laughed in your face. And the way *you* believed her," she added, gesturing to Nora.

"Mila's as crazy about puzzles as I am! Maybe worse. We get in that zone and we don't look up, Rem. You know this. Besides, she never once let on that she liked Boone, so why wouldn't I believe her?"

"So gullible," Remi muttered.

"I'm sorry I lied to you both, but Boone and I weren't exactly..." Mila paused. She probably should have put a little effort into figuring out how to break this news to her family. "We aren't telling anyone because of Sadie. Boone hasn't dated anyone since his divorce, and—"

"No one?" Remi asked, shocked. "Haven't they been divorced a really long time?"

"Ten years," Mila replied.

Nora's eyes widened, and she whistled. "Wow. That *is* a long time. Why hasn't he dated?"

"Sadie was only two when his wife left him, so for the first few years, he was raising a toddler on his own. Boone was working full time, so when he was home, he was all about her."

Nora smiled sadly. "I knew I liked that man. What a stand-up guy."

"He really is," Mila agreed.

"That covers the first five years, tops," Remi countered.

"Boone said he wasn't interested in a relationship, that he's too set in his ways at this point."

"Does he still feel that way?" Nora asked. "Because, Mila, all you've ever dreamed of is getting married and having a family."

"I know. And I still want that."

"But does Boone?" Remi repeated.

"That's what we're figuring out. We agreed to take things slow and see where they go. If he didn't have Sadie, we wouldn't have to keep it quiet, but he doesn't want to introduce her to a woman until he's sure about the relationship. He's not the only one with the potential to be hurt if things go wrong."

Nora nodded. "That makes sense."

Remi obviously didn't agree. "Sadie is a smart kid. I don't think you and Boone are giving her enough credit for being able to handle this. Especially since it's obvious you're already in love with him."

Mila didn't bother to deny it. "I am."

Remi was never one to mince words. "So how long are you going to keep sneaking around? I mean, there's going slow and then there's standing still. Boone hasn't introduced anyone to Sadie in ten years. That feels like zero movement to me."

"We didn't put a time limit on it," she said, trying not to panic over Remi's comment. "It's only been three weeks," she pointed out. "I'd hardly call that too long."

Remi leaned forward, resting her elbows on her knees. "I know that, Mila, but I also know that you won't put pressure on Boone when the time comes. I don't want him stringing you along forever."

"He wouldn't do that," she insisted, hating that neither of her sisters looked convinced.

"I like Boone a lot," Nora said, "but I'm always going to be Team Mila. It's your heart I'm most concerned about."

Mila appreciated that. "It's only been three weeks," she repeated.

Remi and Nora sighed in unison. "You're right. It's still early days," Remi said. "Just know that if this goes on for too long, we're going to hold another one of these interrogation/intervention/interview/come to Jesus meetings."

Mila laughed. "I'll considered myself warned."

Lark knocked on Nora's open door, peering inside. "Sorry to

bother you guys, but there's a woman downstairs in the tasting room, Mila. She's asking to talk to you."

"Wonder who that could be," Mila mused aloud as she stood.

Remi rose as well. "I need to head out, too. Meeting Sadie in the stable in ten minutes. She's going to help me name the new donkey. Oh, and before I forget, I'm pretty sure we're going to have kittens in the next day or two. Mama Mia is nesting and grooming like crazy."

Nora rolled her eyes because she wasn't a fan of the Mama Mia moniker. "Maybe someone other than you and Sadie should name the donkey."

Remi brushed off Nora's comments. "We have things well in hand. We're also making a list of names for the kittens, too."

Nora raised a hand, pointing her finger at Remi. "You are *not* naming my kitten."

"You might not get one if you keep bad-mouthing poor Mama Mia." Remi didn't really help her case, because every time she said "Mama Mia," she used a strong Italian accent, making it sound less like a name and more like an "oh my God" exclamation.

Mila snorted, then headed downstairs to the tasting room. There were only a few people there, as it was still early. She knew the patrons at the other tables, since they were Gracemont locals, so she assumed the woman sitting alone was the one asking to see her.

As she approached the table, she studied the gorgeous blonde. She looked vaguely familiar, though she couldn't place from where.

"Hi," she said, offering her hand. "I'm Mila Storm."

The woman smiled as she shook her hand. "Lena Hansen."

"Oh! You're Sadie's mom." Sadie had a photograph of her and her mom in a frame on her nightstand, but the picture was a few years old. Now, she knew why the woman looked familiar. "I didn't know you were coming to visit."

"I wanted to surprise Boone and Sadie." Lena gestured to the other chair at the table, so Mila joined her.

"Sadie will be over the moon," she said. "She's been dying to show you her bedroom and the stables."

"Yes," Lena said. "She's talked quite a bit about the horses. She helps your sister, I believe?"

Mila nodded. "Remi. Actually," she glanced at the time on her phone, "Sadie is probably on her way there now. She got home from school just a little while ago."

"I'll catch up to her soon. I wanted to stop by and meet you first."

Mila wasn't sure why she would be first on Lena's list over Sadie. "I'm glad you did. Sadie's told me a lot about you."

"Just Sadie?"

Mila frowned, confused by the question.

Until Lena added, "Not Boone?"

"Um…" Mila honestly didn't know how to answer that. Mainly because, despite how much the two of them had shared over the past few months, Lena was the one subject that Boone was decidedly closemouthed about. Mila had tried to initiate the conversation more than once, but Boone was very good at changing the subject or offering only monosyllabic replies to her questions about the woman. "Sure."

Lena laughed. "I was teasing you. Boone's not the most effusive of speakers. If he's not telling you what to do, and when and how, he's not talking, am I right? When we were married, I was hard-pressed to get him to string more than five words together."

Actually, Lena *wasn't* right, but Mila didn't feel as if she could contradict her. With Mila, Boone was quite talkative. And while, yes, he did like to give commands, they were always the sexy variety, and Mila didn't mind those at all.

Mila was saved from replying when Lark stopped by their table. "Did you two want to order anything?"

Mila looked at Lena, who shook her head.

"I just stopped by to speak to Mila for a few minutes," she told Lark, who glanced at Mila.

"We're fine," she added.

"Cool. Wave me down if you change your mind." Lark walked on to another table, striking up a conversation with Edith Millholland and her nephew, Manny. Edith owned quite a few rental properties in and around Gracemont that Manny did the upkeep on. Once a week, they held their "business meetings" at a local restaurant, or here, or at the brewery, though Mila didn't think much business was ever discussed.

"Sadie said you're teaching her to crochet." Lena crossed her legs, leaning back.

"I'm not sure how accurate that is anymore. This is one of those cases of the student surpassing the teacher. She's started making stuffed animals that are so detailed and beautiful, you wouldn't believe it."

Lena swept her long hair over her shoulder. "And you're giving her cooking lessons?"

"Yes. She and Boone are interested in getting better in the kitchen."

Lena snorted as if Mila had said something ridiculous. "Right. I'm so sure Boone wants to learn how to cook."

Her sarcastic tone had Mila's hackles rising. It was clear the woman was here for a specific purpose, and Mila wished she'd just get to it. "He's actually becoming a very good cook." She felt a strong need to defend Boone.

"I suppose I'd have to see that to believe it. Boone's one of those old-fashioned type of guys. A woman's place is in the kitchen and all that."

Mila shook her head. To hell with playing nice and not contradicting this woman. "That's not true at all."

Lena laughed in disbelief. "Well, people can change, I guess." Then she sobered up. "That's why I'm here, after all."

"What do you mean?"

"I'm sure you're wondering why I wanted to speak to you," Lena said, finally getting to the point of this visit.

"I'll admit I'm curious."

"Sadie talks about you quite a lot. She seems to be growing fond of you."

"I'm fond of her, too."

"I'm going to be very frank with you, Mila. You wouldn't be the first woman to cozy up to a man's child to get close to him."

"Excuse me?" Mila considered herself a peaceful person, but Lena was testing that.

"Don't take that the wrong way," Lena started.

"How am I *supposed* to take it? I'm not using Sadie to get to Boone. I care about Sadie because she's bright and inquisitive and fun to be around."

Mila wasn't sure Lena was even listening to her.

"Look. You're a pretty young woman, and I'm sure Boone, with his rugged good looks and slow country charm, must seem very appealing to you. But I need to warn you—whatever you think is going to happen between you and Boone, won't. He won't make you his girlfriend. He won't marry you. And there won't be any happily ever after with him."

Mila narrowed her eyes. "You and Boone have been divorced for ten years. I hardly think you—"

"That's right," Lena interrupted. "We've been divorced for ten years, and he's never once seriously dated anyone in all that time. He's never told another woman he loves her. Has he told you that?"

Mila pursed her lips. "That's none of your—"

"He's never asked anyone to move in with him and Sadie, never wanted anyone else to be a mother to her. Has he asked you to move in?"

"We've only known each other a few mon—"

Lena had a very bad habit of interrupting. "Mila, I was very young when Boone and I got married. Just twenty. We were madly, passionately in love. Our romance was a whirlwind, to say the least, and we got so wrapped up in it that we went too far, too fast. I was too young for the kind of relationship Boone wanted."

"A marriage?" So Lena was old enough to say "I do," but too young to understand what that meant?

"Once Sadie came along, I felt stifled, smothered."

Mila recalled Boone commenting that his controlling nature wasn't well received by someone in the past. Guess Mila now knew who.

"Most of my girlfriends were still single, going out every weekend, having fun. They weren't dealing with baby weight or shitty diapers or sleepless nights. What's that expression? The grass looks greener on the other side," Lena added, with a tittering laugh.

Wow. It was official. Mila hated Lena.

"I thought I wanted what my girlfriends had, so I left. Boone was devastated, obviously, but I figured he'd get over it and move on. I've come to see that I made a mistake. If I'd known Boone would suffer with a broken heart for so many years..."

Lena thought Boone was suffering?

Mila might have refuted that, but Boone's ex-wife was on a roll.

"The timing wasn't right for us back then. I needed time to spread my wings, to grow, and I have. Now...well, now, I think the time is right. I'm older and wiser. And obviously, Boone has waited for me. He never found anyone else because there *wasn't* anyone else for him. I've always understood him best, been able to tolerate his demands and his grumpiness and—"

"Grumpiness?" Mila asked. Boone wasn't grumpy at all.

Lena scowled. Apparently, it was okay for her to cut Mila off whenever she wanted, but the same didn't hold true when she was the one interrupted mid-sentence. "You don't know him as well as you think, Mila. Certainly not as well as I do. I was his wife."

Lena wasn't in Gracemont for Sadie. She was here for Boone. But why now? After all this time?

"I think you can agree that Sadie's at an age where she needs her mother," Lena continued.

Mila wanted to correct her, wanted to say Sadie was at an age where she needed *a* mother. Not necessarily her own. Lena hadn't been batting a thousand the past decade, so Mila wasn't sure why she suddenly thought she'd grown some sort of great maternal instinct.

"You're lovely and young, and I'm sure you could have your pick of any of the men around here. That's why I'm asking you to step back with Boone."

Mila wasn't sure why Lena was so certain there was anything going on between her and Boone. Obviously, there was. But they'd taken care to hide it from Sadie. "Lena, I don't know what you think—"

Lena raised her hand. "We're both grown women. No need to lie to each other. Boone is a virile man with strong sexual needs. But you shouldn't mistake those needs for affection."

Mila felt the strong urge to throw something at this bitch. "Don't presume to know anything about what's going on between me and Boone."

"Please. I'm asking you very nicely to step away from Boone so that we can work out our issues and become a family again. For Sadie's sake. She needs her mom and her dad. You claim to care about my daughter. Prove it," Lena added, attempting to use Mila's own words against her.

Mila drew in a deep breath, weighing possible responses, which was an act of futility since Lena wasn't the type to listen. The woman rose, smiling as if they'd just solved all the problems of the world.

"Well, I'm off to surprise Sadie and Boone. I suspect I'll be around the farm a lot from now on. This winery is absolutely adorable."

What. The. Fuck?

Lena reached out and took one of Mila's hands in hers. "I do hope we can put all of this behind us and be friends."

This woman was off her fucking rocker. As Grandma Sheila always used to say, "Never engage crazy, you won't win."

Lena waved and walked away as Mila remained at the table, reeling.

She tried to piece together the bits and pieces Boone had said about not wanting a relationship. For the most part, they all had to do with Sadie, or him being too old and set in his ways.

But what if those were just the reasons he'd listed out loud?

He never talked about his relationship with Lena. All Mila knew was that the woman left them when Sadie was two, and while Boone had eschewed dating, Lena had not. His ex had moved on, while Boone remained frozen.

Or he *had*.

Mila couldn't dismiss the past few weeks. Boone no longer felt like a man who was holding back or standing still, as Remi suggested.

She'd believed they were genuinely embarking on a lasting relationship.

No. Not past tense.

She still believed they were. Boone cared for her. Maybe

they hadn't said the L word, but there'd been plenty of times she'd felt it from him.

Hell, he'd shown her earlier today when he sought her out, brought her lunch, and worried about her working too hard.

"Wow. That's some hardcore thinking going on. Surprised there's no smoke coming from your ears."

Mila looked up and found her cousin Theo standing next to her. She hadn't even seen him approach.

He tilted his head, concern in his gaze. "Everything okay?"

Mila started to nod, to offer him a generic "fine"—but everything was *not* fine. "I just met Boone's ex-wife."

Theo glanced over his shoulder. "I wondered who the blonde was. Passed her when I was walking in. She here to see Sadie?"

Mila shook her head. "She's here to win Boone back."

Theo crossed his arms, scowling. "But Boone is yours."

She gave him a quizzical look that Theo answered with one of his affable, warm grins.

"You and Boone are about as subtle as a sledgehammer to the skull. The whole family suspects, but we agreed not to say anything until the two of you did first. Mom thinks you're probably taking it slow because of Sadie."

"That's exactly what we're doing, but obviously we're doing a crap job of it." Mila hadn't mentioned her belief in the legend to her sisters, afraid they'd think she was nuts. Theo, however, was a different story. "Theo, you said when you shook Gretchen's hand that first day…"

Theo's eyes widened. "You felt the lightning with Boone, didn't you?"

"I fell off a ladder, taking down Christmas lights. He caught me and… God, Theo, I swear I've been falling ever since."

"Hot damn," he breathed. Theo placed his hand on her shoulder and squeezed. "The legend claims another. Welcome to the club!"

She sighed, afraid the congrats were premature.

"I'm really happy for you and Boone. He's a great guy and lucky as hell to have won your heart. I'll make sure he knows that," he added, in true overprotective cousin style.

Mila closed her eyes, suddenly feeling very tired. "Maybe you missed the part where I said his ex-wife has returned to reunite with him."

"I didn't miss that part. Just don't think it's important."

"Why not?"

"Because you're a Storm. We're fighters, a force of nature. And when we find our soul mates, our true love, nothing stands in our way." Then Theo frowned. "You weren't sitting here actually considering giving up, were you?"

Mila shook her head. That hadn't even occurred to her. She and Boone had something special, something worth fighting for tooth and nail. Mila knew it all the way to the depths of her soul.

"Good for you. Let me know if you need any muscle," Theo offered jokingly.

Mila laughed. "Thanks."

"Got a meeting with Nora, and I'm now four minutes late," he said, feigning horror.

"You're in trouble," she teased, shooing him on.

Alone again, Mila leaned back, her shoulders relaxing, because her path forward was clear.

She was fighting for her man.

Chapter Sixteen

Boone stepped out of the shower, quickly drying off before wrapping a towel around his waist. He'd given Sadie permission to hang out at the stables until dinnertime on the off chance the kittens were born. He told himself it was because seeing new life come into the world would be a great experience for her, but his real reason was far more selfish. He was looking forward to an hour alone, cooking in the kitchen with Mila.

Their alone time was too limited as far as he was concerned. And while she'd been the one to suggest they go slow, he knew she made that offer for both of them. For him, because he was leery of introducing a woman into the life he'd built with Sadie, and for her, because she had zero experience with relationships.

It had been on the tip of his tongue this morning to tell Mila he loved her, but he'd held back. Because while his heart was all-in, his head kept telling him he'd been too quick to leap with Lena, and look how that had turned out.

In the end, he'd held back less because of his own feelings and more because he wanted Mila to have time to make sure of

Caught in a Storm

her own. This was all new to her, and he hadn't lied about his caveman needs in relationships. If she decided to be with him, he knew himself well enough to know he'd be all systems go.

He'd want her to move in. He'd want to be the first person she saw in the morning and the last person she saw before closing her eyes to sleep. He'd want the two of them sharing their locations on Find My Friends, and before the year was out, he'd have a ring—or two—on her finger. Given the fact they hadn't known each other more than four months, a long engagement made sense, but Boone wouldn't be able to hold out.

Not to mention kids. Mila had admitted to wanting them, and at forty, he'd want to start a family with her sooner rather than later.

Boone wiped the condensation off the bathroom mirror and grinned at himself. He was getting carried away, and he didn't give a shit. Nothing in his life had ever felt this right, except the day the doctor put Sadie in his arms.

He finger-combed his hair, brushed his teeth, then hustled out to the bedroom to get dressed. Mila should be here any minute.

He pulled up short in the doorway, scowling when he spotted Lena perched on the edge of his bed.

"What are you doing here?" he all but snarled.

Lena had been smiling, but it faded at his tone. "I came to surprise you. I thought you'd be happy to see me."

Boone had spent the past ten years essentially playing nice with his ex for Sadie's sake. He was always careful to temper his tone with Lena whenever Sadie was around. Clearly, he'd done too good a job if Lena had gotten the wrong impression in regards to his feelings for her.

"Sadie just saw you a few weeks ago," he pointed out. "Did she know you were coming?" Boone couldn't imagine Sadie would keep that a secret from him.

"No. I came to surprise you both."

Boone took a deep breath, trying to calm down. While seeing Lena again ranked at the bottom of his list, it was most likely on top of Sadie's. She'd been dying to show her mom her bedroom and the stables, so he should be glad that Lena was making the effort.

"Sadie's at the stables right now," Boone said. "There's a barn cat about to have kittens and she wanted to watch. She should be home in an hour or so for dinner."

"Perfect," Lena said, slipping off the bed and crossing the room.

Boone frowned, grasping her wrist when she attempted to touch his bare chest.

Her eyes narrowed briefly, unhappy at his rejection. Putting some distance between them, he walked to his dresser and pulled out some clean clothes. He tugged on the shirt, then carefully slipped boxers on under his towel.

Lena smirked at his efforts, not bothering to turn around or shift her gaze away, which pissed him off. Dropping the towel once he was covered, he threw on a pair of jeans, shooting her a dirty look.

"I stopped by earlier," Lena said. "But no one was here, so I drove down to Gracemont. Not that there was much to see. This town is tiny. I did find a market, so I bought some groceries. I thought the three of us could make dinner together."

"We have plans for dinner," Boone said, recalling Mila's arrival was imminent. He was anxious to get his ex out of his bedroom.

He started to walk to the door but Lena beat him to it, leaning against it.

"What plans?"

Boone gestured for Lena to move but she held her ground, looking at him in a way that told him she was up to something—and he wasn't going to like it. "Why are you really here, Lena?"

"I told you. I wanted to surprise you and Sadie."

"I thought you and Alan went back to Florida."

"Adam," she corrected. "And we did fly back. But things weren't working out. Between losing my job and Adam being a complete pain in the ass about it, I decided it was time to move home."

In other words, Adam wasn't going to foot the bills while Lena sat at home, pretending to look for work. Boone felt a spark of respect for the guy, because too many of her ex-boyfriends supported her for months, even years before wising up.

"Are you living with your sister?"

Lena shook her head. "No. We get along fine for short visits, but you know the two of us would kill each other if we tried to live together for any amount of time."

"Okay. So, you've got your own place in Williamsburg?"

"Not exactly."

Boone frowned. "What does that mean?"

Lena's eyes widened with exasperation. "Well, obviously, money is tight right now, and until I find another job, I was hoping I could stay here with you."

Boone laughed out loud. Because she was joking. She had to be.

She didn't share his humor.

"No. *Hell* no."

"Boone," Lena said, attempting again to draw her hand over his chest. "I don't have anywhere to stay."

"Not my problem."

"I should have known you'd be unreasonable about this. So, what? You want me to beg, Boone? Want me to plead?"

He shook his head. "No, I don't. Because the answer will remain no."

"You're not thinking this through," she said.

"What the hell is there to think through?"

"Sadie is at an age where she needs her mother. If you let me stay here, she and I will finally have time to really bond."

Boone wanted to tell her she gave up the chance to bond when Sadie was two, but dredging out all the old anger and resentment would serve nothing.

"Listen, Lena," he started.

"Dad?" Sadie called his name from the living room.

Great. Boone would've liked to have settled the living situation before Sadie arrived.

Lena quickly spun, opening the door and walking out. "Surprise!" she yelled, laughing when Sadie stopped in her tracks.

"Mom!" Sadie rushed over, hugging Lena. "What are you doing here?"

Lena smiled, running her hand over Sadie's hair. "You made Gracemont sound so wonderful when we were together, I decided to come check it out for myself."

"Did Adam come with you?"

"No," Lena said lightly. "He and I are over."

That announcement didn't even make a blip on Sadie's radar, probably because she'd heard those words countless times before. "Oh. That's too bad. He was nice." The words were delivered by rote, with a minimal amount of emotion.

"So, I'm moving back to Virginia. In fact—" she started.

"Don't, Lena," Boone said, trying to cut her off.

"I was hoping I could move in here for a little while."

Sadie's eyes widened. "Really?" Then her gaze shifted to his face, and her smile faded. "Dad?"

"Sadie, it's not a good idea."

"I can share my room. The bed is huge," his daughter offered. Lena stepped beside Sadie, wrapping her arm around her shoulders. Lena was an expert when it came to backing him in a corner, always finding ways to pit Sadie against him.

Sometimes—with smaller things—it worked. Simply because he'd learned to pick his battles. But this? Fuck no.

"She can stay tonight. *Only* tonight," he stressed. "Tomorrow, if she's serious about wanting to hang around, she can get a room at the hotel near Henley Falls."

"But, Dad—" Sadie started.

"I'm *not* changing my mind on this, Donut."

His tone, paired with her nickname, must have done the trick, because Sadie backed down.

Then he reconsidered that assumption when Sadie nodded and said, "Okay. I understand."

His daughter had gotten her huge helping of stubbornness from him…so her easy capitulation was enlightening.

Sadie didn't want her mother to live here.

Obviously, Lena had expected Sadie to fight until the battle was won, because she looked slightly shocked.

"But, Sadie, wouldn't it be better if I stayed here? I'd be here when you got home from school, and we could cook together. You said you liked doing that stuff with Mila, right?"

And just like that, a light went on.

Lena knew about Mila.

Boone should have expected Sadie to mention Mila to her mother. After all, she'd become a big part of Sadie's life here on the farm.

"Yeah, I do." Sadie looked around the cabin, obviously realizing that Mila hadn't arrived yet. Which was strange. She was late.

"You're back early," Boone said to his daughter.

Sadie nodded in acknowledgement. "Remi thinks there are still hours to go before the kittens come. She's betting they come in the middle of the night, just because it would be a major pain in her a—butt."

Boone was pretty sure, despite Mila's assurances early on,

that Remi was making no attempts to stem her colorful language around Sadie. Her comment just confirmed it.

Lena huffed, annoyed by the change of subject and the fact that none of this was going the way she'd anticipated.

Lena gestured toward the kitchen counter, where several grocery bags sat. "I told your dad I went to the market and bought the ingredients to make spaghetti. I remember that's your favorite."

It *had* been Sadie's favorite, before moving from Williamsburg. Mainly because she hadn't been exposed to anything better. That changed in Gracemont.

"Actually, my favorite dinner is meatloaf. Mila taught us how to make it. And she always serves it with garlic mashed potatoes and fresh green beans that she sautés in butter."

"Oh." Lena was clearly taken aback. "That does sound good."

Boone watched Sadie's internal struggle because, while she wanted to be appreciative of Lena's offer of spaghetti, quesadillas were supposed to be tonight's fare, and he and Sadie had both been looking forward to them.

Boone glanced out the front window, wondering once again what was keeping Mila.

"Well," Lena said, recovering quickly. "What if we make the spaghetti tonight and tomorrow, we can do the meatloaf? It'll be fun. The three of us cooking together."

"You're only staying tonight, remember?" Boone said, working overtime to temper his tone.

Lena's smile was pure malice. She wasn't finished fighting that battle.

Which was tough luck for her, because he wouldn't be moved.

"I need to run out," he said. Mila should be here, and Boone was worried that she wasn't.

"What?" Lena exclaimed. "*Now?*"

Boone nodded. "You two don't need me around like a third wheel. You were just saying you were looking forward to spending time with Sadie." Lena wasn't the only one who could manipulate situations. "You two have a fun girls' night, cooking and talking." Boone looked at Sadie. "But remember, it's a school night. Homework still needs to be done, and no staying up late."

Sadie nodded in agreement. "Okay. I only have a science worksheet to do. It won't take long." She looked at Lena. "I'm going to go put on my comfies, Mom. Be right back."

Lena didn't reply, watching as Sadie walked into her room and closed the door behind her.

"Boone. I was hoping we could eat dinner as a family."

He frowned. "Why would we do that, Lena? We aren't a family."

She reared back as if he'd struck her. "But…Boone…"

"Her bedtime is nine o'clock," he reminded her, even though he fully intended to text Sadie at that time to make sure she was in bed. God knew Lena wouldn't enforce it.

"But—" she started again.

"Don't wait up. I won't be back until late." Boone wasn't coming back until he was sure Lena and Sadie were asleep.

Heading to his bedroom, he put on socks and tennis shoes, returning to the living room the same time as Sadie. Lena was still standing in the middle of the room, looking completely lost. If Sadie wasn't there, Boone would have chuckled at her discombobulation.

Grabbing his truck keys, he walked outside, climbing into the cab. He drove straight to Mila's farmhouse and parked.

When he knocked on the door, he was slightly surprised when Mila answered. She was dressed in a similar comfy outfit to the one Sadie had just put on, and her feet were covered with a bright pink pair of fuzzy socks.

"Boone," she said, equally shocked to see him.

"What are you doing here?" he asked.

She grinned. "Last time I checked, I live here."

"It's Tuesday night," he pointed out. "Why didn't you come to the cabin?"

"I didn't want to impose."

"Why the hell would you think you're imposing?" he asked, confused, trying to recall if he'd said something at lunch that might have given her that idea.

"I know you have company, Boone, so I thought I'd, um…"

Shit. "You know Lena's here?"

Mila didn't reply.

"Invite me in," he demanded.

She stepped back, allowing him to pass. Closing the door, she gestured down the hallway toward the kitchen. "I'm heating soup for dinner. Need to stir it."

Boone followed her down the hall, inhaling deeply when he entered the kitchen. "Goddamn, that smells good."

Mila grinned. "It's my take on zuppa Toscana," she said, then listed the ingredients when he gave her a quizzical look. "I fiddled with the recipe a bit. Mine is Italian sausage, potatoes, spinach, and bacon. I made a loaf of sourdough as well for toast. You're welcome to join me, unless…"

"I'm not eating dinner at my house." Glancing over his shoulder, he realized the house was silent. "Where are Nora and Remi?"

"Still at the stables. I just got back from running soup and bread to them. They're both committed to staying with Mama Mia until the kittens arrive." As she spoke, Mila opened a mason jar and added more soup to the pan, then cut four thick slices of bread from the loaf, putting them in the toaster. "Is Sadie with her mom?"

Boone nodded. "How did you know Lena was here?"

"She stopped by the winery when she first arrived."

Boone didn't like the sound of that. The only reason he wasn't losing his shit right now was because Mila didn't look mad or even upset. "Did she need directions or something?"

Mila shook her head. "She came to speak to *me*."

Boone had been leaning on the counter, watching her work, but at that revelation he shifted, twisting her away from the stove so that she was facing him. "What did she say to you?"

Mila bit her lip, and Boone got the sense she was weighing her words.

Leaning down until his face was inches from hers, he narrowed his eyes. "Lie to me about this, Mila, and you'll find out not all spankings are fun."

Her blown pupils told him that threat had fallen way the hell short. And not just with her.

Because her suddenly flushed cheeks and heavy eyelids had attracted the attention of his cock. Now was not the time for an erection, but his dick wasn't getting the message.

"I guess Sadie mentioned me to Lena, and she wanted to meet me."

Boone gave her a look. "I know my ex well enough to know it was more than that. You gunning for that red ass?"

She laughed breathlessly. "Keep up with that threat, and you'll *never* find out what Lena said."

Boone chuckled, wrapping his arms around her waist, tugging her against him and letting her feel his hard-on. "Clearly the threat isn't working for either of us."

Mila's hand dropped, lightly cupping him through his pants. "I know we just had sex at lunchtime, but I swear, it feels like that was years ago."

This woman.

She was fucking made for him.

Boone gently extracted her hand from his dick. "Let's eat and talk, and then we'll make up for all those lost years."

Mila giggled just as the toaster popped. "Okay. I'll dip the soup, you butter the bread."

They worked side by side, then carried their food to the table. Mila went to the refrigerator and pulled out an open bottle of white wine, filling two glasses.

He lifted his glass, tapping it against hers. "To us."

Mila smiled. "To us," she repeated.

"So…you had the pleasure of meeting the ex." Boone hadn't talked to Mila about Lena much, and he regretted that now. Part of him figured he hadn't because he didn't like talking about Lena, period. She was a reminder of a very difficult time in his life. The way she'd walked out on him had left lasting scars. The other reason was less interesting, but probably just as powerful. After ten years, he'd gotten very good at holding his tongue about Lena because he never wanted Sadie to overhear him bad-mouthing her mother.

"She's a very beautiful woman," Mila mused.

Boone's opinion of Lena's attractiveness had been tainted over the years, the inside spoiling the outside. "She doesn't hold a candle to you."

"Can I ask," Mila began, "why did you and Lena get divorced? I know you said she left you, but…what led to that?"

"Lena was young when we married. Probably too young. She was pretty and charming, a social butterfly, the life of the party, and…"

"And?"

Boone sighed. "And restless. She wasn't suited for the quiet, steady life I wanted. When I came home from work, I just wanted to unwind, eat dinner together, maybe snuggle on the couch in front of the TV. Lena hated that, preferred eating out—even though we couldn't afford it—and meeting with friends for drinks. After Sadie was born, things became strained because those nights out were few and far between. When she left, she said she'd had enough of boring nights and my controlling nature. That she wasn't cut out for the whole marriage and baby routine, and that she wanted her freedom because Sadie and I were smothering her."

"Smothering."

Boone saw recognition dawning in Mila's gaze.

"Earlier today..." She pursed her lips. "Are you worried you'll smother me too?"

He rubbed his chin. "It's a concern. I know I can be overbearing. I'd never want to push you away because—"

"Boone," Mila interjected. "Nothing you described today sounded bad to me. It didn't come across as overbearing or smothering. It sounded...wonderful."

He frowned.

"I've spent my whole life dreaming of meeting a man who loved me so much, he couldn't stand to be apart from me. Someone who'd want to spend time with me, worry about me, and want to hear what I had to say. Even if it's boring stuff like what I did at work."

"You couldn't be boring if you tried, darlin'." Boone took a bite of soup and groaned. "Jesus, that's good."

Mila laughed. "You say that about everything I make."

"Because everything you make ends up being the best thing I've ever tasted."

Mila playfully slapped his arm. "No pressure there."

He winked, then took a bite of bread, aware he'd used her food as a way to avoid the Lena topic—again.

Mila realized that, too. "I'm sorry Lena made you feel like it was your fault she left. Because I don't think that's true. It sounds like you were two very different people. Did your other girlfriends accuse you of smothering them?"

Boone considered that, then shook his head. "No. I parted amicably with all three of them. My high school girlfriend went off to college, and while we tried the long-distance thing, it didn't work. Same with the second girlfriend. She got a job in Chicago. I couldn't live in the big city, so we agreed it was best to walk away."

"And the third?"

Boone shrugged. "We were a mismatch in terms of personalities. Realized we were better friends than lovers. She's married to one of my good friends now, Erik, and I see them from time to time." Boone grinned, recalling something he'd forgot. "Actually, the last time I ran into them, she elbowed her husband and joked that it would be nice if he tried to be a little more like me. Apparently, he'd forgotten her birthday. Don't get me wrong. Erik's a great guy, but he's a bit of a workaholic, and he walks around with his phone in his hand like it's an extra appendage. Hard to get his attention and hold on to it sometimes."

"So Lena was the only one who felt smothered?"

Boone hadn't put that together, but then again, he'd never considered those earlier relationship serious enough to attach the word *forever* to them. "Yeah. I guess so."

"I have to ask, Boone. Did you and Lena *ever* get along?"

Mila was asking the hard questions. Not that he minded, because she was viewing things from a different perspective and helping him to see that relationship in a new light. When Lena first walked out, placing all the blame on him, Boone was running on fumes, working all day, then coming home to take care for Sadie. Hell, he'd been doing that before she left, because the first thing Lena did when he got home from work was hand him the baby, claiming she needed a break after "babysitting" all day.

He used to hate the way she referred to raising their child as babysitting.

When she hit him with that smothering line, he was tired enough—and frustrated enough—to believe it.

"The sex was good," he replied, only half joking.

Mila snorted. "Do you and Lena get along now?"

Boone sighed. "I try to keep things civil."

"I feel like there's a 'but' coming."

He chuckled. "*But* she makes it hard. It's like you said, Lena and I are very different people, something that didn't become glaringly obvious until we were married with a baby on the way. As I said, I'm rigid," he added, casting her a sideways glance, grateful when she shook her head and rolled her eyes, disagreeing with him, even if he was right. "I'm set in my ways, Mila, I told you that. I like order and routine, so when I tried to encourage Lena to come up with a daily routine for Sadie—feedings and naptimes—I thought it would make things easier for her."

"It didn't?"

He shook his head. "She resented it. Told me I was trying to control her. Lena is chaos personified, always late, never prepared for anything. She used to laugh at me for making a grocery list. When she shopped, she grabbed whatever struck her fancy, which left us with a bunch of random crap that couldn't be combined into meals."

"Yikes." Mila raised her hand. "I must be rigid, too, because I would never shop without a grocery list."

"If it had just been her and me, we would have gone our separate ways and that would have been it, but we had Sadie. And I know Lena loves Sadie."

"Uh-oh. That's another one of those 'but' statements," she teased, taking a sip of wine.

"*But* our parenting styles are very different. When Sadie's with her mom, rules fly out the window. It makes things difficult for me when Sadie comes back home and suddenly there's a bedtime, iPad and TV limits, and the expectation that she'll brush her damn teeth." Boone ran a hand through his hair. "This is why I don't like to talk about Lena. I sound like a bitter asshole."

She shook her head. "No, you don't. You sound like a responsible, caring dad. Sadie doesn't know how much Lena bugs you, does she?"

"I would never let my emotions cloud the way she feels about her mom."

Mila grasped his forearm. "And *that's* why you're such a good dad."

"Thanks for saying that." It wasn't the first time she'd said it, but as she *was* the first—only—person to ever say that to him, it meant a lot.

"You said you haven't dated since Lena because of Sadie. Is that the only reason?"

Boone shrugged. "No, not really. Although she's the main one. In first grade, Sadie grew close to one of Lena's boyfriends, Bobby. He was a nice guy and obviously in love with Lena. He went the extra mile with Sadie whenever Lena had her for the weekend, buying her stuffed animals, treating her to ice cream, stuff like that. When she was seven, Bobby proposed to Lena, and she turned him down. Obviously, he stopped coming around, and Sadie cried. She couldn't understand why Bobby didn't want to do stuff with her anymore. I knew that if I brought a woman into our lives, it wasn't just me who had the potential to get hurt, but Sadie as well."

"That makes sense."

"What you're not saying is that it makes sense *to a degree*," he added, when it was clear she had more to say on the subject.

"By using Sadie as an excuse, you never ran the risk of getting hurt again. I mean, it was noble, but..."

Boone grimaced. "Cowardly. And you're right. I guess between that and the fact I was letting Lena live rent-free in my head—"

"How so?"

"I let Lena convince me I wasn't good husband material. Our marriage was rocky almost from the start. Lots of fighting. The more I tried to fix the relationship, the more she resented me for it. When she said I was smothering her, I guess I looked back on all the things I'd done—making the baby schedule, writing the grocery lists, setting a time each week to clean the house together—I assumed she was right. She told me I was a controlling bastard, and I believed her. So, I set the idea of dating and marriage aside, convinced I wasn't cut out for it."

"Lena thinks you've never dated because you're still in love with her."

Boone couldn't help it. He laughed hard and loud—because *what the fuck*? "You're joking," he managed to say, once he caught his breath.

Mila shook her head.

Suddenly, a light went on, and Boone's humor faded, his temper piqued. "What did Lena say to you earlier?"

"She asked me to step aside to give her time to win you back, because Sadie was at an age where she needed her mother and her father."

"So twelve is the age when a girl needs her mom? Not before?" he snapped. Then something else clicked. "Is that why you didn't come to the cabin tonight? Were you stepping aside?"

"Good God, no! I'll be honest, I debated with myself all afternoon about whether to stick to tonight's cooking lesson. In the end, I didn't want to ruin Sadie's visit with her mom, since... I wasn't sure how Lena would react if I showed up."

"Why does Lena even think there's something between us? We haven't said anything to Sadie."

Mila shrugged. "I'm not sure she does know for certain. I get the impression Sadie's mentioned me to her mom a lot. Lena knows I taught Sadie how to crochet and about the cooking lessons. She insinuated I was only befriending Sadie as a way of getting close to you."

"She said that?!" he asked hotly, considering revoking tonight's sleepover.

Mila raised her hand, attempting to calm him down. "It's okay, Boone. Water off a duck's back."

Her words did not help. "Mila, I don't want her treating you like that."

She scooted her chair close to his, and he was grateful for it. He hated any distance between them. Reaching down, he pulled her even closer, until her legs were tucked between his outstretched thighs, dinner forgotten.

"I assume Lena's with Sadie now," Mila said.

"Yeah. Guess I understand why Lena hit the grocery store now, determined the three of us were going to cook together tonight, playing happy fucking family."

Mila's eyes widened. "Wow. She's really committed to this idea of hers."

"What she's committed to is *Lena*. I figure two things are at play here, and neither of them have a damn thing to do with getting me back. One, you're the first woman Sadie's ever mentioned to Lena, and I suspect there's some competitiveness and maybe even jealousy at play. Two, Lena's been the 'dumper' in all her relationships, never the 'dumpee.' And she always had the next man lined up and in place. But Adam, the guy in Florida? He kicked her out, which means she's stuck with nowhere to go now. Apparently, she saw two choices—here or her sister's."

"She really thought you'd let her move in?"

Caught in a Storm

Boone understood why Mila was flabbergasted. "As I explained, I've been civil for Sadie's sake. Looks like I was a little *too* civil, because I obviously fooled Lena. I told her she could stay tonight, but if she's serious about staying in Gracemont for Sadie, she'll have to get a room at the hotel outside Henley Falls."

"I'm guessing she didn't take that well," Mila mused.

"It went over like a ton of bricks. I think she expected Sadie to take up the battle and wear me down, but..." Boone smiled as he recalled Sadie backing down quickly. "She didn't."

"That's...interesting."

Boone agreed. "So, my reasons for coming here tonight were twofold. One, I wanted to see why you hadn't shown up at the cabin—I was worried."

Mila squeezed his knee, pleased by his admission.

"And to see if there's a vacant cabin I could crash in tonight."

Mila ran her finger over her lower lip, the action pure seduction. "There is. Or...I don't expect Nora or Remi to come home tonight. They took sleeping bags with them, planning to sleep in the stable with the new kittens once they arrive. You could always stay here."

Boone liked that idea. A lot. "What would we say if they *did* come home?" He was ready to pull back the curtain on this secret romance, but if Mila didn't feel the same, he'd wait. Hell, he'd wait until the end of time.

"They already know about us," she admitted, surprising him.

"Since when?"

"Since last Tuesday, but I only found out today, when they dragged me to Nora's office and confronted me." Mila's cheeks pinkened. "Apparently when I got home last week, my shirt was on inside out."

Boone barked out a loud laugh. "Well, I guess that would do it."

"You're not mad?"

He shook his head. "Not at all."

"Good. Because I ran into Theo after my Lena encounter, and he confessed the whole family knows."

Boone ran his fingers through her hair. "I suppose we haven't exactly been subtle about it. Mav constantly gives me shit about my sudden excitement surrounding the lunch hour. He hasn't come out and said anything directly, but whenever noon arrives, he tells me to "say hi to Mila.""

She giggled, then quickly sought to reassure him. "They know we're keeping it quiet because of Sadie. They won't say anything."

Boone nodded. He appreciated their discretion, though it was obvious the time had arrived to come clean with his daughter.

"Mila," he said.

"Hmm," she hummed.

"Let's finish dinner, and then I want you to show me your bedroom."

Boone laughed when Mila picked up her spoon and started shoveling the soup in like it was her job.

"Slow down, darlin'. We've got the whole night alone and a bed to spend it in. I'm going to make sure we take advantage. Now…tell me about the rest of your day."

Chapter Seventeen

Boone opened his eyes, the early morning pale gray sky telling him dawn was on its way.

Last night had gone from being a complete disaster with Lena's appearance to one of the best night's he'd had in a damn long time.

After dinner, Mila had led him upstairs, where they'd taken turns undressing each other. From there, they'd lain on her bed and he'd made love to her, the two of them kissing, touching, talking, and losing themselves in each other.

It seemed funny that Lena believed Boone had been saving himself the past decade for her, when it was crystal clear to him the one he'd been waiting to meet and fall head over ass in love with was Mila.

He was unsurprised when Mila lifted her head from his chest. Like him, her internal alarm clock sounded early.

"Morning," she said softly.

Boone kissed her forehead. "Morning, beautiful."

Mila shifted to her back, stretching. The movement caused the sheet to slip down, revealing her bare breasts. Boone couldn't resist such a treat when it was laid out right in front of him. Shifting to his side, he cupped one, then leaned forward to draw her tight nipple into his mouth.

Mila moaned in pleasure.

"Sisters home?" he murmured.

Mila shook her head.

"How can you be sure?"

She snorted a breathy laugh. "Remi lumbers around this house like an eight-hundred-pound man. Believe me when I say, we would have heard them come in."

"Good," Boone said, sucking her nipple back into his mouth, drawing on it harder, loving the way Mila squeaked. They were still learning and discovering each other's turn-ons and limits. So far, their sexual desires lined up perfectly.

Mila closed her fists around his hair, her back arching to invite him to suck even harder. He savored that whimper of hers that was half pain, half pleasure. She'd confessed during one of their Tuesday night truck quickies that she liked when he pinched her nipples, enjoyed the flash of pain more than she expected.

If he could, he'd spend the rest of the day focused solely on her gorgeous tits, but the clock was ticking…as always. He swore to himself that one day—hopefully soon—he and Mila wouldn't always have to steal these too-brief moments.

Dragging his tongue through the valley of her breasts, he continued downward, amused when she giggled as he made his way over her stomach. His girl was ticklish. He teasingly dipped the tip of his tongue into her belly button, her hands swatting him away as she laughed harder.

"Boone."

He placed a quick kiss on her stomach, then preceded to journey downward until he hit his true goal. Mila confessed early on that he was the first man to ever go down on her, and then she let him know that she was "a big fan."

Laughter had become an integral part of their liaisons. Despite their short association, they'd grown truly comfortable with each other, Boone feeling more at ease with her than any other person he'd ever known. Mila remarked that it felt like they'd known each other for much longer, and he agreed. In some ways, it felt as if she'd always been a part of his life because she fit so seamlessly into it.

Mila gasped when Boone wrapped his lips around her clit, sucking on it.

"God," she said, her fingers stroking through his hair, her body writhing.

He drew his tongue along her slit, pushing it inside her as she cried out his name.

"So good," she said.

Boone loved how responsive Mila was. She was already soaking wet and ready for him. At some point, perhaps she'd learn how to hold back her orgasms, but right now, as this was all too new and powerful, she tended to come very quickly and multiple times. Boone wasn't going to pretend that was not a huge turn-on—and ego boost. There were times when he felt every minute of his forty years, but that vanished with Mila. With her, he felt as vigorous and virile as a twenty-year-old man.

Returning to her clit, he ran his tongue around the sensitive bud as he pushed two fingers inside her pussy. Within a dozen strokes, Mila was there, her back arching as her climax struck hard.

Boone stroked her through it, drawing it out until the last tremors of her inner muscles faded away. Only then did he pull his fingers out and crawl back over her body. Kissing her flushed cheek, he pressed his lips to her ear.

"Roll over, darlin'."

Mila's eyes lit up. She was also a big fan of doggie style, another of her late-night confessions, when they were cabin-bound during the snowstorm.

Flipping to her stomach, she let him lift her hips, planting her knees on the mattress. When she started to lift her upper body, he pressed on the nape of her neck.

"Head down."

She turned her head to the side, resting it on a pillow. Her eyes were closed, her face the picture of trust.

Boone ran his finger through her slit again, but this time, he didn't stop until he reached her anus. Her eyes flew open as she looked over her shoulder at him. They hadn't explored this part yet, but that didn't mean Boone wasn't interested. He fully intended to claim every part of this woman, and once he did, he was never giving her up.

He raised one eyebrow as he pressed the first knuckle of one finger inside the tight hole.

"Boone," she whispered.

"I want all of you, Mila."

She blinked several times, then nodded. "I'm yours."

It was as close as the two of them had come to truly expressing their feelings. Hearing her admit she was his, impacted Boone more strongly than he would have expected. Those words were powerful and perfect, and, while he'd realized weeks ago that she'd stolen his heart, he didn't know just how much that would mean to him.

He smiled at her, then turned up the heat. Gathering more of her juices, he continued to toy with her anus until one finger was buried deep. Leaving it there, he guided his dick to her pussy, thrusting in as her hands flew upward, palms flat against the headboard, seeking purchase.

Boone took her hard, fucking her with his cock and his

finger, driving in and out of her pussy and ass, claiming the gift she'd just given him with those two words.

There was no turning back from this point. She was his.

Mila came in just a few minutes, her hands curling into fists as she panted, her breathing fast, shallow. Mindless words fell from her lips as he fucked her through that orgasm and into a second.

His name melded with a mix of curses and cries to deities as her body trembled roughly when she came again. Boone tried to hold back—he swore to God, he tried—but she squeezed him too tightly, milking every drop of come from his balls until his vision turned black.

Falling forward, he twisted to the side so he wouldn't crush her. Mila followed his movements, positioning herself as his little spoon, his cock still tucked inside her.

Wrapping his arm around her waist, he drew her back until they were pressed together from top to bottom. He kissed her shoulder, his lips resting by her ear as he told her how beautiful she was, how perfect. How she was made for him.

They remained there for a good ten minutes before Boone realized dawn had broken and time had run out. For now.

He groaned and forced himself from Mila's bed. He wasn't looking forward to the upcoming confrontation with Lena, but he needed to make it very clear to his ex that they were never getting back together. Knowing Lena, she'd put up a fight, unable to accept the word "no" with any sort of good grace.

He quickly threw on his clothes, then bent over the bed, placing a kiss on Mila's shoulder. She hadn't moved yet, looking delightfully relaxed.

"I know I need to get up, but I don't want to," she said, lifting her arms over her head. "I wish we could spend the whole day in bed."

"Wonder what the chances are we'll get an April blizzard this year," he joked. Those days trapped in his cabin with Mila had been pure bliss. If he had a time machine, there would be no question that was the moment he'd return to…over and over again.

"If only," she sighed.

He finished dressing, perching on the edge of the mattress to put on his socks and boots. Mila ran her hand up and down his back, the touch comforting and nice.

Boone was finished pretending this thing between them was a trial run. God, it had never been that for him. Not really. He'd agreed to it because he had Sadie to think of, but the truth of the matter was, Mila had started staking her claim on his heart the day she fell off that ladder and into his arms. "I think you and I should talk today at lunch. About the future."

Mila's hand stopped moving, and her happiness wavered slightly. "Is this going to be a good talk or a bad talk?"

Boone chuckled, putting one knee on the mattress and his hands on the pillow by her head. "I hope you'll think it's a good talk."

Mila's smile reappeared even brighter than before. "Okay, then. Yeah. I'd like to talk about the future."

Bending his arms, he dropped lower, placing a longer kiss on her slightly puffy lips. He'd spent a good hour last night worshipping them as they made love. Boone couldn't call what they'd done "fucking" because it had been so much more than a physical act.

He moaned again, then pushed away from her. It was that or rip off his clothes again and take her once more. Despite the fact her sisters knew about them, Boone had a lot of ground to cover before he and Mila broke the news of their relationship.

First, there was setting Lena straight, then having a serious heart-to-heart with Mila about where they went from here. And finally, he needed to talk to Sadie. Boone was most nervous about that conversation, because it was uncharted water for him and his daughter. He knew she liked Mila a lot, but for most of Sadie's life, it had been just the two of them. He didn't have a clue how she'd feel about expanding their family.

Because if things worked out the way Boone wished, they wouldn't just be welcoming Mila into their family but hopefully a baby or two in the future.

After that, he'd make sure every damn single buck in town knew that Ms. Mila Storm was his.

"Meet you at the winery?" he asked. On occasion, depending on their daily schedules, they'd meet at different places for lunch, but primarily they sat together in the winery kitchen.

She nodded. "Sure. I'll make us something special."

He grinned. "I'm looking forward to it."

He planned to tell Mila he loved her, and he was ready to take things to the next level. He hoped she was ready as well.

Waving, he left her room, letting himself out of the farmhouse. It was still early, not much after six a.m. If he was lucky, he could sneak into the cabin without Sadie realizing he'd been out all night. If she caught him, she'd ask where he'd been, and he really didn't like lying to his daughter.

The cabin was dark when he arrived home. He quietly opened the front door, slipping off his boots before making his way to the bedroom. Lena wasn't on the couch, so he assumed she'd opted to share Sadie's bed with her.

Walking into his dim room, he shucked off his shirt and jeans and was about to head to the bathroom to take a shower when he spotted someone in his bed.

"Where have you been?"

Boone scowled when Lena sat up, just barely holding the covers over her breasts. She was clearly naked.

"What are you doing in here?" he barked, trying to keep his voice down, because God help him if Sadie woke up and found them like this—Lena naked in his bed, and him in nothing but his boxer briefs.

"You were with *her*, weren't you?" Lena spat.

Boone put his hands on his hips, fighting like the devil not to completely lose his shit. "Where I was is none of your business."

"It *is* my business when you're out all night and Sadie's here at home alone."

Boone took two steps closer to the bed. "Are you out of your fucking mind? I didn't leave Sadie home alone. I left her with *you*, her mother. I've never left Sadie alone, *ever*, and I never would. Now get your ass out of my bed."

Boone recognized the moment Lena realized her mistake by starting an argument with him. The angry lines on her face faded. "Boone," she started, more conciliatory, using that sugary-sweet tone she employed whenever she wanted something.

"Get *out* of the bed," he said through gritted teeth.

"I shouldn't have spoken to you like that," she said. "It's just…I was worried about you."

He rolled his eyes. "Save the bullshit for someone who's interested in buying it."

Lena narrowed her eyes briefly but recovered quickly. "I didn't mean to fall asleep in your bed," she lied. "I came in here after Sadie went to bed, to wait for you. I wanted to talk to you about us. About our future."

He held up a hand. "Let me stop you right there. You and I don't have a future, Lena."

"Don't you think we owe it to Sadie to try?"

He huffed out an impatient breath. "I *am* thinking about Sadie. You and I are the biggest mismatch in history. There's no way I'd put Sadie through all those fights."

"We're older now, Boone. We've changed, grown."

He hadn't seen an ounce of growth on her part, but he wasn't going to open that can of worms. "Lena, you're only proposing this because you don't have anywhere else to go."

Boone wasn't sure what was worse. Lena's anger, her fake sweetness, or her fake tears.

She made no attempt to stem them, letting them slide down her cheeks. "I can't believe you think so badly of me. I'm here because I still love you. And I know you still love me."

He scoffed. "No, I don't."

"But you've never dated, never remarried," she said, as if that somehow proved her point.

"Not because I was harboring any feelings for you," he said, going for bluntness, since nothing else was working. "Lena, get out of that bed, put some clothes on, and try to find some self-respect."

Her crocodile tears evaporated in an instant. "You're the same asshole you always were."

She shoved the duvet down, climbing out of his bed, not bothering to hide her nakedness. Boone had seen it all before and wasn't looking for another show, so he turned his back and walked to his dresser, grabbing a clean T-shirt.

Lena pulled on the robe she must have been wearing when she snuck into his bed last night.

He gestured toward the door when it looked like she was ready to start the argument again.

Lena, furious, stomped by him.

He started to follow, but pulled up short when he heard Lena say, "Did you let yourself in here?"

Mila stood just inside the front door of the cabin with a canvas tote bag in her hand. Her gaze traveled from Lena in her damn robe to him in his boxer briefs, pulling a T-shirt on over his bare chest. He grimaced, then braced himself. He hadn't been gone from Mila's bed that long, but the two of them walking out his bedroom like this didn't look great.

Mila offered him an apologetic smile. "Sorry for just walking in."

"You don't have to knock, Mila. You know that." Fortunately, there was a pair of lounge pants hanging on the back of a chair near his bedroom door, so he tugged them on, as Lena shot Boone a dirty look over her shoulder. She probably would have added a few choice words as well, but Mila started for Sadie's room, distracting them both.

"Sadie called me."

"What?" he asked, panicking. Had his daughter heard him fighting with Lena?

He and Lena followed as Mila knocked twice on Sadie's door before letting herself in.

"Hey, Mila," she said weakly.

Boone hurried toward the bed, placing his hand on Sadie's forehead. "You sick, Donut?"

Sadie shook her head.

Mila gently moved him out of the way. "Girl stuff."

"Again?" he asked, aghast. "But didn't she just... I mean, I thought it was a monthly thing. It's only been a few weeks."

Mila huffed out a light laugh at his discomfiture. "It takes a while before it becomes a regular thing." She looked down at Sadie. "Sometimes a few years."

His daughter groaned in pain.

"What's wrong?" Boone asked, hating that Sadie was suffering. The last time she'd gotten her period, Mila had fixed her up in the middle of the night, and the next day, he'd driven her to stay with her mom, so he was flying blind here.

"Cramps," Sadie replied.

Lena had drifted into the room, perching herself on the opposite side of the bed. "Oh, baby."

Mila reached into her bag and pulled out Advil and a bottle

of water. She looked back at Boone. "Is it okay if she takes a couple of these?"

He nodded. "Of course."

Mila shook out two pills, giving them and the water to Sadie. Then she pulled something else out of the bag. "I raided Nora's 'I am Woman' shelf."

Sadie grinned, then imitated a lion, holding her hands like paws. "Rahrrr." She and Mila laughed, though Boone didn't get the joke.

Mila plugged in the electric heating pad and placed it over Sadie's abdomen. "I brought a box of ginger teabags, too. Nora swears by them. I'm afraid there's nothing else to do. You just have to wait for the pills to kick in."

"Okay." Sadie's gaze slid to him. "Can I stay home from school today, Dad?"

Boone had zero experience with this, so he didn't know if this was one of his daughter's ploys to play hooky or not. He looked at Mila.

"Cramps really are painful," she murmured.

"Tell you what, kiddo. Why don't we see if the medicine helps? If it does, I'll drive you in late. If not, you can hang out here today and take it easy."

Sadie smiled. "Okay."

"Sadie," Lena said, leaning forward and taking their daughter's hand. "Why didn't you come find me?"

"Last time, when we were in Williamsburg, you just said I'd learn to get used to the cramps."

Boone's jaw clenched. Of *course* she did. Their daughter had been hurting, and Lena hadn't offered her any real help at all.

"Well, you *will*," Lena said, as if that was some sort of defense. Then his ex looked at Mila, as if expecting support.

Mila, bless her, the sweetest woman on the planet, nodded. "It does get easier to deal with, Sade. Because you'll know what to expect and how to minimize the pain. Advil and heating pads will become your best friends."

"Thanks, Mila," Sadie said.

Boone could practically hear Lena gnashing her teeth from here. And he fucking loved it.

"Can we have meatloaf tonight, Mila?" Sadie asked softly, and this time, Boone could tell his daughter was laying it on thick. Not that he blamed her. Mila's meatloaf was the bomb.

"Yeah, sure. Of course. It's the perfect comfort food, isn't it?" she replied with a wink.

Sadie nodded. "Were the kittens born?"

Mila reached into the back pocket of her jeans. "I got a text from Remi as I was on my way over here." Flipping her phone toward Sadie, she showed her a picture. "Four kittens."

"Aw," Sadie cooed. "They're so cute!" Then she frowned. "But that's not enough."

"Not enough for what?" Boone asked.

Sadie lifted her hand, counting out a kitten per person. "Nora, Kasi, Gretchen, Mila, me."

Boone put his hands on his hips. "When did I say yes to getting a kitten?"

Mila and Sadie simply exchanged a glance and giggled like he was spouting nonsense, which he probably was. He'd known the second Remi found that damn pregnant cat, they were getting a kitten.

Sadie slipped deeper under the covers, yawning. "I think I'm going to go back to sleep for a little while."

Mila ruffled her hair affectionately. "Feel better."

Boone walked over and placed a soft kiss on Sadie's forehead. "Call if you need anything, Donut. I'll be here a little bit longer. After that, I'll just be in the vineyard, and you can text me."

Lena patted Sadie's hand but didn't say anything else before leaving the room.

He and Mila followed, and before he closed the door behind them, he looked back toward Sadie's bed. She was already fast asleep.

Lena dropped down onto the couch, heavily, looking strangely vulnerable. Something he'd never seen in her.

"I think I should go back to Williamsburg."

Boone remained standing, overwhelmed by equal parts relief and annoyance. While he'd be happy to see the back end of her, someone *else* would not. "Thought you wanted to stay close to Sadie." Lena hadn't even been here one full day, and already she was planning to cut and run and disappoint their daughter… again. He wasn't even sure why he was surprised.

Lena gave him a look. "You were right. I'm just here because I need a place to stay."

Mila tried to slowly make her way to the front door, clearly not feeling as if she belonged. Boone reached out as she passed behind him, grasping her hand to pull her next to him. She had a right to be here because, if he had his way, this was going to be her home. Very, very soon.

"Don't go." She started to protest, but he shook his head. "You're a part of my life now. Mine and Sadie's…and by extension, Lena's."

Mila stopped trying to leave, her unease giving way to… happiness. "I'm a part of your life?" she whispered.

Boone wrapped his arm around her shoulders, tugging her close. "Yes," he said simply. The two of them were going to have that talk, but not in front of Lena.

Lena was watching them closely, her lips pursed tightly together. She'd been defeated and she knew it. It wasn't often Lena didn't get what she wanted, so he wasn't surprised she was struggling to accept the loss.

"So, now you're just taking off?" he asked. "Without giving a shit that Sadie will be disappointed?"

"No," Lena said, hesitating. "I mean, yes. I'm not going to stay somewhere I'm clearly not wanted."

Boone pinched the bridge of his nose. Of *course* she was twisting this around to make it his fault. He lowered his voice, praying Sadie was still asleep. It was stupid to have this conversation here, with her in the next room, but Boone didn't want to drag this out. "I didn't say you couldn't stay in Gracemont. You just can't stay in this cabin."

"I have no money, Boone. I spent what little I had for the plane ticket home from Florida. I had to borrow money for a tank of gas from my sister. And I'm driving her car, which I need to return to her by Sunday. I can't afford a hotel, so I'm not sure what else you expect me to do. You've left me no choice."

This was Lena 101. Unable to solve her own problems, she blamed others when they wouldn't do it for her. It was why he'd bought the plane ticket for Sadie to visit her in Florida last summer. Why he'd always been the one to drop Sadie off at Lena's and pick her up. Why he'd covered ninety percent of Sadie's expenses for the past ten years.

And the reason she got away with all of that was because Boone refused to let Sadie suffer. She wanted to spend time with her mother, so he found ways to make that happen when Lena couldn't…or wouldn't.

"Boone," Mila said softly. "There are a couple of vacant cabins."

He turned to face Mila, unable to believe what he was hearing. Even after Lena's rudeness to her yesterday, Mila was trying to find a way to help. "Mila."

"Sadie hasn't even had a chance to show Lena the stables or introduce her to the horses."

Boone sighed, recalling Sadie making those plans one night

shortly after her return from her last visit with her mother. He rubbed the back of his neck...then nodded, just once.

Mila turned to Lena. "There are several cabins on the farm that we rent out to visitors. Quite a few of them are taken this week, but a couple aren't. They're all kind of rustic, but you're welcome to stay in one of those until Sunday, so you don't have to cut your visit with Sadie short."

Lena looked as amazed as Boone felt. "You really wouldn't mind?"

Mila shook her head. "Of course not."

"That's...that's really nice of you, Mila."

"There's one cabin that's pretty close to this one. I'll come back this afternoon with the key. We can head over there together, and you can settle in."

Lena was more subdued than Boone had ever seen her. "Thank you." Glancing at him, she said, "I think I'm going to go lie down with Sadie for a little while. I didn't sleep well last night."

He wondered how long she'd waited up for him. Given the dark circles under her eyes, he'd guess she hadn't gotten more than a few hours' sleep.

He and Mila watched as Lena walked back to Sadie's room, tiptoeing in and closing the door behind her.

Mila sighed. "Well, I guess I—"

She stopped talking when Boone grasped her hand and tugged her toward his bedroom. Closing the door, he placed his hands on her hips.

"Mila, earlier, when you got here... I realize that didn't look good, but—"

Mila laughed softly. "Boone, you'd only just left my bed."

"Yeah, but..." He raked his fingers through his hair. "I was stripping off to get in the shower. I didn't even see Lena in the bed. Apparently, she spent the night there, waiting for me to get home."

"Given what I've learned about Lena, that tracks," she said dryly.

He frowned. "You're not mad?"

Mila squinted, confused. "Why would I be mad about that?"

"I love you." Boone hadn't meant to blurt out those words, but now that he had... "I'm in love with you."

Mila smiled widely. "I'm in love with you too."

He kissed her, deep and slow. "I don't want to keep this thing between us quiet anymore."

"Neither do I."

Boone cupped her cheek affectionately. "Once Lena leaves, I'm going to sit down and talk to Sadie about us."

Mila bit her lower lip nervously. "Okay. Do you think... Should I be scared about that?"

He chuckled. "I was worried about that talk myself until this morning."

"What happened this morning?"

"Sadie called *you* when she was hurting. With her mother in the very next room."

"Oh," Mila said, as if just now realizing that. "Yeah. That's awesome."

"Plus, you've promised to make her meatloaf and garlic mashed potatoes. How could she not love you, too?"

Mila narrowed her eyes playfully. "I'm starting to think the only reason the Hansens keep me around is because of my cooking."

Boone couldn't resist teasing her. "Well, I wouldn't say that's the only reason, though it is pretty high on the list."

"There's a list?" she asked, giggling.

"Of course, there's a list."

"What else is on it?"

Boone grinned, because she'd set herself up without realizing it. "The most obvious one is because you're so sweet."

Mila gasped angrily, slapping his chest. "That's the meanest thing you've ever said to me." She might have sold the line if she wasn't laughing.

"Now, now. I just said that was one reason. Another is because you're so sexy."

"Ooo," she purred, running her hand down his arm. "The list is getting better."

Boone gripped her hips, pulling her lower body flush against his. "But the number one reason is because you're my very, *very* good girl."

The color on her cheeks and the way her eyes dilated told him just how much she liked that reason.

"So we're all systems go," he said, wanting to make sure she understood what that meant to him. "I'll talk to Sadie, and then we make it official with your family. We're a couple. We can date for a while if Sadie needs some time to get used to the idea, but... Well, how would you feel about sharing a kitten with Sadie?"

"Sharing? Why?"

"That way, when you move in, we'll already have the family cat. The ONE family cat."

"Move in?" she whispered, clearly in love with that idea.

"Yeah. The Hansens have gotten used to fine dining. So we're going to want it every night," he joked.

Mila laughed, and then they sealed the deal with one hell of a kiss.

Chapter Eighteen

Boone claimed the seat next to Mila, just as he had the previous three weeks for Sunday dinner. Lena had left a couple hours earlier, after what was a surprisingly pleasant visit. Of course, Boone knew who he had to thank for that. Mila had joined them for dinner Wednesday night, making Sadie's favorite meal as promised.

Lena had been quite friendly and charming, regaling them with stories about her humorless sister, Carol. The evening reminded him why he'd been attracted to her all those years ago, and made him feel just a little less stupid about marrying her.

Mila had kindly shown her around the farm when Sadie was in school, and on Saturday, Remi took his daughter and Lena on a trail ride, which his ex raved about for the rest of the evening.

There were still more than a few times over the past four days when shades of Lena's self-centeredness showed, but rather than get annoyed, Boone was able to be amused. Because Mila always managed to sneak him a wink or make a horrified face that only he could see. She helped him to laugh it all off.

When Lena left, she promised to return soon, giving Sadie *and* Mila hugs before driving away. Boone had intended to talk to Sadie prior to dinner, but she hadn't even come back into the house, following Mila instead to the B&B to help Claire cook.

The Storms were a chatty group, the mealtime conversations always entertaining. Sam was grumbling about some shit the former mayor was stirring up with the city council. Unhappy with his loss to Sam, Scottie Grover had apparently decided to become a pain in the ass, bitching about the city's proposed budget to anyone who'd listen.

Gretchen was talking to Kasi about the wedding that had taken place at the event barn the day before, sharing some of the cool things she thought Kasi might want to include in her own reception. From there, the discussion branched into what food Kasi and Levi might want for their rehearsal dinner and the reception.

Mila's suggestions were met with a lot of enthusiasm.

"You are so good at this!" Kasi gushed.

"She should be a caterer," Boone said, shooting Mila a grin. She rolled her eyes—but when he said the word "caterer," her family sat up and took notice.

"Oh my God, you totally should," Theo chimed in. "If we could offer that as part of the event barn's options…"

The second he said *that*, Gretchen and Nora jumped in, also excited.

"Finding a good caterer is the number one complaint we hear from people renting the barn," Gretchen added.

"Tell them your ideas for the winery and brewery menus." Boone was aware he was putting Mila on the spot, but he also knew she was facing the dreaded tasks of cleaning all those damn cabins this week after yesterday's wedding.

"What ideas?" Nora asked.

Mila described her idea for the grilled cheese and wine pairings, then talked about her plans to expand the brewery menu, as well.

"If we served meals instead of just appetizers, we could keep people at the brewery a lot longer," Theo observed, clearly impressed by the idea.

"The truth is," Mila admitted, "catering would be my dream job. I love working in the brewery and winery kitchens." She lifted one shoulder. "There's just never enough time with…"

"The cabins," Remi filled in. "I thought you liked running the cabins? Decorating them and all that stuff."

"I…I…uh…" Mila stopped talking.

"You kept doing it to help me," Claire said.

Mila started to shake her head, then stopped. "It's pretty physically grueling, Aunt Claire, and with your back issues—"

"I'll take over the cabins," Remi offered. "I would have offered before, but I honestly thought you liked running them."

"It's a nice offer, Rem," Mila said, "but there are a lot of times when the cleaning duties overlap with your trail rides."

Once again, Remi had the answer. "Then we'll hire Lark to work here full time. She's already waiting tables part time and performing on the weekends. She was just saying the other day she really needs to find a job with more hours. She can help clean cabins. She's tired of living at home, and she's trying to save enough money so she can move out."

"She'd *have* more money if she wasn't constantly spending hers on concerts and trips," Jace muttered.

Remi rolled her eyes. "Who cares what she does with her money? She's a free spirit. Point is, Lark's a great worker."

"When she's here," Jace stressed. "You better nail down her hours up front."

Boone was surprised by the hint of anger in Jace's tone. Of

all the Storm brothers, he was the most easygoing, which was saying something.

Rex nodded. "I think hiring Lark is a fine idea, Remi."

"Then it's settled," Claire announced. "Remi is now in charge of the cabins, we're offering Lark a full-time job, and Mila is Stormy Weather Farm's kitchen manager and, more importantly, our official caterer."

Mila blinked a few times, then turned to him, smiling widely. "Dream job," she whispered.

He patted her hand. "Congrats."

She laughed, leaning closer to whisper, "Thank you."

The rest of the meal felt like a celebration as Rex opened a few bottles of wine, everyone toasting Mila's new job title.

Once dinner wound down and the dishes were cleaned, he, Sadie, and Mila said their goodbyes.

As they approached the fork in the path, one lane leading to Mila's farmhouse, the other to his cabin, Sadie turned to face them. "When are you guys going to tell me you're dating?"

Mila and Boone stopped in their tracks.

"What?" Mila asked.

"I'm not an idiot," Sadie said, with enough exasperation that Boone couldn't help but smile.

"No one thinks you are, Sadie," Mila was quick to reassure her.

"How long have you known?" Boone asked.

"I saw you kissing by the car the night I snuck out. I got up to get a bottle of water and," Sadie shrugged, "there you were."

"That was well over a month ago, Donut. Why didn't you say anything?"

"I figured you'd tell me when you were ready."

Damn if Boone wasn't proud of the young woman who was blossoming before his very eyes. Of course, that pride was mingled with sadness, because Sadie wasn't his little girl anymore. Part of him wanted to keep her five years old forever, the two of them spinning in the kitchen, her in her yellow dress, him playing the Beast.

"To be honest, I planned to talk to you about this tonight," Boone admitted. "I know I haven't really dated much since your mom."

Sadie snorted. "You've never dated *anyone*, Dad."

Boone glanced at Mila. "Sometimes I wonder why I taught her to talk."

The three of them laughed.

"Are you okay with me and your dad dating, Sadie?" Mila asked.

Sadie's expression said it all. "Of course, I am." Then she looked at him. "You're happy with Mila. You weren't before."

Boone wanted to argue, but Sadie didn't give him a chance.

"I'm not saying you weren't fun or nice, but that's different. You were whistling in the kitchen the other morning." Sadie turned to Mila. "*Whistling*," she stressed, like it was the most unheard-of thing in the world. "You laugh more. And talk more."

Boone didn't realize until that moment just how quiet their fall had been. Sadie was furious about the move, and after too many arguments about it, and then her silent treatment, he supposed he'd stopped trying to convince her that coming here would be a good thing.

Then…he realized their house had *always* been too quiet, even before the job offer. They sat together for dinner, and he asked about her day. But after the meal, they tended to drift into silence, watching television together without much conversation.

Boone hadn't considered himself unhappy, but now that Sadie pointed it out… God. He'd always thought protecting Sadie was the most important thing, but by denying himself happiness, he'd been sending her a horrible message. Choosing fear and a risk-free life over love and happiness.

"I *am* happy, Donut," he admitted. "Happier than I've ever been in my life."

That confession left both his girls smiling widely.

"I'm glad." Then she turned her attention back to Mila. "Are you going to move in with us?"

Mila's gaze flew to Boone, slightly panicked. "No. I mean, not right away. And not unless you're okay with it. Or…"

Boone wrapped his arm around Mila's shoulders, taking her off the hot seat. Now that they'd started this conversation, it was time to drive home—to his daughter *and* Mila—just where he saw this going. "I want Mila to live with us, but you get a say in that, Donut."

"I think she should move in tomorrow. Think about it, Dad," Sadie said, eyes wide. "Meatloaf and buffalo wings whenever we want. No more frozen lasagna or yellow dinner."

Boone laughed, ruffling Sadie's hair. "Chip off the old block. The way to a Hansen's heart is through their stomachs."

"Tomorrow might be too soon," Mila replied, but Boone didn't agree.

He shook his head. "Tomorrow's not soon enough."

Mila studied him…and he realized he and Sadie were going to get their way. There was no reticence, no hesitation in her eyes. Just excitement.

"Can I spend the night with Nora and Remi?" Sadie asked. "Since tomorrow's the start of spring break, they invited me. We're watching both the *Mamma Mia* movies in honor of the kittens being born."

Boone nodded. "Sure. That's okay."

"Just Nora and Remi?" Mila added. "What about me?"

"Remi said you and Dad wanted to start a puzzle tonight."

Mila flashed him a look, while Boone tried to keep his poker face in play, because he honestly couldn't tell if Sadie understood that was code for sex.

"Oh, um, yeah, right. I forgot we'd planned to do that," Mila replied. She was going to have to work on banking her expressions. She was currently bloodred and slightly twitchy.

Boone covered his mouth with a hand, trying to play his chuckle off as a cough.

"Do you need anything for tonight? I can grab it and bring it over to the farmhouse," Boone offered.

Sadie shook her head. "Remi said she had a T-shirt I can borrow, and I can raid Nora's CVS closet for a toothbrush."

"Great." Boone ruffled his daughter's hair, as she tried to swat his hand away. "You sure you're good with everything?" he asked, because as many times as he'd played out what he would say to Sadie about Mila, he hadn't anticipated the conversation going so well or being so…easy.

"I'm great with everything." There was no question that Sadie was completely sincere…and that was when Boone realized what true happiness really felt like.

MILA WAS SLIGHTLY STUNNED by everything that had just happened. In one night, she'd gotten her dream job, the love of her life, and a family. She had to fight back tears when Sadie stepped over to her, hugging her tightly.

"I'm glad he picked you to fall in love with," Sadie whispered.

"Me too," Mila said, aware her voice was thick, clogged with emotion.

"I'm going to walk to the farmhouse. Y'all don't have to come," Sadie said, stepping on the opposite path. "Have fun doing your puzzle." This time, there was no question that Sadie got the code, as she gave them an all-too-knowing grin.

"I'm going to kill Remi," Mila murmured.

Sadie giggled. "She didn't say anything. Just said you wanted to do a puzzle. I believed her until you two just started acting all sketchy."

Mila shook her head, trying not to laugh.

"Shouldn't have taught her how to think, either," Boone said, reusing the earlier joke.

"I'm not a kid, Dad. I know you and Mila are gonna kiss and stuff." Sadie waved and walked on to the farmhouse. "See you tomorrow."

"So…" Mila started, once Sadie was out of hearing distance.

"What the hell just happened?" Boone asked, shaking his head, his disbelieving expression matching her emotions perfectly.

Mila was wondering the same thing. "I think we got Sadie's blessing?"

"Yeah, we did."

"And I think she knows we're having sex, if that's what she meant by kissing *and stuff.*"

Boone barked out a loud laugh. "I had 'the talk,'" he finger-quoted, "with her last summer."

"You did? Not Lena?"

Boone snorted. "I suggested Lena have it with Sadie when she was down in Florida, because I knew they were going to teach sex ed in seventh grade. Lena claims she forgot, but I'm sure that was intentional when she said I'd handle it better than her anyway."

Mila wasn't sure why anything Lena did or said still surprised her. After all, she'd met the woman, and it didn't take long to figure out Boone's ex would always choose the path that best suited her…and *only* her.

Then Mila grinned, trying to picture Boone having the sex talk with Sadie. "How did it go?"

Boone rubbed the back of his neck as the two of them started heading toward his cabin. "I did some research online and bought a book I saw suggested. It had cartoon pictures, and the two of us sat down one night on the couch and went through it. Longest twenty-seven minutes of my life."

Mila giggled.

"She asked a couple questions," Boone said. "Nothing too tough. Then I told her if she thought of anything else she was curious about, she could ask me or her teacher when it came up in class."

"No follow-ups?"

Boone shook his head. "Not so far. How much would it piss you off if I said I'm kind of hoping she comes to you if she needs further clarification?"

Mila rolled her eyes. "I wouldn't mind. As long as it's not specific to you and me kissing *and stuff*."

"We'll cross that bridge when we get there." Boone took her hand, and they walked together peacefully, neither of them talking as they let the dust settle on their Sadie chat.

Once they entered the cabin, Mila headed to the bedroom, oh so ready to get down to the "stuff" part of their evening.

Boone clearly had other plans, because he tugged on her hand, pulling her over to the couch instead. "Not so fast, darlin'."

"Boone," she started, but his chuckle cut her off.

"Cool your jets for a minute. Now that we've got Sadie's blessing, I'd like to hash out a few more things."

"Listen," Mila said, hoping to head him off at the pass and set his mind at ease. "Sadie was kidding about me moving in here tomorrow. Or at least, I'm pretty sure she was."

"She wasn't," Boone countered. "And neither was I."

"I didn't think you wanted to rush things."

Boone sighed and ran his fingers through his hair. "I've been working under the assumption for the past decade that my instincts when it comes to relationships are bad. I kept looking at all the mistakes I made with Lena—jumping in too fast, falling in instalove, moving things to the next level at the speed of light without really getting to know her as well as I should—as reasons to hold back with you, even though…"

"Even though?" she prompted.

"Even though I was doing all those things with you."

"The Sadie concern is a legitimate one, Boone."

"*Was* a legitimate one," he stressed. "And my daughter just took it off the table. She's as crazy about you as I am. I know Sadie, darlin', and I can see that. She wouldn't have said any of those things she just said if she didn't mean them. The fact she knew about us for a month and still reached out to you for things, still grew the relationship, speaks volumes to me. She didn't pull away or try to create distance because she was upset about this thing between us. She loves you."

Those words were as welcome as a fleece blanket on a winter's day. "I'm crazy about her too."

"And she knows that. Kids are astute, Mila. They know when adults are faking it with them. You've never offered her anything less than genuine friendship."

"So what are you saying, Boone?"

"When things started heating up between us—fast and furious—I freaked out, assumed I was doing it again. Making the same mistakes as before."

She tilted her head, trying not to get too excited, because while it didn't sound like he believed that anymore, she was terrified she was reading this wrong. "Are you?"

"I was young and stupid when I met Lena. I wanted to keep up with my buddies, wanted to be married with a family, and I tried to shoehorn her into that place with me. Even though it should have been obvious she wasn't ready or interested in the same things I wanted."

"The things you want, Boone…I want them, too," she tried to reassure him. "I've always wanted them."

He grinned, lifting her hand from her lap to kiss her palm. "I know we said we'd take things slow, but, well, I'm older and wiser now, and it turns out, I'm one hell of a judge of character these days. Because I know beyond a shadow of a doubt, you were meant for me, Mila. And if you'll give me the chance, I'll prove I was meant for you, too. For the rest of our lives."

Mila's eyes widened because even *she* hadn't let her thoughts go that far. She'd been sitting here hoping he'd invite her to move in with them. But this sounded like…

Like a proposal.

"The rest of our lives?" she whispered.

Boone gave her a crooked smile. "I'm not getting any younger. I'd like to have kids with you while I'm still able to pick them up."

Mila could barely catch her breath. Because while she loved Boone with her whole heart, a large part of her had been petrified he'd say he didn't want children. And she'd known if—when—that conversation came up, she would be forced to make a very difficult decision. "You want kids?" she asked, blinking away the happy tears threatening to fall. "Because you said—"

Boone cut her off. "Everything I said that first night was a big pile of bullshit. The ravings of a lunatic. I want *everything* with you, Mila. A home, marriage, family. What do you think? A couple kids? Sadie would be over the moon with siblings, the world's most doting sister."

"That sounds amazing," she said, her voice husky from emotion.

"I want to grow old with you on this farm, where we'll grow

grapes and make wine. Where we'll dance in the kitchen every night to your cooking music, watching my waistline expand."

Mila giggled.

"I'll have to take up running," he added, though she wasn't worried about that. Boone's job was very physical, and he prided himself on staying in shape.

Regardless, she couldn't help teasing him. "There will just be more of you to love."

He ruffled her hair. "I want to sit out there on that front porch, watching our grandkids run around the yard, playing. We'll spoil them rotten."

She nodded, swiping away a tear. "We will." Boone had just drawn a picture of her dream life, and Mila was struggling to believe it was all real. It simply sounded too wonderful to be true.

"So, while I'd like you to move in tomorrow, I'm willing to wait until next weekend because I figure you'll need time to pack."

Mila laughed. "Oh, wow. You're giving me five whole days?"

Boone wrapped his arm around her shoulders, tugging her toward him and placing a kiss on the side of her head. "You're right. That's more time than you'll need. Especially since I suspect Sadie and your sisters are sitting in that farmhouse right now, making plans for your move."

Mila couldn't argue with that. "Nora's probably dragged empty boxes from the basement and is currently labeling them, so everything is packed appropriately in a well-organized manner."

"I sincerely hope she is." Boone gave her a quick kiss, resting his forehead against hers. "Sadie was right. I *am* happy. Shit, I didn't know it was possible to feel this happy."

"Neither did I," she confessed. "Boone?"

"Yeah?"

"Can I heat my jets back up?"

He barked out a loud laugh, hopping up from the couch. The second Mila rose, he bent down, picking her up and carrying her to his bedroom, bridal-style.

He placed her on the edge of the bed, stepping away to pull his shirt off over his head. Mila was never going to get sick of that view. Shirtless Boone was a work of art. She ran her hand over his chest, toying with his light smattering of hair. There were a few sprigs of gray interspersed with the brown.

He joked about his age on occasion, but she sure as hell didn't consider him old. While there was thirteen years between them, Mila appreciated his maturity. Guys her age tended to value stupid shit—like their cars, getting drunk, or getting laid.

Her fingers drifted lower, and she pushed them into the waistband of his jeans, using that grip to pull him closer. He looked down at her, his eyes smoldering with a hunger that took her breath away.

She popped the button, then slowly slid down the zipper as Boone watched. Once the jeans were open, she pushed them and his boxers over his hips, licking her lips when his thick erection sprang free.

Boone cupped her chin, tilting her head up as he drew his thumb over her lower lip. "Open, darlin'."

She didn't need to be asked twice. Mila bent forward as he closed the distance. Wrapping her hand around his girth, she stroked him several times as she slid her tongue around the head of his cock, tasting the tiny drops of precome there.

Boone held still, letting her explore and play, though she knew her dominant lover well enough to realize he was using great restraint. However, she didn't want his restraint. She wanted him to lose control, to let her experience firsthand just how much he desired her.

So, Mila teased him, loosening her grip, not taking him into her mouth, even though that was what he wanted. That continued for a couple minutes before he got wise to her game.

Gripping her cheeks, Boone tilted her head back. "Naughty girl. You playing with me?"

"What do you mean?" she asked coyly, her expression giving her away.

"Don't poke the bear, darlin'." Boone shifted one hand behind her, gripping her neck, while he used the other to cover her hand on his cock, showing her exactly how much force and friction he wanted.

Rubbing the head of his dick over her lips, he narrowed his eyes, tapping twice, an unspoken demand for entrance.

Mila opened her mouth, then held on as Boone pushed his rock-hard cock deep inside. He knew from their past encounters how much she could comfortably take, and he took care to make sure he held that line, not shoving against her gag reflex. With his hand—and hers—still working the base, he thrust in and out of her mouth.

His breathing became labored, and she thought he was close, so when he pulled out, she frowned.

"Boone—"

He shook his head. "I'm taking advantage of this night, Mila. Which means you and I have miles to go yet."

She liked the sound of that. "What did you have in mind?"

His jeans had fallen to his knees, so he sank next to her on the bed, pulling off his boots, then boxers and pants. "First thing we need to do is even the score because you're wearing way too many clothes."

Boone quickly corrected that oversight, her clothing joining his in a pile on the floor. "Crawl to the middle," he directed. As she did so, he pulled back the duvet so that she was reclined on the soft cotton sheets. She lifted her arms, intent on pulling him atop her, but he leaned just out of reach.

She tilted her head but didn't question him. So far, their sexual encounters had been straight-forward, mainly because of time and location issues. Between sneaking in quickies during lunch or in the front seat of his truck, their options for variety had been limited.

Tonight, the world was their oyster, and Boone seemed ready to capitalize on that.

"You ever read any romance books where the guy ties the woman up?" he asked.

Mila sucked in a deep breath because holy hell. He'd just hit on one of her top five "Sexy Things I Want to Try."

She nodded. "I have."

"Does the idea of that turn you on?"

"So much," she whispered.

Rather than reply, Boone rose from the bed, walking across the room to his closet. "I placed an order online a couple weeks ago. Had to hide the box in here so Sadie wouldn't come across it." Boone shifted stuff on the floor of the closet, returning to the bed with a box.

Mila sat up excitedly. "What did you get?"

Boone chuckled at her enthusiasm. "Hope you're still excited when you see what's inside."

Flipping back the lid, Mila's eyes widened as she took in the array of sex toys. "Holy shit!"

"Mila, if you never want to try any of these things, we won't."

"I want to try them all," she gushed.

Boone had already unpackaged the toys. "I washed them already because I knew if we decided to play with them, I wouldn't want any delays." He pulled out restraints, handing them to her. They were soft, with Velcro cuffs. "Thought we could start with something like these. If you enjoy being tied up, I'd love to graduate to handcuffs and rope eventually."

"Okay." Her heart was racing a million miles an hour, not with fear but with anticipation and need.

Reaching back into the box, he lifted out a tube of lubrication and…

Mila gasped. "Is that…"

"A butt plug. It's a smaller one, because I know you're new to anal play. We can start slow, but, darlin', there's not a single part of you that I don't want to claim."

"I want that too," she admitted. Boone had toyed around with her ass, but he'd never breached her with more than a finger. The plug he'd purchased wasn't freaking her out size-wise. Or at least, not completely, but it was definitely bigger than his finger.

Boone didn't pull anything else out of the box. Instead, he tucked it under the bed.

"But there was more," she said.

He shook his head, amused. "Greedy girl. Let's start with these. Lie on your back."

She did as he said, shivering in anticipation as he attached the restraints to the headboard, then reached for her arms. Pulling them over her head, he attached each wrist, her arms outstretched. She tested the hold, aware she wasn't getting free until he released her. The idea of being helpless was a much bigger turn-on than she'd expected.

She waited for him to hook her ankles to the footboard, but he tossed those straps to the side.

She frowned, confused.

Boone booped her nose. "We'll get to those in a minute. For right now, they don't work with my plans."

She loved that he'd thought about this, planned this night, even going so far as to buy the toys. It was touching to realize that Boone was thinking about her even when they weren't together.

Climbing back onto the bed, Boone knelt between Mila's legs, pushing her knees apart to make room as he lowered his head.

"God!" she cried out as he took her clit into his mouth, sucking hard enough that she saw stars almost instantly. The man had a magic tongue...and teeth...and fingers. Pressing two thick fingers inside her, he continued to stroke her clit with his tongue. Boone went down on her like *she* was his favorite meal, not the beef stew.

"Let me see one of those pretty orgasms," he demanded, his voice rough with need. "Then we'll get down to business."

Mila always felt a slight tremor of panic when he talked like that, because the orgasms he gave her were almost painful in their intensity.

Thrusting hard and fast, he nipped her clit, and just like that, she was there.

Exploding.

Erupting.

Free-falling with no net to catch her.

Boone stroked her through her climax, drawing it out until she cried, "Can't. Take. Any more."

She knew those were the famous last words of a fool, because Boone, with his cocky grin, was going to push her to the brink and beyond again. And again. And...

Rising back to his knees, Boone lifted her legs until she was completely exposed to him. He gripped her beneath her knees, holding them out, her ass slightly lifted from the mattress.

"Time for the other restraints." Boone hooked the Velcro cuffs around her knees, before attaching the ends to the headboard, alongside the straps holding her hands in place.

Mila released an unsteady breath that captured Boone's attention.

"You only have to say stop," he reminded her.

"I know," she quickly reassured him. "But I'm not going to. This is... God, I love this so much."

Boone ran the back of his fingers over her cheeks. "You're so beautiful like this. I love having you bound, completely at my mercy."

She closed her eyes, smiling.

Best. Night. Ever.

Her eyelids flew open when she felt something cold brush her ass. The lube.

Boone circled her anus with the tip of his finger, applying more lube before pushing inside.

He slipped in easily, thanks to the lubrication. As he slipped that one finger in and out several times, Mila found herself anticipating his return thrusts, her hips rising to meet him.

She froze when, on one return, he pushed a second finger in with the first.

"Oh," she said, feeling the pinch.

Boone studied her face carefully, making sure she was okay. He always took such good care of her. He pushed her limits, but he let her adjust and gave her time to find her way.

Just as she was enjoying the stretch, Mila groaned, upset when his fingers left and didn't return. That was when he lifted the plug, covering it with more lube.

"Take a deep breath and hold it," he instructed.

She did as he said, pressing her eyes shut tightly as he worked the plug inside. She probably should have been a little more freaked out earlier, because the thing was deceptively bigger than she'd thought.

She lost hold of her breath and was forced to draw in another, though this one was shallower.

"Almost there," he said softly. "This is the widest part. You're being so good, Mila. Such a good girl, taking this plug for me."

She melted when he praised her and called her his good girl. Literally…melted.

Her body relaxed, the widest part of the plug breached her ass, and Mila was finally able to draw in a deeper breath.

"Okay?"

"It's tight," she said. "And it feels sort of strange. But not a bad strange."

"It's going to get tighter," he warned her.

Her brows furrowed until Boone's hands pressed flat into the mattress by her head, his cock dancing along her pussy.

"Oh," she breathed, when he reached down and guided the head into place. He was going to fuck her with the plug in. Mila wasn't sure, but she sort of thought she could come just from the idea.

Not that Boone gave her a chance to test the theory.

Cock in place, he slid inside in one relentless thrust, not stopping until he was buried all the way.

Mila trembled, shocked to realize just how close she was to coming again.

"Boone," she said, his name more air than sound. "So good!"

He smiled at her…and then he set himself loose.

Mila was grateful for the straps on her wrists and knees, aware they were the only things keeping her in place, grounded. She came after a dozen thrusts, and it felt as if she'd left her body.

Boone didn't give way, fucking her through that orgasm and on to another. Mila screamed his name, along with some four-letter words, followed by a half dozen "I love yous" right in a row.

Boone grunted, his body going stiff when he came, filling

her. She wished they were making their baby tonight. The idea of carrying his child was a powerful one, and she was grateful he didn't want to wait long.

Dropping to his elbows, Boone planted kiss after kiss on her cheeks, forehead, lips. "I love you too, darlin'," he said, once he was able to speak again.

Then he pushed himself up and unfastened the restraints, massaging her shoulders and thighs as he did so. Kneeling beside her, he gently lifted one of her legs, gripping the base of the plug.

"Ready?"

She managed one weak nod. He'd fucked her boneless. She hissed slightly when he pulled out the plug.

Unable to move, she followed Boone with her eyes as he rose from the bed, heading to the bathroom to wash. He returned with a warm cloth, cleaning her as well, before joining her in the bed and pulling the duvet over them.

Mila curled into his arms, his chest her pillow.

They were quiet for several minutes, but Mila knew that, like her, he wasn't sleeping. Tonight, they were standing on square one, at the very beginning of something new and wonderful and forever.

"Can I tell you a secret?" she whispered.

"Of course."

"I knew you were mine the day we met. I fell into your arms, and, Boone, it was just like Theo and Levi said. It was as if I'd been struck by lightning."

Boone cupped her cheek, lifting her face so he could see her eyes. "You felt it?"

She nodded. "Love at first touch."

Boone's smile, so huge and bright and beautiful, told her just how much he liked that.

"I felt something that day too. Because I was an idiot, it

scared me. I knew right in that moment that you were dangerous."

Mila huffed out a breathy laugh. She'd never once—in her entire life—been called dangerous. It beat the hell out of *sweet*.

"I never believed in second chances, Mila. But you made me want one. And then…you gave it to me."

"I love you," she said, kissing him softly.

"Love you, too."

Boone deepened her kiss, and she felt it again.

That same electric jolt, even stronger than their first touch.

She was caught in a beautiful, powerful storm with this man.

And she never wanted it to end.

Epilogue

Maverick leaned back and looked around the room, wishing he was in as celebratory a mood as the rest of his family.

Kasi and Levi had exchanged their vows five hours earlier—just in front of family and close friends—in a beautiful outdoor ceremony in the large backyard of Maverick's childhood home, which was now the B&B. The weather had been perfect, offering them a cloudless spring day.

Following the wedding, they'd taken no less than seven million photographs, Aunt Claire armed with a two-page list in terms of groupings she wanted. From there, they'd all moved to the event barn, where nearly every single citizen of Gracemont had gathered to help the newlyweds celebrate with a huge barbeque feast and some amazing deejay, Randi, a guy from Winchester whom Gretchen had found. His playlist had kept the dance floor packed for the past two hours.

Levi and Kasi were currently dancing and laughing in the middle of a circle of loved ones. Dad had already led two conga lines—mercifully without taking a tumble—and Maverick was certain there would be at least one more before they all called it a night.

He'd tried without success to find his own party mood, but he just wasn't feeling it tonight. Levi was the first of his brothers to take a trip down the aisle, and while Maverick was over the moon—because his brother had found one hell of a woman in Kasi—the wedding was shining too bright a light on things he'd never have himself.

A wedding.

Marriage.

A family.

His own happily ever after.

"Did someone forget to tell you it's a party?" Boone dropped down into the chair next to him, wiping sweat from his brow before taking a long swig of his beer.

"No one forgot," Maverick grumbled.

"Then did you forget to tell your face? Because your eyebrows are going to stick that way if you scowl any harder."

Maverick attempted to soften his frown, but Boone's chuckle, paired with the shaking of his head, let him know he'd fallen short.

"You're usually the life of the party," he pointed out. "What's going on? Pissed off because you're related to all the bridesmaids, so you don't have a chance to score?"

"Ha-fucking-ha." Maverick and Boone had grown to be good friends over the past few months. Working together day after day for long hours ensured they'd had plenty of time to go from acquaintances to good buddies who gave each other shit.

Boone placed a hand on his shoulder and squeezed. "Seriously, man. What's wrong?"

Maverick sighed, then found himself confessing something he'd never admitted out loud. "I lied about the curse."

Boone frowned, confused. "What?"

"The family legend, about love at first touch? I said I didn't believe in it. But I do."

Boone leaned back in his chair, studying him. "You realize Levi, Theo, and Mila don't believe it's a curse."

"That's because it didn't bite *them* in the ass."

He tilted his head, suddenly curious. "But it did you?"

Maverick nodded. "I got struck by lightning in high school. Met my soul mate junior year."

Boone's eyes widened. "You're kidding. Why didn't you ever say so?"

"Because the family curse doesn't always go both ways. She wrote me a letter. A horrible letter about how I'd ruined her life, and then she left Gracemont."

"I'm sorry, Mav. I didn't know."

"No one does. And I'd appreciate if you kept it that way."

He hesitated just enough that Maverick snickered. "You're going to be one of those guys who doesn't keep secrets from his girlfriend, aren't you?"

Boone's grin gave him away. "I don't have to tell Mila if you really don't want me to, but I'm not sure why you're shutting your family out on this."

Maverick took a long swig of beer. "What good would talking about it do?"

"Maybe the legend got it wrong. Or you did. You were only what? Seventeen? That's a bit young to find your one true love, don't you think?"

Maverick had considered that before, even tried to convince himself he hadn't felt that strike of lightning. But the truth was… he had. And he'd never felt anything even close to it since. Though God knows he'd tried.

Rather than argue the point, he shrugged. "Maybe it is," he lied. This conversation was why he hadn't brought the subject up to his brothers. He knew they'd do the same thing as Boone. Try to explain it away to console him because they loved him, and they were determined to see him happy.

But Maverick knew what he knew.

He'd met and fallen in love with his soul mate when he was just seventeen years old.

She'd been his for one glorious summer, and then he'd lost her.

Forever.

Glancing up, he watched Levi kiss his lovely bride as they danced, and he quietly mourned the life he'd never have.

Nope. There was nothing to do but ride out this storm.

For the rest of his life.

Be sure to read the entire Perfect Storm series.
Taken by Storm
Shelter from the Storm
Caught in a Storm
Riding out the Storm

Calling all fans of Mari Carr AND Facebook! There's a group for you. Come join Mari Carr's Facebook group for sneak peaks, cover reveals, contests and more! Join now.

And be sure to join Mari's mailing list to receive a **FREE** sexy novella, Midnight Wild.

About the Author

Virginia native Mari Carr is a New York Times and USA TODAY bestseller of contemporary romance novels. With over three million copies of her books sold, Mari was the winner of the Romance Writers of America's Passionate Plume award for her novella, Erotic Research. She has over a hundred published works, including her popular Wild Irish and Italian Stallions series, along with the Trinity Masters series she writes with Lila Dubois.

Follow Mari:
www.maricarr.com
mari@maricarr.com

Join her newsletter so you don't miss new releases and for exclusive subscriber-only content.

Made in United States
North Haven, CT
02 October 2025